*My sister is a
formwanderer: she is a mirror
of want. Each person she meets sees
what they want, when they look at her.
And she changes for each pair of eyes.*

Two sisters, fleeing the city of Paradon, find their
way to a village by the sea, where Old Kelp's cottage –
and her recipe book – await them.

Amber feels this is where she finally belongs, baking
honey cakes each night for the villagers to collect in the
morning, using a set of bone spoons that allow her to add
truth, lust and confusion to her pies and puddings.

Her little sister Maya is a formwanderer, engineered to
reflect the wants of others. All her life she has been like
a twin to Amber, but now Amber has changed her mind,
and wants Maya to learn how to be herself.

Kip, a child growing up amongst the songs and
stories of the village, delivers Amber's ingredients.
When an act of terrible violence stirs and
sets free the secrets of a generation,
only one of these three can reveal
the truth . . .

Jess Richards was born in Wales in 1972, and grew up too fast in south west Scotland where she lived with her English parents and three brothers, watching the ferry boats going to and from Northern Ireland. She left home at 17, went over the border to England, and lived for a year in Carlisle, before moving to Devon. She gained a first class degree from Dartington College of Arts when she was 21. After brief stints busking and carrying on in both Leeds and London, she moved to Brighton aged 23 where she has grown up a bit slower, and has lived and worked ever since. Her debut novel, SNAKE ROPES, was shortlisted for the 2012 Costa First Novel Award and longlisted for the Green Carnation Prize.

www.jessrichards.com

JESS
RICHARDS

COOKING
WITH
BONES

SCEPTRE

First published in Great Britain in 2013 by Sceptre
An imprint of Hodder & Stoughton
An Hachette UK company

1

A CIP catalogue record for this title is available from the British Library.

Hardback ISBN 978 1 444 73803 2
Trade paperback ISBN 978 1 444 73804 9
eBook ISBN 978 1 444 73806 3

Typeset by Palimpsest Book Production Limited, Falkirk, Stirlingshire
Printed and bound by Clays Ltd, St Ives plc

Hodder & Stoughton policy is to use papers that are natural, renewable and
recyclable products and made from wood grown in sustainable forests. The
logging and manufacturing processes are expected to conform to the
environmental regulations of the country of origin.

Hodder & Stoughton Ltd
338 Euston Road
London NW1 3BH

www.sceptrebooks.co.uk

For the real life 'crones' I've known:

Betty, who liked birds and animals and had big lips.

Jessie, who loved to cook and made a magic fountain real.

Joan, who fancied a man a quarter of her age.

Val, who said 'don't be serious' when she was old
enough to know better.

and for Luke:

who died far too young, and made a rip in the sky.

'O wad some Power the giftie gie us
To see oursels as ithers see us'

'To a Louse', Robert Burns, 1785

AMBER

My sister is a formwanderer: she is a mirror of want. Each person she meets sees what they want, when they look at her. And she changes for each pair of eyes. Though Maya's three years younger than me, when I was really little I desperately wanted a twin. I'm the one who's closest to her. I've cared for her, brushed her hair, fed and comforted her. I've given her games and stories and pictures to imagine. I've slept in the same room as her, borrowed her clothes and watched her wear mine.

But now we're grown.

She's grown for sixteen years.

As I've grown, what I want from Maya has changed. Now, part of me desperately wants her to be herself.

But she doesn't know what that is.

This morning Maya sleeps in curtain-sieved sunshine. I perch on the edge of her twin bed and blur my eyes. Her dark hair streams over a pale yellow pillow. She dreams. I don't. So within her somewhere, something is separate from me. I look at her face and see mine. With a want, strong as marble, I force her to show me how other people have seen her.

Different faces flicker on hers like masks. Her expression distorts with a thousand reflections. She murmurs, cries, laughs, cries again. Whispers. Shouts. Whimpers. Smiles. Her fingers grip the rosebud duvet, she scratches, touches the fabric.

She's dreaming away echoes of what others want.

Some of these faces are beautiful. A child: a boy, a loner. A woman hunting miracles, an old man hankering for faith.

We all hope we want good things, but this isn't true.

That face, yes, that one. I'd swear that's a face of a killer.

It wavers away, becomes wider, sweeter, the lips mouth the whispers of someone newly in love.

If I let my sister go everywhere and anywhere and no one cared, I could learn the secret desires of everyone in this city. These faces show me that many people who Maya's met are seeking hope.

Maya wakes as if she's inhaling the sky.

She sees me and her face shifts into a mirror image of mine. As she sits up, her hair twists into long dark layers. She blinks her eyes into sight and says, 'A dream of death. Something's about to change.'

Crashing from her bed, she runs out of our room. After the sound of a flush and the smell of orchid air freshener, the shower splashes. I pick up Maya's worn toy hyena that she dropped on the floor, hug it to my chest and sit on her crumpled duvet.

Her voice chirps, 'I've steamed up the mirror!'

I call, 'So now you're invisible!'

She laughs like an overgrown child and kicks the bathroom door shut.

Our city has collected and sucked up all things powerful, beautiful and useful. Paradon is a city that hoards. Our hopes are fine-tuned, carefully channelled to root and grow and twist along straight lines made from pavement and marble, metal and glass. We spread our desires as apparitions: they are attached to us like invisible wings and scaffolds.

In the living room I open the curtains and the sun dazzles in.

As I watch the news with the volume low, I can hear Maya upstairs in our bedroom, thudding around.

The overexcited reporter smiles out at me as she explains, '*The media can't show photographs or film footage in case the public are enveloped by a formwanderer's manipulation.*'

Image wipeout. Blackout.

I say, 'You mean we could see someone who should be cared about.'

Another image: a blue suit with a grim face at a spotlit table.

An expert, impassioned voice:

'*Our initial intention in genetically engineering these humans, using nanotechnology, was to enhance the development of their mirror neuron pathways and make them deeply empathic. The surface of empathy is indeed positive – most people who know formwanderers view them as cherished friends or treasured family members. With nanotechnology also causing their skin cells to be reflective, technically speaking they are astounding creations, able to mirror desired behaviours and appearance. But we now know there are also the psychological aspects of projection to consider. Children, for example, often see formwanderers as all kinds of creatures; adults have complex needs and wants of which we aren't always consciously aware. Alarmingly, it's recently come to light that our unconscious desires are being acted upon by formwanderers.*

'*In the most recent case, and we can't name the parties involved for legal reasons, x and y lived together, seemingly happily. X's friendship with a formwanderer was long and devoted. But the relationship between x and y broke down, because of y's infidelity. The formwanderer listened to x, was a perfect friend. X talked, expressed her anger, took the offer of a sofa to sleep on. The next morning the formwanderer provided x with breakfast*

3

– her favourite foods, of course – pineapple, cherries and yoghurt, it's been reliably reported. After breakfast, x returned to the marital home to find y had been brutally murdered. The form-wanderer claims to have no memory of anything that night after x went to sleep on the sofa. However, the bloodstained murder weapon was found in the formwanderer's possession.

'*So formwanderers not only act as others knowingly want them to, they may also enact underlying, darker desires. This is just one of many recent cases. Culpability is in question – does it lie with x for that moment of wishing y dead rather than unfaithful, or with the formwanderer for killing y? Or the blame could be placed on the parents, and there are many, who commissioned a formwanderer baby to complete their family. To provide the ideal son or daughter, or to present an only child with a perfect playmate, for example.*'

I bite my lip. My face is reflected on the TV screen.

I say, 'Or a perfect twin.'

The man frowns at his notes, and continues:

'*Some parties are calling for ethical investigations into the organisations which still genetically engineer these humans. It has been posited in several publications that formwanderers no longer function as they were originally intended to; they are not fit for purpose, and should be considered mutations rather than human beings.*

'*The current advice is to keep our desires as pure as we can make them. Aim for emotional self-sufficiency and avoid negative emotions, especially conscious or unconscious hedonistic or vengeful desires. Emotions must be boxed, kept for solitary moments. Watch for sudden spikes or flares, and endeavour to flatten them.*'

The two-dimensional face stares out at me from the screen.

Maya's footsteps on the stairs. I switch off the TV.

She comes in and bashes her shin against the coffee table. 'Here you are. What are you doing?'

'Nothing.'

She folds her arms, says, 'Liar,' with a smile in her eyes.

'You don't mind.'

The smile spreads to her mouth. 'No, I don't.'

Next to the TV is an aquarium. I sit on a cushion and watch the angelfish swim in and out of hollow castle windows.

Maya shuffles across the carpet and sits next to me. We've always loved these fish. We often stare at them for hours.

Through our childhood we lived as twins might; we shared our ambitions. When I was very young, I flunked all the tests at school, so I could be put back into Maya's classes.

I say to Maya, 'Do you remember we used to want to be beauticians?'

She's staring blankly at a guppy with black and white stripes and a rippling tail. 'We did. But they said we were too ugly.' The guppy changes colour from black and white to ghost pale. Maya laughs.

She's right. We were physically examined, and advised we'd never achieve the required perfection; we were too short and there was *an inherent lack of prettiness*, the careers adviser said, displaying a perfect set of teeth, *though a lot of character. But. It's not character they want.*

The careers adviser was taken with Maya, wanted to keep her there after our session. She said to her, *You don't look at all like your sister. You just remind me so much of my aunt Sis, who brought me up. She made the best egg and mustard sandwiches. She was locked back in time. She was such a good listener. Could I talk to you? It's just there are these thoughts which start as crumbs and turn into lumps when there's no one to hear them.*

You know what I mean, I can tell you do. She stroked her neck as if smoothing out bumps and seemed on the verge of tears. Maya leaned forward, nodded at her with sympathy. But I dragged her away, and we left the careers advice behind.

We rethought our future plans and reluctantly decided to study hard. We were going to soar in our exams and get into university. Maya studied hardest for the particularly keen teachers of arts and I worked for maths, classics and some of the sciences. So we two could have achieved excellence, and might have been able to advance to the next level of learning. If we'd done so, we may have qualified for a university place.

Between us, I'm sure we could have. But not without each other.

We stayed on at school, taking the only qualifications they'd allow us to. These were enrichment courses in customer absenteeism, consumer picnicking and responsibility pie-charting. We failed all the assessments. Our parents realised that though Maya was trying and failing, I wasn't trying at all. I wasn't just killing time, I was slaying it, hacking it up. Often, I'd get Maya safely home, find an excuse to go out alone, and come back after three a.m. looking like a raggedy doll. They wanted Maya to stay good, amenable and innocent, and not to follow me. At the end of the year, they removed us from school. Neither of us had learned anything useful enough to obtain jobs and earn our own way.

Maya's eyes are like glass.

I say to her, 'We aspired too high and achieved too low, didn't we?'

She taps her finger on the aquarium, next to a novelty rock. She's eyeballing a hidden catfish. 'I've got something to do today. A drawing for our cleaner. She likes fruit and bold colours. Black grapes and red peppers.'

The angelfish move steadily and the air-pump froths. Our aspirations are lost in the sludge at the bottom. All our hopes have blipped away and neither of us can catch another one.

Tonight we all eat together, which is a rare occurrence. Our parents' sky-high careers keep them absent and when they're home, they're so exhausted that they want a sanctuary from work, from long hours, from facades and perfections.

Since school ended, I've taught myself to cook. We used to rely on pre-prepared meals, but now I arrange the shopping and have made this evening's dinner. The few cookery books we have contain recipes designed to keep us healthy and slender. Tonight we're having salad with thin strips of chicken. As I dish up dressed leaves and artichokes, Maya pours vitamin juice into our glasses. Our parents blink secrets at one another with tired eyes.

Maya is calm and silent as they help themselves to chicken and talk to each other between mouthfuls.

Our mother twirls her fork in her hand, eyeing her frosted fingernails. 'How are your hours looking? Mine are doubled for at least a month.'

Our father licks his teeth and replies, 'And mine for weeks. Deadlines are crashing into other deadlines.'

They go on in this vein, self-consciously glancing at me when they think I'm not listening. They're now telling each other how much pride they gain from their careers.

I nudge Maya's foot, under the table.

She nudges mine back.

Our parents talk us upstairs into the soft room with white sofas and sit us down. Our mother perches on the edge of a cushion, clasps her hands in her lap, and smiles us a fuchsia-lipped smile. 'You're going to be Lab Assistants.'

She beams up at our father, who nods back at her. Her hands outstretched, she says, 'We've done it.'

Our father hugs himself and pats his own shoulders. 'We've got you jobs.'

Our mother's highest voice: 'Such an achievement, because you really aren't that good at anything. Sorry, but honesty is best?' She surveys my face for hurt, finds none, and glances at Maya.

Our father's deep blue suit creaks as he reaches into the breast pocket and hands us each a letter. He leans an arm on the mantelpiece, where lilies curve tall in a green vase. He looks like a photograph of himself as he turns only his face towards us. 'Amber, your letter tells you where you need to be tomorrow, and at what time. So early to bed, and sleep well. Maya, you'll start in a couple of weeks, when your predecessor has moved on.'

Our mother says, 'I'm sure you'll be given the dullest uniforms, but we've bought you each a new outfit as congratulations presents. They're in your wardrobes. Surprise!' She says to me, 'You'll feel clean and swishy all the way there and all the way home. We'll get takeaway food tomorrow night, and we'll both be here . . .' She frowns at our father with her eyebrows, not her forehead, 'Won't we?'

He nods, but slides an organiser from another pocket and turns away from the mantelpiece. He taps a pointed shoe on the floorboards beside the white fur rug as he pokes and flicks his finger over the touch screen. He slips it back in his pocket and grimaces. 'I'll need to renegoti—'

Our mother continues over him, '. . . to celebrate Amber's first day.' She clasps her hands together, her eyes shining. She says to our father, 'Oh, so grown-up. Remember our little . . .' Her voice trails away and she yawns.

He turns to us, one shaped eyebrow raised, 'You can say thank you.'

'Thank you,' Maya responds, smiling up at him.

Though I'll never know exactly what our parents see when they look at Maya, I can tell she mirrors something which can melt our father's eyes to a softness I can never invoke myself.

'Are we to work alone or with others?' I ask, forcing the words from my tight throat. 'Because though each person sees what they want –'

Our father, his eyes still on Maya, says, 'Stop it, Amber.'

'– people think all the time of how to annoy each other, hurt someone, and Maya could just grab onto one of those desires . . . What if someone there hates the boss – what if they all do? Maya could—'

He looks at me and snaps, 'I said *stop*.'

Our mother says to me, 'It's not Maya I'm worried about. She'll fit in anywhere, just fine. It's only a handful of form-wanderers who've done anything criminal. You're the daughter who causes us trouble.'

I grab Maya's hand. 'Maya, you're confused, aren't you, around lots of people – you don't know who you are, you won't be able to—'

Maya tears her gaze away from our father and nods at me, her eyes wide and fearful. 'Yes, it's confused now. Bam smash colours. He wants yes, she wants yes, yes is yellow, you want no, no is black. I'm a bit middlish jumblecon—'

Raising my voice, I say, 'See? And don't you think that what people want from other adults is more dangerous than what they want from children? Maya's going to have to be a real grown-up in just a couple of weeks—'

Our mother shakes her head as if she can't find any language. When she finally speaks, her voice cracks. 'She's an innocent!

Not like the others.' She looks at our father, her hands extended.

I say, 'She's innocent for you. Or perhaps you want to keep her ignorant, but in an adult workforce not everyone is going to want her to be innocent, are they?'

Our father says, 'Amber, leave this alone.' His voice drops away as he sighs. 'Your mother and I are just off, what, twelve-hour shifts?'

Maya leans forward, her face in her hands.

Our mother says in a tight voice, 'Thirteen. This is a good news night. Aren't we all here? Can we all be here?' She wipes her palms on her magenta pencil skirt. 'I need to get out of these work clothes. I feel like I'm still – what were we talking about?'

Our father says to her gently, 'You're home.'

She exhales.

Maya raises her face from her hands and looks up at our father. Confusion drains from her expression. 'Don't worry. I won't let you down. I'll be perfect.'

'Maya, stay with me?' I coax her, but our father's caught her attention again.

As he looks back at her, his face slips into relief and so does hers. He smiles and says to her, 'Of course you will. You'll be absolutely brilliant. When it's your first day, we'll all be cheering you on. But for now, congratulations.'

She beams him sunshine.

Our mother taps her hands on her knees, and slumps her shoulders. 'Sorry, darlings, I'm drooping. Bed?'

Maya looks at her and yawns. Says, 'You're so tired. Working too, too hard for far too long. Don't want to argue. Night night. For sleep.'

'You're so understanding, Maya.'

I lay my head on my knees and close my eyes. I murmur,

'She's the exact opposite of an emotional vampire. Perhaps you could tell everyone you know that Maya's died. Then we'll keep her as an eternal child, hide her in a cupboard for years. I'm sure you could even persuade her to enjoy living in the dark . . .'

The white door clicks shut behind our parents.

Maya's heard me. Her eyes have darkened. 'Do you want me to pretend-dead?'

'No, just trying to . . . Don't worry. I'll think of something else.'

She clenches her hands together. 'You think up amazing things. Like when we made helicopters out of tin cans and dropped them from the windows out the back, they went clangfly, clangfly . . .'

'Thanks. Feeling a bit stuck. I need reminding I'm good at ideas.'

We turn to face each other.

I say, 'Serious now. We have to talk about sensible things.'

We nod, take a deep breath and tear open our letters.

They've got us jobs through a friend of a friend of a friend. They must have been online for hours through the nights and been tested and retested and managed to obtain fairly decent personality profiles for us both: they've given us skills we don't have. I read my letter. Have a quick look at Maya's.

Two jobs, different labs.

My heart thumps. 'So we're to be separated.'

Maya smiles at her letter. 'I'm going to be useful.'

I look closely at it. She's meant to work in a lab, testing how glass can be made stronger against differing strengths of flame. She'll have goggles and be trained to use a dangerous blowtorch.

She'll be with a workforce of twenty others.

Maya tells me, 'Around my neck I'll wear a necklace of magnifying glasses.'

I show her my letter. 'I'm supposed to work in the Tear Lab. The profile they gave me must have showed me as having an emotional intellect, which is a complete lie.'

'What's the Tear Lab?' Maya asks, with doubt in her eyes.

'Where sadness is measured. Somehow. It's woolly wording. There are experiment rooms in a basement. It's psychology and I'll have to sign an "I don't care about ethics" form.'

'I'd hate that.'

'I know.'

'I can't cry. Tearstop.'

'It's not that you can't, it's that you won't. You cry in your sleep.'

She looks at me with wide eyes. 'Do you have to cry to work there? What happens if you don't?'

'I'm not going to tell you what happens to people who get fired. You'll get upset.'

Her expression seems relieved. 'Oh. OK.' Maya doesn't mind not knowing about things I don't think she'll like. She's reading her letter again, smiling a little as she runs her fingers over the words.

Fired employees have to work on what's called a voluntary basis, though it's a legal requirement. At school we were taught they do things which are designed to give them self-respect, but which are essentially useless jobs. The pastoral counsellor said, 'They have long poles with nets on the end of them. The night volunteers reach out of the highest windows in skyscrapers to rescue moths that are heading for the moon, and the day volunteers capture escaped helium balloons.' He was trying to make it sound gentle, as our teacher had recently been fired for straying from the curriculum yet again. This time she'd been telling us the truth about wild animals. I'd loved the vicious details: teeth and claws and skeletons and blood and survival instincts. She'd been drumming on her desk, yearning for a glint of enthusiasm from any one of us.

In a group of people, Maya's attention is grabbed by the person who wants the most from her. She locked onto this teacher's desire to inspire passion. Maya enacted the role of a wildcat and tore down one of the blinds before I shooed her out of the classroom and calmed her in a broom cupboard by stroking her hair in the dark. The teacher thought Maya should be an actress. When we came back into the classroom, she said, 'I've always wanted to nurture a talent like yours. I could really see the brutal spirit of the animal – how do you do those teeth?' and she clapped her hands when Maya snarled at her. Maya wasn't seen as a gifted actress for long, as the teacher was fired soon afterwards. Apparently, at our age, she was only meant to teach us about the pollination and cross pollination of flowers.

If this was all, and there was only myself, I wouldn't care.

Maya's not going to be safe, because what people want isn't always safe.

We all have instincts to fight, freeze or run. We can all hate, want revenge, fantasise that someone is maimed, but then we banish these thoughts in a second. If a formwanderer is there, they might act instinctively. Now that formwanderers are all over the press, suspicion will increase and spread fear like a virus.

Maya reads and rereads her letter, hugs it to her chest, strokes the envelope.

'Maya, we're going to have to leave.'

She looks at me. 'But you're going to bed early.'

My voice trembles a little. 'No, I'm not.'

'I'm going to learn to use a blowtorch – look, the personnel department said they wanted to give me more skills!' She waves her letter at me.

'You only want the job because our parents have made you want it.'

She shakes her head, clutches the letter with both hands and stares up at the ceiling, which is what she always does to stop herself crying. She looks like a vulnerable version of me, awestruck, her eyes full of fear as she nods in determined agreement and crumples up her letter. She crumples my letter as well, goes into the hallway and clunks them both down the recycling chute.

I feel guilty. So I beckon her back into the soft room. 'Try to think about this really hard. What do *you* want?'

We sit on a sofa, holding all four of our hands.

She says, 'To run away.'

'That's what I want, and that's what we're going to do. What else do you think you want?'

'To be useful.'

'That's what our mother wants. Try again?'

'To be liked.'

'Yes, that's probably yours, but it could be a whole bunch of other people's as well. Something more certain. Again? You want to . . .'

'To . . . have a beautiful baby that stays tiny-little and never cries . . .'

'A very old one of our father's, before he got wise. One more go?'

Her eyes have gone darker. 'You're making me tired!' Her breathing is strained.

She doesn't understand I'm trying to get her to express a splinter of herself rather than facets of everyone else. I persist, 'One more thing you think *you* want – try really really hard – even a tiny thing and we'll stop.'

Maya looks at me and leans her head back a little. The set of her jaw matches my determination. It's like looking in a mirror. She takes a deep breath. Unblinking, she says, 'We don't have time for this. We have to pack.'

'That's definitely mine. Well, you've tried. Come on, then.'

Maya grabs her mobile and glances around our bedroom at the plug sockets for a charger.

I tell her, 'We won't need things like that.'

She drops the phone on her bed. When she reaches for our box of nail varnishes, she catches my gaze. She shakes her head and leaves it where it is.

She picks up my notebook and passes it to me. I hold it for a moment, consider how to spell out a meaningful goodbye to friends, and discard the notebook and farewells in a drawer.

'Maya, don't take mementos.'

'Why not?'

'Nostalgia makes people fusty.' I don't want to tell her that once we've gone, we'll never come back.

I pack some of my clothes. They're tight, bright, and designed for summer. Rummaging through our wardrobes for anything warmer, I realise we've got countless occasionally worn and never-worn items. Our hangers are crammed with combinations of lace, linen, cotton, silk and every colour from black to neon bright. If our mother has hung new outfits in here, I can't tell which ones they are.

I stop yanking cramped hangers and turn and look around our bedroom at the pastel bedspreads and pale striped wallpaper, the pictures on the walls of thin women in ball gowns gazing at moonlit skies. Our bedside tables are cluttered with electrical cords, drawing crayons, silk flower arrangements and frosted bottles of perfume.

We're really leaving.

For Maya's sake. And if I'm honest, for mine as well.

Just as Maya has been engineered, so has everyone who lives here, one way or another. In Paradon, our whole lives are constructed. There are images to fit ourselves to, the right clothes to sheathe ourselves in; these arc lives with pre-determined paths which speed along parallel lines. We're all meant to want this but I don't. I wrap my arms around my body and realise if I stayed here, my whole life would be spent believing that nothing I am and nothing I do will ever fit.

Maya's in the bathroom searching for the toothbrushes I've already packed. I get my radio from a bedside drawer and plug in the headphones. The weather report tells me the sun will shine tomorrow, like it did today and yesterday, as the weather is designed for the eternal summer we always have.

The female newsreader's voice announces: '*Breaking news. In the last three hours, another formwanderer has been arrested on suspicion of violent crime just as the latest murder trial reached its conclusion. In that case the formwanderer was deemed culpable, and has been removed.*'

They don't explain what *removed* means. But I know. For the last few days I've left Maya at home, gone out into the streets and listened to the whispers. In a city this size, there are conversations stinging everyone's mouths.

I've discovered that when formwanderers are removed, they're incarcerated in concrete cells underground.

The whispers say:

no human contact
fed via conveyor belt, lights off, water provided in drips
a living burial
as good as a death sentence.

I've always listened to whispers.

*   *   *

Downstairs, we fill the remaining space in our bags with packets of multigrain biscuits, oranges, nutrition drinks and rice cakes. I scrawl a note for our parents, take a carving knife from the drawer and remove its safety shield.

There's nothing that eases the thought of this unknowable journey more than the certainty of a fine blade to cut away any obstacle which has to be cleared. Whatever we find barring our way, be it an overgrown path, an overeager man or an overcrowded forest, this blade and the singing sharpness of the metal means our route will be clear, and if it isn't, I'll clear it.

We close the front door behind us and walk along the deserted pavement.

My heartbeat flutters in my temples as I talk to Maya about how much I love her, how she's so like a proper twin, more than just a sister. And more than any words, I build a feeling of *want*. I think of our lifetimes in duplicate. Never alone, never lonely. Glancing at her, she looks exactly like me, in her face, hair, age and build. Her brightly coloured clothing is identical to mine.

The cameras on the poles at the end of our street turn and fix their Cyclops lenses on us. I grip Maya's hand, and her grip is as tight as mine. The cameras falter, click, and look away.

Dawn comes as we pass an early morning fashion shoot. Water-print outfits flood from models who adopt weeping poses; we can see them above the flashes of crouched photographers.

The recorded female voice that speaks in every lobby or crowded area comes from some speaker or another. It says, '*Move along. Cluster alert.*'

I whisper to Maya, 'Keep your eyes down,' as we squeeze past.

We're about to cross the road when a curly-haired woman in a waist-pinched suit steps in front of us, a camera between her fingertips. She's wearing a press badge. She narrows her eyes at Maya.

The woman steps closer, her hand outstretched. 'You look familiar.'

Putting my arm around Maya, I draw her away. 'We're identical, in every way. Twins. Aren't we.' I squeeze her shoulder.

Maya shakes my arm off. She's looking at the woman.

The woman says to Maya, 'Identical? Not at all. You've got a story to tell. Something different, I'm sure. Would you come with me for a sec?' She leans her head to the side and smiles.

Maya frowns at the woman, steps towards her. She says in a self-assured voice, 'Of course I have. I've got something amazing. It's absolutely scandalous and it's all yours.'

The woman slips her camera into a pocket and clasps her hands together.

I grab Maya's arm and wrench her away. Though she struggles, I'm stronger.

Dragging her quickly from the main street, I yank her into the deserted pedestrian passageways, along one narrow street, into another. As she stops pulling against me and lets me lead her, I stop and catch my breath in a doorway which smells of bleach.

Maya leans against a wall. 'Where?' Her breathing slows to match mine.

'We'll find a map soon. But this is the right direction. Ish.'

'A direction?'

'The direction to leave.'

Maya puts her hands on her waist and squeezes. Kneads at her stomach with her knuckles. She grimaces and looks down at her body. 'I'm corseted, suited. Tear me out! This is a painful thin!' She groans. 'I need something incredible!'

'It's that woman's feelings. Let it go, Maya. It's not yours.'

Her hands grip her waist and her knuckles are white.

I grab her hands and hold them. 'Look at me. You're leaving.

With me. We want to leave. Both of us. Because we want the same thing. You look exactly like me, don't you?'

She pulls her hands from mine and presses her temples, her expression confused. She shakes herself. 'Yes. I look like me. No. You.' She holds out her hands, palms up. As she stares at them her face clears. 'I do, don't I? Always, when I look in a mirror, I look like you.'

'Yes.' I smile at her and say, gently, 'And that's how you look, to me.'

'Because you want the most from me.' She looks down at herself. Touches her cheeks with her fingertips, says, 'I do. I'm just like mysister.'

'You called me that when you were really little.' I glance along the passageway. Three invisible people are here, wearing high-visibility clothing. The street sweepers and cleaners make sure the marble is dusted, the pavements are scrubbed and the windows are polished. They don't look at us at all. They aren't used to being noticed; they believe they're invisible.

Maya approaches the nearest one, who sweeps the pavements with a six-foot wire brush. She says, 'The sound of your brush tastes of sad.'

The sweeper sweeps, chasing dust.

Wants nothing, expects nothing, sees nothing in Maya at all.

I say to Maya, 'You're jumbling. Come on.' She does this when she's confused. Sometimes it's words, sometimes flavours and scents or colours and emotions.

She walks beside me. Says, 'Let's find what's out. Outoutout.'

We walk along the river path. The wall next to us is lined with polished mosaics depicting leotard-clad dryads, a Pan in designer pyjamas and Bacchus in blue chiffon, floating in grapes. A couple, staggering, approach us. I turn Maya away from them and say, 'Look how many colours have made this picture.'

She touches the tiled face of a nymph with pink cloud hair.

When the couple have lurched past, we continue walking alongside the blue-rippled river. Warm in the sunshine, too warm, I jump as a car beeps on the road above us.

We cut through a park as the morning sun brightens. We can see some of the highest office buildings and skyscrapers.

Maya stops for a moment and stares up at them. She beams as if greeting old friends. I follow her gaze to the mirrors on top of each of the skyscrapers. They're enormous convex circular mirrors which rotate, flex and swerve. The mirrors are linked to satellites that capture the sun or the moon, and reflect their brilliances into the city. Each mirror throws rays into other mirrors; silver nights and golden days curve around and around the streets of Paradon. The sky is tinted with currents of synthetic white clouds. When the clouds occasionally fall, their mists smell of ammonia. For Paradon alone, the meteorological industry controls the weather.

All we've ever known is a mirrored summer.

Maya is still smiling up at the enormous mirrors. 'Can they come with us?'

I don't reply.

On a narrow bridge at the very edge of Paradon, we look down through railings at the main road leading in. The sun shines on small metallic booths, wasp-striped barriers rise and drop. Androgynous figures stride, clad in bulletproof clothing and dark glasses. Vehicles wait in queues to drive into tunnels.

We can see the high walls of a detention centre. There are the sounds of traffic and, from somewhere, barks of dogs.

Maya glances around us at the empty bridge, and I look

along the road that leads out. Grass and thistles have cracked the concrete. Further along, lilies tangle through bulrushes in the verges. There's a landscape of uneven hills and disorganised clusters of trees. In the distant sky are textured clouds, the darkest I've ever seen.

Maya says, 'No one's stopping us. Nothing looks.'

I loosen my grip on her hand and release it. 'Paradon doesn't care who leaves, it cares who comes in.'

Just outside the city is the sound of birdsong, eerie as flutes. My fingertips feel cold. As I breathe them warm, I realise the summer being reflected into Paradon is leaking. In the fields next to the road, dandelions and wild roses flower alongside daffodils and snowdrops. Crumbling stone walls are overgrown with passion flowers in all the colours of fireworks.

We'll travel north like birds in a reverse migration. We're winged creatures who've freed ourselves with our claws. Our fingernails are the deepest shade of purple.

KIP

My name is Kip and Mammy says I'm ten, and she's better at birthdays than me so she's probably right. Every day is the same for me even if it's colder than the one before. And that's what winter's like, but by each day being the same I mean I do the same important job, so early no one else is awake.

Each morning, my ankle gets yanked at by a rope lead that's tied to Dagger's collar. He's our dog who's not a very good dog, as he can't bark, and never has, not ever. And he's no good at picking anything up in his chops without dropping it, and he pulls so hard on the lead he near enough breaks my ankle each morning but it wakes me up. It's not his fault I'm rubbish at waking, or that he yanks so hard. He needs to get outside and piss. Every morning I hop him back up onto my bed, untie the lead and tip him off gentle, as I don't want him to spark at me because even though he'll not bark, he'll bite. His good tooth is so hidden under his scraggled black fur, I can never see it coming.

I brush my teeth and put on my dress and wellies and duffel coat. My important job starts the moment I pick up the round wicker basket and get whatever our fair is from the table where Mammy's left it. I put ours in the basket first, so it's mine and Mammy's and Dad's fair that's going to be the best till last. I strap the basket on the trolley, open the latch to the front door, wheel the basket outside and make a wave at the sea. Then I walk every narrow street, lane and alleyway in our village, and pick up the fair from all the doorsteps.

It's called fair because we make sure it *is* fair. We go through the alphabet of all our first names so everyone in the village gets a turn for two seasons. Before me doing the fair, it was Kerry. This is my first ever turn and I've had autumn and now it's winter so when spring comes, I'll stop. Next it's Lizzie, who's after me on the list that's kept on a notice board outside the school.

We all know the rules, and this has been the biggest rule for the longest forever; the fair has to be taken up to Old Kelp's cottage every morning, before anyone else is awake.

When my turn started, Mammy said to me, *It's the most important job there is. It's more important than me looking after the empty houses, and more important than the farm work and odd jobs your dad does, so you'd best learn to wake up early and go early to sleep.* The first morning she got up with me, and she brushed her curly brown hair into a frizz. She had tears on her cheeks as she told me, *I feel all puffed up and proud.*

Today, the fair that Mammy's left out is a pat of butter wrapped in paper, a pack of dried apricots and a lemon. I put our fair in the basket and shut Dagger indoors.

It's still not quite dawn. I look across the shore at the hills, and can't see the jackdaws in the fuzzy-looking trees though they're loud and jack-chacking. Along the ledge there are tied-up fishing boats lying slanty in the mud-sludge till the tide comes to lift them straight. A seagull lands on the concrete steps that lead down to the beach. It looks right into me with its yellow eye. It decides I'm not breakfast and flaps onto a blue plastic box of rusted chains and fine nets. The seagulls are the squall-ishest birds of all – they're grouchy as they have to get up even earlier than me.

I wheel the basket away from the beach, up a steep narrow lane between tall thin houses, and pick up the fair from the doorsteps. There are trays of eggs, bags of flour, and baking powders. At the top of the hill I come back down another cobbled lane. There's a carton of milk, some vanilla essence, a few jars of jam and suet.

At the top of another street, I'm outside Lizzie's house. She lives alone and she's left out a jar of thick honey. At the Quiet Woman's doorstep, I pick up the bunch of violets she always leaves for the fair. She came here last summer and stayed, but doesn't want to know us. She's got some quiet blessing in her hands because the violets flower for her all the year round. There's a row of them inside her kitchen window on the sill. Something moves at the side of my eye. I shiver and look round at an empty narrow space between two houses.

Here, at the very top of the village, there are the three rows of empty houses Mammy looks after. They've got signs on posts outside that call the houses 'Holiday Lets'. They stand empty most of the year till the spring and summer people come. I leave the basket at a corner, and go along the first street of Holiday Lets. There's a wavy feeling in my stomach.

The Holiday Lets houses look like blank masks; the windows are empty eyes and the doors are mouths. I feel prickly on my neck, like I'm being watched from one of the windows. I've got scared breathing.

A seagull yells loud from one of the mossy rooftops. I make sure I don't slip on the icy cobbles as I run back to the basket and wheel it away.

The spring and summer people stay in bed late, then get up

and walk around. At first they say everything is sweet and rustic and pretty. The next day they take photographs of us and the sea and the boats and nets, and our houses and cottages that aren't Holiday Lets. Then they climb the hills all round here and hold their little phones up in the air and say *no signal no signal* and when it rains they go indoors.

They spend a lot of money in the corner shop. In there, Jessie sells them fudge, eggs, bread and elderberry wine. She says it's got a good percent of proof. Drinking just a little of that wine makes them walk wonky and *that's the proof of Jessie's proof,* or that's what Dad says, anyway.

After they've been in our village a few days, they often wander out of the village all the way up to the verge where their cars are parked. They turn the keys in the engines and make the cars growl to check they still work.

While the Holiday Lets are empty, Mammy goes in to dust and dry them out as they smell so damp. She says she feels like she's haunting all the empty houses. But she likes doing the gardening and pot plants, so they look nice for the spring and summer people. The spring and summer people leave their rubbish out on all the wrong days: Jack takes it to the tip on Tuesdays. The seagulls have feasts and our cobbled streets have dirtied plastic blowing up and down the alleyways. The spring and summer people don't know about the fair because it's done before they wake.

I turn into a narrow alleyway and get more fair: jars and jars of honey and marmalade and a bottle of cooking wine. After the street through the middle of the village, I turn another corner and get the fair from Aunty Pippa and Uncle Finn's doorstep. Finn is Dad's brother. They live with my cousin Adam, who barely speaks and has ginger hair. They've left out a pack of raisins and two jars of sugar-pickled beetroot.

Opposite their house, there's vinegar on George's doorstep. I look through the window at his flying taxidermy seagull. On his workbench there's a new white animal model. It could be for a dog, but I hope it's a fox or a badger. The bleached skull is where the face is to go, and he's set in the painted eyes.

At the cottages near the corner shop there's potatoes, onions and a block of cheese. Someone always slips in sensible food. Yesterday our teacher, Mam Vann, left out half a roasted chicken. There's never any fair outside the three craft shops.

When the spring and summer people come, Mam Vann and George take down the wooden boards and fill the three shops. My Aunty Pippa makes perfumes, and anyone who's made stuff through the winter puts in crochet socks, patchwork bags, thick jumpers, woollen trousers and all the warm clothes the spring and summer people don't bring with them. They're never cold where they come from so they don't know what real weather's like.

The most expensive things are George's taxidermy animals – the spring and summer people love them. Dad often says, *George makes the best living out of all of us because he has an artistic eye.* I think his other eye must be glum, living with a houseful of dead animals' soggy bits. That's what makes him a grouch.

The craft shops also sell the paintings Mam Vann makes us do at the school, of boats and hills and the sea. Just before the spring and summer people come, our pictures are stuck on cardboard and put in the craft shop windows with a sign saying: Local Artist. Mam Vann signs them, and the visitors buy near enough all of them. The money she gets is used for our school.

The school used to be a chapel. Next to the arched door, there's a bunch of sage. It's probably my friend Caddy who's left it there, so there's a little bit of fair extra, just from her. She loves the school but I don't know what for. It's been closed for the last week because we've used up all the coal we had. It won't be closed for long, as there's more coal coming. Unless *someone* steals it.

I walk out of the village up the steep hill, wheeling the heavy basket. I pass the thick spider pole that sends wires to our phones. We use our phones for each other if the weather's bad. Sometimes when our phone at home rings, there's a plastic voice that says we've had an accident and could get paid.

Further up the track, I pass the red letterbox. There's little we want to write, apart from to people who've moved away. The postman comes every week or so, parks his van at the top of the hill and brings down boxes for the corner shop.

On the hill, the fir tree wood creaks. Old Kelp's cottage is crouched in a hollow not far from the trees; her thin chimney wheezes smoke into the sky. Old Kelp has lived longer than time and older than age. We're all afraid of her, so we take her the fair and she bakes us honey cakes. We don't want her to curse us. She's learned some of her worst curses from listening to the fir trees that grow far too close together. She can curse in the languages of trees. They drop so many needles that turn into dust. Nothing lives under them. Mammy says, *Plants need light like we need our lungs.* The trees breathe stale badness inside their cramped stretched trunks.

I creak open Old Kelp's rusted gate. With my head bowed, I wheel the basket up the path to the front door of her cottage. Keeping quiet, I leave the ingredients on her doorstep. Barely breathing, I pack the honey cakes she's baked and left outside into the basket, one by one.

Keeping my eyes on the ground, I creak the gate closed behind me as I wheel the trolley away. I go back down to the village, to put the cakes on the doorsteps of everyone who left out fair.

This afternoon, Dad's out in our back yard and I'm standing in the doorway watching him plane and sand the wood on a set of shelves he's just built. It's spitting with rain, and his brown jumper and grey overalls have rain freckles on them.

I ask him in a whisper, 'When did she make the worst troubles?'

He looks up at me. 'Old Kelp? Mostly when new people moved to our village.'

'Did she do that when Aunty Pippa came here from Paradon?'

'That was bad trouble.'

'Did anyone tell her to go away, because Old Kelp didn't like her coming?'

'Pippa fell in love with Finn, and he fell for her too, so no. No one ever told her to go.' He grins at me, straightens up and sets the shelves upright. He looks me up and down as he stretches his back. 'Old Kelp doesn't like outsiders, and double doesn't like the ones from a city that wants the gifts of the whole damn world for itself. I'm glad for Finn, though. He wasn't built to be alone.'

'What did Old Kelp do?'

'She put a curse on the sea to flood over our village. That was to tell us that if others came, we'd be flooded out by them.'

Mammy comes to the doorway and says quietly, 'She stood outside her cottage that night, and the grey stones it's built from were snarling.' Then she says, 'Brack, it's about to chuck it down.'

Dad frowns at the thick sky. 'I've got another three to do. I promised to get them to George by the end of the day. He's been waiting, said he'll pay then and—'

'Then you'll have to finish them indoors.'

He picks up the shelves and hands them to Mammy. She takes them through to the living room.

Dad shoves the sandpaper in his toolbox, picks up his plane

and rubs it down with a cloth. He wipes his brow with the damp arm of his jumper.

Mammy comes back, puts her hands on my shoulders and says in my ear, 'On the night of the flood, Old Kelp stretched her spindly arms to the sky. Her fingers had crescent moons for claws. All kinds of badnesses swam out of her mouth in shrieks and groans on the night of the first flood, and a year later, on the night of the second, and two years after, on the day of the third. Now careful, Kip. You know all the stories about her, but you mustn't talk about doing the fair. It's the same for all of us, and I'm not saying I saw anything or didn't when it was my turn, but I'd never risk my eyes or tongue, and neither should—'

'I haven't—'

She puts her finger on my lips. 'Well, good. Keep it that way.'

Dad shakes his head at Mammy. 'Crescent moons for claws. You've got a sense of drama, I'll give you that.'

She squeezes my shoulders and lets go. There's a rule that whoever is doing the fair can't talk about anything they've seen or heard up at Old Kelp's cottage, not ever. I know from all the stories that she'll curse us if we speak. Someone from our village once did, years ago. All he said was that when he opened her gate, he saw her face at the window, and her skin was as ancient and cracked as a cliff. Soon after saying this, he went blind and lost the use of his tongue.

I check Mammy's gone into the kitchen so she'll not hear me. At the back door, I quietly ask Dad, 'Were more people moving to our village when those other floods happened?'

'Never can remember dates and years.' He puts the plane on top of his toolbox and gives them both to me. They're so heavy I nearly drop them.

He grabs a broom from against the brick wall and brushes away the wood shavings. I can hear Mammy filling the kettle in the kitchen as I put his toolbox and plane on the doorstep next to my feet.

'Did anyone *see* Old Kelp do the flood trouble?'

'Ah,' he says, still sweeping, 'that's the question, but everyone's sure she did it. We all had to help build the tunnels to stop her floods coming in so high. And when the tunnels stopped the village flooding, Old Kelp put trouble on the land not to grow potatoes.'

I whisper, 'Who saw her do that?'

The sky throws down heavy rain. Dad curses under his breath and says, 'Your mammy knows weather. Enough about Old Kelp.' Rain soaks his short black hair and the shoulders of his jumper turn dark brown with wet as he puts the broom in his outdoor tool cupboard. Water runs off his nose and stubbled chin as he bolts the cupboard closed and pushes past me to get indoors.

He stubs his foot on the toolbox and growls. 'You could bloody help more, not just watch!' He picks up the toolbox and plane and takes them through to the living room.

He's left drips on my dress.

I stand in the doorway and watch the rain make moving puddles on the cobbles in the yard. I think about what might happen if I drop the fair and spoil it or break the rules or don't do it right. Old Kelp might do another curse on the land, and if the earth grows potatoes to spite her, they'll grow with human eyes. Or she'll go up near the graveyard on the far side of the wood, and shake the worst fir trees with the rotten fungus that grows round their trunks. She'll shake up those graveyard trees and think of us, and make us all stink till we're dead.

AMBER

'What are seasons for?' Maya asks me, after we've shared an energy bar and are crouching down for the night. We're in a deserted bus shelter with only two unbroken panes of glass, on the edge of an empty road. She rubs her fingertips together, breathes warmth on them.

I say to her, 'Huddle up. Body heat. That's how our warm keeps warm.'

She lays her head on my shoulder and I put my arms around her.

An animal huffs cold air in the field behind us.

Maya doesn't breathe till the sound moves away.

She whispers, 'How do you know?'

'Know what?'

'About how to keep warm.'

'I listened when people told me things. Try to sleep.'

I hold Maya and close my eyes, as we sit cold and silent. The sound of a bird's wings whirrs somewhere in the dark.

Maya's eyelashes blink against my jacket.

'Amber, I can't sleep.'

'I can hear that.'

She leans away from me and her eyes are wide. 'I didn't ever listen much to anyone apart from you. I must be lucky. Having a sister like you who listened to everyone so I didn't need to. You'll tell me what I didn't hear?'

I smile. 'You didn't miss much.'

'Especially, I didn't listen at school. In the second school, the big one, I only really listened in archaeology, architecture and art. Now I'm not at school and we don't have a home, will I have to listen more?'

'We'll find a home.'

After a pause, she asks again, 'What are seasons for? Did anyone ever tell you that?'

'No. No one ever told me that.'

She untucks her hair from behind her ears, puts her hands to her mouth and blows.

'Come back.' I hold out my arms. 'Keep the warm shared.'

'Your nose is freezing.' She grips me again, and I shift my knees so my legs are leaning against hers. Cuddled in the corner of the bus stop, I can smell her greasy hair.

'Amber,' Maya whispers. 'Were we sharing more warm when we were walking? It's just, this sharing warm isn't making me warm. Is it making you warm?'

'Come on. Let's keep moving.'

We stagger to our feet, leaning against one another, and pick up our bags. The lamp posts glow along the main road we left to come down here and huddle. I know that road must lead somewhere, so we go back up to the lights and cracked concrete.

As we walk, I watch Maya. She jumps each time there's a noise, a branch scraping in the trees on the verge, the sound of a distant car, night whoops of birds. She blows on her fingertips, rubs her arms.

She turns and stares along the empty road behind us. 'Amber, can't we . . .'

I turn as well as I follow her eyes. On the distant horizon

there's a glow that's the halo of moonlit Paradon. 'Maya, no. Come on.'

'It's so cold . . .'

'We can't go back.'

We turn away and keep walking.

Maya's quiet for a while.

I say, 'We're not going to stay this lost. We'll land somewhere, and that's going to be our new home.' I grab her hand. 'I'll tell you all about seasons. There are four of them; you remember we used to talk about them when we were little?' I'd found a children's geography book about them. It didn't say very much.

'Only indoors, in secret.'

'The season code.'

We were taught at school that we were lucky to live in a controlled climate, the weather reports rarely altering apart from the precise brightness of sunshine or the degree of moisture in the air. When we were really little, I was fascinated by seasons. So at home, me and Maya played the season code. Winter meant *cheer up*. Summer meant *be nice*. Spring meant *I've got a plan*, and autumn meant *we've been found out*. Our parents overheard us and saw me hugging the book to my chest. They copied some of its pictures; they painted the attic windows: orange leaves for autumn, sunshine for summer, snowflakes for winter and flowers for spring. The constant sunshine bleached the paint off the windows but even when the paint was years gone, we could still see the traces of seasons in the sky.

Maya glances at me. 'Why are there four seasons?'

'I don't know. Maybe because four is a tidy number. Like a square or a box.'

'Are seasons tidy?'

'No, not at all. Seasons are wild and chaotic and beautiful and unpredictable and exciting and bright and murky and all kinds of temperatures and we're going to live in all four of them.'

Her voice is shrill. 'All at the same time?'

'No, one at a time. Not this way around, though. The Paradon summer is leaking, so we're going through spring into winter. When we're further away, we'll know, as the seasons will happen the right way around. We might not see autumn this year. We could have a double winter.'

'Why are seasons one at a time?'

'Because they're polite and they wait for one to finish before the next one begins . . . I don't know, exactly. But we'll find out.'

'Can't there be five seasons?'

'What for?'

'For when we're a bit scared of seasons changing. We can have a season that's blank and still and clean and not changing at all. It could jump in between all the other ones, like a gap. We'll need a season-rest, won't we?'

'No. We'll love them.'

'But we've only ever had summer and that's the good one.'

'Nothing's best of anything when it's the same all the time. Look, we're nearing—'

'Where's summer gone?'

'Stop it, Maya. Look.' I show her the surface of the road. 'We're nearly as far as winter. The glitter. Look – it's frost. And the sky is so clear. Look up, above those clouds, those shining things, those tiny bright—'

Maya's eyes look at where my fingertip is pointing, and when she sees the stars for the first time, she screams as if everything we've ever tried to believe in is erupting from her mouth.

I look at the stars and see hope swarming in clusters. I've calmed Maya, and now she's catching the tremblings of excitement I feel all over my body. Soon we're both shivering as we walk.

The stars glow brighter, clearer, as we walk further into winter.

Maya is more than trembling, she's shaking, glancing upwards every so often; her eyes are still vividly afraid.

I tell her, 'The white dots are called stars.'

Fear clenches her jaw. 'They're holes in the sky.'

Putting my arm around her shoulder, I say, 'The stars have always been there, we've just never seen them. The brightness from the moon and neon lights blotted them out.'

Maya says in a tiny voice, 'The further we go from home, the nearer we'll get to the holes. They'll suck us away through them; we'll be bleached dead in the bright on the other side of the sky . . .'

I feel as if light years are reflecting into my eyes. Full of hope, I want Maya to feel this as well. I rub her shoulder. 'No, stars are old burning suns. Though we can see them all from here, some of them don't even exist any more. We're looking into the past, aeons and aeons ago.'

Maya pales, pulls away from me, stops walking, frozen. She wraps her arms tightly around herself and says, 'Deadstars.'

I shake my head at her, not quite sure what she's feeling.

Her voice sounds desperate. 'What's the point of anything, then? Why do we have houses and food and news and each other, why do people bother sleeping and waking and eating and working or baby-making more people or hoping for anything at all, if things glow so bright when they're dead?'

I look at the sky again, still shivering with excitement. 'Those are galaxies spreading above us.' I grab Maya's hand. 'Don't be sad or fearful. Make your eyes see them as not-dead. Then you won't be scared.'

Behind the brightest ones, I show her the swathes of more distant stars burning blue-white. 'Look at those ones, they're the most alive stars of all.'

35

She frowns at me. 'You're pretend-talking me.' She's caught some other feeling that I have, one I don't even know myself.

'Think of them all as alive.' I'm trying to make her feel the hope I want to keep, but she's still shaking.

Maya says, 'We could stand here forever and never know which are alive and which are dead. Ancient deadstars should be blotted out. If they're still shining while they're dead, there's nothing worth having, nothing to burn for.'

I squeeze her hand. 'Let's keep moving. We'll find something to burn for. I'll want it enough for both of us.'

When we're crouched breathing dust in a broken cowshed, I ask Maya, 'Were you scared in Paradon when I wasn't there and you met new people?'

She nods. 'Sometimes. Most people are confusing. Saying something pretend and thinking so many unpretend things all at the same time. Especially when there are crowds of them. Bash crash bam.'

Maya seems stronger than she ever has before.

I ask her, 'Do you feel different, away from Paradon?'

'A city has a lot of things to want. It pulses electric.'

'Like a heart?'

'It's made from electric and wire and pipes: the ones you can see and all the hidden ones you can't. It breathes in people-sounds. All the sounds of talk and music and breathing and running and shouting and dancing and working and crying and laughing and screaming and driving and singing and every noise anyone can ever make. They're all the sounds of the city breathing. But the people who are doing all those things don't know they're making the city stay alive. If one person decided to switch everything off and be completely silent, then another and another, the city would stop breathing and die.'

I persist, wanting her to think about how *she* feels. 'And what does it feel like to be here, away from Paradon?'

She cuddles up close to me. 'I'm learning-up new things. But the soil's scary.'

'Why?'

'It wants things to put inside itself. It's hungry. The sky tries to pull things out of the soil again, that's why the plants and trees rise up. But the sky's frightening as well, because it watches everything. And it doesn't think at all before it does weatherish things.'

'Does it help that we're together?'

'Still everything's confusing. Sky wants up, soil wants down. Our parents wanted easy things. Good child. Sweet Maya.' She smiles to herself.

Now I feel guilty for taking her away from them.

She says, 'What are we not talking about?' She frowns as she opens her half-empty bag. She rubs her arms, shivers.

'We might meet new people out here. And I don't know what they'll be like. What they'll want. What they'll see when they meet you. I'm worried.'

She hums to herself.

'Maya?'

She still hums.

I try to be less confusing for her. 'You're getting less like me the further away from Paradon we get. Which is what I want, and what's best for you. I think. Maybe we should live on our own, not see other people at all.'

'So, we're hungry now, aren't we? What's left to eat?'

Rummaging deep in my bag, there's no food.

Maya delves in her own bag. She holds out her empty palms at the same time as I do. 'Me too. Nothing.'

Maya blows on my nose and says, 'Winter.'

The season code – cheer up.

My jaw feels tight as I blow on her nose. 'Spring. In a little while, maybe.'

'Maybe spring. Make it a good one.'

Days pass. Sometimes we leave the main road and walk along snaking roads lined with crumbling walls and tangled bushes. We spy on dilapidated villages.

In the daytimes, people gather outside small shops. They wear woollens, long drab coats, mismatching scarves and hats knitted in yellows, browns and bright oranges. The sky is as grey as the crumbling cobbles and cracked paving stones that they walk along. We would stand out like neon lights in our layers of summer clothes. We muddy ourselves up and hide behind walls and in overgrown graveyards. We're learning to duck and run. We're learning the signs other people are near, and the sounds to listen for. Not only speech, but a whistle or a hum, feet squelching in mud, the panicked flight of birds, cows or sheep running. We're motionless, peering between branches or over walls, spying on villages till dusk. We wait till these people have disappeared behind the painted doors of their small houses, or left the villages to go back to mottle-walled farmhouses in the fields.

I often look at Maya as she watches them. Ask myself if she would be dangerous for any of these people. If Maya would catch what they wanted, and give it to them. If the people who live these weathered lives outside of crowds and cities also harbour rage or yearnings for revenge, camouflaged by worn faces. If she'd kill someone's herd of cows, perhaps, for the envy of their fields. Torture someone for fathering the wrong baby. Slap a child for loving one parent more than the other. Maya eyes them with the curiosity that I feel, mirrored.

When their chimneys are smoking, the village streets are silent and the stars come out, we scuttle in. We take sweets from small shops, milk from fridges, we grab bruised apples and the foul raw onions that Maya eats, from sacks in sheds. Doors are never locked.

As we leave a village, the fields are black lakes and the trees are shadows. I'm watching for somewhere sheltered for us to sleep.

Maya bites into a raw potato that in the dark looks like an apple. She grimaces, spits, and throws it over a fence into a field. 'Why are there no old people outside Paradon?'

'Have you seen any hospitals?'

'There was a chemist shop a few villages back.' She takes an onion out of her bag.

'Poorly stocked chemists can't do much about collapsed veins or old hearts or crumbling bones.'

'Why aren't there hospitals?'

'Our father told me part of their tax funds external services. I don't think people in Paradon realise how minor the services are.'

Maya seems pale as she swallows a mouthful of raw onion. 'We're going to die young, aren't we?'

'We're not going to die for a long time. We have to live first.'

She smiles to herself, and stinks of onion. I feel lighter because she's eating something I don't like and thinking a thought that could be her own and not mine.

We drink stolen milk in a night which has rain clackering through it. We're sheltering in the skeleton of a barn under a corrugated roof, where the aroma of cow shit mingles with our own unwashed smells.

Maya asks me, 'When are we going to land?'

'Soon.'

'When?' she demands, a determination on her face that matches my own.

I swig from the carton of milk. 'I think we're near.'

'Near where?'

'The place we're going to land.'

'How do you know?'

I say, slowly, 'I feel different since we left Paradon. There's this dream I keep having and I've never believed in dreams. Never even remembered them till now.'

'What's the dream about?'

'It's a low cottage with walls made of old grey stones. Inside the cottage there's some kind of fire. Warmth. And something dead that's filling the cottage with life. I can't see what, but I keep dreaming of the feeling of it. It's an ancient place, waiting. I dream of it for longer each time we sleep.'

'I have strong dreams.'

'I know. You've always remembered yours.'

'So now you're having strong dreams too. That's good.'

'Why's it good?'

'You're getting to be more all of yourself than half of yourself.'

'I didn't think I had halves.'

Maya taps her head. 'Everyone does. Sleephalf and wakehalf.' She glances at me, rolls her eyes and says, 'The insidehalf and the outsidehalf.'

'Well, my insidehalf must be getting bigger since we left.'

'So that's good.' Maya taps a finger on my head. 'Inside and outside, they want to be the same size, otherwise you're lopsided. Rolling around, wonky egg-like, thinking and feeling nothing's ever the right way up.'

'What does dreaming about a cottage mean?'

She raises her eyebrows. 'That's your outsidehalf wondering. What does your insidehalf say?'

'Inside . . . there's this feeling that it's going to be our home. But a home with a heartbeat, not simply walls of stone, a liveliness inside it that's like—'

Maya smiles. 'Inside, the air feels like it does in an empty room after people have been dancing?'

'Something like that.'

'Well, the insidehalf's usually righter than the outsidehalf.' She lays her head against my shoulder.

After a vivid dream of the same cottage, where I'm watching sticks and bones drumming in an empty fireplace, I wake to the reek of dung. I can see through the holes between bricks that it's a white-skied day. Dreaming still feels so new to me that now I'm awake, I don't want to speak.

Maya's sitting cross-legged on a pile of planks, plaiting straw. She's caught my quietness. We drink icy water from a trough, pick up our bags and leave the barn.

Maya eyes the branches of trees with suspicion as we walk along narrower roads. My feet feel as if they're treading a path they already know.

By dusk we're on a narrow road at the peak of a hill. Across a field there's a thick forest of fir trees; down from the trees there are chimneys and tiled rooftops. Past the chimneys, there is the sea, pale, flat. Everything around us is still. My pulse races and my feet move faster, my heart beats, come on come on come on.

Next to a lay-by, there's a well-trodden path through a field that leads towards the chimneys. Our broken shoes soak up rain from the grass as we walk down the path. Maya rushes ahead, looks to her left, and stops. She looks over her shoulder at me.

I rush past her.

In a hollow is the cottage from my dream. Behind a rusted metal gate. A small garden to the right with a strong wooden shed. This is the cottage: ancient greying stones, small windows. This is the cottage: a worn wooden front door, rocks lining the path. This is our cottage: the curtains, closed. A thin, smoking chimney.

Come on come on. Come in. My feet guide me towards it, through the gate, up the path, to the door.

My hand turns the cold handle and the door opens into darkness.

Warmth.

I step inside.

The click of another door, closing.

Smells of honey and ginger and cinnamon.

A sound as soft as falling sand,

and silence.

Maya comes in and switches on the light.

The kitchen is that of a professional baker. On the shelves are bowls and pots, pans and jugs, jars of herbs and spices and essences. A browned mortar and pestle are on the counter. There's a fire burning in a wood-burner. The oven door looks like a mouth. I open it and the inside of the oven is like an enormous stomach. In an oversized orange ceramic jar on the counter is a vast assortment of misshapen spoons.

Maya calls, 'Hello, hello?' as she crosses the kitchen and goes towards a closed door. I'm certain there's no one here but us. Maya opens the door and disappears behind it, still calling.

The kitchen cupboards are filled with flours and powders and flavours.

Maya's voice: 'Hello?'

I open another door, and there's a narrow living room, the black curtains on the far wall pulled closed. There are two sagging chairs by an empty fireplace. A sewing box with a broken lock. A basket of coal. I drop my bag on the floor. Under the metal grate is a slump of pale sand. Above the mantelpiece there's a mirror flecked with stains.

Maya's voice, louder: 'Hello?'

She comes into the living room and says to me, 'No one's here. There's one bedroom and the walls are painted with black paint. The wardrobe's full of a woman's black clothes. The double bed's made. There's a cabinet in there full of dangerdanger things. Oh, there's a bathroom. All the windows are hidden behind dark curtains. There's a side door that leads out to an overgrown garden.'

'The cupboards in the kitchen are full of baking ingredients.'

The electricity fizzles, the lights flicker off and back on.

As Maya rummages in the sewing box and shrieks at the pins, I go back into the kitchen.

A thick book is on the wooden table and I switch on an old-fashioned table lamp that shines a halo of light over it. The book is a cake and pudding recipe book, the pages covered in smudges of flour and brown rings from mugs. The ingredients are fattening, sweet; there are ingredients I've never heard of, flavours I've never tasted. My mouth salivates and I feel a little nervous because I've never cooked anything as rich or complex as some of these puddings. The recipes are in old shaky handwriting, and there are aged notes folded between the pages with lists of additional instructions.

Inside the front cover, there's a note. The words are written in spidery writing, with a thick black pen:

COOKING WITH BONES

Bake through the nights,
put honey cakes on the doorstep in the mornings.
Sleep through the day.
No one to say, go away, come here.
No one to knock.
No one to be near.

I'm so tired I can almost hear the recipes whispering to each other inside the pages. Reading this note, it immediately makes sense. Perhaps because I'm exhausted, perhaps because I need it to enough. I know what I have to do, and if I do what this recipe book is asking of me, we can live here.

Maya bangs and crashes, rummages in the cupboard beside the side door. She pulls things out, frowns at them, and puts them away again. There are multipacks of toilet and kitchen rolls, bin liners and sanitary towels, batteries, washing powder and toothpaste, old cooking utensils, light bulbs and fuses, ancient strips of unused stamps, unwritten postcards, washing-up liquid, bleach and shampoos.

She leans both hands on the cupboard door to make it close.

I say to her, 'We've landed.'

I open a kitchen cupboard and get out a ceramic mixing bowl. From a hook I lift down a dented copper saucepan. I turn the dial up on the oven and open the recipe book at the stained page. I'm going to be baking every night from now on, perhaps forever.

HONEY CAKES

Honey, 72 fl oz
Butter, 27oz
Flour, 108 oz
Baking powder, 5 medium spoons
Salt, 9 pinches
Bicarb of soda, 5 medium spoons
Spices
Eggs, 27
Milk, 14 fl oz

Place the honey with the butter in a saucepan and heat till melted, stirring with a medium spoon in an anti-clockwise direction, continuously.

Before sifting the flour, baking powder, salt, bicarbonate of soda and spices into a bowl, stop. Consider the nature of the particular spices you've selected, and keep this thought at the forefront of your mind at all times, imagining your thoughts are buzzing in the air between the powders as they fall from the sieve.

Beat the eggs and milk together, until both are submissive and exhausted. Perhaps add lemon peel, if a notion of sharpness would benefit the effects of the particular spices used.

Make a well in the centre of the dry ingredients and imagine this well is empty and awaiting rain. Add the honey mixture gradually, beating well between each drop, and think about a sprinkle of nuts if a sense of earthiness would benefit the effects of the selected spices.

Bake in cake trays until the cakes are firm yet springy. You could add honey or some further spice to the surface of the hot cakes and bake further, if you are experimenting with a variety of spices for different purposes.

Leave to cool in a location at ground level, free from damp.*

* Whilst the cake is cooling, the cake breathes. The direction of breathing for honey cakes should always be upwards, because of the honey's memory of the flight of bees. The breath of honey cakes needs to spread as if flying, in as much available air as possible, in anticipation of a shared consumption and shared effect.

As I find and measure out the ingredients, I realise I'm going to need to use a much bigger mixing bowl and saucepan. The cake trays are stacked in the drying rack beside the sink, and are made for small, individual cakes – enough for a lot of people.

The honey is stored in a clutter of jars which line the kitchen shelves and huddle in cupboards. It has a deep caramel colour and scent. I dip my little finger into one of the jars. It tastes as rich as toffee.

I extract a misshapen spoon from the orange pot. Turning the spoon over in my hands, I realise it's carved from a bone.

My skin feels flushed. I kick off my broken shoes and the brown tiles of the kitchen floor are cool under my bare toes.

As I'm greasing the cake trays, Maya opens the kitchen curtains.

I say to her, 'Tell me when the sky gets even lighter, when it's closer to dawn.'

'Sea-looking.'

'What about it?' I spoon the mixture into the cake trays.

'It tastes of open.'

'What does open taste like?'

'Clouds made of salt.'

She's quiet for a while, and I can hear her breathing.

'It's all right, Maya, it's only a jumbling feeling.'

Once I've slid the cake trays into the mouth of the oven, I switch off the kitchen light. We both look out of the window at the dark sky and chimneys and, beyond them, the horizon of grey sea. I feel a draught on my ankles and the tiny hairs rise on my forearms. I shiver. 'We're meant to keep all the curtains closed.'

Maya watches me close them. 'No daylight for us?'

I switch the light back on again and tell her, 'We'll be sleeping in the daytimes. And baking through the nights. That's what the note in the recipe book says to do.'

'Why do we have to?'

'Doesn't it feel right to you as well?'

Maya fidgets with her hair and frowns at me. 'You're getting new feelings, aren't you? But I can't feel them all.'

'Yes. Dreams of this cottage, and now the instinct to keep the curtains closed. The feeling that this cottage has been waiting for us. I'm so excited about the recipes; I'm going to learn to bake properly, with real ingredients. I'll bake every single recipe in the book, one at a time. We're going to eat all of these puddings! We're going to get really fat. I can't wait!' I laugh and grab her hands.

Maya isn't smiling back at me.

I let go of her hands. Feeling a little hurt that she hasn't caught my excitement when it's such a new feeling, I say, 'Maybe we're both going to be very different, away from Paradon.'

Maya taps the edge of the deep ceramic sink. 'I've got instincts too.'

'What about?'

'If we have to live here, we'll shadowsmell.'

'What smell do shadows have?'

She picks up an onion from a bowl on the counter and sniffs it. 'That spice you sprinkled into the bowl with your fingers. It whooshed smell.'

'That was cardamom.'

Maya strokes the brown skin of the onion. 'Well, cardamom shadowsmells.'

'You're still jumbling. Would you be able to sleep?' If she sleeps, I'll have the kitchen to myself. Let myself feel this excitement, make it grow.

But Maya says, 'Not yet without you.' She puts the onion down and rubs her earlobes, her eyes glancing around the kitchen. She bites her lip as she looks at the closed curtains.

I open the curtains a slit and tell her, 'So we can watch together for dawn. Then we'll put the honey cakes out and see what happens.'

When the sky lightens, we open the door to the cold and put all the cakes outside on the doorstep in rows. Back in the kitchen, we eat one honey cake each. Though the browned surface is cool, they're warm and melting inside. They taste of toffee and honey and there's a bitter-sweet tang which must be the cardamom. I want to spread everything out, look at all the cooking utensils, have a proper rummage through the cupboards. Read every page of the recipe book.

Maya's still wide awake and looking anxiously out of the window between the black curtains. I switch off the kitchen light so we can watch the path and cottage gate without being seen.

I put my arm around her as the sky lightens to pale grey and the sea brightens and glows.

She yawns. 'Eating's made me travelstink. Can I have a bath?'

I say, 'Good idea. Go and run one, I'll keep watching.'

She thuds through to the bathroom but comes back again, quickly, her eyes wide, her fingers fidgeting with each other. 'There's no water living in the pipes.'

In the bathroom, the greening pipes that lead from the bath to the ceiling are rattling and shaking. They look like they're going to come off the wall so I instinctively bash them with a square block of cracked soap. They stop vibrating. Boiling water comes out of the tarnished tap in spurts. Steam fills the bath and wets our faces pink.

Maya clutches the edge of the bath with tight fingers. 'Angry water.'

'It's boiling.'

'Same but different. How can I not-burn?'

I thump the pipes again, in case they shiver when I turn on the cold tap. The waters mix.

Back at the kitchen window, I see a young girl turn to close the gate behind her. She's got scruffy short hair, and under her coat she's wearing a blue dress and wellies. She wheels a basket.

When she's out of sight I open the front door. On the doorstep, the cakes are gone. She's left eggs, bacon, milk, butter, cocoa, sugar, honey, flour, potatoes, spices, chicken . . .

Everything we could possibly need, and much more.

I smile to myself at how fattening it all is, compared to the tentative diets and vitamin hygiene that were regimes in Paradon. As I bring everything into the kitchen, I stroke the table, the counters, the chopping boards and the cupboard doors before I put all the ingredients away.

Maya splashes in the bathtub as she hums out of tune.

KIP

Aunty Pippa comes round to our cottage after tea. She comes in quietly and doesn't take her coat off. Standing in the living room beside the front door, she fidgets with her blonde plait and looks at the floor.

Mammy touches Aunty Pippa's new crocheted beret. 'Green suits you. You look pretty in this – ooh, what's up?'

Aunty Pippa says in a choked voice, 'Can I talk to you alone?'

Mammy tells her, 'Set yourself down by the fire.' She helps her out of her coat. Mammy glances over at me, watching them from the kitchen doorway. She does a serious-eye face which means, scarper off.

So I scarper to my bedroom and get changed out of my blue dress and into my nightie. Dagger's still in the living room to sniff Aunty Pippa. He won't be long because he doesn't like her perfume smells.

I stand behind my open bedroom door and watch for Dagger through the crack between the hinges of the door and the frame. I can hear their voices talking and I think it's about Uncle Finn.

Aunty Pippa's saying, 'I don't know for sure.'

Mammy says, 'Well, you sound sure.'

'But I can't stress his weak heart . . .'

'I'd not put up with it from Brack. As brothers go, they're not as alike as they could be. When did this start?'

Aunty Pippa sounds sad. 'I think he's wanted her for years, and it's been almost a year he's been lying to me. That's what my instinct is, anyway. Not knowing but knowing is gut torture.'

They're quiet for a while.

Aunty Pippa says, 'I left one set of failed expectations behind me in Paradon. And I thought I'd got away from all that, but I've made another failure, in the expectations I found right here: that marriage is life. And I made the choice to marry him. He asked, I answered. I should stick with it, no matter what.'

'Unless it's unbearable. And is it?'

'When I think about leaving him, I remember that evening he asked. It was something about the way his hands looked with the light from the sea reflecting across them. We were sitting on the beach. I found myself saying yes and yes and yes again, to marriage, to a home, to a life with him. He's much older than me, so I thought he'd be safe; that he'd know what he wanted, and stick with it.'

Mammy says, 'Your own parents parted, didn't they?'

Aunty Pippa doesn't answer.

'How old were you?'

'About six. You know, I wish there was something in his words when he asked, that could weigh me down more. But he only said the words that were needed. Even so, there was something about the setting sun catching the ripples of the sea, the taste of salt on my lips, and the texture of the skin on the back of his hands. I thought that evening, and for all these years since, that we'd grow old together like fading sunlight.'

'And now?'

'Whenever I've doubted him, I've always thought of that evening. Him with his long auburn ponytail, wearing his dad's flat cap with the fishing flies pinned in, his big hands and the creases around his green eyes. You know, he smiled when I danced. I loved the damp cold sand between my toes.'

Mammy says again, 'And now?'

'His heart must be protecting him.'

Mammy sounds cross. 'You mean his weak heart tells him to lie to you, so you don't get angry about the truth and upset it?'

Aunty Pippa's voice is quiet. 'Something like that.'

'I'd say it's his mouth doing the lying. You've got to say something.'

Dagger flashes black in the space between the door and the doorframe, comes into my bedroom and licks my ankles. I put him on my bed, click the door closed, and whisper stories about wedding dresses into his ears.

Mammy comes in and sits on my bed. She looks a bit fierce in her eyes but the fierce goes away as she strokes my hair. 'She's gone. Sorry to send you off like that.' She scratches a dried soup stain off her jumper sleeve. 'How much of that did you hear?'

'Not much.'

She shifts herself back against the pillow and puts her arm around me. 'Keep it to yourself.'

'Got nothing to say.'

'You're good, Kip. Can't sleep?'

'I tried but I'm wide awake.'

'It's hard not being allowed to talk about Old Kelp, isn't it?'

I nod with my mouth tight shut.

'Sometimes being told not to talk about something makes that something the biggest thing in your head. Sorry to ask you to keep quiet about anything you heard me and Aunty Pippa say tonight as well. She's not in a good way. Would a story help you sleep?' She rubs my shoulder.

I nod again.

'Which one?'

'The one about Gilliam.'

Mammy says, 'This is a story of the oldest woman there ever was, and what happened when she took herself a lover. Some call this woman a witch or a crone, some call her ancient, some call her wise. No one knows how she'd describe herself, for the wisdom of age is a mystery to those who are still young. She's lived for all of her own years and all of ours, in her stone cottage, alone. No one knows what age she really is, but she's generations older than everyone else. She lives next to a forest, where owls may shriek, and wolves may growl, and the branches are so angry they scratch back at the wind. But the old woman is the only one who hears them.

'Down the hill from her cottage, there is a village. She used to go to the village at dusk. She'd knock on every door, and say just one word to each person who answered: *Flour. Eggs. Honey. Sugar. Butter. Milk. Spice.*

'She'd not look at the person she was asking, and they'd scurry to fetch whatever she demanded. For there's nothing so fearful at dusk as an ancient woman in black, who won't meet your eye and asks for the one thing she seems to *know* you have.

'Each night the scents of cinnamon and allspice crawled through the sky all the way from her cottage and down the chimneys in the village. The air thickened so sweetly that it clogged up everyone's sleeping heads, and no one could remember their dreams.

'On a farm nearby lived a man who flogged his horses and forced life from the land. The fields were never rested, year in, year out. The earth gave him whatever he troubled it for, though all the plants that grew for him came up bruised. He strode and strutted all over his land, night and day, taking and taking from it, without listening to what the soil needed back from him. Now one night he met the old woman in black. She must have put a curse made of sugar on his eyes, for he saw her as fairer than she was. He was headstrong in his wooing of her, and he believed spices scented her skin. That farmer became her lover.

'But there was a hidden trouble between the old woman and her lover, as he never told her he already had a wife. Each day he came to the old woman, and each night the scents from her cottage smelled as if they came straight from flowers, or honey-comb, or perfume, and those sweet smells, they hung in the air.

'A farmer's life story travels the land he lives on, it's dug into the soil and it's trampled by the cows, it's spread in the silage, it's drunk from the milk pail and smeared over breads in the butter. But when the old woman came down to the village to demand what she needed, no one talked about her lover's wife.

'Now his wife knew full well what he was up to. But when anyone mentioned her husband and the old woman, she'd laugh so hard no one could stop her, and, well, it's told that hers wasn't the kind of laugh you'd ever want to hear.'

I whisper, 'What'd it sound like?'

Mammy takes a deep breath. 'Like a wail of a—'

I put my hand over her mouth. 'Stop it!'

She smiles on my hand.

I take my hand away. 'Why did she laugh? Don't do it.'

'That farmer's wife was all mixed up because he'd been so rough with her. Her eyes were wide and a vivid blue, but her lips were thin and cracked, from years upon years of biting her tongue. While he was with the old woman, he let his wife well alone.

'Now the old woman, she wasn't of a mind to care about his roughness. She'd got bruises on her face but she gave as good as she got. There was a medicine in the bruises he'd come out of her cottage with; she'd blacken both his eyes, put purple bruises right across his mouth. He was overcome. Over time, he stopped walking like a bantam cockerel, and limped like a lame dog. His face was flushed, and he couldn't see out of his crumpled-up eyes. And yet still he was smiling. He was sucked and beaten and loved dry as a stone. One day he toppled over, climbing a hill.

'He was found hidden in a ditch. He called, *End it for me, or I'm as good as dead.* He was dragged from the ditch by a few villagers, who laughed while he begged them to tell the old woman he had a wife, so she'd end it, and he wouldn't have to tell her himself.

'No one wanted to tell the old woman about her lover's wife, because everyone was afraid of her. But a young girl who hated people keeping secrets overheard all the talk. When the old woman knocked on her door, demanding *Spice*, she told her, *He's got a wife. That's not fair for you.*

'The old woman stopped coming to the village. For years upon years, people used to sneak food up to her, leave practical supplies on her doorstep, fill her coal hole, so she'd keep fed and warm. But she didn't come out of her cottage.

'The farmer's wife found herself to be a far better farmer than her husband had ever been. She had a way with the land. She gave to the fields, and they gave back, more than thrice whatever she asked for. So for each seed she planted, she got three plants, and when she put cows to those fields, for each calf she birthed, there'd be another two slither out after she turned her back. For each milk pail she filled, there would be another two brimming after she'd thought the milk had run out. They say that's payback, for being stuck in a tangle of three and getting out of it again and coming back to being herself as she once was. And that farmer, well, he just disappeared.'

'You have to say the farmer's name.'

Mammy's voice almost sings as she says, 'You know his name was Gilliam, and he was never seen again. All the ditches were searched in case the fields he'd troubled and strained over the years were getting their own back by swallowing him whole. The villagers even got the police to come from miles away. The police wandered round the village, and after a long think, he couldn't find any clever thoughts, so he pinned up a sign that said: *Come and get me if there's a clue.* After a winter and a summer and another winter had passed, it's said that everyone thought if Gilliam was to be found, he would have been found. They all decided he'd fallen in some deeper ditch.' She kisses my cheek.

'Did the police never come back?'

'Oh, this is generations ago. So that one's long dead. He had a son who grew to be the police as well, and he must have been told about it. That family have kept it as some mystery handed down. That very first police always wanted to know what had happened to Gilliam, and it ate at his bones. He passed that hunger on to his son and his son passed it down and so forth. I remember the last time the police came down this way. I was a young thing. He was sniffing round Old Kelp's cottage. But George and his dad got to him, told him she was harmless, a mad old woman who'd lived over-long and wouldn't pain a moth.'

'So no one knows what really happened to Gilliam after Old Kelp found out he was married?'

She shakes her head as she tucks me in. 'No one knew then, and now no one ever will.' She whispers in my ear, 'I think he must have been cursed. Think of the stories I've told you about Old Kelp's curses; the tales of the blind and dumb man, the shock-haired girl, the three-legged hare, and the boy with the twisted spine. Always keep to the rules. Now you've got to be up early for the fair. So, try to sleep.'

AMBER

Tonight, Maya's in the living room by the fire, a pile of black clothes on the floor in front of her. They're all the garments from the wardrobe in the bedroom. She's trying and failing to thread a needle.

I reach to take the needle and help her, but she shakes her head. 'It's like getting an ice cube through a plughole but it gets there in the end . . .'

'What are you doing?'

'I'm going to have another try at taking up the hems. All the clothes here are too long for us. I've done that one now too. What do you think?' She nods at a black skirt on the back of a chair.

Picking it up and looking at the hem, it's wonky, like the hems of the black elasticated trousers we're both wearing. Maya's uneven stitches pull all the fabrics tight and slack. 'It's . . . quite good. You'll get even better if you keep practising.'

'I'm very determined.' She smiles up at me.

I smile back. 'Yes, you are.' Squeezing her shoulder, I say, 'I'm going for a walk, won't be long.' I think what a dangerous thing a needle is, and think of Maya last night, yanking the thread and complaining it doesn't do the same as elastic.

One of us needs to learn to sew, so we've got enough clothes.

We've already eaten so much in the few weeks we've lived here that none of our own tight clothes fit.

Maya's eyes narrow to focus on the needle.

I close the living-room door so she's warm by the fire.

Wrapped in a wide black coat, I slip on the wellies beside the front door and go out into the night. I go round the side of the cottage, through the garden, over the wall and through the field. My feet crunch on frost.

I can smell burning as well as earth and bark. Further down the hill, the chimneys in the village are smoking. Above them, the sky is thick with stars.

Maya doesn't like it when I go outside in the nights and come back smelling of earth and bark and salt air. I want her to learn how to be alone. Last time I went outside, I came home to find her inside the wardrobe. She said she thought she'd feel less afraid if she hid.

When I asked her what she was frightened of, she couldn't remember.

Maya's started to mention a few things she likes here: the pillows and black duvet, the smell of rose soap, the depth of the bath and the taste of gooseberry jam. But she talks a lot more about the things she liked in Paradon. She also often mentions things she doesn't like here: the cracks in the cottage walls, the low ceilings, weather in general, the wind in particular, loud noises, and me ignoring her while I'm learning to bake.

I feel somehow bigger, here. As I cross the field my arms feel long, my body feels taller, wider than it really is. As if I've got invisible roots growing from my feet and leaves growing from my fingertips, branches bursting from each hair on my head. My body is a solid core as I stride across the field towards the fir trees.

I realise how small I felt in Paradon.

Looking after Maya, and as I got older, not looking after myself.

Maya was made for me.

As a toddler, I made too much noise, I wet the bed, upset the nanny, babbled to soft toys as if they were real people, broke the heads off skinny dolls when left alone. When I began to talk, I cried for a twin, over and over. This was what my parents found most disturbing; they couldn't understand it. The nanny asked my mother if I'd started out as twins in the womb, but I hadn't. I was taken to a child psychologist who told our parents I was desperate for attention. My parents thought I was too clingy, too needy, too chaotic, never content. Like all parents, they'd been trained to nurture connections, not attachments. They must have found a rogue psychologist, because she disagreed with this approach and warned them about a myriad of potential long-term disorders. They got rid of the psychologist.

I didn't get any easier for them. I remember crying a lot. I remember the nanny's bitten fingernails but not her name. She left, and was never replaced.

And then came Maya. She's genetically related to both our parents, though she must have started her life in a Petri dish. When they first brought her home in a crackling silver blanket, her skin was shimmering all the way to her tiny fingernails. She looked at me with wide black eyes and I loved her instantly. I knew she was for me.

It took Maya around a year to mirror my emotions and mimic my gestures, to reflect me and form her enhanced self into the perfect twin. Our parents saw her as their solution. For them she was the calm, pleasing, well-behaved child they had always wanted, and they knew she'd bond to me and make me contented.

I didn't feel alone any more. She became my other half, my companion, my doll to take care of. She was perfect. She was for all of us, really.

Now, I want her to be all for herself.

I walk into the wood.

In this moment, Paradon seems like a city fast-forwarded through time. A place where people run to catch up with themselves in the future, and never notice what's happening to them now. I couldn't have been contented, living the rest of my life in Paradon and never smelling this rich soil. I'm filled with new feelings: premonitions, intentions, dreams.

Now. I weave in and out of the trees along the edge of the wood. Now. My feet sink in mounds of moss. Now. I lean on a trunk, break off dead twigs, smell the bark. Now. Go further into the wood. Now. The pine needles tremble on the branches above me.

The sky twists.

My arms reach out. The earth tilts.

A flash behind my eyelids – blinding sun on glass. Maya.

The feeling of someone falling through my arms. Maya.

A smash.

The crash of a branch. Maya.

The earth spins. Maya.

Pine needles scratch my face as I fall. Something's happened to her. The snap of twigs as I stagger to my feet. The weakened feeling in my arms thuds into my stomach, and I almost throw up.

I run, caught by branches, tripped by roots, out of the wood, my feet slide on frost through the field, I clamber over the stone wall and into the garden, lurch around to the front door, push it open and—

Maya's fine. She's standing in the middle of the kitchen,

looking exactly like me. There's something red on the kitchen floor.

'She's dead. Warm dead. But dead dead,' Maya whispers, her fingers over her lips, as I slow my breathing. My face burns from the sudden warmth of the kitchen. I lock the front door. Stamp mud off the wellies.

Look at what's on the kitchen floor.

Stop stamping.

Look at Maya.

Look at what's on the floor again.

Look back at Maya.

Maya's staring at me, but my eyes are pulled back to the woman's dead body.

I say, swallowing nausea, 'I thought I felt you—'

Maya drops her hands from her mouth. 'I've blinked, and she's still here. She doesn't go away. She's not wearing black so it's not her cottage we're living in. She's someone else.'

I ask, 'Is her dress really red, or white with blood all over it?'

'Crimson.'

'I thought I felt you fall through my arms. But it was her.' I poke at my arm, pinch the fabric on the sleeve of my black coat. Fidget with it between my fingers and thumb. 'Maya, I felt her—'

She shakes her head. 'No. It wasn't me made her dead. I didn't fall her. Drop her, smash her over the head, I didn't, not with that rock.' She gestures at the lump of grey stone, bloodstained, lying on the floor. 'She looked like this, her face smashed in. Dead on this floor when she was never here before. Like she's always been here. Only she wasn't. Not last night or the night before. She's not been here ever, not since we found this cottage. And you were here too, when she was not here this afternoon.'

I try to move my feet but they don't work. My body sways a

little and the room spins. I lean on the door to steady myself.

Maya seems dizzy as well. 'She wasn't here when we ate cheese omelette. We were talking about the colour black. So we'd have noticed that dress, even if we didn't see her lying dead inside it. I'm almost noticing it now, though her face is more distracting. We were sitting at the table.'

I shake myself and nod at the wooden table against the wall where we eat our meals. 'We . . . were. We mixed an omelette together and you used too much pepper.'

Maya takes a giant step over the woman and leans down to look in the slops bucket. She points at the brown and white eggshells on top of stale cake. 'Look. You remember. If she'd been here then, we'd have tripped over her. Fallen on top of her. Maybe have screamed, or maybe we wouldn't –'

I turn away from the dead body. 'I don't want to look at her face. How could—'

'– no, we would have screamed. If we'd fallen on her, seeing her face close up, we'd have screamed . . .'

I frown at her. 'Maya, I felt her fall, so it must have been your arms—'

'No, Amber, it wasn't. I didn't. It must have not been—'

'Here you are, looking at her. What do you want me to think?'

'Did you not see anyone outside, not anyone running away?'

'No. Slow down.'

Maya squats on the floor next to the dead woman and looks at her split eyelid and her other half-open eye. 'Her iris is green-blue-dark. But unseeing blank. She might have been beautiful.'

I say quietly, 'Maya, what happened when she looked at you?'

She still talks too fast and sounds confused. 'No, no remember of looking. Apart from now, looking. The skin of her neck. It's smooth-pale. So she might have been beautiful. But we'll never know. She's not old. And the colour of her eyes, she might have had beautiful eyes. She might have had the kind of eyes fish could want to swim in.'

I snap at her, 'Fish don't want to swim in anyone's eyes – water's the only thing fish want. There's no room in eyes. The eyeballs are in there and they need all the room they can get, otherwise they wouldn't move. They'd be clogged up with unswimming fish.'

'Tears are salty. Do you think there's sea in her eyes, though she's dead and her face broken and drowned in blood . . . oh.' She covers her mouth as if about to be sick. 'When she was alive, do you think she never, I mean ever, cried waves—'

'Oh for . . .' I step over the woman's legs, and turn a dial on the cooker. 'The oven's on –' I spin around to face Maya '– so we'd better clear her away.'

We take her outside to the shed and the night is made of thickened dark, the moon's hidden in clouds so we're invisible with dark coats and scarves on, bandaged in black, a torch clenched under my arm as we carry this dead woman in a dress that looks brown in the dark like old blood.

Maya's supposed to be carrying the woman's legs. She says, 'She aches my arms with heavydeath.'

So I've got all her weight.

I close the shed door, with us inside it.

Right now I'm glad it's still winter, I'm glad for this cold. The wind scratches the branches of trees and the wooden shed creaks. The shed's draughty, and I'm breathing so hard that everything seems askew: the spade and fork look like cutlery for a very big plate. Leaned up against a wall there's an old mattress behind some planks and a ladder, and I shiver when I drop the dead body on the floor.

I almost say sorry to her, but I don't in case she answers.

Her body lies on the rotten floorboards in between the old plant pots I've kicked over and sacks filled with bulbs which are kept in the dark.

Maya's watching me. She shivers. 'I don't want to be next to a body that's so dead but still feels a little bit warm.'

'No.' I shiver as well. 'Death shouldn't be warm.'

In the garden the pale moon flickers between clouds. I try to dig a hole with the spade but the earth is frozen solid.

I lean on the spade. 'Any fire we burn to thaw the soil could be seen from the village.'

'Well, try digging again.'

'You dig!' I thrust the spade at her and she drops it.

So I grab the fork from the shed and bang the prongs against the soil. I stop and lean a foot on it, breathing hard. 'This won't work. We'll have to wait for the earth to thaw. So we'll bury her in spring. Or summer. Till then, she stays in the shed. So, I'll bury her in there. You're no help – not like this.'

Maya is pale and her hands are shaking.

Trying to speak more gently, I say, 'Go and find her some flowers.'

I go back into the shed and lean the torch so its light shines upwards. I grab the woman under the shoulders and pull her away from the middle of the shed floor. Now there's space to move things around.

I move out the stepladder, plant pots, planks, rake, rusted tins of paint, a toolbox and cardboard boxes. I put them all in the garden, stacked next to the shed.

Back in the shed, I grasp the old mattress. There's a brown bloodstain all across it. I force myself to imagine it's from a bad nosebleed or period, rather than anything else. I thud the mattress onto the floor.

Heaving the woman's body, I pull out the wide crimson skirt of her dress so it hides the blood on the mattress. I cover her with paint-splattered dustsheets. They look like death shrouds and I can breathe now her broken face is covered.

The shed is her mausoleum; this mattress and these sheets are her grave. She's had a dustsheet burial.

I go outside and Maya is in the corner of the garden hunting absent flowers.

And the dead woman does need something, to mark this moment. Tearing up handfuls of grass and ivy, I go in and out of the shed till I've covered her, the mattress, and the shed floor with green.

As we go back indoors, I think that the cold shed is good for this woman, and for us, because we don't want anyone coming to this cottage. A body could bring people, and what we've got to remember is: though there's a dead body which might bring live ones to find it, we're lucky it's winter, and lucky it's so cold and lucky that there might only be a few weeks each year, on a good year, when the sun might shine enough to warm up *anything* enough to really, well, stink.

To carry on as normal, when nothing feels normal, is the only thing I feel able to do. So I mop the kitchen floor while Maya watches. She looks afraid of death and its shadows. Each time I look at her, I feel fear as well. In a warm rush that feels like an internal rebellion of life against death, an instinct pulses through my body. It makes me want to do things that make us both feel solid and vivid and real and alive.

So I bake puddings and cakes, and we stay up through the night with good smells and heat blustering from the oven. Soon we're down to our black knickers and vests and singing at the honey cakes to rise, and they do rise, like little suns in the oven. When it's nearly morning we're dancing around trying not to bump into one another, laughing about how we really can dance, though I'm a bit wonky, a bit wobbly because I've got a bellyful of toad-in-the-hole and crab-apple crumble, which Maya couldn't even eat as she's so dizzy from death and life and dancing.

The whole cottage is alive with the smell of nutmeg and a whiff of violet, because there is a small bunch of violets left with the ingredients on the doorstep each morning. They must somehow be lucky, because flowers aren't meant to grow in winter.

I put a small violet petal on the top of every honey cake, a few heartbeats before they're fully risen. I've been doing that for a while now, but opening the oven door makes all the honey cakes I bake sink.

But I must be right about the luck in the violets, because we are lucky. We've got this cottage and all the things in it, and no one bothers us and as long as we leave the honey cakes out on the doorstep, they're taken away at dawn, and there are more ingredients in their place and everything is the same, night after day after night.

So on this night of the dead woman with the bloodied face and crimson dress, I know that hiding her away is the only thing to be done, so we can keep this cottage and the recipes and the life we've found here. After I've put the sunk honey cakes out on the doorstep and later, brought in the ingredients, we go to bed.

Maya sleeps on her back, almost on the edge of the bed. Since we've shared this bed, she sleeps further from me when she's annoyed or overwhelmed. I build a feeling of want, and will myself to see past her face which looks the same as mine. I whisper, 'Show me what she saw when she looked at you.' Soon another face flickers on hers, a sad woman's face with desperate eyes. I feel sorry for this face, there's an ache in my chest. I don't know what it means. The face flickers a few times, till Maya's face settles back to mine, and remains, unchanging. The ache fades away.

Maya's whispering, so I listen to her.

'Not outside in the shed, not under the grey clouds . . . weathery sky. Sky is looking down at the shed. The sky can't see . . . not behind the shed door. Sky doesn't have a telescope . . .'

I lie on my side, clasping the cramp in my stomach that's from too much crab apple. Under the wash of black paint on the wall I can see the wallpaper bumps of flower petals.

Maya's crying. She murmurs, 'Don't like it. I want mysister.'

My heart clenches because she never cries when she's awake. Tears that only flow in dreams must spring from the deepest places.

And perhaps she needs to cry, now. Cry and howl and scream the woman's death out of herself, but I know, when awake, she never will. While we were in the kitchen after hiding the body in the shed and I was baking for hours, and we were high on sugared smells – oh, those puddings! I thought, though I didn't say it aloud, that though we felt so alive – filled with dancing and sugars and whirlings and spice – I was thinking Maya must have killed that woman.

If we never have to look behind the shed door again, she'll be out of our thoughts. If I forget the dead woman, and Maya forgets her because I do, we won't have to think about her. She'll stay there, undiscovered. She'll lie there quietly, for the rest of all time, being forgotten.

Being dead in the shed.

*   *   *

Maya comes into the kitchen and nearly crashes into a stack of plant pots while I'm putting dusty boxes under the table. She looks around the kitchen at the garden tools and bags of bulbs. 'This is all –'

'– the stuff from the shed.'

Maya whispers, 'Is she out there, still?'

'We didn't dream it. But let's try to forget her.'

'I thought maybe she'd have . . .'

It doesn't feel like we'll be able to forget her. 'She's still there.'

'It might be better being above the ground, not under it. There's more space for her to feel—'

'She doesn't have feelings any more. We do. So, think about something else.'

Maya looks at the stepladder propped against the wall. 'Where are you going to put all this stuff?'

'Oh, somewhere.' Crouching down, I rummage in a rusted toolbox which has screws and bolts, hooks, hammers, screwdrivers and nails in crackling plastic bags. 'These things are so gloriously dangerous. Ow! I've scratched my wrist.'

'Wash it clean, quick.' Maya goes towards the sink, reaching for the tap.

She stops. Turns away from the sink. Paces backwards and forwards between the wall and the sink as she hums, fast and faster.

Straightening up, I go to the sink to see what's upset her. It's the rock that killed the woman. I've left it clean and dry on the draining board.

Maya continues to pace with her hands over her ears, her eyes half closed and a hum loud in her mouth.

I pull out a kitchen chair. 'Sit here, Maya. It'll be all right.'

She sits on the floor, still humming.

I put the rock on the kitchen table.

Maya hums with her hands over her ears as she watches me mix flour and water together in a bowl.

I sit down and cover the rock in the paste and sprinkle salt all over it.

When her hum stops, Maya says, 'It's finished. The scared tune in my head.'

I wipe my hands clean on a tea towel. 'There. It's a murder weapon disguised as a snowball.'

She sighs, quietened.

We're in the living room sitting in the chairs on either side of the fire, the cushions bumpy beneath us. Maya's leaning forward, blowing dust off her slippers. 'Are they done?'

I close the recipe book and clasp it to my chest. 'The cakes?'

'I can smell honey.'

'So they're nearly done.'

'Do you think they mind sunk cakes?'

'The scraggy-hair girl still takes them.' I glance at the closed black curtains, faint traces of polka dots all over them, shutting the night outside. 'I should watch her.' I drum my fingers on the recipe book.

Maya watches my hands. 'What if she sees you?'

'Well, I can't let her see *you*. Anything could happen.' I bite my lip.

Maya's pinching her fingertips and frowning.

As I stand, she looks up at me. 'Maybe they only care about food, so they won't come here looking for whoever the dead red woman was. Is. Was. Do you think if people knock on a door and it isn't answered, they'll come back and knock and come back, knock-knock—'

'Stop it, Maya.' I rub my temples. 'The woman will be missing from some home or another. She might have a family

70

who'll look for her; they could find us and stop leaving the –'

'Well, we could go—'

'– ingredients. And we won't know if they're looking for her or not while we're asleep when they're awake, and they're asleep when we're awake. It's only a locked door that keeps them out. Easily broken down.'

Maya's staring at the mirror over the fireplace as she whispers, 'A threshold. Do you remember that word? It was in the ghost stories . . . a half-in-half place on a stone bridge that led to a town full of stench-ridden half-in-half ghosts . . .'

I follow her eyes as they alight on the snowball that sits on the mantelpiece.

'What if the dead woman haunts us?' She looks up at the ceiling.

'She won't. Do you like making yourself frightened? Come on, come here.' I hold my arms out to her, wait, and drop them again. 'Come on, you could choose not to be scared of ghosts. Stop thinking about her – we don't both have to.'

Now I'm the one who's staring at the snowball, my heart flickering in my throat, imagining Maya raging to the point that she smashed up the woman's face.

I'm making a loaf of bread. Maya sits at the table with her head in her hands. She seems as if she's in a heavy grey cloud. I scatter in more flour, knead the dough and try to concentrate.

Maya sighs, loudly.

I stop kneading. 'All right. What are you thinking?'

'That if I watch you, I feel the things you're feeling in your body, but I don't feel them if I'm not looking at you.'

'Perhaps your brain's sending messages to your body, trying to tell it we're still the same. People feel like that when they've lost a limb. They can still feel sensations where it used to be. So if you're feeling my sensations, maybe it's because we're becoming separate to each other, but your brain's clinging on.'

'I could cut my brain and body apart from each other if I had invisible scissors.'

I thud the mixing bowl down on the counter. 'That would mean cutting through your spinal cord.'

'Well, it can't be much thicker than invisible string. And I've got another feeling that's my own and not yours. I have it all the time.'

I try to smile at her, but don't feel like I mean it enough. 'That's a good thing.'

'It's not. It's a missing feeling. A gapspace.'

Picking up the bowl again, I want to focus on the texture and smells of the dough. But I hear myself say, 'I know. You won't feel it forever.' Even to my own ears, the words sound unconvincing.

'I miss summer and clean windows. This cottage hasn't got any stairs and that frightens me. There's nowhere to run away to. The old woman stuck her pins in the arms of the living-room chairs. A chair is meant to be upholstery, not a pincushion. I keep finding them. And these.' She looks down at the black jumper and trousers we're always wearing. 'And these, they're even worse.' She extends a slippered foot. 'Old woman things.'

'What's wrong with them?'

'Why do we have to wear her slippers?'

'Our shoes are worn out.'

'If our shoes died in Paradon, we'd throw them away and get new ones.'

I put down the bowl, sit next to her and fold my arms. 'Is this really about the slippers, or are you still thinking about the dead woman?'

She frowns at me but doesn't reply.

I used to be able to make Maya think and feel whatever I wanted her to. Now, I can't tell if she's hiding what she's really feeling behind what she says. Though part of me wants her to have her own thoughts and feelings, another part of me misses knowing what they are.

Especially now. Her eyes are shields.

I say, 'What's wrong with the slippers?'

She sighs. 'They miss the old woman's bare feet. They make me feel I'm made of old-woman. Sometimes all I can smell is talcum powder and toe-skin.'

'Well, sniff other things. Try some of the spices – don't spill them. Or the violets. Washing-up liquid?'

Though I don't say it aloud, I also think a lot about the old woman. Because when we found this cottage, she hadn't taken her hairbrush. It's still in the bathroom, a mist of hairs smudged through the bristles. And the length of her hair – she wouldn't want to go away without a brush as her hair would get so matted. I unteased one of the strands and measured it with a tape measure from her sewing box. Her hair was over three feet long. And though we've lived here with no one knocking on the door, no one noticing we've taken her place, sometimes – well, quite often, and now more than ever – I worry the old woman will come back.

KIP

This morning I'm doing the fair and I'm at Lizzie's doorstep. Something's not right. There's no fair but there's a black leather glove lying here with no hand in it. It would be scarier if there *was* a hand in it, but it's still a bit scary because it looks like a big dead insect with not enough legs. She can't mean for me to take Old Kelp a glove. Can't bake anything with that.

Lizzie's probably gone away to her sister's again. She lives a few hills away from here, in a much bigger village called Fastleigh, which has the doctor, the chemist, the police and the fire-outer in it. Mammy says they're full of it over there, and they call our village a back-water but we call our village Seachant, after all the songs we've remembered for gazillionations of years.

Though we don't go to Fastleigh often, some of us go forwards and back when there are farmwheels to be had – the farmers will take us along in their trailers if we've got a good enough reason to go.

I put a rock over the glove so it doesn't blow away.

And next door to Lizzie's house, the Quiet Woman hasn't left out her fair either.

No violet flowers for Old Kelp.

Not sure what she'll make of that.

*   *   *

Kip

Old Kelp's curtains are always closed. But this morning the curtains in the window nearest her front door have a little triangle of light between them. I look down at my wellies as I open her gate and walk up the path. I look at the doorstep as I empty the basket and pack in the cakes. I'm breathing quiet and fast and I know I should walk away. But that little triangle of light is still there in the window. I listen at the door and can't hear a sound. I'm not going to look. But the window calls my eyes like trouble. It calls me with the shape of a triangle and stops me breathing as I'm pulled towards it.

I creep to the window and a looking-in accident happens with my eyes and the gap in the curtain.

I've always wanted to see Old Kelp.

But there's something very wrong.

There are two of them.

The light is on in the kitchen and both of them are dressed in black. One has her back to the window. The other one is looking right at this window with badness in her eyes. She's tall and like a skeleton she's so ancient and stretched. All around her, the kitchen is full of clouded badness and twisted thoughts and brewing storming curses. I can't breathe as I back away and wheel the basket of cakes out of the gate and run all the way back to our village. My eyes are flicking from side to side because they want to have another looking-in accident with the window.

But I know not to look back at Old Kelp's cottage because that's another rule and I haven't broken that one. And I'm not meant to knock on her door and I haven't broken that rule either. And the biggest rule I haven't broken is that I can't talk about anything I've seen or heard at her cottage and now I've really seen her that means no talking, *right now*, and I mustn't ever, or I'll be cursed.

I've always really wanted to see Old Kelp for myself, and now I have.

But I didn't know there were two of her.

No one knows there are two of her.

I'm not sure if I'm very good at keeping secrets.

On the best rock on the shore, it's like being sat on the lap of a sleeping giant. There's a dip in this rock that fills with stones whenever the tide comes in. Rocks are a good place to settle squirms because rocks are solid and cold. But these squirms are frisky and hot in my legs. I press my feet on the rock in case it can pull them out. The things I want to say about seeing two Old Kelps are trapped in my legs and that's what these squirms are all about.

But the squirms are still big. I lean back and wave my feet at the sea and whisper, 'Catch them catch them.'

I can tell from the buried sun it's still really early in the morning. I'm meant to take the cakes and leave them on all the doorsteps of anyone who left out their fair, but I haven't done it right today. The cakes are in the basket with me up on the best rock.

I'm feeling full of not doing things right, so I throw stones at the sea and tell the splashes about seeing two Old Kelps but not out loud. I should keep this secret shut up so hard it won't break out of me at all. Because if she's split in half and doubled herself, and I talk, I'll get twice the badness and madness and curses that run through her twisted veins.

Mam Vann comes down the beach in her purple velvet swishy coat, leaning on her walkerstick but moving fast. I blink and she's already further down the wet sand. I blink again and she's here at the rock on the edge of the waves where I'm still throwing stones. Mam Vann is stumped over with all kinds of old bad in her face, though I know she's for good.

She says, 'What're you on a rock for, Kip?'

I say in an angry voice, 'There's never two stones look the same.'

'Don't get to thinking now, will you. Turn your head around, that will. You keeping all the cakes for throwing down your gullet at your own belly, are you?'

'No.' I bite my tongue as I climb down and my dress catches and snags on the barnacles.

Getting the basket down from the rock, I tell Mam Vann, 'I ran but I didn't break them. And I've been looking after them, see?' I put the basket back on the trolley.

She looks at the cakes and shakes her head at me. 'Don't be running, Kip. Not what you're best at. Get these cakes round the houses. Do it right. And give me mine now.' She grabs one of the cakes and it fits in her palm like a small sun. She smells it, closes her eyes and talks like a song, 'Perfect cake, perfect day.'

I want to dance a bit, as I feel better knowing I didn't tell Mam Vann about the Old Kelps. I'm wheeling the basket up the wet sand towards the houses. Most of the houses in our village are tall. They're made of brick, some painted ice-cream colours, and some plain, and they stand close and narrow. But one or two along the shore are cottages, like ours, and they're more like Old Kelp's cottage. They're older and they're made of dark grey stones and they've got white lichen like tiny stars all over them. Even with all the wobbly stars that make the cottages look like they're made of outerspace, they sit so firm and squat, they look like they should be croaking.

Me and Mammy are eating our dinner at the table and I'm staring out of the living-room window at the sun. It's between rain clouds and it looks like two suns. They're both spying on me.

Mammy pinches my arm, says, 'Wake up, starer, put some juice in your bones. Eat.' We're having brown bread and leekie-garlic soup. She slurps her soup and tells me, 'Love you, Kip.'

I tear off a lump of bread. 'Did I do something good?'

'You're mostly good these days.'

'Dad doesn't think so.'

'He'll come round.' She ruffles my hair and I blow it off my face. When I've finished my soup too, she clatters up our bowls and takes them into the kitchen.

I don't much like being proper good. I used to make up stories all the time when I was smaller, and it was more fun than true things. But it went a bit wrong because there really *was* a girl trapped in a tunnel and no one believed me because of my too many made-up stories. The girl was Kerry and the tide came in fast and she had to swim out by herself in a storm. Everyone said she was bloody lucky to have made it and they all called me a scanty liar and went on and on about crying wolves, but I've never seen a wolf laughing.

But now I've got this secret about Old Kelp and I don't want it, a bit of my old bad wants to break out.

So I call to Mammy, 'There was a black glove with a hand still in it.'

'A what?' she calls back from the kitchen.

'Nothing.' I bite my lip.

She comes to the kitchen doorway wiping her hands on a tea towel. 'Are you telling me something important?'

'Maybe yes.' I look out of the window at the sun again. It's hiding.

She leans against the doorframe. 'Out with it, then.'

'I found a black glove with a hand in it and no arm on the hand. And the hand was as puffed up as a dead thing.'

She frowns at me. 'Where was this, Kip?'

'In a tidemark. It was tangled in sea-bleached rope, and the hand was holding a mermaid's purse bit of seaweed, those little brown pockets?'

She nods, her eyebrows raised.

'And it leapt up and ran away like a crab but not sideways.'

'Oh Kip, I'll not even pretend to believe you with that one. Best to keep with telling the truth, eh. Especially when it's your turn on the fair.'

And I sit here for ages looking at the sun in the clouds wondering how I can tell the truth when I can't talk about what I've really seen.

Dad's due back the day after tomorrow. He'll have slept in a barn on Jock's farm. Jock had a wrong delivery of coal – the truck brought too many sacks. He only paid for three but ended up with thirty. So Jock's hidden the coal in his ruined out-house, but he's got to run it down quick so when he orders more he can say he only had the three. Everyone here thought they'd get some cheap, but Jock's saying he won't sell it for money; he'll give it for work.

So Dad's gone to work for Jock's coal, milking cows, fixing the electric fences or barn roofs, building walls up again that got crumbled in the gales – whatever Jock says. When Dad's done, he'll bring back the coal, piled up in our trailer. It's a great big barrow with handles. Dad made it himself. It's so big it takes a man who's as strong as a tractor to pull it. Dad will go back to the farm again, when he's rested from the work. We'll get more coal for us than all the other grown-ups who are talking loudly enough about getting work done for coal, but not getting themselves up there and working.

Dad has to be back then, as Mammy says she's going to have

a birthday. She's going to put her hair up in white rag knots all day tomorrow so she can have tidier curls for her birthday.

In Seachant, birthdays pop up when people want them most. A lot of the birthdays are in winter and not when it really is the date someone was born out. It's a long time since Mammy had her last one, and she says she's well overdue. She said it'll be the best birthday that's happened for her in a long time, *Because we never want the fire to go out, and this year it won't.* So though I'd swear on Dagger's good tooth that Mammy's birthday was in summer the last time she had one, if she's having one so we'll have plenty of coal and not let the fire go out this winter, it'll be a good birthday not just for her, but for me and Dad as well.

In my bedroom, everything's blue. I've got a blue bed and a blue carpet and blue walls, and a blue globe that's my bedside lamp, and a blue dresser with a mirror on it. All the blue makes me want to get to sleep fast most nights because it gives me up-in-the-sky dreams. Dagger's curled on my feet. I nudge at him and he snores.

Tonight I can't sleep because I'm thinking of half-in-half things, like half of a bowl, and half of a bucket or half of a bed. When things break or split in half, they're usually useless. So two Old Kelps might not be more dangerous if they make the same amount of trouble as one. Old Kelp's curses might go wrong unless both halves of her are doing the same thing at the same time. What use is half a spoon without the other half to stop anything spilling?

I'm at Old Kelp's cottage and I just quickly glance at the curtains, which are proper closed. I look down at my feet and the rocks along the path all the way up to her doorstep. The cakes are hidden under a torn bin liner held in place with stones. It's been raining. Next to the door, there's ivy clambering the wall, and I wrap a strand around my finger and say, 'Shh!' in case it speaks to both halves of Old Kelp from hidden tiny mouths in its leaves. I can hear the wind shushing with me.

I lift off the bin liner. The cakes are burned around the edges. They've not been burned like that for a long time, and not since I've been getting the fair.

Old Kelp saw me look through her window.

Maybe she's been watching me all this time. Maybe she knows I'm never proper awake in the mornings and am clumsy with my fumble hands and squirm legs. And now she also knows I'm bad at the rules.

Don't know what the grown-ups will make of these cakes. Flattened burnt trouble. The cakes have tasted sweeter for a while now; the grown-ups say sweetness is a sign there's a good summer coming. They always find some kind of meaning. But these ones are flatter than the ones yesterday, and the ones yesterday were flatter than the day before.

Emptying the basket, I take out the jars of jam and honey, the packets of butter and margarine, dried fruit, nuts, sugar, bacon, flour and trays of eggs. The least burnt cake, I put flat at the bottom of the basket for Mammy. I put my cake, the next least burnt one, next to Mammy's, and pile the other cakes on top. I pack them round the edges so they don't get crumbled.

Today, the cakes haven't got any violet petals on top of them. Don't know why Old Kelp took to baking with violet petals. Maybe while we were asleep, she sent a seeing gale down the chimneys and looked at us all through her wind eyes. She must have seen the Quiet Woman watering her violet flowers in the night, and decided to like her the best.

But again today, there weren't any violets for Old Kelp and Lizzie's not left out her fair either.

Walking away, I wheel the basket so it doesn't rock. But I swear Old Kelp's eyes are looking out of her kitchen window at me as I walk away. I want to look back and check, but I walk one foot and then the other, faster and faster. The sea stretches wide under a sky full of grey chaser clouds. They're moving so fast they make my eyes see the whole world spinning. It's like when I make my globe lamp go so fast all the little invisible people who live on it go flying.

I can feel Old Kelp's eyes hot on the back of my neck. I close my own eyes to stop them wanting to have a looking-over-my-shoulder accident and try to work out from the hot on my neck how many bits of hot there are – two eyes from one face or four eyes from two . . .

I trip and bump the basket off the trolley. It falls hard on the ground. I check the cakes. They're split in half. I crouch and lift out the half cakes and the crumbs stick to my sweaty palms. Mammy's cake and mine, right at the bottom of the basket, they're the only ones still in one piece.

Our cakes are on a plate on the living-room table, and I can hear the kettle boiling in the kitchen for Mammy's tea. I put a leaf of ivy for a blessing next to her plate. She's clattering around in their bedroom, getting up and dressed loudly.

There's knocking at the front door.

I open it and it's three of our neighbours. Their faces are frowned up. Above their blustering hair the sky has gone grey.

I say, 'Please be nice.'

George is so tall I could get a crick in my neck from looking up at him. He mutters, 'Why are the cakes broken?'

'I got—'

Jessie barges in and looks at our cakes, all round and not split. 'So these ones aren't broken. Ours are.' She folds her arms over her green pinny. 'Now I've got to get the shop open, so talk fast.' She raises her eyebrows.

I say, 'I tripped. Never meant to—'

'So you broke them yourself.' George rubs his grey beard with a scritch noise.

'I was scared.'

Kerry flicks her red hair off her pimpled cheek and leans over our cakes. 'Of what? But if it's about *her*, you know not to speak.'

'I was frightened of . . . breaking Mammy's cake. It's her birthday tomorrow and I want it to be good.'

Jessie puts her hands in the pockets of her pinny and rocks back on her heels. Her round face still isn't smiling. 'So you broke all the others. How come—'

Mammy comes into the living room. She's got her hair in rag knots and she's wearing a bright orange jumper and her favourite trousers: the purple ones with the red bow patterns. She's polished her blue shoes and smells of rosewater. She looks at us all. 'What's this, a cake share I didn't know about?'

Jessie says, 'Kip broke all the others, kept the only ones not broken for you pair.'

I grab Mammy's hand. 'I tripped – I didn't mean to.'

Scratching at his beard again, George says, 'Kip's making you out to be better than us, if you pair get the best ones.'

Mammy shakes my hand out of hers. She strides to the table and picks up a knife. I run and grab her arm, but she's strong with her hair in knots, and she cuts our cakes in half.

I bite my lip and can taste it's bloodied.

Mammy turns around. 'There. Are we even or odd?'

'Fair is fair. That's even.'

George says in a growl, 'Don't favour yourselves again, Kip.'

'Settle, George.' Jessie pats Mammy's arm. 'We're all to have the same, so it's as fair as the fair.'

George has bent himself in half to look at Dagger, who's glaring back at him from the kitchen doorway. He knows George is thinking about taxidermying him.

I step between them and glare at George. 'You can't have him.'

George smiles a little, mutters, 'Not yet.'

'Not ever.'

'His skin's the only bit of him I'm after. You can keep the rest.'

Mammy calls, 'George, ease it on the winding up!'

He mutters, 'The burned bits are darker on my cake.'

The other two are fussing over Mammy's hair, telling her how lovely it'll look tomorrow when she lets it out of the rags, and she doesn't hear him.

I say to him, 'They were not.'

He looks back at Dagger. 'Good healthy fur. Could last a long time, a dog like that, even if he can't bark when he needs to.'

'Leave off him.' I pick Dagger up, though he's squirming, and shut him in the kitchen.

George's eyes glint at me as he goes outside. He leaves the front door wide open.

Mammy asks Kerry, 'How are your monthlies going – any lessening of the pain?'

Kerry looks at me and her face goes redder than it usually is.

'Oh, sorry, pet,' Mammy says, 'I've forgot how shy you feel when you're young.'

I wonder if they'd be so bothered about me splitting the cakes if I had monthlies like Kerry, but that's never going to happen. I go to the table, where the cakes cut down the middle are looking back up at me from the plates. Mammy and the others are saying goodbye and they aren't looking at me. I'm glad – my eyes are spilling a bit. The cakes are half in half, split in two. They look too flat, the burnt bits look too dark and I don't like the look of them. Not one bit.

Mammy comes over and sits down at the table.

There's another knock on the door.

'Not yet more cake gripers . . .' Mammy murmurs as she goes to open it. 'Oh, it's you. Come in.'

I know, from reading bits of the detective books Dad likes, that you're never meant to say *oh, it's you*, to someone who knocks on the door, in case it's a murderer. So I go and stand next to Mammy to protect her.

It's not a murderer. It's Uncle Finn and Aunty Pippa. She's wearing a crochet skirt and beige coat and her blonde hair is in a bun. She gives Mammy a small bottle. 'Happy birthday.'

Uncle Finn's wearing his flat cap and a long raincoat. He nods at Mammy and says, 'She knows we don't do presents, but she wanted to for you.'

Aunty Pippa glares at him.

Mammy turns the bottle over and over in her hand. 'That's kind. But it's not today, it's tomorrow. When Brack's home. Come in?' She steps back from the door.

Aunty Pippa says, 'We won't just now. I wanted you to have it.' She nods at the bottle in Mammy's hands. 'It's a new scent. An experiment with myrtle. If you don't like it, I'll try with something else.'

'It'll be lovely.'

Uncle Finn says, smiling, 'Grand sense of smell, she's got.'

Mammy says to Aunty Pippa, 'That you have. You've been lying low the past few days. All right, are you?'

She looks down at her shoes.

Mammy says, quickly, 'How's Adam?'

Uncle Finn says, 'He's always fine.'

Aunty Pippa says to him, 'Is he?'

He waves his hands. 'All right. Shut up, Finn.'

Mammy says to Uncle Finn. 'I'll send Brack round as soon as he's rested up.'

'Tell him I've been breathless again. Won't be well enough to go up the cliffs with him for a while.'

She nods, and says in a sharp voice, 'Should be staying out of trouble, no doubt. Don't over-exert, will you?' She puts her hand on Aunty Pippa's arm. 'Come round for a chat soon. You must need a bit of looking after yourself, sometimes.' She looks at the perfume. 'Thanks for this. I'll wear it tomorrow. Are you sure you won't come in? You should see Brack's latest – a great deep trunk for the shop. Jessie needed more storage, out back. Now you two could do with—'

Uncle Finn shrugs. 'We're off for a slow walk. Dishes dull, but there you have it.'

Aunty Pippa says, 'Kip, will you call in on Adam later?'

'Maybe.'

They turn away and Mammy closes the door.

I say to her, 'Last time I was round, Adam read a book about asteroids the whole time.'

She opens the bottle and sniffs it. 'He's shy. Needs to be drawn out. Mmm. Unusual. Maybe it'll even out when it's on the skin.'

'Let me sniff?'

She holds out the bottle and the leafy smell is so strong it makes my nose rumple.

I say, 'Do they give each other presents for birthdays where Aunty Pippa's from?'

She puts the lid back on the bottle. 'Maybe, despite all the medicines and hospitals in Paradon, people still have to try really hard to be born so they need a reward. With us, we're lucky to have been born out, rather than born in. That's the gift in itself.'

I say the line from one of our songs. 'Born into the earth.'

Mammy puts the bottle on the mantelpiece. 'Well, we were both born out. And that's all the gifting we need.' She kisses my head.

Mammy and me eat the cakes for breakfast and we eat every crumb. My stomach gurgles. So does Mammy's. She says, 'It's all right, Kip.'

'You sure?'

'If it's bad, we'll make ourselves better quick by pretending it's not. Mind over stomach.'

'But what if—'

'Oh, de-glum yourself.'

My stomach gripes. 'Can't.'

She smiles but doesn't look like she means it. 'Don't tell your dad, but I've been making you a new dress. Keep it quiet.' She puts her fingers over her lips.

'What colour?'

She shakes her head. 'Not telling you till it's done.' She sits on the baggy chair – a pile of cushions under a patchwork blanket. She pats the cushions beside her. 'Bunch up.'

Cuddled up to her, I say, 'Can I have a story?'

'I'll tell you the story of how the fair came to be set up. You've heard it many times, but you must always remember why it's so important you do it right.' She strokes my hair and says, 'There is a city that shines bright as any star and the streets are made of polished stone. Some say it's filled with all of the gifts there are in the world. Others say it's filled with all of the troubles, but I prefer to think of the gifts. A long time ago, it had enough gifts of its own to keep, and plenty to give away. It rushed its gifts in and out of itself like a tide, spreading jewels far and wide.

'But one day, that great city caught a sickness. It cut itself off from the world that lay outside. It called all useful things back in and closed the doors behind them. It called in all the doctors and staff from the hospitals that it had trained and sent out; it brought them back home, to where it believed they were needed the most.

'But outside of the city, the sickness spread as well. What is caught on a tide isn't ever pulled just the one way. The people outside were left doing their best, but they didn't understand which medicines did what. And then the medicines ran out anyway. There was talk of superbugs stinging. Viral, like a pestilence.'

'Were they giant insects?'

Mammy shakes her head. 'It spread so quick. The city forgot all the people living and dying outside. They wouldn't let anyone in. And they cured themselves using medicine, like the miracle medicine can be.

'The people outside tried everything they could think of to clean themselves out. But there was no miracle in bleaches, in charcoal or vinegar, even in salt, when death had spread its wings so wide. The whole older generation died, they were weakest, you see. Few slow. Most fast. Filled the graveyard here. If you look at the dates on the headstones, you can see it.'

Mammy has tears in her eyes.

I ask, 'Would a superbug be too big to keep in a jar?'

'Whatever that virus was, it was too big for an enormous city, even one as shining and gifted as Paradon. Some say it buzzed airborne. It liked festering in hospitals and sickrooms the best.' She kisses my head. 'It took both my dad's parents within days of each other. My mum's within weeks. You've seen their graves. It's died off now. But still, we've never had the medicines back, and all the hospitals are derelict or gone. We'll none of us live as old as people once did. You know, the hospitals used to put clocks into dying hearts to make them tick a pace. A miracle, a blessing, call those ticks and tocks what you will. Now hearts just stop.'

She shivers and her face looks pale. 'Back then, that's the one time the villagers had to knock on Old Kelp's door.

'They knew Old Kelp was still alive, as the supplies some were still leaving on her doorstep disappeared each day. She'd survived, as she survives everything, even time. She was the only old person left. She'd not come to the village for many, many years, not since Gilliam disappeared. The villagers were fearful of her curses, but there's a terrible courage that comes when people around you are dying. Two of the bravest knocked on her door in the night. She answered it, and they saw a storm brewing behind her in the kitchen. At first she didn't speak a word, just looked at them with eyes so deep that they could feel her sight tunnelling through their veins. They thought they were cursed in that moment, but all the same they threw the words they needed to say from their mouths. They told her all the other old ones were gone and begged for her help. She turned her back to them, and said in the lowest, quietest voice, *You'll bring me something from each of yourselves, let me alone, and take what you're given in return. That's what's fair.* Then her door slammed shut on them, and they found they were still standing, still breathing, their hearts were beating furious and wild, but nothing had changed. They knew they'd been blessed, by not being cursed.

'So the remaining villagers met together. Everyone agreed to leave something out for Old Kelp. A list was drawn up. Turns were to be taken so only one person was ever to go near her cottage, and she'd always have the privacy she wanted. In return, she left out enough honey cakes for everyone on her doorstep. And that's how the fair came to be set up.' She nods at me.

'Honey is a natural medicine. Kills bacteria. Must fend off superbugs as well. We give her the thickest, rawest honey from the farmers who grow fields of foxgloves and thistles for the bees they keep. And with the blessings of her ancient hands, Old Kelp's the only hope we have to stay well and alive as long as we can. She may curse us at any moment, but she understands our need for time to live, even if we'll never have the ancient time that belongs only to her.'

'There's a doctor in Fastleigh now, who comes here for Uncle Finn.'

'He was another of those, like Pippa and probably the Quiet Woman, who didn't do well with the Paradon ways, and left. Even he can't get his hands on much by way of medicines. So he has no miracles but knowledge. I worry over you, Kip.'

'I'm fine now.'

She looks at me and her eyes are dark. 'When you were little you had fits, three times. Thought I'd lose you.'

'But I never have since. Years and years of you not losing me.'

'I know.' She kisses my head. 'But there's no medicine for fits.'

Dagger pads out of my bedroom and the fur on his throat quivers. He's trying to growl at Mammy as she's got her hand on my arm. We're at the table with the window open a crack, drinking too-strong mint tea.

I take another sip as Mammy pours herself another mug from the yellow teapot.

She looks out at the sky through the window. 'Indoor storms. Weather goes wherever people do, have you ever noticed?'

I shake my head but she's still looking out of the window.

'Sometimes clouds follow us. Sometimes hail. That's what happens when a person lives so alone. Old Kelp stirs how she feels into the cakes, and we eat it all up. If she's joyful one day, we'll get her sunshine and feel bright, if she's clouded with trouble, we'll get a gutful of storm. She's no one to take anything out on, be it rage or joy. But sometimes she must be content in her home, as the cakes make us feel so light, like rain sheeting through sunshine, or as if we're all being whirled around in a warm soft wind.'

'I'd like to see weather inside a house. Like when our kitchen rained.'

'It was only a tile that had crashed off the roof.' Her eyes are far away as she shakes herself and bites her lip. She puts her hands over mine. Dagger glares at her with black angry eyes. Her belly grumbles again.

Mine growls back at hers.

Mammy frowns. 'These cramps are taking time to settle.' She sips her tea, slams her cup on the table and puts a hand on her middle. Her face shows me her cramps are much worse. She pants, 'We watch the cakes . . . being burned, or too flat, or risen . . . too high. It all depends on how she's feeling, locked away as she is . . .'

My belly aches. I scrape my chair away from the table and lean over. 'The cramps aren't . . . too bad.'

Mammy rubs my back. 'They are, Kip. It's because today, the cakes were broken.' She shakes her head and the rags in her hair jiggle. Her face pales even more. 'She's showing us her heart's broken. We're eating her sadness.'

'No, it really was me who broke them.'

'Doesn't matter, Kip . . . fair is fair . . . No such thing as always sunshine. We still have to eat them if we want to live well. For what do we say about the cakes?'

'Not a crumb wasted; no illness to come.' My stomach stabs a pain through me.

'But the cramps . . . may come . . . all the same.' Mammy's chair tips and thuds as she lurches to the bathroom and sicks.

AMBER

There's a separate sheet of stained tissue paper, clipped to one of the recipe pages. The spices are listed in a badly drawn grid. Some of them are in their pure form, like cinnamon, cassia or ginger. But some of them are blends which the old woman must have mixed herself. They're labelled in jars on the shelves. For the last batch of honey cakes I used the jar labelled Brown Spice. It was a fine powder which smelled faintly of dried mushrooms. The effects of the spices are written in the grid, and opposite brown spice she's written:

To bring muddied or ignored events into full view.
(only one pinch - unless the intention is to induce vomiting)

The brown spice is running low because, without having read this properly, I stirred a large spoonful into the honey cake mixture. The cakes were a little overcooked, slightly burned, which may take the edge off, but I wonder if they will induce vomiting. Or expose ignored events.

I'm washing the cake trays, bowls and bone spoons in the sink when I sense Maya behind me. 'Don't creep. I thought you were asleep. Have you calmed down yet?'

Maya looks at me blankly.

I say, 'About the girl looking in the window? I really don't think we need to worry too much about her. She looked scared to hell.'

Maya's voice sounds bleary. 'From dead to here is string-tied. We should bury Dead Red further away, deep in those fir trees. Dead's a pull-tight knot. She should be six feet down, aren't graves sunk?'

'Wake up, and don't speak till you can. There's a small grave-yard up on the far side of the wood.'

'Well, could we bury Dead Red there?'

I turn to her, wiping my hands. 'The earth will be as frozen there as it is here. Anyway, they'd notice a fresh grave. Bury her in your head.' I frown at her. 'You've got extremely sentimental over a corpse. It's lovely you've made a friend, but if she was an alive friend, she wouldn't let you give her a nickname she mightn't like. Now, I can't stop thinking about the old woman who lived here. I'm worried what will happen to us if she comes back. I want to find out where she's gone. Come on, help me search.'

I go into the bedroom and call, 'Come on!'

I stand on the edge of the bed, my body straining forward, my hands reaching into the wardrobe, right up to the back of the top shelf where I can feel something square. I step a bare foot onto the shelf at the bottom. The whole wardrobe leans, leans, and crashes down on the bed, with me trapped in the dark underneath it.

I shout, 'Moyu, got moy out. Got moffballs iyn mouff!'

We've decided, from everything we already know and everything we've found, that the old woman who lived here was *very* old. We gather up proof and put it all on the kitchen table once we've decided what each bit of proof proves.

She had a posy of dried pink roses in a rusted biscuit tin on the top shelf of her wardrobe, which is proof she was sentimental about someone who gave her flowers.

The three tubs of lily of the valley talcum powder and two bottles of rosewater are proof of the old woman's smell. Her lace gloves prove she liked her hands to look pretty.

Her bed linen, towels, curtains and clothes are proof that she dyed all the fabric in this cottage black, which might mean she was mourning for someone who died, perhaps the person who gave her the flowers.

She had five pairs of slippers in different sizes and one pair of wellies with a torch inside one of them, and the biggest shoes are a pair of black stilettos which have never been worn outside because the soles aren't scuffed. So the old woman didn't know her own shoe size, but whatever their real size, her feet were still larger than ours. The slippers are also proof that she didn't go outside often; the wellies with the torch inside them prove she did gardening at night, and the stilettos are proof she liked to feel sexy but only when she was indoors.

We're in the bathroom. Maya's frozen, staring at the mirror.

I hold out a red lipstick and antique jar of aqueous cream. 'More proof she must have had a sex life and dry skin.'

Maya's voice shakes. 'Let's mirrorsmash.'

'Why?'

'Something's wrong.'

'With the mirror? No there isn't. It's you and me, looking the same.'

Maya shakes her head, her eyes fearful.

'There's nothing!' I put the jar down, knock on the mirror, and wave at Maya. 'See, my hand. Stop scaring yourself.'

I'm eating freshly baked fruit scones in the kitchen. The lamp is lit, the curtains closing the daylight outside. I'm reading, leafing, sifting my fingertips through the recipe book.

A thin piece of paper, folded into four, is caught in the binding at the back of the book.

Maya comes in from the living room and watches me ease it out with one finger. I don't breathe as I smooth the paper flat.

I read it with my hand over my heart.

Turning to Maya, I say, 'I haven't seen this note before. I almost missed it. Her handwriting is tremulous, she must have been ill when she wrote it – or very, very old. The ink hasn't faded. This must be the last thing she wrote.'

We read it together. It says:

I leave for the next
spoons from the last
lifetime lived
lifetime passed

My hand is shaking.

Maya says, 'What does it mean?'

'It means when she left here, she knew she was going to die. I've read everything. I can understand her now; this book seems like a lifetime in recipes. The herbs and spices, the sting in salt, the air in the flour, and all the fruits, nightshades, the spices she stirred . . . she wouldn't have wanted to die here. She'd have gone outside. A cliff, a forest, a lake, rock or stone, sea, bone, earth. She knew what things were made of. How they lived. How they died. She wouldn't have wanted to die within walls.'

Maya says, 'She won't ever come back.'

'Never.'

She exhales, loudly.

'You're relieved. Maya! She left here, to die!'

'I'm relieved because you're relieved.'

'Don't tell me how I feel. I've read her recipes, her notes and footnotes, grids and diagrams, her languages, codes, and now I'm really sad. I feel like I knew her.'

'The note says "leave for the next". Us. We're doing what she would have wanted. So it's all right.'

I mimic Maya. 'What she would have wanted. When living people say that when someone's dead, they mean it's what *they* want.'

She points at the words. 'But look, it *is* what she wanted.'

I wipe away my tears and read the note again. I nod. 'Yes. You're right. What I'm doing already. For me more than her. Is that wrong? And look. The final recipe. Her handwriting is frail. She wanted someone to take over from her. She was *calling* me – I mean, us – here.'

I show Maya the page:

SAND CAKE

Cornflour, 8 oz
Sand, 1 oz
Butter, softened, 6 oz
Caster sugar, 6 oz
2 large eggs
Icing sugar / dust

Turn on the oven and grease and line a round cake tin.

Sieve together the cornflour and sand, thinking of sand clocks, of life cycles, of beginnings and endings, of cliffs crumbling to rocks to stones to sand, and footprints leading along an inevitable path.

Gather the intention of a call in your throat. Use a large bone spoon to cream the butter and sugar in a mixing bowl. Once the texture is fluffy, grip the spoon, close your eyes and send out the thought as high as stars and as deep as oceans that the end is now, as is the beginning. Imagine footprints having already crossed a circuit of the whole world now approaching the place where you stand; footprints of the one who is to begin where you end.

Break each egg separately, considering the potential new life erupting inside each yolk. When you discard the shells, imagine them ground to sand and blown by winds. Beat the mixture and then fold in the flour and sand. With a circular thought, release the call from your throat and believe that it has been heard.

Put the mixture in the tin and bake for about one hour until the cake is brown on top and a skewer comes out with no trace of sand. Leave to cool in the tin and think of an hourglass, tipping.

When cold, as you sprinkle the top of the cake with icing sugar or dust, your hand should move with the motion of beckoning.

Consume half of the cake in one sitting, and place the other half in an empty fireplace* in your home, so using the directions of vertical and horizontal air, the cake can continue to breathe and spread *the call for the new one to arrive the moment you depart.*

You will hear footsteps. When you do, be sure to leave unseen, and close the door behind you.

* The other half of the cake will crumble to sand in the grate when the new one arrives.

I don't want Maya to speak. So she doesn't. Instead, she sits on the kitchen floor and watches me light a candle.

I whisper, 'Cooking with bones is elemental, physical. No. Not even that. Bones are at the core of anything living. They're the strongest part. Cooking is for pleasure, for feeding ourselves to overflowing sometimes. Cooking and eating, with such flavours, such spices to stir, we can fill ourselves up – it's all about being alive. Bones survive even death. Both together, enchantment.'

Maya's got her arms resting on her knees and she's watching me, wide-eyed.

I turn to her and say, 'I'm not sure if I believe in enchantment. Not a blind kind of faith.' I hold my hands over the book and feel cold air between the pages and my palms. Closing my eyes, I can smell earth and pine.

I say, 'I've got to go outside.'

Getting up, I kick off the slippers and shove my feet into wellies. I check the front door is locked as I swathe a black coat around me, grip the torch in one hand and pick up the posy of dried pink roses in the other.

Maya says in a small voice, 'But it's daytime outside.'

'It's dark in the wood.'

*   *   *

As I lock the side door behind me, I touch the handle with my fingertips and whisper, 'Look after Maya, don't let anyone in.'

I walk through the garden and climb over the wall, glance around as I cross the field to check I'm not being seen. As I go into the wood, there's a feeling of being pulled. Under my feet, twigs crack. I shift the branches of needle-fine spikes. The branches thicken and the daylight goes and all around me it's dark. I feel something pulling me into the middle of the wood, to the darkest place. I shine the torch on the ground as I go deeper into shadows, to places where terrible things could hide sleeping, and I wonder if I'll wake them. My heart feels stuffed full of dry leaves, scratching the internal cavities as it pumps.

Dark as night.

The sound of branches, creaking, crunching, a howl in the distance. Something sniffing, scurrying nearer.

The torch lights up the thick trunks. There are shadows that look like the outlines of people, and as the beam shines on them, they look like trunks again.

My heart tight thumping, my feet are pulled on and on, the trees cluster darker, closer, thicker, and I wonder if I'll be able to find my way out. But still my feet step with the feeling of being pulled towards something I'm meant to see. My heart pounds as if bound with a leather belt.

Squeezing between trees, spines catch at my hair. I hunch under the branches. Beneath my feet, dead needles sink.

A small clearing. The grey sky is bright after so much darkness. In the middle of the clearing is a mound in the shape of a woman's body. I put down the posy and, using my fingertips, stroke away the brown pine needles which are decomposing into dust and soil around the woman's head.

I find the face of the old woman. I know it's her. She smells faintly of cloves and cardamom. There are pine needles through her long hair, over her eyes, her lips. Her face is deeply wrinkled. Her forehead feels like paper.

As I whisper to her, 'Sleep, sleep, sleep,' the wind in the highest branches of the trees seems to hiss, 'Wake, wake, wake.'

There's a sinking tiredness in my limbs as I cover the old woman's face again. I breathe for her, smell for her, see and hear for her. I whisper, 'Here, you're still, and there's so much life. I heard your call.' I put the posy of dead roses over the old woman's heart.

I lie next to her and look at the trees from beneath. As the clouds shift above the highest branches, the sky changes colour from dark grey to light. The scents of growth are all around me.

The colours in the trees light up. I never knew before now there were so many different shades of green. Deep black-green, blue-green, grey-green, and high above, a pale tinge along the edges of the spines. The trunks and branches are the colours of earth, dark brown, rust, deep red.

There's too much colour in this world. My eyes drink the colours and tears roll into my hair because I'm lying next to a dead woman who can't see any of it. There's a deep ache through my body. It isn't too much colour at all, it's *so* much.

It's so much colour, I'm full.

As I sit up, I see there are other graves in this clearing. No head-stones, but shapes the length and width of humans in a line in the pine needles. I crawl and look at each one; they're in varying states of decay. The oldest graves are dents in the soil, the newer ones are slight mounds. Even after decades, perhaps hundreds of years, all the graves smell of spices, yeasts and flour, all the baking scents from the cottage mixed with the smells of soil. The one I was lying next to is the clearest grave of all, because the old woman is still on the surface. She hasn't yet sunk.

And next to her, there is room enough for me. And after me, others.

But not yet. The branches above me are silent, still.

Not yet.

The cottage, the wood-burner lit, the oven warm, the spices clamouring in their jars.

Not yet. The recipe book glowing.

The recipes whispering between the pages. Not yet.

The bone spoons, dancing in rhythms of stirring, whisking, beating in the kitchen.

Calling me back to my home.

All of the women in these graves have lived in the cottage, cooked in the kitchen, and when time has called the end of their years, they've come here and died.

As I breathe in the scents of spices that merge with the smells of decomposition, my skin feels flushed, warm, alert. The tiny hairs on my spine are raised.

My body has woken.

When I unlock the side door and go from daylight back into the cottage, my eyes can't adjust to the darkness in the kitchen. I can just about make out the chairs, the sink, the cupboards. I can't see Maya.

Silence.

I call her name.

Nothing.

I find the switch and light fills the kitchen.

Maya's hiding under the table, jammed between dusty boxes. She's staring out at me with her hands over her mouth.

I crouch next to her. 'What is it?'

Her eyes seem haunted. 'Don't know what to do here alone.'

'I want you to be yourself. Being on your own sometimes

might be the only way to work out what that is. You're trying, I know.'

'You'd *like* me to want all the same things you want.'

'But I don't really *want* you to. That's sisterhood for you.'

Maya's shivery. She says, 'I don't like-argue.'

'Well, that's something else you don't want, all by yourself. So don't let's argue. Finding something you like rather than everything you don't might make you happier.'

As I take the wellies off, I think about the row of graves in the wood. I'm not going to tell Maya about them. She'd want us to bury the shed woman there, with them. It doesn't feel right. It's a silent, private place. For them.

And one day, for me.

But if Maya dies before I do, it wouldn't be a place I'd want to bury her.

She crawls out from under the table. 'It was horrible here without you. I found charcoal and did drawings. Of all kinds of vicious ghosts. They scared me so much I had to burn them. Burnghost haha. So you can't see them.'

I snap at her, 'You're still such a child – what if I don't want to look after you any more?'

She staggers to her feet and smiles at me. 'Only a child for you, mysister.'

I melt to her. 'Come on, then. I want to know everything there is to know about the old woman's life, now more than ever. Let's look for more proof.'

I've got my hands in the cupboard under the kitchen sink. I show Maya that up the back there are damp packets of black fabric dye and bags of salt.

Under the washing machine there's wet orange rust and seventeen dead ants.

Back in the bedroom we find a coil of rope tucked under the mattress between the last spring in the base and the headboard. I tell Maya that's proof the old woman liked kinky sex.

Maya lies on the bed. 'The ceiling's the colour of cream. With the dusty cornice it looks like an inside-out wedding cake.'

In the bathroom I find a rusted cut-throat razor jammed behind the pipes at the back of the sink. I call Maya in and show her. 'Look – this is the kind of thing that might be sold on the black market.'

We sit on the floor and I open and close the rusted razor blade.

Maya says, 'They had one of those in the museum in Paradon.'

'This would have belonged to the old woman's lover. How dangerous is it?' I try to cut my thumb and it doesn't even scratch.

We talk about our visits to the museums in Paradon and all the dangerous exhibits. Along with cut-throat razors, they displayed particularly brutal cooking knives and products containing banned dyes, preservatives and cancerous e-numbers. The signs next to these items told us how people used to live, risking lacerations and cuts, allergies, hives or their lives, on a daily basis.

I say, 'A few dangerous things are still sold in chemists. Safety razors under the counter. Soap bars with slippage warnings and pictures of injuries on the boxes. But a lot of things we saw in the museums, we've found in this cottage.'

'Sewing needles and rickety ladders.'

'And nails and screws and axes.'

Maya laughs. 'If I'd known we'd be living as dangerously as this, I might have listened a little bit in the health and well-being class.'

'You didn't listen—'

'I listened to the ghost stories the teacher told us when we were little.' She shivers.

'Well, no wonder you're scared. Your growing brain was filled with ghosts.'

'Was health and well-being useful?' She looks at me with raised eyebrows.

'I can't work out how much real danger we're putting ourselves in while holding a rusted razor. So I'm guessing not.' I grin at Maya and drop the razor in the bath. 'The blades in the bedroom are much more dangerous. Come on.'

We go into the bedroom and look inside the cabinet on the wall at the hatchet, meat cleaver and rusted saw.

I say, 'Now these really should be kept locked up. Why would she have these in her bedroom? It's like a museum display. Or a shrine? She must have wanted to see them before she slept, wanted each time she woke for them to be the first thing she saw. A collection of blades. Individually they're extreme anti-safe. But put together, they're murder weapons.'

Maya is biting her lip.

We say together, 'The bone spoons.'

In the kitchen Maya lurches towards the orange ceramic jar.

I step in front of her. 'No, I need them. Think about bodies. Not that you do. The bones are the strongest part. And all the foods a body has ever eaten – all the flavours must be absorbed into the bones over a lifetime. The precious stem cells and all kinds of blood cells are buried in the marrow, as long as they're never broken. Stem and marrow, it even sounds organic, doesn't it? That's why bones make good spoons.'

Maya looks at the recipe book.

I flick the pages back and show her the note behind the front cover. 'Look. "Cooking with Bones". She meant these spoons.'

The food in Paradon was tasteless, lifeless – limp lettuces, more nutrients in the bacteria on our tongues than in the leaves. No cream, bland flavourings, few spices, nothing fresh. Biscuits were like cardboard. Nutritional drinks tasted of sad cabbage soup.

I stroke the recipe book as I tell Maya, 'These recipes and her notes, all the extra instructions are the work of a genius. She spent years and years learning, writing it all down. She was a pudding alchemist.'

Maya nods at two of the misshapen spoons lying on the table next to the recipe book. 'We had wooden spoons, chrome, aluminium, clear pink and blue plastic ones in Paradon. That one's tiny, and the other one –'

'– is a femur, expertly ground into the shape of a ladle. You know what this means, though. Since no one's ever taken the bone spoons away and buried them, there's a strong chance that no one will find the shed woman's body.'

'What's a femur?'

'Oh, come on. In biology we spent at least two months on bones! The femur's this one.' I draw a line with my fingertip from my knee to my hip and feel my skin flush at the sensation.

Maya wrinkles her nose and frowns. 'Your pupils are big wide.'

I snap at her, 'The old woman who lived here had a lover. Maybe one day I will. Some of the stains on her black bed sheets still won't quite wash out. She must have let the stains soak in and never washed them. She must have loved him. Kept them stained from him and her together – now I wonder where the bones of the pelvis ended up . . .'

'Amber!'

'Prude. People do have lovers. Some people *want* one.'

Maya stares at me, her eyes full of fear. 'Amber, I don't want to touch human-inside bones.'

'That's another thing you don't want. Well, fine.' I go to the cupboard next to the side door. There's a set of antique wooden spoons tied together in a knotted piece of string crammed between two boxes of rubber gloves.

I put the wooden spoons on the table next to Maya. 'She must have used these before the bone ones. Don't cook from the recipe book; all those recipes want bone spoons. But if you're cooking lunch or breakfast and need to give eggs or anything a stir, use these. Let's have our own things, yours and mine. I'll have the recipe book and bone spoons. I'll clear a drawer for you.'

'I don't want a drawer!'

'I'm helping you feel at home!'

'It's nothing like Paradon, and I don't want these!' The wooden spoons clatter onto the floor.

Maya says in a small voice, 'Are you sure we're right?'

'What about?'

She points at the bone spoon in my hand.

I say, 'Yes. They're human bones.' The mortar is a skull. It sits on the counter, lopsided, brownish-white, with three tiny bones fixed to the base to keep it upright. Though this is a terrible thing to know, I've thought this all along but it feels different saying it aloud. I've got sobs trapped in my chest. Instead of crying, I laugh. 'I think the spoons are made from the old woman's lover – do you think she ate the rest of him?'

And at exactly the same moment, Maya says, 'Let's put the bone spoons in the shed with Dead Red.'

'No! I'm still going to cook with them. Maybe we should take the shed woman's bones out of her body and cook with them as well.'

'If you touch Dead Red, I'll make bone spoons out of your inside-bones.' She glares at me as she goes into the bedroom.

*   *   *

Lying under the black duvet next to Maya, her face is half light and half dark. There are pillows in a line between our bodies. She's still angry with me, and she's put them there as a wedge.

I say to her, 'Close your eyes, and before—'

'Before what?'

'Before you say what I want to hear, don't think. Don't give me what I want at all. Speak from yourself.'

She closes her eyes and frowns. 'I can't.'

'With your eyes closed, can you concentrate harder on not seeing me?'

'People invented mirrors. Do you know why?'

'So we can look at ourselves.'

Her eyelids move a little though she doesn't open them. 'Because we want to believe what our eyes see. We think mirrors are proof we're right. Mirrors must have been made because no one's quite sure enough.'

I ask her, 'And what about you?'

'I'm a mirror for you. You want to know you're real, you're alive, you matter. I only exist at all because you wanted a twin. I'm like a toy our parents bought you when you cried too loud. You've always looked after me, because you've really needed to learn to look after yourself.'

I feel sad. 'But they loved you the most anyway.'

'They loved me anyway, yes. Because they wanted to.'

'And now I don't want you to be my twin any more.'

Maya doesn't say anything for a while.

When she speaks, she says, 'I've got thoughts you don't know. Not the same as yours. So you do mean it a bit, but I still look like you.' She runs her fingertips over her face, her eyelids squeezed shut.

Her voice is quiet. 'Want is stronger than thoughts. Seeing

isn't only done with eyes, though most people think it is. You'd have to mean it all the way through.' She rolls away and her hair merges with the dark pillowcase.

KIP

At the window I watch Mam Vann as she shuffles down the concrete steps and onto the beach. Her purple coat is buttoned tight against the wind.

Mammy comes out of the kitchen. 'We'll have our honey cakes and set out to meet your dad on his way home.' She's wearing her best dress for her birthday, a blue corduroy one with pink flowers.

The honey cakes are risen and golden this morning. No violet petals, but an extra layer of honey on the top. They taste sweet and kind.

As I finish mine, Mammy wipes her mouth. She ties a blue scarf over her smooth neat curls. As she puts on her coat, she looks out at Mam Vann. 'I'm glad we get to walk together, Kip. She lost her parents far too young. George's dad took her in, but she and George fought like cats. When she was a little girl, she wanted to be a grandmother.'

I pull wellies on over my thick socks. 'No one has one of them.'

'People used to, before the hospitals went. When I was a child, we all used to wish we had grandparents. We used to talk about what they'd be like, all the things they'd know.'

'What did you want grandparents for?'

'My mum told me about hers. She said they played games and told stories and gave treats but it was strange to spend time with them. She didn't like the way they looked for the faces of their own parents, brothers and sisters in her face. You'd think they'd have given her a feeling of belonging, that she'd have liked the attention. But she didn't like being told she looked like anyone else.'

Mammy looks out at Mam Vann again. 'But she wanted to *be* a grandmother. Gave herself the name Mam Vann when she was little, as she thought it sounded like a grandmother's name.'

'What's her real name?'

'Don't remember, so it can't have suited her. As a child she collected things she called *histories* for these grandchildren she was to have – like sweetie wrappers, alphabeti-spaghetti . . . oh, bear-shaped dried pasta and those bright rubbers for the ends of pencils, elastic bands, yellow washing-up gloves, tin foil and sink plungers – all the things she thought were a little bit odd, so one day they'd not be around any more. She kept the histories in a wooden box under her bed. She showed me them once, when I was really small. I told her she'd have to get a baby quick, get that baby to grow fast and have a baby of its own.' Mammy laughs. 'This is before I knew how it was done. But even as an adult, Mam Vann never wanted the children. She looks old from a distance, doesn't she?'

'But she is old.'

'She's not. She's a few years older than me. It's all in how she carries herself. It's because she knows none of us will grow very old, so she wants us to see her as old, so we'll think she's wise. Look at her shambling along. She knows someone's watching.'

'Does she like teaching because she thinks all us children are her grandchildren?'

Mammy kisses my head. 'You know, Kip, you might be right.'

We both watch Mam Vann through the window. The tide is a long way out and she walks along the edge of the waves.

We're walking up towards Old Kelp's cottage as we have to pass it to get up to the road. Dagger strains at his rope lead and tries to bark and I tug, but he shoots off and the lead slides through my hand and trails away. He's caught the smell of something and goes haring from the path. He squeezes through Old Kelp's gate and he's off round the side of her cottage.

Mammy pales. She whispers, 'Get him, quick. I'll be right here. I've not been through that gate in a long time. She'll be more used to the sound of your footfall.'

I pull up the hood on my coat and follow the trail in the grass that Dagger's left behind him. I creep through Old Kelp's gate without looking at her door or windows. I go to the side of her cottage and look back at Mammy holding her brown coat closed tight around her. She nods at me, her eyes fearful. My throat thumps with heartbeats as I go into Old Kelp's garden. There are stakes tied with fraying string, stuck in the frosted earth in lines. The beds are overgrown with dead white stems. A cold wind blows and makes the tips of the long grass quiver.

Dagger's at her shed, clawing the door.

I crawl up the path towards him, and look back at the cottage. The side door is shut and the curtains of the two small windows are closed. I grab the lead as Dagger strains at the rotten wood at the bottom of the door. I yank but Dagger holds firm, his nose is stuck to a smell. I pick him up and he squirms.

At the gate, Mammy's watching for us, her face clouded with worry. She reaches over the gate and grabs Dagger from me, so I can open the gate and try not to let it creak. But Mammy yelps and the gate creaks and clicks shut behind me. She's holding Dagger too tight. He's bitten her wrist and as she drops him I grab his lead. Mammy's face is hollering red and there are tears in her eyes. The blood from Dagger's bite is splattered on her coat. I take off a welly, rip off my thick sock and she wraps it round her wrist like a bandage.

I keep watching Old Kelp's windows as I shove my foot back into my welly.

We walk away fast.

Mammy whispers, 'We weren't really there. Say nothing. Not a word.'

Dagger's padding along happy, but Mammy's not speaking to us. She's gripping my sock on her wrist and she ducks through a gate into a field. Dagger and me follow her down to a brook. The water whooshes over the rocks and she wets the sock and washes the bite from bad Dagger's good tooth.

She says, 'Bloody dog. No use for anything.'

'You've only got one bite mark. If he still had his other tooth, you'd have two.'

'Small reward, Kip.' She uses my sock to wet her coat till the blood splatter is gone.

I sit on a cold flat rock beside the brook and hold Dagger tight though he wriggles. I whisper in his ear, 'Stay put, stay put.'

Mammy flaps her coat in the wind to make it dry. Her scarf comes undone and blows off her curls. She curses, but catches it, and shoves it in her pocket. I think about Old Kelp's curtains, and I'd swear when we were walking away, one curtain opened a slit. The width of an eye.

The road we're on is narrow, wide enough for only one car, a tractor, the postman's van, or the tip trailer. Mammy's not saying much. I want to take her thoughts away from her ouch and back to her birthday but she sits herself down on the grassy verge. 'I need a breather.'

'Sorry Dagger bit you.'

Dagger's sniffing at a dead jackdaw on the road.

She glares at Dagger, and says, 'He's no good for anything.'

'He's good for waking me in the mornings, when nothing else can—'

'There's your dad!' She staggers to her feet and runs up the hill towards a man pulling a small trailer. I can hear the squeak of the wheels. I can't run with the blisters from my welly with no sock so I limp after her, pulling Dagger hard.

As Mammy gets to him, he puts the handles down and stops the squeak. He opens his arms, and she goes running into them.

Dad's chin is bristly and his wellies are covered in mud.

He's muttering, smiling into Mammy's birthday hair. 'You're smelling fine, Dorcas.'

She puts her hands on his cheeks. 'You're well, no troubles or grumbles?'

He puts his hands over hers. 'Nothing's wrong. Missed the cakes, though not as much as I've missed you.' He kisses her lips.

He looks at me over Mammy's shoulder. His smile drops as he glances down at my muddy coat and stained dress. He says, 'All right, Kip? You've been looking after Mammy for me, then?'

'Yes, Dad.' I grab his hand for a squeeze, but he shakes my hand like a man and lets go.

Mammy burrows into the nook under his arm.

Dad says to me, 'You wheel the trailer. It'll give you strong muscles.'

Mammy slaps Dad's chest. 'No, Brack, you wheel it. Kip's too young, nowhere near strong enough yet.'

'Well, it's time he learned to be. Nonsense, a boy wearing dresses. He's an embarrassment. You know they've heard about him all the way at Jock's farm, and all the hands from the next farm along. Had to bury my face, the laugh they were having at my expense. It's to stop.'

AMBER

Nothing can be found in this remote, rustic place. I can't imagine anyone ordering people who aren't lost to search for someone who is. I doubt anyone here ever looks properly for anything. People who value nostalgia must holiday in places like this – a remote coastal area – staying in villages which, in Paradon, are marketed as 'the quaintest step back in time'.

I get out of bed, leaving Maya murmuring in her sleep. Closing the bedroom door quietly, I go to the bathroom to run a bath. My newly awake body is tingling. I need to warm myself and scent myself sweet.

All the water in Paradon which ran from taps, through pipes, into washing machines, sprinkled from showers: every splash had a slight scent of swimming pools. Even the river was over-chlorinated. So with the combination of the sun and chlorine, our clothes, all our fabrics, even our thoughts were bleached and grew pale.

I test the temperature of the bath. I get vanilla and almond essences from a kitchen cupboard, and drip a few drops in the bathwater. I lock the bathroom door and stir up the water. The steam coats my face with aromas of cake.

Holding out my fingertips I look at the slash of purple on the edge of the nail of my little finger. All that's left of the nail varnish.

It's all that's left on my body, of Paradon.

In the bathroom cupboard, I find jars of lemon moisturiser and salted lotions, and line them along the edge of the bath. In Paradon, skin is protected from the sun by an array of sun-blocks, guards and screens. People spritz, rub and lather them on in vast quantities. The relentless sun burns into anything which soaks up light. And though the sun is worshipped, it makes everything old before its time.

When we left, the labs hadn't yet perfected the hair dyes; they were still attempting the longed-for permanence. The latest experiments were designed to find a permanent colour which filled the hair follicles like ink. Then hair could be coloured in as it grows. But science is too slow; it doesn't keep up with the speed of dreams.

I watch my reflection ripple in the bathtub.

'Our little gargoyle' our parents had called me, when I was so young they may have believed I wouldn't remember. Sometimes, I think the phrase was some dazed mind-speak of new parents. A huge amount of infantile excretions, a lack of sleep and therefore probably hallucinations, could easily lead parents to see the ugliness in a difficult toddler, if their eyes weren't seeing them through a filter of desired or inherited beauty. When they were quite young, our parents both had surgery: my father's hooked nose was smoothed, his curved back braced; my mother's square chin was rounded, her cheeks pulled taut, her forehead injected. Perhaps, in searching my face for familiarity and remembering the faces they were born with, they found their own discarded ugliness.

Since living in this cottage I've learned I can only mirror any kind of beauty if I believe I'm beautiful. If I look into a mirror and believe I'm ugly, I'll see a beast, yes, a gargoyle. If I believe I'll see an erotic exotic or some alabaster nymph, that's what I'll see.

I take off my nightdress, leave it in a pool on the floor and look at my naked body. I'm a landscape of hills, valleys and creeks. I was meant to live here in the country. I've become solid. Now, I *am* a country. Here, I've become a woman; a landscape of breasts and belly, buttocks and thighs. I am a mountain.

With no one to scale me.

My eyes can see clearer, my taste buds are budding, and my body has expanded. This new weightiness of my body is something which would be despised in Paradon. But my ever-expanding waist isn't clenched, cinched, clamped or stapled. My breasts are ripe fruits which bounce when I dance, and have no need for underwires, overwires, highwires or corsetry.

I look over my shoulder as I'm dancing in front of the bathroom mirror. There is so much more of my body. I have doubled in size. I can see my enormous backside dancing of its own accord, the flesh jigging to the sound of its own tune. I can certainly feel it. My backside has grown to the size of a bustle. And doesn't it love to sway.

Boom boom bum.

Everything echoes.

As my body sinks into the bathtub, the water rises. I lean this way and that, block the water behind me, tilt myself and cause a warm waterfall to rush around my thighs. I smell of vanilla essence, cardamom and nutmeg, flour and butter. My flesh has absorbed these flavours. I've grown curves from all the baked and steamed and grilled puddings I've absorbed and digested.

My new shape is just like my old self, but risen.

I grab handfuls, pinch and squeeze myself. My fingers find a hidden place, tucked under layers of sweet-smelling skin. I think of the colour of dandelion petals, the brightness bees vibrate themselves for. I lie back in the bath, vibrate myself all the way through and ripen into honey.

I breathe in the damp scented air. My skin smells of cakes. Over an hour has passed. More than one, I'm not sure. In this bathroom there's only my own mind and body to navigate. I tremble a little, touched by hands I've never felt before.

In the mirror as the steam clears, my eyes shine bright. Seeing myself without the uglifying filter of our parents' gaze is a new feeling. I now like what I see in these mirrors. But keeping my body just for myself, I'm not sure I want to. I cover my lips with my fingertips and they smell of salt. Sweet, slightly bitter. A pheromone warning.

I should boom boom bum my sister from my bed, and get myself a lover.

In the bedroom, I put on knickers and a vest which rises up over my belly. My thighs are melting honey, with no bones in there at all. I pull one of the old woman's black dresses on and it sits too tight across my breasts. I sit on the bed and a seam rips.

I think about what the old woman must have felt like, living this solitary life but having a lover in this bed. And I imagine having the bed to myself, without Maya; having a lover who comes and goes, scales me and dismounts, lies down and drowns in me . . . a lover with bones . . . I wet my lips with my tongue.

Without Maya sharing my bed, I could go outside under a dark moon, naked, my arms outstretched, and chant that I want a lover, and see what comes running at me from the night . . . drag them in here with my teeth, wrestle them onto the bed . . .

Maya's lying there watching me.

I say, 'Don't spy,' as I grab the damp bath towel from the floor and drop it on her side of the bed.

She says, 'You think I'm cramping you in, don't you?'

I go into the kitchen, switch on the light, and pick up the

recipe book. Flick the pages forwards and back, look away and let go as they fall open.

I read the page.

STEAMED SUET PUDDING

Flour, self-raising, 6 oz
Salt, pinch
Suet, 3 oz
Sugar, 2 oz
Milk, 5 fl oz
Spices

Place the flour, salt, suet and sugar in the mixing bowl. Use a medium spoon. Stir diagonally. Stir horizontally. Allow the spoon to be the guide for a clockwise or anti-clockwise direction.

Dissolve your intention* into your fingertips.

Add enough milk for a soft dropping consistency. Drop your intention from the spoon into the mixture. Stir again. Clarify your intention. Stir again. Select spices according to the strength which is required. Sprinkle in the spices.

Cover the bowl and place it in the steamer. Steam for as long as it takes for your own mind to either clear or fog.

Let the pudding sigh before eating.

Serve piping hot, with jam, marmalade or honey, depending on the precise amount of sweetness required to disguise all traces of your intention.

* The intention in the baker's mind needs to be particularly focussed with this recipe. Keep it held in the fingertips whilst stirring. The intention with any recipe involving steaming should involve some aspect of clouding the eater's vision, or the opposite: inducing clarity after foggy thinking.

Maya sits at the table, pressing her fingertip onto the pepper grains on top of the pepper pot. She says, 'Pepper's so greenish.'

'Is there something useful you could be doing? You could make our clothes wider as well as shorter. If you really tried to learn to sew, you could take in sewing. I could use more butter and margarine in the cakes, make the cake-eaters put on weight so their clothes split too. You could say, there there, to them. By letter. Not in person. You'd need your own room . . .'

Maya frowns and leans her head to the side. 'Sewing needles are angry little creatures.'

Intention. This bowl on the counter. The ingredients, ready. A picture of fog, filling my mind. Push the thought into my fingertips. Let it flow through the spoon. Stir it in horizontally. Stir it in round and round. See if it works. Practising on Maya. Clouding her mind. Rapid heartbeat. Ejected sister, evacuated from bed. Almost explosive. No. An internal explosion, not so dramatic. Clouding. Maya wandering somewhere else to sleep, the whole bed mine, spreading out my arms and legs across the sheets. The curtains, slightly open. A lover looking in at me through the window. No. Too directional. Think of Maya. Fogged-minded Maya. Her uncried tears, evaporating into mist. Vapours of steam.

She interrupts. 'I don't like how you think of me.'

'Which thought don't you like? Is it one I've mentioned or one you're guessing at?'

She clenches and unclenches her hands. 'You think I killed Dead Red.'

I turn the heat on under the steamer pan and turn to face Maya. 'I did think you killed her, but I'm toying with the idea that you didn't – you like her far too much.'

'Then how did she die?'

'That night, I didn't lock the front door, so she must have come in here with the person who did kill her. You were sewing. You didn't hear them. Perhaps you caught a glimpse of them but were scared and don't remember. And the person who really killed her ran away. It was dark. I didn't see anyone leaving, but that doesn't mean they weren't here.'

I pick up the bowl and hold it in the crook of my arm as I continue to stir the steamed-pudding mixture.

She frowns, thinking hard. 'Or you could have killed her. You could have come back in much earlier than you seemed to. One day I might go outside too, and might not . . .' She bites her lip and looks at me.

I'm still stirring. 'Ah, it's not just about what I think of you. You're homesick and wondering how you could find your way back to Paradon . . . Is that it?'

'Might be.'

'You'd get thin again. No one's curved, they're tightly stretched. They've all sold their souls, to something.' I put the bowl on the table and sprinkle in a pinch of chilli, a slap of ginger, and a punch of cardamom.

Maya stands up. 'You don't like me any more.'

'I love you, but that doesn't mean I have to like you all the time. Don't sulk. You've just come over all out of sorts. Unsorted. You'll feel better when we've had this steamed pudding. Do you want jam or marmalade or honey with it, or all three at once?'

She smiles. 'Ooh, three colours at once. Red, orange and gold explosion!'

'Glorious. Let's change our names. I'll be Gloria. Someone with a name as good as Gloria could never feel bad about anything. She'd only ever feel glorious. What name do you want?'

She folds her arms. 'I like Maya.'

'Try something more earthy. Someone who lives contentedly with her sister in the country, but sleeps alone and doesn't mind at all. Rosalie . . . Meg . . . Lottie . . . Peggy?'

'I'm keeping Maya. When I was a baby, our mother thought my skin was like the surface of a shimmering spyglass. That's why she chose me a name that means dream or illusion. She said I was a delicate mirror-thing.'

'Well, you soon grew out of delicate.'

'Our mother told me when you were born, you were so grotesque you didn't look like any human she'd ever seen.'

'When I was born, there was just one person in the world that looked like me, and that was me. Till you turned up and copied my face!'

Maya steps towards me. 'Look at me. No matter what you say, you still want a twin.'

I don't tell her she looks completely identical and is unarguably right. She even looks as angry as I feel. Instead, I say, 'Poor Maya.'

'Why not poor Amber?'

'Because if I tell you what I saw today, you'll be frightened.'

'*You're* not.'

'I'm braver than you.'

Maya says, 'Or you're secretly a murderer, and that makes you feel stupid-courageous.'

I breathe in, give the bowl another stir and think about fog. I feel as if someone else is holding my hands, stirring with me as I say, 'There are people out looking for the dead woman. I heard something in the garden. Saw a dog at the shed door. Scratching at it. There's a woman, the scraggy girl and a dog. They all have claws. The dog wears a small death shroud. It was scratching scritching scratching . . .'

Maya backs away. 'Nonono,' she murmurs as a plate falls to the floor and smashes.

'They didn't find her.' I point at the broom. 'Clean it up. It just means one of us has to be awake all the time.'

She stares at me, her face pale. 'No, they know. Not that she died here. Not on this kitchen floor.'

I stir the bowl and think of thickening mist . . . and that . . .

Maya's face is stricken. 'What if they find her, what if they take her away, what if they find the snowball, what if they . . .' She shakes her head, her eyes wide.

'The snowball once was a rock, covered in her blood.'

Hands in my hands, a gale in my ribs, someone else breathing my breaths through the recipe, stirring a thick dark fog. Not a light to be found.

Stir stir stir.

I say, 'You should have seen them, Maya, as they scuttled away, all three of them – their teeth were pronged. And they had limps. You know how frightening people seem when they're skew-whiff. Step. Drag. Step. Drag. They looked hungry. Starving, I'd say. Sometimes hunger gives people a terrible strength. When they want something badly enough. They wanted her dead body. Can you imagine what starving people might do to a human corpse? One of them might even have had a wooden leg. Not the dog. What's more ferocious than a starving peg-leg mother and her starving daughter?'

Stir, stir, stir.

She looks at me.

Stir stir stir.

She says in a whisper, 'Their dog, was it dogstarved—'

'A hound. Some unearthly beast, made of fogged darkness and growling pure killer instincts. Glow-in-the-dark dog drool. It would tear your throat out and plunge you into some underworld oven. There, demons toast you with goblets, and torture you by forcing you to cry so you can drink your own tears. And you think that'll keep your temperature down, but your tears are salt on your tongue, the taste of them is drying you from the inside, your skin is blistering from the heat of raging fires. Smoke, all around you, too thick to see . . . do you remember the dead woman's eyes?'

Maya puts her hands over her ears and hums.

Still I stir, stir, stir the pudding bowl, watching the pale mixture thickening. 'Her bruised dead eyes. They're staring at nothing in the dark, a great black nothing that's filling her now. Creeping through her, a dark fog. If she could cry real tears, she'd never be able to stop . . .'

'Nonono . . .' sings Maya, her eyes dark, her cheeks paling.

The pudding mixture, still thicker.

Maya groans.

I put the bowl down and say, lightly, 'I won't sleep. I'll watch to make sure they don't come back. You sleep after this steamed pudding is cooked and you've eaten your fill. You can have all of it. I'll have dumplings. Jam dumplings.' I lick my lips. 'You can sleep while I have my dumplings and make the honey cakes for the doorstep. I'll wake you; we'll have bacon and eggs. I'll sleep, and you can watch for them.'

Maya's hands are shaking.

I get the greaseproof paper and cut a circle out.

Her voice sounds confused. 'But we'll never not see each other. You'll not sleep when I'm awake and I'll not sleep when you're awake and we'll never not be together, untogether, never at all—'

'You're double- or triple-jumbling. It'll just be till we know if they're coming back to look for her or not. By then, we'll be so used to sleeping apart we'll have to sort out having a bed in the living room as well as in the bedroom and we can—'

She takes a deep breath and talks more clearly. 'I won't be able to sleep on my own. The wind's always screeching outside. Wind's gruelling. Is there a reason for it, or is it spite?'

I fasten the circle of paper over the pudding bowl. The bowl hums in my hands as I put it gently in the steamer. My forehead is coated in condensation. I grip the counter to steady myself. Steam fills the room and it should be warm but it feels cold. It's moving towards Maya.

I clang the glass lid on the steamer and it mists.

Taking a deep breath I turn around.

Maya's eyes are murky.

I whisper to her, 'That was too much, I'm sorry. What I haven't told you is that, as searchers, they didn't seem particularly clever. The girl didn't try to break the padlock. The mother didn't even come through our gate. I got carried along by something. I'm feeling a bit . . . what's the opposite of dispossessed?'

I wave my hand in front of her face.

She doesn't flinch. The damp which fogs the kitchen has filled her up.

There's something in the corner. A shadow, grey against the

patched plaster wall. A human shape. Something nearly there. Something almost watching. My heart skips beats. I've got the feeling it will suddenly move closer if I don't keep my eyes fixed on it.

KIP

There's a fire lit on the beach. The grown-ups are singing into the dark at the sea. Mam Vann's leaning on her walkerstick with one hand and conducting driftwood at the crowd of them with the other.

Jack's playing his fiddle. George twists back and forth drumming a fast and steady beat on his bodhran with his drumming-bone.

Mammy's got the best voice; even in a whole crowd of people, she sings loudest and highest. Dad's beside Mammy with his arm around her waist. She wanted the singing for her birthday because it's her favourite ever thing to do. They're singing a jigging song called 'Drowning the Houses', a song about the floods.

About six of the boys are down the far end of the beach, playing ogres-beat-waves. I'm sitting on the second-best rock where they can't see me. This rock's only here when the tide's out and it's the shape of a seal. The fiddle sounds louder and the voices get higher and the bodhran's beat drums up the singing.

Dagger's lead is wound too tight around my wrist. He's slouched on the sand next to me looking tired. I untie him. He sparks wide awake, dashes past the fire and down to the edge of the waves. He smells a lump of something he wants his nose soaked in, and rolls in it.

I chase after him and drag him off a dead jellyfish. He stinks, so I take him to the smallest waves and splash and rub him down. He wriggles and tries to bark; his neck moves like he's giving it a good go. He looks skinny soaked, half the size of himself dry. The boys have found a rope tangled with stringy seaweed and they're yowling off up the beach.

The song's changed to a slower tune about Gilliam, called 'No Flowers', all about how he was never seen again. I listen to the words of the chorus:

'Don't let yourself go,
get loved at too hard
else you'll drop in a ditch,
right under the stars.
There will be no flowers,
to lay on no grave:
when you thump what you love
then you'll die not so brave.'

I sing along so quietly I can only hear it in my head, but even in my head I can't carry a tune. Just like Dagger not being able to bark, it's the same for me with singing.

Dagger shakes the sea and the jellyfish stink onto my dress and coat. Grabbing his lead, I creep through the crowd to get to Mammy. Dad's eyes water as he gets a whiff of me. I make a come-here wave with my hand, and Mammy leans down to hear what I'm saying.

I tell her, 'Got to go home to wash.'

She says in my ear, 'What's he rolled in now?'

Dad leans down as well. 'Long dead by the smell, get off and cleaned up, but get back down here quick. Wear only the clothes I've put on your bed, or I'll give you what for.'

Mammy says to him, 'Not tonight.'

Dad shakes his head and sings with the horde of voices again. He's joined in the chorus: 'there will be no flowers . . .' He holds the last note steady.

Mammy looks at him with a smile, her eyes shining. She flushes at the sound of his rich voice, puts her arm around his waist and joins in with 'to lay on no grave'.

I haul Dagger away. Though he wants another go on the jellyfish, I yank him up the beach so hard his back legs leave drag tracks in the rippled sand.

When I come back down the beach clean and without Dagger, the fire's gone dim. The grown-ups aren't singing any more, they're bickering. The moon is shining and they look like shadows of who they are. There are three other children left on the beach. One of them's my cousin, Adam. They're climbing on the second-best rock. Caddy's standing on the part of the rock that's the seal's head.

The huddles of grown-ups keep moving, breaking and coming back together in different bunches.

I get near the second-best rock, but not too near Dad. He'd put a pair of his old woollen trousers on my bed, and he'd cut the legs short to fit me. He'd also left me a belt, and my cable-knit jumper. I'm not wearing the trousers. I'm wearing my nightie and the jumper because he said *the clothes on your bed*, and my nightie was under my pillow, so that counts.

I go over to Adam. 'Why have they stopped the singing?'

He's watching his mum and dad who are in a huddle of their own, talking to each other and no one else.

Maeve waves her spindly arms in the air. 'Someone's goneded missing.' She grins up at me under her curly hair and holds out her arms. Her face looks like a cranky kitten's. I pick her up.

She leans her head on my shoulder. 'Like you, Kip.'

'Like you too. Who's gone?'

Adam nods at me. 'None of us. We're here. The others are all off somewhere.' He waves at the houses. 'Playing pirates. I've to look after Maeve, and Caddy has to stay too – the pirates wanted a girl to tie up. The grown-ups got wind and it's outlawed for these two, but not all the grown-ups are bothered about their own right now. So I'm the mug who's been roped in to see neither of this pair gets trussed.' He's talking much more than he usually does.

Caddy points at each of the adults. 'Kip's mum and dad, Adam's mum and dad, my dad, my mum, Ben's dad, Pike's mum and Maeve's—'

'Yes, I know.' I stop her before she lists the parents of everyone who goes to the school.

Adam says, 'Maybe George has shut himself indoors again – no, there he is. Or Kerry? She was looking peaky.'

'She's over there,' I point.

Caddy grabs my arm and hisses, 'Have you seen her? Is she so so old she's made of bones bones bones?' She jumps off the rock and draws circles with her feet in the sand. She means Old Kelp, so I don't answer.

Caddy spins around, her arms outstretched, the bobble on her hat so big it looks like an apple thumped on the top of a cake. She sings, 'You can't say, can't say, can't say . . .' There's a note off key in her voice.

Dad's looking over at me and he's seen the nightie. He takes two steps towards us, his hands clenched. Mammy pulls him back.

I tig Maeve, Caddy, then Adam. 'All waves.' We tear across the sand, swerve past the clutter of grown-ups and climb up onto the rock that's the lap of a giant. I pick up a stone and throw it at the sea and soon we're all doing it. Caddy's chucking her stones the furthest, much further than me, but I'm not trying as hard.

Mammy comes over. 'Kip, we're just going to go round and knock on some doors. Can you keep this lot with you?'

I'm a giant looking down at her. I've got two stones in my hands and I'm knocking them together for giant footsteps. 'Has it been good singing?'

'That it has.'

Caddy hurls three more stones.

Aunty Pippa and Uncle Finn still aren't talking to anyone but each other. They come over to the rock and beckon Adam. He bends down to hear them as they talk to him quietly.

Mammy says to them, 'Can Adam stay here with Kip – else he'll be on his own with the two young ones, and, well . . .' She watches Caddy roaring as she hurls about five stones in the air. She says to Aunty Pippa, 'Oh sorry, thanks for the perfume. It smells so different on the skin to how it does in the bottle – don't you think? I like it.' She holds out her wrist.

Aunty Pippa sniffs it. 'It suits you. I wasn't sure. Not everyone can take such a strong scent and make it really sing.' She looks round at the other adults who are walking away back up the beach. 'Where's everyone going?'

Mammy smiles at her, quickly. 'Probably nothing to fret over. You two get yourselves home. Thank you.' She smells her wrist as she glances at Caddy. 'I'm just worried about Kip getting overwrought. I'll bring Adam back to yours later.'

Aunty Pippa looks at me. 'What's wrong?'

Mammy answers, 'You remember when he first started school, he had these fits—'

I say, 'I'm fine!'

'Still.'

Aunty Pippa nods. 'I remember. A frightening time, that was. I'd be the same. Adam. Adam!'

Adam looks round at her. 'I'll talk to Kip.' He keeps grappling with Caddy.

Aunty Pippa looks at my hands knocking stones together, and smiles at me.

'Do you want these?' I hold them out. 'You can do giants knocking with them.'

She takes them and puts them in her pocket. 'Thanks, I'll have a bash with them later.'

Uncle Finn scratches his bare top lip and murmurs something to Aunty Pippa. They turn and walk away up the beach. Uncle Finn stumbles and reaches to steady himself on Aunty Pippa. She stops and holds his arm till he can walk again.

I whisper to Mammy, 'He's loads older-looking than Dad.'

'Only four years.'

'And even older-looking than Aunty Pippa – like he's *her* dad, not her husband . . .'

She watches Adam as she tells me, 'Shush it.'

Aunty Pippa and Uncle Finn swerve past the others who are clustering outside the cottages along the shore. The street lights shine on everyone's heads and I look for the one with the blondest, curliest, longest hair. 'Lizzie's still not back yet, is she?'

Mammy's voice is sharp. 'Not back from where?'

I shrug.

She says, 'No one's seen her for a few days at least. Jessie's passed by her door over and over again, to open the corner shop, and she did knock to see if she'd mind the shop for her yesterday, but there was no answer. She thought she'd gone off again to visit her sister. But she can't remember if Lizzie said that or not. And Mam Vann thought Lizzie had gone off as well, but up

Jock's farm. And now she's not sure either. No one listens right. But Kip, has Lizzie been leaving out her fair?'

'There was a glove.'

'A what?'

'I didn't take it for fair. A black glove on her doorstep. I put a rock over it.'

'For what?'

'Are you cross?'

She breathes in hard, and out again slowly. 'No. Yes. I am a bit cross, Kip. She put out no fair? You should have said.'

'I'm not meant to talk about—'

'You can talk about the fair. Just not about Old Kelp. How many mornings has there been no fair at Lizzie's?'

'Three. No. Four. The Quiet Woman hasn't left out her fair either.'

'You don't know how many days?'

'I'm no good at seeing things right in the mornings. Or remembering how many of anything after.'

'Oh Kip. This isn't one of your stories?'

I shake my head. 'No, I'm full of truth.'

She looks pale. 'Three or four days. Flipsake, Kip. You stay put.' She lowers her voice, looks at Maeve, and back at me. 'Keep them away from Lizzie's house.'

Maeve's too near the edge of the rock so I pull her back. She says, 'Where's my mum goneded?'

'She's with the others.'

She wails, 'Tired!'

I clamber down, reach up and her eyes are shining as I lift her down. She clings on, so I give her a bounce around.

As Adam climbs down too, Caddy pinches and grabs at his ginger hair. He shakes her hand off.

I put Maeve down and Adam says, 'Kip, why do you wear dresses?'

'I like them.'

Maeve says, 'Butterflies!'

Adam says to me, 'But what for?'

'Just feels best, wearing them.'

'Better than these?' He grabs the sides of his thick black trousers, stretches the trouser legs wide and makes his legs move round in circles like a puppet.

Caddy scrambles down and says, 'Tomorrow I'm going to wear trousers and I'll wear them better than you.'

Adam undoes his trouser button and zip. 'Wear them better right now. Swaps. Give your skirt here, Caddy.'

'Give me your jumper as well, chickenlegs.' Her hands are on her hips. Adam's trousers slide down his legs. 'Will not. Too bloody cold.'

'Keep your trousers on.' She takes off and runs along the sand towards the waves, twisting and turning.

Adam pulls up his trousers. 'So Lizzie's sick or something.'

'Looks that way.'

Maeve bends down and she's reaching for another dead jelly-fish. I pull her away and pick her up again.

Caddy's got her shoes and socks off and she's kicking up the waves. She shouts at us, 'I don't feel any cold! Not ever, and I'll be the one to make my legs the bluest!' By the looks of her bare feet and ankles in the bright moonlight, she's getting blue fast.

Adam says, 'Would you want to be a girl if you could, Kip?'

I glance up the beach but no one's coming back for us yet. 'What are you asking for?' I frown at him.

Maeve strokes my cheek.

Adam says, 'Just. Dad said so. I told him I didn't think you did. He said I'd best not be getting any ideas from you.'

'Right.' I walk along a tidemark of tangled seaweed.

Adam walks fast to keep up with me. 'Kip?'

'What?'

'Have you got any ideas I *can* get from you?'

'No.'

'Well, that's good for Dad, but no good for me.'

'He'll be proud of you, then.'

Caddy's spinning around with her arms outstretched, and she stops knee-deep and beckons to us. I hold Maeve tight and head towards her.

Adam's beside me. 'Can I try your dress on?'

I turn to face him. 'No, it's mine.'

Maeve reaches out and grabs a chunk of Adam's hair and laughs as she holds on tight with her hand and buries her face in my neck. She pulls him so close I can see every one of the freckles on his nose.

He eases Maeve's fingers off his hair and says to me, 'Do you wear frocks so the girls like you best?'

'No. I like them is all.'

'All right. Just always wondered, eh.'

'Well, don't.'

He turns and splashes into the icy waves after Caddy, with his shoes still on.

In our cottage, the fire's burning in the grate and Dagger's asleep in front of it on the rug. Adam fumbles for the light switch as I plonk Maeve down on the baggy chair. She settles into a curl.

Adam goes into our kitchen and I can hear him rummaging in the cupboards. 'Ooh, what's this for?'

As I go into the kitchen, he's holding a can of wood-brightener and reading the instructions. 'Your kitchen's always so tidy.' He squints at the instructions on the can. 'Flammable. Interesting.'

I look at the pottery hen, the folded tea towels, and a stack of clean bowls next to the deep white sink. 'Do you like cleaning?'

He puts the can away again, in the cupboard under the sink. 'I like cleaning if there's not too much stuff stacked everywhere for it to ever look proper clean. Mum and Dad can't tidy up because their hoards are in the way. Always going on about storage but not making any more cupboards. Now Dad's heart's this weak, they've got excuses for no more anything.'

'How come you're talking to me more now? When the grown-ups have told us to play before, you've barely said a word to me.'

He looks at the floor, his cheeks flushed. 'Just.'

'Just what?'

'Talk most to Mum, don't I? She's always told me stuff then said *keep it to yourself*. I thought she meant everything we talk about. But now she says she didn't mean *all* of it. She says I don't talk enough and I've got a genetic. Can't remember what that was. She thinks she's messed my brain up because she's not an insider.'

'She's an insider now everyone's used to her. I want to ask her about Paradon – are there swarms of giant insects they kill with medicine?'

He frowns. 'She's never said so. It's just, well, Mum says I'm going to need someone else to talk to.' He picks at his ear. 'Before she came here she learned psychology, so she knows the right thing to do when there's troubles at home.'

'What's psychogee?'

'Where people look in your head, and ask you what you want to do.'

'You don't want me to do that to you?'

'No, you won't see in. My brain's in the way. I've got to talk to someone that's not her, else I'll have problems. She says I've got her . . . outsider complex? Something like that.' He frowns at me. 'I'll check what she meant later. See if I'm doing it right.'

'So you're trying out talking on me?'

'That all right?' His cheeks are still flushed as he glances at me.

'You're good at it.'

He beams. 'Knew you'd be the right one. Always have thought you're all right.'

'Thanks.'

'So. Have you got cinnamon sticks and matches?'

'For what?'

'Smoking.'

'Cinnamon?'

The front door rattles and opens.

Caddy's standing in the doorway and her eyes are wide. 'You've got to hear this,' she says, panting. 'No wonder they're not bothering about us. They're all indoors at Lizzie's place—'

'What for?' says Adam.

Caddy's near-on shouting, breathing hard from running. 'Lizzie's not there, and her house is a mess. Someone's been all through it. Wrecked, and her knickers are everywhere!'

Maeve sparks awake. 'Knickers everywhere?'

Adam says, 'Is Maeve big enough to know knickers?'

Caddy slaps his arm. 'Dimwit. Lizzie's been done! Done in! That's what they're saying. Heard them through the window. They've got the lights on – opened one of the windows and everything, so there must be a right stink.'

'Maeve, come here.' She clambers off the baggy chair and I put my hands over her ears. 'Is there blood?'

'Come on,' Caddy beckons us. 'We'll spy.'

'Me with,' says Maeve. I hold her ears tighter.

Adam says, 'Is Lizzie's tongue black? Do you remember, Kip – we saw a rat like that once—'

Caddy says, 'Didn't see her yet. But if that's what dead looks like, she'll have a good black tongue.'

I take my hands away from Maeve's ears and ask her, 'Could you stay here with Dagger and be still?'

'No.'

'Come with, then.'

Looking in the window, Lizzie's front room is bright from the bare light bulb. The grown-ups are lifting up two yellow chairs tipped over on the rug. There's a broken vase on the coffee table and smashed glass all over the green sofa, from a picture of a bonfire that's hanging off the wall.

Adam whispers, 'Is that it?'

Caddy beckons us round to the windows at the back. Her mum and dad are in the kitchen with Jessie and a few other grown-ups. They're drinking tea and looking pale, and Jessie is picking up bits of broken plates off the floor. Maeve's flustered mum is washing a stack of dirty dishes. We creep past the back door. The other window's open. It's Lizzie's bedroom.

'Can't see,' whispers Maeve, jumping.

Caddy kneels down and shushes her as me and Adam look in. Mammy and Dad are in there with Mam Vann and George. They're all on the other side of Lizzie's rumpled bed, looking at something we can't see on the floor. Her underwear has been tipped out of the drawers all over the bed. A pair of blue knickers are hanging off the lampshade.

Mam Vann looks at the window and we duck.

Maeve says, 'What's in there?'

Adam sits on the back doorstep and thumps his fist beside him for me to sit down too. 'My mum and dad aren't there. That's no good at all for my outsider complication. They could try harder.'

Kip

I squat down under the window. 'A lot of the grown-ups must have gone home. So only this lot think something's up.'

Caddy hisses, 'Lizzie must be there, dead, on the floor beside the bed. That's why they're not tidying that room. They'll have to get the police if she's gone and got herself murdered.' She beams.

We all listen at the open window.

Mam Vann's saying, ' . . . if she's not here, it doesn't have to mean anything's wrong. We just have to find her.'

Mammy's voice says, 'Too far to Fastleigh in the dark. How many miles?'

Dad says, 'Has anyone got her sister's phone number?'

Adam whispers, 'You're full of seascrag, Caddy. Lizzie's not done in at all. She's gone off and her house is a tip. They're not even going to traipse to get the police for her. Best thing ever, walking in pitch dark. If she's not even dead, let's go.'

'Is my mum in there?' says Maeve, thumping her chest.

Adam whispers to her, 'What are you thumping yourself for, young one?'

Caddy looks at him like he's stupid. 'Sometimes, she's a monkey. Maeve, go in and yell for your mum. Tell her you want your bed.' She turns the handle, nudges Maeve through and closes the door. She wrings out her wet socks and pulls her shoes on. She mutters, 'Thought Lizzie was dead and everything.' She stomps off into the dark towards her house.

'Come on,' says Adam, standing up. 'Me and you, we'll go back to yours.'

I reach for the door handle. 'No – I want to go in—'

There are yells from the boys playing pirates round the narrow lanes and their shouts are coming this way.

I freeze. Hold my breath.

A hurled rock misses my leg. The shout comes. 'Oyoyoy! Girl-boy!'

Adam backs away from me.

I say, 'Do what you want,' and leg it. I don't stop running till I'm home and I've slammed the front door behind me.

Dagger lifts his head and blinks at me under his ragged black fringe. I sit on the rug by the fire with him. He slumps his head onto my lap. I can feel his good tooth resting on my knee, through my lilac nightie that's frayed along the hem.

I bury my head in his fur. I whisper, 'No good for protecting, are you? Neither's Adam. He's probably gone off with them. Thought he was meant to be an outsider.'

Rain whaps hard on the window. The coals glow in the grate. Dagger moves his head and lies on his side with his paws stretching out. I lie beside him and stroke his soft ears. He blinks at me. I tell him, 'You still won't be any good for protecting, when they've got some of Jock's coal for the school and it's open again, because Daggers aren't allowed.'

A half-hour has passed and Mammy and Dad still aren't back. The telephone is ringing. I can't find it but it keeps ringing till I do. It's under a pile of yellow fabric Mammy was measuring for new curtains.

I pick up the phone. 'If you're Jock, it's bad ringing time because Dad's out.'

'It's Aunty Pippa. Is Adam with you, Kip?'

'He's gone off with the other boys.'

'Hm. Are you sure about that?'

'No, but he probably—'

'Is your mum there?'

'Did you and Uncle Finn go straight home?'

'Things we had to do. Where's—'

'Mammy and Dad are at Lizzie's.'

Her voice sounds sharp. 'Why?'

'They all think something's happened to her. Her house is wrecked.'

I can hear muffled talking.

'Are you still there?'

She's got her hand over the phone.

'Hello?'

She sounds distracted. 'Sorry, Kip. It's all right. Well, not. At least, yes. Adam must have sneaked in. Finn's just come down and said he's in his room.'

Again, muffled voices.

I say, 'Tell Adam sorry I ran off.'

'So are you there on your own?'

'I'm with Dagger.'

'Do you want me to come round?'

'I'm fine.'

'Is your fireguard on?'

I look at the fireplace. 'No, it's in the corner.'

'Put it on and get to bed. Night, Kip.'

AMBER

The kitchen smells of allspice and is oven-warm. Apart from this corner. I pass my hand through the air and my heart beats faster, because the air is different here. My fingertips feel icy.

Maya comes in. 'The mirrors here have ghosts living in them.'

I drop my hand. 'What do they look like?'

She moves her fingers in front of her eyes. 'Faces made of smokethreads. Have you ever seen upset-despair? It's just . . . they don't seem despairing. Ghosts should, don't you think? They're saying words they want me to listen to but I can't. It's not right. I should be able to hear them if they want me to.'

'Not if they're not real.' I grab a tea towel and swish the colander and grater dry. 'Don't look at the mirrors if they frighten you. Did you ever see ghosts before we lived here?'

She shakes her head.

'So what's making you see them here?'

'This cottage is like it's from a ghost story.' She stands next to the closed front door and runs her finger over the wood.

I glance at the cold corner and back at Maya. 'In what way?'

'The smells of damp and dust, mould . . .' She shivers. 'There really could be ghosts in the mirrors.' Maya looks at me closely. 'Those people with the dog; do you think they'll come looking for Dead Red again?'

'Is her ghost in the mirrors?'

She whispers, 'No. First there's my face that's our face, then a flash of red, and red's wiped out by the ghost faces. I never see Dead Red's poor wrecked face.' She looks up at the ceiling. 'I'm glad I don't. Sometimes I think about what her face looks like now. If it's worse than it was.'

Feeling nauseous, I tear a mint leaf from a dried bunch and chew it. The clean flavour settles on my tongue.

Maya says, 'What if Dead Red wants us to go out and check she's all right, but we can't bear to look. Can you imagine how lonely she feels?'

'She doesn't feel. Don't ever go and look at her.'

'I'm too scared to. But it's not fair for her that no one's looking at her. No one's looking after her.' Maya looks really sad. 'You don't think anyone's even properly looking for her. Will anyone ever look for us?'

As I put the kettle on, I realise she's not really talking about the dead woman any more. 'Our parents know we're safe.'

Maya stands next to the table. 'How?'

'There's a postbox not far from here. I wrote, just once.'

'When?'

'Ages ago.'

'They haven't written back?'

'I didn't ask them to.'

'Do you miss them?'

'Sometimes. You do, a lot, don't you?' I get two yellow cups from the cupboard and spoon camomile from a tin into the teapot.

Maya wraps her arms around herself and looks up at the ceiling. 'You asked them why they didn't hug us more. Our father said, *But you know I love you, I'm working so many hours.* He felt sad and guilty and his phone rang and his feelings changed direction. Then our mother said, *Can you imagine how children would grow up if their parents didn't work so hard, but spent all their time with their children? Those children would have no toys at all, nowhere to live* . . . She went pow-pow with her fast words so she didn't get hurt by yours.'

I strain our tea and think of the phrase: *connections rather than attachments.* They said it often enough. I say to Maya, 'You're not meant to rely on closeness. They believed they were looking after us, psychologically. Night class before they had me. Refresh class before you. But you're not meant to feel like you need them – if you do, they didn't get the balance right.' In Paradon, children were encouraged to speak in archetypes. Our father, our mother.

Maya says, 'Well, I do miss them. More because of Dead Red. More because of you, not wanting to look after me when for always before, you did.' She looks at the cup I've put on the table in front of her. 'I don't like this tea. It's got a brown smell.'

'It's calming.'

'I'm already calm. You see, now I can feel in jumps. From scared to calm to scared. Sad and angry and lonely and out-of-place. I can miss everything or nothing, and you're not stopping me.'

I sit on the chair next to her. 'I meant the hugs I gave you, every single one.'

She says, tightly, 'This cottage wants only you; I can feel it in every room. Especially in the kitchen. I'm a spare person. Nothing will make it home for me. Not even you, loving it.'

My heart feels dislodged from whatever tissues bind it in place. What she's saying feels true, but I don't know what to do about it. She seems angry that I love the life I've found here. Perhaps there's only so much love inside me. Now the recipes and this cottage also take pieces of it, there's not enough left when Maya's been used to having all of it.

I say, thinking hard, 'Do you think all your feelings are somehow caused by my feelings, whether they're the same emotion, an opposite one, or a hidden emotion?'

Her voice is still tense. 'Yes, I do. It's how I've always been. It's how I was made to be. It's who I am.'

'And you can't choose for yourself how to feel?'

'Of course I can't. It's how I was designed.'

I say, quietly, 'Then I don't know what to do.'

Maya leaves her camomile tea steaming on the table as she disappears into the bedroom.

The sadness I feel spreads in rings, like a stone dropped in water. I sit in silence for a while and let it ripple, till I can find how to let it be still.

During the night, I get the cake trays out and take the jam jars of spice blends down from the shelf. Putting them on the table, I close my eyes and follow my instincts. I run my fingers back and forth over the spice lids, grasp one, and put the rest back on the shelf. The jar I've picked out is labelled Red Spice.

I look at the table of spices stapled into the recipe book, and scan the list till I find:

Red Spice: Adds whatever red will bring. Bloodlust, anger, love, lust or rage. Bloods, rusted metal, sunset.

While I polish each bone spoon with a soft cloth, my body feels flushed, my skin tingles, sweat gathers in the bumps of my spine. I stroke my neck and imagine my own hand is someone else's.

I open the red spice lid and sniff. There's a flash of chilli in the scent. Getting a bowl and the sieve, I sift in the flour and other powders; I add a spoonful of red spice, pause, and think of the old woman and her stained sheets. I feel as if she's here with me, a bone spoon in each hand, whispering in my ear.

And what might she whisper, this woman who knew all about red spice?

I want to know all about red spice.

Dropping the honey mixture spoon by spoon into the bowl, I beat it in. I imagine I'm the old woman as I whisper, 'Bring me a lover, bring spice to me, let someone's hands touch me, scale my body, let them not stop till I tell them to. Let me fall underneath and cascade on someone. Let me roll my living flesh over and over and under and over and into some other living flesh . . .'

Red spice wants to burn. It wants space to breathe and spark and blaze and spread. I'm flushed on every inch of my skin. I put down the bone spoon.

A sigh.

I grease the cake trays with butter and listen as I give the mixture a final stir.

Another sigh, louder.

I spoon the mixture into the trays. My hands are warm as I slide the cakes into the oven.

Yet another sigh, a cold draught on my wrist. And it's gone.

I feel as if I'm being watched. I turn to see the shadow, flickering in the corner. I say to it, 'Whoever or whatever you are, it won't work on me if fear's what you're after.'

Nothing changes.

I whisper, 'Do you want me to live here alone?'

The shadow fades away.

KIP

Mammy shakes my shoulder and her voice says, 'Get up.'

'Am I slept in – got to go to Old Kelp's?' I'm still lying on the rug with Dagger and the fire's nearly out.

Dad growls from somewhere. I grab Dagger and he sparks awake. Mammy's opening the curtains. It's nearly dawn outside.

Mammy looks really tired. 'Not quite time for the fair yet, Kip.'

Dad comes out of the kitchen doorway. He strides across, leans over me and his voice growls up to a shout, 'Wake up, will you? And you can get bloody dressed right!'

Mammy screeches at him. 'Not now!'

I hold onto Dagger. There's a growl jiggering in his throat that can't come out. I grip him even tighter in case he decides to use his tooth on them.

They push and pull with angry voices. Mammy's yelling at Dad, 'You promised me!'

They disappear into the kitchen and slam the door.

I rest my chin on Dagger's head and whisper to him, 'They're barking because you can't.'

Dad comes storming out of the kitchen and goes into my bedroom. He comes out with the pair of woollen trousers from my bed, hurls them at me and roars, 'Trousers. Put them on!'

Mammy's shouting, 'Let him alone! Don't you think he's got enough to fret over!'

He yells back at her, 'If he wore the bloody right clothes, he'd not be bullied!'

I want to make them stop shouting, so I put the trousers on under my nightie and they're too wide for me with no belt. I tie them together at the top.

I drop the nightie down over the trousers.

Dad looks at me, so angry he doesn't even see I've put them on. He comes at me and grabs for the nightie.

I leap away from him onto the baggy chair. My foot gets stuck in the cushions. The room tilts. My arms flail. My hands can't catch anything. I fall slow, slower . . .

and my head thwacks on the hard wooden floor.

Dagger's licking my face and my head feels like it's set to split open. Feet thud on the floorboards against my cheek.

A hand shakes my hip. Dagger's got his paws on my shoulder and I can feel him jerk and jerk, trying to bark.

I open my eyes a slit and Mammy and Dad's faces are near mine. Their mouths look like they're not shouting or screeching, but doing slow slow slooow baaarrrrkksss . . .

I open my eyes wider. Dad's mouth is still moving. Mammy's holding a towel to the side of my head.

She's got tears on her red cheeks.

Dagger's running backwards and forwards. It's like watching them all on the other side of a window and I can't tell if they're speaking or shouting but whatever they're doing, their mouths are moving without noise.

I sit up and my head screams with giant ouch. But I lean my chin on my knees and want to smile, because my ears have switched off the shouts.

Kip

I'm lying on the baggy chair under a blanket. Mammy's gone outside with the wicker basket and trolley for the fair.

Dad gives me a cup of sugary tea. He isn't blinking with his eyes; he's blinking with his mouth.

Mammy comes back in without the basket. I point at the window with the dawn in it and try to say, 'Got to do the fair,' but Mammy shakes her head and I shout, 'The fair!' but can't hear myself.

Her mouth blinks something at Dad.

Dad scoops me up and carries me into my bedroom. He lies me down and Dagger jumps up and lies on the end of my bed. There's sick in my belly. All the blue in my bedroom is puddling.

Mammy comes into my room and sits on my bed next to me. I hold onto my head because my sore brain wants to fall out.

Watching her lips, she's blinking one word over and over and I think it's 'talker', but that makes no sense.

Mammy was saying 'doctor', not 'talker'.

The doctor is here. Every pearly button on his shirt is sewn on with a different colour of thread. I'm standing by the fire and Mammy and Dad are watching him.

The doctor has wavy short brown hair and his arms are made of big muscles. The thick hairs on his arms show through his white shirt. He's much younger than Mammy and Dad, and he's got all his doctor things in a cream suitcase. He's kneeling on the floor and sticking a metal thing with a light in my ears and putting his eye to it. His breath smells of toothpaste.

He puts a stethoscope all round my chest and back. His mouth moves as he feels my heart in my wrist. I can feel boots thump on the floorboards and Dad comes storming across the room.

I think the doctor called me a girl, because Dad reaches down and grabs at the nightie I'm wearing.

Mammy drags him away.

The doctor lifts the skirt of the nightie, rolls up a trouser leg and looks at one of my red blotchy ankles. I yank down the nightie and my sore brain is full of throb throb churn. I sit on the floor and hold my head still and that doesn't work. So I lie on the rug and don't feel the falling.

I look up at the doctor and Mammy and Dad. They're all giants standing over me. The doctor's lips are moving and they're all looking glum. The floorboards pitch and settle and Dad goes into the kitchen and the door shuts him away.

Mammy goes over to the front door, opens it and Dagger comes in and licks my face. She grabs him and puts him behind the kitchen door with Dad. Her blue shoes cross the room and she gets a notepad and pen, gives them to the doctor and goes and stands in front of the closed kitchen door.

The doctor is on the floor next to me and his trouser knees are scuffed.

He holds the notepad in front of my face and he's written:
DOES YOUR HEAD HURT
I say, 'Yes,' but can't hear it.
He nods. Flips over the pad.
'Can you hear me?' I say.
He nods, and writes:
ARE YOU DIZZY AND FEELING SICK
'Yes. Why aren't you writing question marks?'
He smiles at me and though he's got young eyes, they crinkle up.
WHEN YOU HIT YOUR HEAD DID YOU STOP HEARING STRAIGHT AWAY?
'Yes. I like question marks.'
He laughs.
DID BLOOD COME OUT OF YOUR EAR? ? ?

'Don't know.'

He looks at Mammy and their lips blink at each other for a long time.

I say, 'Was there blood?' and still can't hear my voice.

The doctor writes on the pad again:

I THINK YOU HAVE INNER EAR CONCUSSION. IT WILL GO BUT IT COULD BE QUICKLY OR IT COULD BE A LONG TIME BEFORE YOU HEAR ANYTHING

'And feeling dizzy?'

SHOULD GO QUICKLY

He writes something else down and holds out the notepad again:

YOUR LEGS ITCH

'Yes.'

He nods. The notepad says:

CAN I HAVE A QUICK LOOK? ? ? ? ? ?

'Only because of the question marks.'

He lifts the bottom of the nightie and rolls the trousers up to my knees.

DOES IT ITCH WORSE WHEN YOU WEAR THESE TROUSERS?

'All trousers.'

He looks over his shoulder at Mammy again and she goes out of the room and comes back in with three pairs of trousers I used to wear before I stopped. She shows them to him. He asks her something. She answers. He asks her something else. She answers again.

He writes on the pad and holds it out to show me:

YOU HAVE EITHER AN ALLERGY TO WOOL OR VERY SENSITIVE SKIN. YOU NEED TO WEAR LOOSE CLOTHES

'Can Mammy make them?'

He turns and looks at Mammy and her face is pink; she

glances at the closed kitchen door, turns back and looks like she's talking quiet. She goes out of the room and comes back in with two of the dresses and three nighties that used to be hers and she made smaller for me. The doctor looks at them by stroking the fabric with his fingers, and moves his lips at Mammy.

He writes:

YOU DON'T ITCH WITH COTTON

'I like dresses best.'

The doctor writes on the pad, tears off the page and hands it to me. He's drawn in great big letters:

? ? ? ? SEE YOU SOON ? ? ? ?

I count the different thread buttons on his shirt and there are six I can see and the rest are tucked in his trousers. He puts on his raincoat, picks up his cream suitcase and Mammy follows him to the front door. She stands in the doorway moving her mouth at him and the early morning light shines her brown hair red.

Mammy's got Old Kelp's cakes in from our doorstep, and she puts them on the table.

I say, 'Who did the fair?'

She shuffles her feet, miming someone stooped. She must mean Mam Vann. So they've not found Lizzie yet, because she's after me on the fair list, and Mam Vann is after her.

I say, 'My belly doesn't want me to eat today.'

She writes on the notepad and holds it up. It says: *You don't have to do anything today, you're sick.*

She crouches next to me and puts her hands over her ears. The way she moves her head and face makes me want to laugh. I know she's showing me she wants me to keep my head still. She takes the trousers off me from under the nightie and pats my knees. She opens the kitchen door. Dagger comes rushing in and licks my cheek. Dad picks me up and carries me back to bed as everything spins and spins.

In my dream Dagger's rolling on the dead jellyfish in the sand. I pull him away. We're on the road to Jock's farm and Dagger's rolling on the dead jackdaw. So I pull him away again. Dagger's sniffing at the door of the shed up at Old Kelp's cottage . . .

I wake and sit up in bed, not dizzy any more. My head is bang sore, and my throat is hoarse like I've been shouting for hours. My legs are full of squirms. I know that means I need to say something out loud.

If I do it quick, it *might* be allowed.

Dagger's curled in a ball on my bed. He watches me with one eye wide open under his scraggy fringe. I grab him and his throat jiggers and I know he's trying for a growl. He thrashes one way and the other but doesn't spark to bite. He settles on my lap.

I close my eyes and say what I want to say.

When I open my eyes, everything's still blue and nothing bad has happened. Dagger licks my hand. Now I need to say it to someone who isn't Dagger.

In the living room the fire is burning. Mammy and Dad are at the table, reading and eating their tea. Mammy is in her pale pink dress. Dad looks up at me from his detective book. His lips move and Mammy beckons me over. The notepad is there and I pick it up and hold it out to her.

She writes: *You still can't hear?*

'No, but look, I can shake my head – dizzy's gone.'

She smiles at me and writes: *That's very very good.*

Dad frowns; I think she's kicked him. He takes the pad off her and writes:

I'm really sorry, Kip.

He pats my back and slices off a chunk of bread. He puts it in front of me on a plate. Dad leans forward and takes Mammy's hand, his mouth moving from chewing, not talking.

She blushes and squeezes his hand, and her other hand strokes a dark mark on her neck that isn't a bite from Dagger, so it must be a kissing bite from Dad. So they've made up.

I sit at the table and ask Mammy, 'Is Lizzie back yet?' and she shakes her head. I ask her, 'Is Mam Vann doing the fair tomorrow or is it me?'

She writes: *Mam Vann till you're better.*

'If I can't hear myself speak, can I be allowed to talk about Old Kelp?'

Both Mammy and Dad's lips move at the same time, and Mammy shakes her head at me, really hard. She writes: *Never, never say anything about what you've seen while you were doing the fair. Not when you can hear or can't, not while you're doing your turn or you've ended your turn, not ever.*

I say, 'Can I talk about her window?'

Dad shakes his head, looking angry.

'Can I talk about her shed?'

Dad frowns and asks Mammy something. Mammy puts her hand on his arm but she's still looking at me, closely.

Before they both say no to me again, I close my eyes, take a deep breath and say, 'This isn't a lying story. Remember Dagger running into Old Kelp's garden? He found a smell in her shed. Dagger only gets stuck to a smell that hard when it's a *something dead* smell.'

It doesn't feel like I'm talking when I can't hear it. I'm not really here.

I keep my eyes shut and the air I'm breathing feels like it's full of thick thunder clouds. Maybe Old Kelp knows I've spoken about her shed, and, now there's two of her, she knows twice.

Kip

Something touches my arm and I open my eyes. It's Mammy's hand and she's standing beside me.

She writes: *Never, ever say that again.*

Dad slides the notepad away from her and writes: *It'll just be the smell of a dead rat.* Mammy and Dad are looking at each other with faces so pale, I know they're scared about Old Kelp cursing us.

Mammy puts her hand gently over my mouth and shakes her head.

Though neither one of them's even written so much as Old Kelp's name on the notepad, Dad tears out that page, crumples it up, and burns it in the fire.

AMBER

There have been people walking up from the village on the shore, passing our cottage, all day. They follow the path which runs up towards the road. Some have climbed over stone walls and gone into fields and the wood. The ones in pairs kept stopping behind the fir trees. I saw them through the bedroom window, their legs meshed between low branches, wandering in all kinds of directions like a disorganised flock of birds.

Some of these people were holding hands and some of them were bickering and nudging at each other, and some of them stopped and kissed each other or slapped each other's backsides. All slightly frisky. They've caught the effects of the red spice from the cakes I made.

No one has looked at this cottage. They've bowed their heads as if they believe I'll come roaring out of the front door and rip through them, taking the effects of the cakes away. Any love, bloodlust and rage torn from their throats, clenched in my teeth.

Red spice was meant to bring all that is red. To me. I'm at the kitchen window, clasping the curtains beneath my eye. No one else is coming up the path. Nothing red comes towards me. My intention is scattered in these people's stomachs, being digested into them. Lost lust wanders away up the hills.

After time filled with no one, the sky darkens to dusk. A man walks down the path by the wall. He's wearing a thick green coat. He's young. Thin. He glances at our cottage, and looks away.

Now, that's flirtation if ever I saw it.

There's a glint in his eyes that's some kind of bloodlust and I imagine lying under him or spilling over him and I'd like that glint of bloodlust in his eyes to look right at my burning body before I plunge him—

Maya's voice says, 'What are you looking at?'

I snap, 'Go away.'

But she comes to the window and looks out between the curtains. She gasps, 'He's not been in the ungarden, has he – looked away in the not-shed?'

'Stop jumbling! He's just some man from the village, walking past.'

'Amber?'

'What?'

'You believe me that I didn't kill her, that she didn't fall through my arms . . . and you say it wasn't you . . .'

'That's what I've said.'

'What if it was him?' Maya's got her eye to the curtain-crack.

'He's gone.'

We come away from the window and she says, 'Maybe he's not come into this cottage while we weren't asleep. Seen her not unlying there on the floor where he left her. He could have not killed us in our beds. We could be not here now, believing we're unbreathing, but we're undead.'

'You're still jumbling. Half dreaming. Wake up.'

She goes to the bedroom doorway. 'Oh, poor us, all dreams and innocence, sleeping unawares like children . . . Look, if you stare hard enough at the bed, squint your eyes a bit, you can see us deadlying there in it, can't you?'

'No. I'm here looking at you. We're. Not. Dead. Pinch your-self.'

She pinches her forearm.

I say, 'You smell over-ripe. When did you last wash?'

'Have we kept locking the front door every time we've put out the honey cakes or got in the ingredients?'

'We, meaning me. Of course I have. Lots of people have walked past today, but no one's come near. So don't worry. You're still half asleep.'

She gets back into bed and closes her eyes, because I really want her to.

In the bathroom, I rummage in the cupboards and find the red lipstick. It's dry like a wax crayon but the colour is still bright. I look in the mirror and rub the lipstick so hard into my top lip, it numbs. Coloured in. Just a touch, and it lights up my face.

Finally. I've seen strangers, here. A man. I imagine our paths, meeting. Fate, playing a game.

As I crayon the dried lipstick into my bottom lip, I think about going out with a boyfriend in Paradon. I felt sick when he went home with someone prettier, because he left me in a club. I'd never been to one before and I drank too many bottles of something neon green. I felt as if I'd walked into the middle of danger. Alone in a crowd, something changed. Surrounded by chaotic strangers dancing, the smell of unknown chemicals, their faces seemed like demons. One of the demons shoved me into a corner, bruised my wrists. I struggled, hissed, spat. He was monster-sized. There was a fight. Someone pulled a knife, another a broken bottle. The demon let go of me and joined in. The lights spun and burned ice-blue, time froze. I froze as well. I looked at a wall of faces for someone who could help me thaw and get away. There was no face I could trust

When I finally got home, I locked myself in the shower and sobbed into my knees.

And when the next boyfriend came along, I went right back out again.

I run a brush through my hair and think of the man outside, glancing at the cottage. I whisper, as if to him, 'Be that face in the crowd I wanted to see. I might . . . want you need you keep you, open my arms and run to you. Be someone who could drag me out of danger and love me without hurt.'

Looking at the lipstick, I don't want this red. I do want it. In the mirror, my eyes look deeper, my pupils dilate, there's something about the vivid colour of the red . . . the rich deep scent of red spice in the honey cakes . . .

I stroke my cheek with my fingertips as I close my eyes and try to picture the face of the man I saw outside on the path. But too fast, his image has faded. I wanted to be rescued that night in Paradon, but I don't want to be rescued now.

Old feelings of frozen hurt clash with the new warmth in my body.

Nothing melts.

The scent of red spice fades.

I open my eyes again, unable to fantasise without freezing. Unable to fantasise about someone faceless.

In the kitchen, Maya's sitting on the floor in the cold corner, her hands over her mouth, her face pale.

I snap at her, 'Maya, don't stare at me, your eyes are too intense.'

Her voice is strained. 'I tried to sleep. But I felt like Dead Red was dragging my face towards hers. She was trying to force me to see the dress—'

Feeling frustrated, my body aching, I say, 'No. Don't make everything about you.'

She burrows her face in her arms and shakes her head. Looks up at me again. 'Your talk-style is too big. All the things you want since we've lived here make my insidehalf and outsidehalf feel invisible. Now I've got feelings that jump, I've got to learn how to bitelip and swallow-words.'

My voice rises: 'Paradon made you the way you are, and now you're not there you have no idea what to do. You're enhanced, but for who? Designed, but for what? There's only me to mirror, and I don't want you to. So what are you? Who are you, without what other people want?'

Her body seems to shrink. Her eyes, for a moment, look black. Her skin, for a second, shimmers like it did when she was a baby. Then she looks just like me again. She closes her eyes to hide their expression.

But not before I've seen deep hurt.

I crumple. 'I'm so sorry. I'm not angry with you. Just frustrated with myself.' I can't tell if she's heard me. Can't speak in case I make it worse. Guilt leads me away from her into the bathroom. I bolt the door.

Time slows as I stare at my face in the mirror with my hands covering my red mouth. I think about glass, shattering.

Maya's lurking around the bedroom. I haven't slept very much, as the wind has only just stopped yowling. Maya kept getting in and out of bed making cold draughts under the duvet. She slept fitfully, murmuring about how vicious the wind is. Now I'm drifting awake and asleep.

She whispers, 'Dead Red,' as she passes the closed curtains.

I watch her in half-light as she creeps around the bed and whispers, 'Murder weapons should live together.'

Opening my eyes a slit, I see she's looking at the snowball that's in the cabinet with the blades. I'm not sure how long it's been there, or which of us decided that's where it should be kept.

I close my eyes again and the pillow sinks under my cheek as I slump back to sleep.

As I wake, I stretch my limbs across the whole bed. I wrap a black dressing gown around myself and my hair feels moist and tangled at the base of my neck.

In the kitchen I switch on the light. The table, chairs and oven, the worktops, spoons and cupboards all gleam with warm colours. The fire in the wood-burner crackles, and quiets. I blink my eyes awake.

I call, 'Maya?' but there's no sound.

The kitchen is still, silent. A few onions are missing. The bathroom door is open and the bathroom is empty. As I walk through the cottage, my hands clench, cold. My feet are numb, my face, draining.

Maya's nowhere.

There's a letter on the table next to the recipe book. It's on a narrow piece of torn greaseproof paper in Maya's handwriting.

She hasn't written my name, or her own.

You've buried Dead Red in your head.
But I can't.
Thinking about her feels like
snapped elastic stings.
She smells of metal.
Her face aches the teeth
in the back of my jaw
and when I look out at the shed
I can taste rot.

You say you want me to be myself.
I can't do that with you.
Don't know if I can do it
without you.
Might not be part of my design.
Don't know.
Never tried.
Trying now.
Still doing what you want,
really, aren't I.

My heart stops. Maya's gone. My heart beats.

KIP

When people talk, the sounds of voices distract us from seeing people being angry or glum or tired. Now I can't hear talking, our home is crammed full of feelings. Mammy and Dad are glum and I think it's because they're worried about me. Seeing them so miserable is making me glum too.

After tea, Mammy and Dad are in the bathroom cheering each other up with a bath running and the door locked.

So I sneak outside and go round to Adam's.

Aunty Pippa opens the door. The light shines on straggles of her blonde hair which are coming out of a plait that's not as neat as usual. She looks like she's been crying. I point at my ears and tell her I can't hear. She smells of lemons and nettles so she must be trying out new perfume smells.

I say, 'Is Adam here?'

She shakes her head. Her mouth moves.

I make a writing-down shape with my hand.

Her face changes and she nods. I follow her into their hallway that's filled with piles of books and spare light bulbs on shelves made from planks of wood and stacked old bricks. She rummages in a sideboard drawer that's full of sticky tape, boxes of paper-clips and wooden buttons. She pulls out a strawberry-coloured pen and a notebook with daffodils on the cover. She holds them out to me.

I write Adam a note:

Dear Adam,

Please come round mine soon.
I'm sick, and fed up. I'm living with glum people.

From Kip

Aunty Pippa squeezes my shoulder.

She tears out the page with my note and folds it in half. On the next blank page in the notebook, she writes to me: *So is Adam.*

I ask, 'Sick?'

She opens my note and points her forefinger at my words: *fed up.*

As she sees me out, her eyes are welling up.

'Are you all right?'

Her mouth smiles.

'Tell Mammy if you want to talk because she can hear you.'

She nods and takes her coat off a hook in the hallway.

As she puts it on, I say, 'Don't come home with me right now; she's in the bath with Dad.'

She swallows, takes her coat off and hangs it back up again.

'Sorry,' I say. 'Maybe come round a bit later?'

She rubs my shoulder and closes the door. She's got a lot of glum herself because if she was smiling proper it would be in her eyes.

Dad's working up the lane on Jessie's roof. The tiles fell off; last night was full of gales. The wind without noise was like being

stroked by a cold hand. Mammy wouldn't let me go outside in
it for long, in case it blew too hard in my ears.

Mammy keeps wandering in and out of the living room. She's
in here again now, poking at the fire in the grate. She smiles at
me, and uses her fingers to flatten and pat at my blanket. She
goes back into the kitchen and makes frying garlic smells.

Under the blanket, I'm wearing my favourite dress. Neither
Mammy nor Dad nor the doctor has noticed I don't itch with
woollen jumpers. I know my legs itch when they're wearing what
they don't *want* to wear. But Dad can't get angry now the very
clever doctor has given me a diagnosis: I'm allergic to trousers.

Early this morning when the doctor was here, he decided I'm
not interesting after all. He's realised my skull isn't broken and
he looked a bit bored. He wrote on the notepad that he'd thought
it might be, but he's sure it isn't. I could have told him that
myself, because if my skull was broken, my head would rattle.

Caddy is here on her way home from the school. We're drawing
pictures of flying rugs and firework mountains. She shows me a
trick where she puts her finger through a candle flame without
burning it, and I can do it too. She's got a wobbly tooth so I try
to pull it out for her. I only stop yanking when Mammy gives
us chocolate frogs and goes back into the kitchen.

We eat them under the table as we write on the notepad to
each other.

I write: *Why's Adam not come round? I asked him to, has he
said anything?*

Caddy writes: *He's got family stuff exploding up.*

I write: *Has Aunty Pippa or Uncle Finn popped?*

She puts her hand over her mouth. So someone's told her not
to talk.

She writes: *Mam Vann's teaching us volcanoes again because everyone but me forgot their bits. Vent, crater, magma. And the best bit is* . . . She looks at me and waits for an answer like she's being my teacher.

I write: *the explosion.*

She looks smug as she writes: *lava. While we're not learning volcanoes, she's getting us to make up new songs.*

She looks at me and I'm smiling. She pinches my arm, kicks me and writes: *You'll miss it all – that's a bad thing!*

I write: *Missing the school is the best thing ever.*

Caddy's mum comes in through the front door with blustering anger all over her face. She sees us under the table. I don't think she knew Caddy was here. She must have got herself into a state out looking for her, as she looks really angry. Mammy comes out of the kitchen folding a sheet.

Caddy shouts something; her mum grabs her arm and pulls her out from under the table.

When they've gone, Mammy sits under the table with me and strokes my hair.

She sees the notepad me and Caddy wrote on. She picks up the pen and writes: *I asked Mam Vann about you and school, and she says you can't learn anything without working ears.*

I grab her for a cuddle because I'm so happy she's forgotten my eyes work.

Mammy, me and Dagger are in the corner shop watching Jessie put our cheese in a brown paper bag. We had to pass two of the boys on the way here. They were on their way home from the school. They stopped and jumped on a wall to watch me from high up. But they didn't spit on me, because Mammy did a good angry face at them. They stood giant-still and watched me all the way along the street. I've still got goosebumps. Kerry is here in the shop with her spotty face all red and she's paying for a bottle of vinegar.

Behind the counter is a wall full of tiny drawers. Zippers of all colours and liquorice string and balls of pink and orange wool are spilling out of them.

Jessie says something to me, but Mammy shakes her head and touches her ears. I stand next to Mammy as she rummages in her bag and finds the notebook with our shopping list on it. It's open on a page where I drew a picture of a sugar boy cut in half, with sugar spilling from his mouth. Mammy baked sugar boys this afternoon – they're nutty biscuits in the shape of boys in trousers. When they were fresh out of the oven, we covered them in sprinkles of brown sugar. It spread as it melted and made them look like they were getting dressed in brown clothes. In my picture, the brown sugar is made out of dots. Mammy wrote down to me: *If these boys are nasty, you can bite their heads off.* I wrote down to Mammy: *If there were sugar boys at the school instead of real ones, they'd never be mean.* She wrote: *Because they'd be so scared of you eating them up*, and that made us both laugh.

Jessie's wrist-deep in a big jar of red boiled sweets. She pops one in her mouth.

Maeve comes into the shop, runs to me and grabs my legs. I give her a cuddle, and pull a face at her. Her mum comes in, takes her hand and leads her to the counter.

Mammy's talking to the others. They've all got sweet-bumps in their cheeks. No one's smiling. Maeve hides herself from them in the corner. She tears open a bag of chocolate powder, licks her fingers and plunges them in.

Uncle Finn comes into the shop, and Mammy's the only one who talks to him. She glares at the others when he's getting some milk. Kerry goes into a corner and reads the ingredients on a can of pineapple. Maeve's been found out; her mum scrubs her chocolate mouth with a spittled hankie.

Mammy puts her hand on Uncle Finn's arm but he glances at the others, slams money on the counter, turns around and walks out again.

The others go back to the counter and talk in a huddle.

'Am I still here?' I ask.

Mammy's got her hands on her hips and none of them look at me.

I don't want to be a real invisible person.

Dagger's gazing up at me, one paw limp. I say to him, 'Am I?' He puts his paw down and leans his head to the side, which means, yes. I'm here.

But if the grown-ups don't know that, I can do what I want. So I open the door and watch the brass bell jigger without noise. I look up and down the street to check none of the boys are waiting for me outside the shop. They're not, so I let Dagger lead me away.

Dagger's led me to the school. It used to be a chapel, years ago before I was born out. The arched doorway is shut and the cream walls are stained from winter sea-rain. At the top of the roof, the cross has rusted. One of the side bits has broken off. It looks like an odd letter that doesn't mean anything in our language.

Dagger yanks too hard on his lead and pulls me towards the school door as it opens.

It's Mam Vann. She'll be going home for her tea. Her lips move and the wind blows her hair out from under her patterned scarf. She tucks it away and her mouth moves again. I shake my head. She grabs my arm and pulls me and I pull Dagger, and we're all three of us inside the school. She switches the light on.

The fire is burning low in the knocked-out fireplace. The pews are empty and her teacher's desk at the front is lit by a light bulb hanging on a long black wire from the rotten beams. The school smells of dust, rain and coal. I let go of Dagger and he slumps down next to me on the worn blue carpet.

Mam Vann hobbles down to the front and climbs the steps to her high desk like she's about to teach me something, so I sit in a pew. She opens her desk and gets out a song sheet.

She comes back down and sits in the pew next to me. She pulls a pen from her pocket and writes on the back of the song sheet: *We're learning this one now. Read the words and fix them in your head while you're ill, or you'll never catch up.*

The song is called: 'Tangle of Three and Away'.

I ask, 'Is this about Old Kelp and Gilliam?'

She writes: *No, we wrote it in class yesterday.*

'Who's it about?'

Her cheeks flush a little. She sucks the pen and looks up at the light bulb.

She writes: *Perhaps it's a little bit about Lizzie.*

'How is Lizzie in a tangle—'

She turns over the song sheet and reads the words with her fingers on her lips.

Her eyes go wide.

I ask, 'What is it?'

She looks like she's swearing. She turns it over and writes: *We're going to have to change the words. Don't take this home after all.*

She grabs a book and doesn't even look at the title as she puts it next to me. She writes: *Read this instead.* She always talks to us in a proper voice when we're inside the school, and we have to be polite back to her.

I say, 'Thank you very much, Mam Vann.'

She looks closely at me and writes: *You don't look ill.*

I'm about to say I'm fine, I just can't hear, but she might think I'm well enough to come back. So I tell her one truth: 'The doctor's coming back the day after tomorrow to check me up again.' And I tell her one lie: 'And I still feel really dizzy.' I pretend to be ill so hard I deliberately accidentally forget to pick up the book, and pick up Dagger instead. I walk a bit wonky and bash into a couple of pews.

She's still watching me, so I crash into the doorframe on my way out.

MAYA

Don't look up at the deadstars or hear the sound of branches scraping against the smells of another night's frost. In this wood, the tree needles hide my dig fingers.

I'm not too far away from mysister. Not too too far away.

Am I safe where I curl curl burrow for warm, and there is none.

What there is: an onion sharp tang smell. It's a food for breathing in.

An onion is a skin-away.

My cold head thinks of warm, of place, of home that is Paradon, a city with mirrors that pour in light, pour in sky-brightness, pour in moon and sun.

Here, I'm in this no-name place, alone. Where memories are safer than real.

How to be who I am when other people make me up?

What is real, is that mysister isn't here with me.

This hasn't ever happened before.

I've got shiver-like shock.

Memory is safer than real:

Our mother. I called her a nickname, loud in my head and not with speak. I called her: Buttereyes. And Buttereyes, she always said, over broken platecupbowl: *Just a mistake, nothing to cry over*. Her carefulmake creamcake was smooth as white sea. My fouryear fingernails were kittenclaws. Ten scratch crescent shapes made spoiled creamcake. Buttereyes was all cry. She wetcheeked a voice screech at me. Buttereyes was so so tired. She screamflagged the kitchen red. So I kitten-stopped in cornerland and dripped *nonosorry*. Slapped face with no hands. Over-cried to nothing.

Still this real: am burrowed in a hole under trees with scratch branches. A screech-spite wind pushes my eyes so I close them and think another memory, safe from gales.

Our father, he dressed up nice. He'd got a work crowd to impress. He wore his late-suit for night-dinner. There's me in the bath and he came in and said, *Goodnight goodnight*. He gifted me a blue boat. I shouted, *Splash*, and washed his suit with bath waves. I said, *Wishaboat for bathtub* as the door closed him gone. I shout-wished after him: *You want to be a sailor*, but he did a no-come-back. So I made sailor farts with wet lips at the closed door, again, again.

But here, place is too real for memories to keep-safe. Too cold, too many smells, too much dark, so many shriek noises. Feelings jump too high, dig too low.

Now I'm without mysister, am I no one?

There's a smell of scare.

KIP

The lights are off and the curtains are open at Lizzie's house. Dagger's caught another smell and he pulls me round the back where the door is open a crack.

Inside the hallway are four doors.

The air isn't moving right. Someone else is in here.

I push open the door on the right. Adam sits on the floor next to the neatly made bed. His school satchel lies on the floor next to him.

All Lizzie's underwear has been cleared away. Adam's got Lizzie's comb in his hand, and he pulls out a strand of her frizzy blonde hair, snaps it in half, and flicks it onto the floor.

I say, 'Oi!' and switch on the light.

Adam drops the comb and looks up. He's got tear shapes drawn with pen on his cheeks, three from each eye. I let go of Dagger; he gives Adam a sniff and dashes out of Lizzie's bedroom.

I say, 'What's wrong?'

His lips blink a word that might be, 'Nothing.' He frowns at his shoes.

'Not nothing, is it?'

He shrugs, stands up, climbs over the bed and closes the curtains. He turns to face me, his lips moving fast.

'Can't hear you.'

He looks like he's shouting.

I shake my head. 'I can't . . .'

His face is red and his lips are still moving.

Putting my hands over my ears, I shout, 'Can't hear!' and stick my thumbs in my ears. My right ear goes pop.

Adam's shouting, '. . . that must have been why I was sent to bed so early whenever Mum was out – he pitched in with something I'd done wrong, made me out to be bad for something or other and sent me off to bed. He must have waited till I was asleep, right upset at being told off, then he must've snuck out and come here to her!'

'I can hear you!' I put my thumb in the ear that doesn't work and waggle it.

'Course you can, I'm shouting loud enough!' He folds his arms and kicks Lizzie's bed.

'Who came here?'

He says, quietly, 'Dad.'

'What for?'

'Whatever he got off her in this.' He punches his fist on the mattress.

'Your dad and Lizzie?'

'That's all everyone's bloody talking about.'

'So that's what they were chattering on about in the shop. Couldn't hear them. Think they upset your dad.'

'When are you coming back to the school? I'm going to be a school refusal. Now you're not there, they've bloody turned it all on me. Hate them.'

I shake my head and say again, 'Your dad and Lizzie?'

'Shut up!'

'Did you draw . . .' I touch my cheek and look at his pen tears.

He kicks the bed again and a real tear comes out. 'I just want them to bastard know, I'm so, I'm so – oh bastard hell.' He clenches his fist and punches his stomach. 'I didn't even bloody feel that, see?' His face is bright red and real tears run over his ink ones. 'Ow.' He doubles over and sits on the bed.

'But your dad's so—' I sit next to him and look at the purple and orange flowers on the curtains.

'What?' he chokes out. 'Dad's so, what?' He glares at me, his face flushed. He smears his eyes with his hand and the pen tears smudge across his cheeks.

'He's so . . . quiet.'

'Well, they're all saying, *it's always the quiet ones*, and I'm quiet too, so I'm sick of it.'

'It's always the quiet ones who what?'

'Don't know.'

I say, 'Who do things they shouldn't?'

'Suppose. Or it's always the quiet ones that do things quietly that the loud ones do loudly, but the loud ones feel shocked when they find out that the loud things they do loudly are also being done quietly by a quiet one.'

'What?'

He shrugs his shoulders and sighs. 'Do you want a smoke?'

'I'm glad I'm not as quiet as your dad, or they'd say all sorts about me.'

'They do say all sorts about you.'

'I know.'

He reaches for his satchel and pulls out a bundle of cinnamon sticks. He hasn't got any matches; he says his mum's been hiding them from him.

Dagger's in the kitchen, sniffing at the oven.

Adam says, 'Don't open it. Lizzie left half a chicken in there. It stinks.'

175

There are four boxes of matches in a drawer, so we close the curtains and smoke the cinnamon sticks at her table, using a pudding bowl for an ashtray. I don't feel anything at all and mine keeps going out. Adam smokes two in a row, lighting them over and over again because they don't burn. He picks up the telephone and says into it, 'Hello, Lizzie, are you loving my dad? Oh, no one there.' He slams it down. He shuffles through her kitchen cupboards.

'What are you looking for?'

'Wine.'

'Lizzie might have been teetotalled, because that's what Mammy said to her she should be. Lizzie was so drunk she was kissing her bottle but wouldn't share it around.'

'She would be, eh.' Adam tells me, 'It was Mum.'

'What was?'

'That broke everything and threw all Lizzie's knickers all over the place.'

He gets down on his hands and knees, and soon he's laughing under the kitchen table. 'Kip, I'm high!'

I lean down from the chair I'm sitting on, and say, 'You're not, you're low.'

He laughs till tears run down his face.

I try to smoke another whole cinnamon stick but still don't feel like laughing.

'What *are* you doing here?' I ask, as Adam crawls out from under the table, wiping his eyes.

'They're fighting at home, kind of. They were till the doctor came and as soon as he knocked at the door, they pretended they weren't. Well, Mum pretended everything was the same as it always is. And Dad was just quiet. Of course.'

'The doctor's done with me now. Reckons my ears just need time to sort themselves out. Looks like he's right. I've never heard your mum and dad fighting.'

'Proper fights should have yells in them. But they fight without shouting; they use angry eyes. Pew-pew!' He fires an invisible eye-gun at me and drops his hand. 'They come into my bedroom one at a time and say all kinds of stuff to me. Can't get a word in, not once it's the one of them and the one of me. I don't want to know about why he came here to Lizzie or what Mum and him do or don't get off each other. Wish they'd bloody fight. It's not that Mum can't get angry – she must have been to have wrecked this place, mustn't she? She just won't get angry with Dad. And he says he feels guilty. And that's not going to fix anything.'

'Why not?'

'Because she wants him to keep feeling guilty. Bloody hell, listen to me. I get what's happening more than they do. I've got a grown-up brain too quick and I don't want it.' He folds his arms and slumps on a chair.

'So, you're hiding here.'

'I'm not hiding. I've got my toothbrush, a loaf of bread and an apple. I'm pilfering. Like a pirate stealing a ship.'

'Pilfering what?'

'Lizzie's house! She owes me.'

'She owes you her house?'

'She owes me somewhere I can get away from the trouble she's caused.'

'If your mum trashed this place, she's got her own back and you don't need to—'

He leans his face on his hands and frowns at me. 'Would you break everything if someone took your husband off you?'

'Don't know.'

'I'd break everything. Good fun breaking things. Probably cheered her up.'

'But Lizzie's not taken him anywhere; he's there fighting with your mum.'

'Well, if she had taken him, they wouldn't both be at home fighting wrong. Dad says he loves Mum *and* Lizzie. Says he feels torn up. So is his heart splitting into bits, one part for each of them – could he have pockets growing in his heart?'

'Don't know.' I glance at the door that leads into the hallway. 'That night – what were they all looking at on the floor in Lizzie's bedroom?'

'I saw that. Came in here after you ran off. It was a dirty sheet. Someone –' he looks at his bitten fingernails '– had pissed all over it.'

'Your mum did that? That's rank.'

'She won't talk to anyone now – she won't even go to the shop. She's embarrassed they've all seen her wee. You must have heard what they're saying?'

'I couldn't hear anything.'

'So that's why you don't know.' He walks his fingers on the table top like little people's legs. 'Mum followed Dad here one night when he came to see Lizzie. Dad legged it as soon as Mum walked in. She smashed things up and hurled Lizzie's stuff at her. So Lizzie legged it as well.'

His hand people act out the scene on the table, and jump off the edge.

He says, 'The day after the grown-ups found this house wrecked, some of them had a look for Lizzie around the fields and up in the wood. They didn't find her. So that night, Mam Vann and a few of her cronies were on and on about sending some of the lads to Fastleigh to get the police. So Mum ended up in the corner shop telling Jessie that she'd trashed Lizzie's place, and Lizzie had gone haring off. Mum told Jessie she was to tell everyone why, so she'd not have to say it twice.'

Both his hands mime mouths talking, and he pays close attention to both.

He sighs and drops his hands down. 'Everyone says if Lizzie had to leg it out of here quick, the only place she'd have legged it to would be her sister's. No one has her phone number, though.' He folds his arms. 'No need to get the police for that.'

'That must have been when she dropped the black glove. I hid it under a rock.'

We talk about what a single black glove could have for a meaning: a death wish, or that Lizzie's a one-handed slapper, or hands are useless, or one hand can be warm and the other cold when you're caught in a tangle of three like Old Kelp with Gilliam and his wife, and Aunty Pippa and Uncle Finn with Lizzie.

I open a can of beans, find a fork and eat them cold from the tin as Adam rummages through Lizzie's kitchen drawers.

He says, 'I love being high because everything's more interesting.' The ink tears have gone from his cheeks.

Dagger's scratching the floor and worrying at the oven. Adam looks at him. 'Do pilferers have to clean ovens? Don't want to. Lizzie should've at least got her chicken out before Mum smashed up her house.' He slumps down at the table, his head in his hands. 'Bloody hate Lizzie. All her fault I'm here and it's teatime and everything.'

I put the rest of the can of beans in front of him. 'It's not Lizzie's fault it's teatime. Wasn't just her fault for anything. It was your mum and dad as well. Tangle of three, isn't it.'

He pushes the can away. 'Not even bloody hungry. So Mam Vann's doing the fair for you?'

'It's just till I can hear. And I'm not going back to the school till then either. So don't dare tell anyone that's now.'

He stands up. 'Lizzie's going to miss her turn on the fair. If she ever comes back it'll be ages till it's her again.' He whispers, 'Have you had a blessing? While Dad was doing the fair, he whistled a lot. Wouldn't say a word about Old Kelp, but whistling's meant to be happy, isn't it?' He frowns. 'Though it wasn't a happy whistle.'

I keep my lips tight shut.

'I reckon blessings feel like a wallop across the head, when they're from Old Kelp. I can't wait for my turn, though it's not for a long time. You should try for a blessing – you'll probably feel all puffed up and golden. Like a mini-Midas. That's a blessing you'd want. Imagine if you could turn your toothbrush gold and get gold teeth from brushing them. It'd be like the sun shone out of your mouth, and you'd be able to bite really hard – you could gnaw through electricity wires . . .'

'She'd probably rather curse me. Stop talking about her!' I clamp my mouth shut again.

'Or, you could ask her for a doppelganger and be two of yourself. Good Kip and Bad Kip. You could tell lies again like you used to. Now, that could be fun.' He grins at me. 'You take turns and I'll be Bad Adam for all the time.'

'Is that how people could make two of themselves? Do they get a ghost half and a real half, and make a double-ghost gang?'

'Ha! Maybe yes. Mum met a ghost once. She said it didn't know it was dead and she felt rude even having mentioned it. It threw one of her perfume bottles at her and she stank of lavender for a month. I'll have to think about double ghosts. Hm.' He rolls his eyes up to the ceiling. 'I am high, eh. Let's me, you and Dagger sneak out and go up to the wood one night. We'll hide in the trees and tell each other ghost stories.'

AMBER

Maya hasn't come back.

On the first night of missing her, I say to the shadow, 'Well, you've got what you wanted. I'm here alone and she's gone. So what are you going to do now?'

The shadow doesn't reply.

As I slide the honey cakes out of the oven, I think:

She'll have to come back. She's no one if she's not my sister.

But while she's gone, she'll not only be somewhere else, but someone else. Depending on who she meets, she could be many someones. When she meets other people, they won't know she's a formwanderer, because everyone sees what they want. They'll love her, want her, need her. She could be anywhere now, being anything for anyone. Doing whatever they want her to, believing she has to. She could forget me entirely; cut away the part of her identity which I gave her. Lose the bond between us which I've created. I wonder if I made it strong enough to tie her to me, even when we're apart.

To pull her back.

On the second night of missing her, while the honey cakes are cooling, I reread her letter and think:

It's what I wanted that's taken her away from me.

She can only become herself without me.

But now I want her back and I don't know how far want can stretch.

On the third night of missing her, as I stir the cake mixture, I think:

At the heart of Maya, she isn't really the sister I want back, she's not even the twin I've invented. She's only what my eyes have wanted to see.

As a baby, her black eyes and silvery skin were beautiful. Neither I nor our parents wanted her as she really was. I wanted a twin. They wanted a loving normal child who was easy, malleable, and would make me calm. As she began her life, so we continued it. We wanted her into being who she is now. Or worse, who she isn't. We engineered and constructed her.

Now what is there of herself to find? It could be nothing.

Maya might peel away every layer of herself that's been formed by other people. The twin I adored. The amenable daughter our parents loved. The behaviours each teacher wanted from her in the classroom. The sweetness a pregnant woman in the park saw in her. The loss that a man on a scaffold threw to her instead of a whistle, as he cried his ache down to her: *My life, you're the spit of my dead brother!* The compulsion that a bruised woman handed her when she stopped her in the street and said, *Avenge me.* With her enhanced mirror neuron pathways making her empathic, with her reflective skin that lets everyone project what they want to see, everyone she's ever met must have left their trace in her very cells. All these traces have become the layers of who Maya is.

Peel the layers off an onion, and at the heart of an onion . . .

At the heart of an onion there's nothing left but a sharp living smell.

And the person who's peeled away an onion is left with tears stinging their eyes and a pile of dead layers of skin.

Wanting Maya to become herself is an invitation to cancel herself out.

Skin herself into absence.

On the fourth night of missing her I sit on the floor, staring at the oven door as the honey cakes rise, and I think:

Before there was Maya, I was a small child who craved affection and felt desperately alone.

Without Maya, part of who I am feels dismantled, cut away.

A missing leg or arm. An ear. A slice of a lung, twenty fingernails, mine and hers, torn from the roots.

After a few nights, I realise Maya's not coming back.

So I need to stop wanting her to because want doesn't stretch as far as wherever she's gone and I'm stretching myself thin and thinner, by wanting something I can't have.

Torturing my thoughts into believing that she's going to be manipulated and damaged, changed beyond recognition, or stripped, flayed, as good as dead, now she's away from me.

Yet even so, often I steal a look between the curtains of the kitchen window, in case Maya comes walking along the path, in case she comes home to me.

One night, the light switches don't work and silence crowds in. I want to cry and scream and bite. Sob and yell and throw things. I'm physically craving something and I don't know what it is. My jaw is tight because I've been grinding my teeth in my sleep. I'm frantic to talk. To anyone at all, I don't care who.

I find the torch and examine every corner of the cottage. The shadow must find desperation repulsive, because even it's not here.

After hours of looking out between the curtains, I watch as

a cream suitcase floats in the dark, moving up the path towards the road. Someone is leaving.

Grabbing the torch, I creep out of the cottage and follow. Nearing the road, I call, 'Come back!'

The suitcase pauses. Spins, and bobs back down the path towards me. I look more closely as I see the suitcase has a man attached to it.

I switch on the torch.

His face and bright eyes are illuminated.

'Who are you?' I ask, wishing I could change like Maya does, but be in control of how others see me.

'I'm the doctor, just heading back home.' His face is young; his eyes are interested and intelligent. His eyebrows meet in the middle.

I will him to see my face as beautiful, and yet slightly pained.

His warm voice says, 'And you—'

'Oh, I'm in pain. Agony, almost.' I look down, and back at him. The wind blows my hair over my face and I sweep it off, imagining I'm a washed-up mermaid or an overworked goddess: feminine, strong, strained and beautiful.

He seems concerned. 'If you're ill, you shouldn't be out in the night, not when it's so cold. I'll help you back home. Where do you live?'

'Down there.' I wave my arm gracefully in a sweep which could mean the cottage or the village.

He looks towards the cottage. 'There are so many empty homes down this way. It's sad.'

'Do you know much about this place?'

Still, he looks at the cottage. 'I only come here when I'm called. Which is rare. You've never called me.'

'I've not been sick. Till now, of course. So you don't know many people who live here?'

'Know doesn't seem to be an option. You all seem so private.'

'It's mine. The cottage.'

He looks at me, his head tilted. 'With the curtains always closed. Do you like living in the dark, or are you a bit low?'

'There is electricity. It fizzles, sometimes disappears for a few hours when there are storms. Is it the same where you live?'

'Not so much, but this place is remote.'

'Would you come with me now, and check—'

'Your electricity?'

I laugh. 'My pain. You said you were a doctor.'

'Did I?' He looks slightly vague. 'Of course. I was. Well, I am. It's been a long time since I've felt like one. But it's surprising how much I remember when it's needed. But yes, you. No daylight at all. You're very pale. Or perhaps it's the light from the torch.'

I realise I'm shining the beam in my face. I imagine myself looking tragic, but ripe tragic, not dying tragic. I can feel his eyes glancing at me as we walk back down the path to the cottage.

My hand sweeps across his, at the gate. An accident. A crackle from his hand to mine or mine to his. The electricity comes back on inside and shines grey through the black curtains. Our eyes meet and he smiles, a caring-doctor smile. I smile back, a ripe, tragic smile. I think of pomegranates, slightly bruised, but filled with pips and juices. And I will him to be hungry for sugars.

I open the front door. He waits for me to go inside first and I do, swaying my boom boom bum just a little. I can feel his eyes on me.

Holding the door open, I turn and face him. 'Come in.'

His eyes lock onto mine, his pupils black. There's a tension in his body, and his voice has a playfully sadistic tone. 'You don't have the feeling about you of any kind of illness. In fact, you don't seem to be in any kind of physical pain at all.'

'Come in,' I say again, making my own voice a little stern.

'I'm sure it won't take us long to work out what's paining me. Perhaps it started with a feeling of loss. Or a pinch of betrayal. I've every faith you'll help me recover.'

'A cure for betrayal.' He raises his eyebrows and his eyes spark. 'Now that could be intriguing. Have you ever heard the old expression: the hair of the dog that bit you?'

I look back at him, unblinking, and say, 'Like which cures like.'

KIP

I've been listening. All kinds of things are said when grown-ups think children can't hear. A whole bunch of people have been in and out of our cottage for the last few days, collecting things to talk about in each other's homes.

Uncle Finn comes round and talks to Dad while Mammy isn't here.

He says, 'Can't we grab life with both hands? How I felt for her hit me like a wallop in the chest.'

Dad says, 'You could have thumped that hit right back and stuck with just the one, like the rest of us.'

'I don't know how long I've got left.'

They don't say much else but go off for a walk together.

Dad's still out with Uncle Finn, and there are more of the grown-ups here again now. It's talk-turns for Jessie and Mam Vann and Caddy's mum; they're standing by the fire with Mammy, eating biscuits.

I'm blanketed over on the baggy chair half pretending to read one of Dad's detective books so my eyes don't show the grown-ups I know what they're saying.

Jessie's saying, 'Finn's heart, what a pressure to put it under. I mean, he's thinking of his loins in the now, and they'll not leave him anything for the future.'

Mam Vann says, 'It's Adam I'm worried for. He's always been a silent mite and he's not been at school for the last few days. All that going on at home. They could split him right down the middle.'

Adam was here earlier, when Mammy went out to help Jessie with a delivery at the shop. He was really angry with his dad, so we gagged each other and had a pillow fight.

Mam Vann's watching me, so I stare at the book. I'm on page ten and there are three and a half dead bodies already.

Caddy's mum says, 'What if Pippa's, you know . . .'

Mammy says, 'What?'

'You know.'

'What?'

'Done something. To Lizzie. Her smashing Lizzie's place up – wouldn't think it to look at her, but that kind of rage . . .'

'Not Pippa, she'd never—'

Mam Vann says, 'Give us a biscuit here.'

On page eleven in the book, there's a poisoning.

'Some people might seem gentle, but after simmering awhile, they just blow.'

Caddy's mum holds the plate of biscuits out. Mam Vann takes two and reaches to steady herself on the mantelpiece.

'You all right standing?'

Mam Vann drags a chair over to the fire and sits on it with a creak. 'Pippa's never going to have been that much out of control she'd hurt her. Though she does love Finn.'

On page twelve in the book, there's the first suspect. Mrs Beesting, who keeps a paperknife in her handbag for protection.

Jessie says, 'Right enough. Can't say why, but she does. He's so quiet, and with a beard and no moustache, he's drawing a lot of attention to his mouth.'

Mammy says, 'Finn's got reason to be quiet. His dad was hard on him when he was a lad – he slammed a ruler across his hands whenever he spoke before being spoken to. Brack had the same treatment but he went against it, and took to shouting where Finn took to silence.'

Mam Vann says, 'Remember when Finn was around eighteen – he had a thing with two girls at the same time, couldn't make up his mind and ended up with neither. Maybe he was born indecisive. We could have told Pippa about them but I'll bet no one did. You know, we should have. Warned her.'

Mammy says, 'People change. You know, even with that tangle of three having to come out, she only told Jessie the bare facts, isn't that right?'

Jessie says, 'Didn't get into complaints over it at all.'

Mam Vann says, 'Poor lass. Why Lizzie had to go for Finn, when he's taken and they've got a child. She's not stupid; she could have gone for anyone.'

'Well, she never went for mine.'

'No one ever went for yours apart from you.'

'Well, my eyesight's not been right for years.'

'What if Finn . . . oh, I shouldn't say it here.'

Mammy has a growl in her voice. 'What if Finn *what?*'

On page thirteen, there's another suspect. Mr Carnival, who always wears a tie, but never around his neck.

Caddy's mum says. 'Did away with Lizzie?'

Mammy is so angry she doesn't speak.

Caddy's mum keeps talking. 'I mean, if something went wrong . . .'

Mam Vann says, 'Like in a sex accident?'

'Ssh.'

I can feel they're all looking at me.

At the bottom of page thirteen, Mr Carnival and Mrs Beesting are tongue kissing and it's slimy, so I put the book down. I curl up facing the kitchen door so they can't see my face.

Mammy's tight voice says, 'Mam Vann, you should bed someone yourself one day, then you'd know those kinds of accidents don't just happen.'

Caddy's mum says, 'But there could have been something like that, don't you think? When people are behind doors, eyes aren't seeing. You know bottled-up guilt could make an already bad heart much worse.'

Jessie's come back and she's here with Mammy. The wind's blowing outside and the electricity is off again. Jessie said to Mammy she needed to have a *private chat* and kept looking at me, but Mammy told her over and over I couldn't hear a word.

So I'm sitting under the table drawing a picture of a raggedy star doll. Mammy and Jessie are sitting at the table drinking bramble wine because they can't boil the kettle for tea. My raggedy star doll has broken universes in her hair and a dented moon on her dress and dusty galaxies on her boots and she's got a sad and happy face.

Jessie says, 'You remember all those years ago when the last of that family of police was here?'

'The one George and his dad saw off? With the wall-eye?'

I make a new drawing of the police with bricks in his eye.

Jessie says, 'The police was on about Gilliam. Said he'd read over the . . . what was it . . . *Archived Case History*, and he said, *That cottage was never searched.*' She lowers her voice. 'He wanted to knock on Old Kelp's door.'

'I remember some of it. They talked him out of knocking, though?'

'Yes, George and his dad said they'd seen him off. Told him it should *stay* archived history.' Her voice goes quiet again. 'Told him the poor woman who lived there now was far too frail and mad to be bothered.'

'The police gave up. Well, then.'

'Oh flip, Dorcas. George was teenage. Little more than a lad.'

'Well, ask him; he might remember. Why do you always have to know everything that's ever happened?'

'That's not what I'm saying. I'm not doing anything about this, and I don't want anything done. But there's something in that attic of George's . . .' Jessie's voice sounds tight. 'You'll not tell a soul? It's still, it's such, well . . . It's a terrible thing.'

'You know I'll not tell any souls.' Mammy is talking in her quiet voice, so she means it. I draw a picture of her quiet voice hiding in a shell.

Jessie says, 'Always been good at keeping things to yourself, haven't you?'

'Well, some people are and some people aren't.'

'Point took. I found a dead bat up at the Lets.'

'There's only a couple of bookings so far for this spring. The Lets Agency wrote. They're still paying me to get all of them ready, though I'll not bother till I have to. There's fewer and fewer people coming here each year.'

'Well, the bats can probably stay on then. There's a mass hibernation going on in one of the roofs. This one didn't have enough fat on it to make it to spring. Gorgeous thing though, all brown fur and those leathery wings. Not a mark on it. So I took it to George's. He didn't answer my knock, so I went on in. Couldn't find him downstairs so I climbed the creaking stair-well, and up again. George was in the bathroom with the door shut. I shouldn't have, but I've always wanted to see over his house. He never lets anyone further in than the ground floor. His kitchen and living room, his taxidermy skins and feathers and skulls are all I've seen. Same for you and your Brack?'

'He's just private, is George.'

'I was curious. George was in the bathtub humming, so I knew I'd hear if he came out. Oh Dorcas. I shouldn't be saying this.' Jessie crosses her legs and winds one ankle round the other.

'Yes, you should. That's why you're here.'

I tear the picture of Mammy's quiet voice out of the book and on the next page I start drawing a picture of George humming in the bathtub surrounded by a fox, three mice and an angry bat.

Jessie's voice is quieter. 'So up George's stairs I crept, and up, and up again. Had a look in his bedroom – he's got a badger and a fox. And in a spare room, there's a table with the legs made from four hares standing on their hind legs.'

'I remember that one from years back. His dad made it out in the street, wanted everyone to see it. He made moulds of hares, covered them in the skins of real ones. Painted the eyes onto marbles. It's a skill, that I'll say.'

'Along the stairways, there's squirrels on the wall with their tails curved into hooks. And up in the attic . . . Well.'

'What?'

Jessie's voice drops to a whisper and I listen hard, but she must be leaning right into Mammy's ear.

Mammy talks with a thin voice. 'His dad's long dead. Oh Jessie, George would have been, what – about fourteen? There's nothing can undo it now. If you need to talk of it again, I'm here. And I know where to find you. But say nothing.'

'Not even to—'

'Not even to anyone.'

I draw a round face with enormous ears and its mouth hammered shut.

It's really dark tonight. Me and Adam are in the fir tree wood. Dagger's slumped on the ground with his nose on his muddy paws; he's looking glum because he's tied to a tree trunk. We found a shallow hole in the ground with onion skins in it. The hole was covered in branches that must have crashed down in last night's storm. That gave Adam an idea and now he's snapping twigs from the branches. He's building a great nest around us. His torch shining through the twigs makes shadows of branches on the tree trunks. We've smoked two cinnamon sticks each and it took ages.

Adam says, 'Let's do ghost stories now.'

'Have you got one?'

'Oh, I'll make one up.'

'All right.'

We sit in the nest.

Adam says, 'There was once a village full of people, and to any visitor, it seemed like any other. The houses were warmed, the fires were lit, the summers were short and the winters were hard.

'Each person who had always lived in that village had lived there too long. Each person had lived as long as the life of a tree in the nearby forest.

'And each of those trees in the forest had the heart of a human who lived in the village. The hearts grew inside the trunks, hidden away.

'The trees grew with no branches. And the trunks grew tall and wide to hide the hearts. There was blood running through the grain of the wood, so no one ever went near. No wolf would go there to howl, no rook would roost, no bats squeaked, and nothing burrowed.

'People visited the village from far away. They didn't know about the hearts in the trees, and fell soppy in love with the villagers. Outsiders married villagers, and for years they lived together. They had children and those children had children and more and more trees with no branches grew in the forest.

'A distant city wanted wood to make bonfires for a celebration – people were coming from all over the world to see athletes compete. The city sent out people who wore bright coats, and they came with silver machinery and felled the forest.

'As the trees collapsed the people in the village with no real hearts of their own cried out in voices like cracks of wood, and disappeared.

'When the trees were cut down, the outsiders were left with a grief that lasted the rest of their lives; they could never bury their soppy loves because there were no bodies. They felt like ghosts themselves, living in a village with no heart, and their own hearts were filled with splinters.

'The people in bright coats hauled their silver machinery and the tree trunks back to the city. They piled the trunks into bonfires. When the celebration happened, the bonfires smelled of woodsmoke and red meat.

'When the trees were cut down, the soil they were cut from was soaked in blood, and nothing ever grew there again.'

I shiver. 'Is that it?'

'That's the end. No happy evers in ghost stories.'

I say, 'I'll do one too. Just need to think one up.'

'Come on. You were good at stories till they got you in trouble.' Adam leans his elbows on his knees and waits.

He's quiet while I tap my lips and think.

I say, 'Once there was the ghost of a bad man and his face was long.'

'How long?'

'His chin was down to his shins.'

Adam beams. 'Ooh. Go on.'

'He lived a bad, long-faced afterlife. He ate up anything and everything that got in the way of his chin.'

'Did he have hairs on his chin?'

'He did as well. And he had lice on the hairs. And everything at shin height went in mortal terror.'

Adam frowns at me. 'What shin-height things are there?'

'Hares. And tree stumps. And footstools and buckets . . .'

'Come *on*, Kip.'

'Babies. They were the chewiest shin-height things of all. And he ate them all up and spat out their teeth.'

'Babies don't have teeth.'

'And he ate them all up and spat out their . . . tongues.'

Adam wrinkles his nose. 'Eugh. Is that the end?'

'Unless you want a happy ever.'

'It wouldn't be a proper ghost story then.' He picks bark off a twig with his thumbnail. 'Didn't really think mine up tonight; I've been practising it for ages.'

'All right. For that, you get a happy ever. All the babies' tongues wriggled and squirmed and bunched together and made themselves into an enormous ghost-eating slug. And the ghost-eating slug slimed the bad ghost man over and over again for the rest of all time. That was really the end. See, for ghost stories a punishment is a happy ever. Not like in real life. If we died and had to be ghosts and then we got punished *as well*, that would be grim.'

'Yuk.' Adam rolls on his back and kicks his feet in the air.

'What?'

'The slug made of babies' tongues! Yuk, yuk, yuk. Kip, let's smoke another one.'

Adam cracks the twigs and weaves them together, his pale hands working fast. He tells me, 'This isn't a nest any more; it's a ring of fire for us to explode invisible atoms and get boomed into outerspace.' He rattles a box of matches at me. 'What if the invisible people in these woods are boomed there with us?'

I take the matches from Adam and put them in my coat pocket. I look over my shoulder into the creaking fir trees and shiver. 'If we see them, I hope they don't look too . . . twiggish.'

Adam cracks and weaves and cracks and weaves around us both. 'I'll make the ring of fire enormous, like a stick igloo. We'll boom it from underneath. You scared?'

'No.' The branches creak above us and I jump.

He nods. 'You are a little bit, eh.'

I don't want him to know he's much braver than I am. 'No. It's only that Mammy, well, she'll fret. She still thinks I can't hear. She's a bit upset about some secret thing and I never told her I was going out.'

'Well, she'd not have let you. What secret thing's she got?'

'Not sure. Something about George. You ever been inside his house?'

'I did when Dad took him the duck. The light bulb in its bill is the best thing ever. It's amazing, isn't it?'

I nod.

'Mum doesn't like it, that's why it's in our downstairs just-for-men-and-boys loo.'

'Go upstairs at all while you were at George's?'

'No . . . Said I needed to piss, but he didn't offer me his bathroom. Told me and Dad he had things to do and sent us home. He had a badger skin on the table and a glass snake eye in a metal clamp. What are you asking for?'

'Ah, probably nothing.'

'George has a secret project on the go. Maybe your mum's got wind of that.'

'What is it?'

'He told Dad about it because he wants him to keep a lookout for swans. He's going to make hybrids for when the spring and summer people come. Someone wrote to George from Paradon and told him to make them a whippet with a swan's wings on its back. He wrote back to say there's no whippets round here and if they want something skinny they'll have to wait for spring and make do with a lamb. Dad said it was foul, mixing animals like that. But George said one of the summer people had taken his address and asked for it special. Going to pay him top whack because it's for an ad.'

'For what?'

'Cosmic surgery.'

'He could do lots of hybrids if that's what they pay him top whack for. A cat and a seagull.'

'An elephant and grizzly bear.'

'Too big! A hedgehog and a miniature pony.'

'Nice. We can see his attic window from our spare room.'

'What's in there?'

'Don't know. He keeps the curtains shut.'

'Does he?' I shiver.

Adam's trying to get in my pocket; he's after the matches. I push him away, he grabs me and I grab him harder. He stands still with his arms around me and my arms are around him and we're hugging birds in this nest-ring-of-fire he wants to burn.

We let go of each other.

I say, 'Dagger's gone!' He's unravelled his lead from the tree trunk. Adam stamps his way out of the nest, walks further into the wood, and calls him.

Rushing to the edge of the trees, I shout, 'Oh no, he's going . . .' I can just about see him running through the field towards Old Kelp's cottage, the lead trailing behind him.

Adam is beside me. He hisses, 'No, we can't get him from—'

'We're going to have to,' I whisper back, as I watch Dagger

clamber over the crumbled rocks in the wall, and go into Old Kelp's garden.

Adam makes himself seem taller, and he looks brave. He puts his finger over his lips at me, then quickly runs through the field towards the cottage. I follow close behind. I trip on a rock in the field and get up again. I limp to the wall.

Adam's pale face appears in the dark and makes me jump. He grabs my arm with a trembling hand and says quietly, 'I heard something groaning. This place is haunted.'

'I know where Dagger will be,' I whisper back.

At the shed door, I yank and tug at Dagger but he's stiffened and stuck to the smell.

Adam hisses, 'Come on!' as he glances over his shoulder at Old Kelp's cottage.

Dagger claws the bottom of the door and breaks off a chunk of rotten wood.

As I reach for Dagger, Adam grabs my arm. 'Did you hear that?'

'What?'

Adam doesn't look brave any more. He whispers, 'Listen!'

This time, I hear the low groan as well, a deep moan, and another, coming from the cottage.

Adam stares at the cottage as he backs away, his eyes terrified, shaking his head. He disappears around the side. I hear the creak of the gate.

He's gone.

One side window is dark and the other lit just a little. If I concentrate on breathing really quietly, and listening to my heart fast-beating, I can't hear anything else.

Turning back to the shed, I crouch next to Dagger, as small as I can, and sniff the gap he's clawed away at the bottom of the door. I cover my mouth and swallow to stop the sick coming up.

I've got a horrible thought that won't go away. What if Lizzie hasn't gone to her sister's at all? What if she's been cursed by Old Kelp for being in a tangle of three? If I don't find out what this smell is now, I'll never be brave enough to get this close again. And something inside the shed smells very, very dead. It smells the rottenest kind of rank, so it has to be something much bigger than a dead rat.

The shed door has a hole at the bottom, where the wood was damp enough for me to break it quietly, one small chunk at a time. Dagger's already crawled in. Now I lie flat on the ground and push myself inside.

It's coal black. I strike a match, and it lights up my hand. The match has its own smell. I'm breathing through my mouth so I can't smell the stench. But it's worse, because I can taste it.

Blowing out the match, I get four burning at once. I take a sniff of match smell, cover my mouth, and hold out the flames.

Dagger's lying on top of a sheet with bumps under it and dry grass and ivy scattered over it. He's grabbing the sheet with his mouth and pulling and rubbing at it. I burn my fingers but don't shout. I drop the matches on the floor and they spark on dry grass. I stamp out the flames.

My feet bump against something soft. I crouch and feel with my hands. Something fabric. I push at it. A mattress. I kneel and reach to find where Dagger is. He jerks when I touch the fur on his back; his spine twists; he's rubbing his chops and won't stop.

Sitting up on my haunches, I strike another bundle of matches. They spark and make a bright light. I crawl onto the mattress and as my knees sink into it, damp seeps through my dress. Dagger twists and wraps his face in stench.

I blow out the matches, light more and hold them out. I reach to pull the sheet away and see what lies in bumps and lumps underneath.

MAYA

Stop it stop it, scare is too big. The sky's a wind spite gloom place with deadstars.

I'm not too far from mysister. Only two roads walk and the cold is the same.

Not to go back to her, she doesn't want. Not till I'm myself for her.

Follow light.

Not too many more steps on broken road.

This is more real: light is here.

Bright through glass.

Red door of a phone box.

Inside, I slump down under light.

A concrete floor with grass cracking through.

There's no wind now.

Above my head: a plastic telephone, metal shelves, light bulb.

Around the light bulb skitters a grey moth which might die.

Poor skitterish gabblish mothish moth.

Safer than cold is memory:

Up and up and up, once I saw inside Paradon weather-mirrors. We were waiting in our mother's skyscraping carpet-grey office block. Me and mysister were small and smaller. We'd played-up all the filing box games and the archives were emptied. Floor mountain of old paper. Our clothes wore Sunday smells.

We saw the mirrors out of the high windows, across across. These mirrors, enormous. Made from maths-shape hexagons and the sun reflected and swooshed in. Our reflections, caught. Mysister grabbed my hand and said, *Stop it, satellites send the sun in. They're too strong.*

The sun shone into my eyes.

I was dazzle blind.

Our shrinking silhouettes danced with my laughing sound: clang clang! I brimmed yellow-joy. Every reflection that lives in infinityland was blanked out HAHAHAHA!

My voice said, *My eyes are getting strongererer . . .*

Mysister covered her eyes, she said, *Stop it, stop it, it'll make you blind.*

The mirrors turned away to shine something else bright.

My laughter clangs ended.

Mysister, sad. She said, *I should have covered your eyes as well. I'm going to look after you more properly, it's my job.*

In the park, mysister's hands passed me mint ice cream for lunch food.

I whispered into her ear curve, *I can see right into people.*

I know, she said. *I know.*

Here, in a phone box. There's only cramp sleep.

Moth still alive.

Air smells of piss.

I can find mysister voice without going back to her. I learned-up her voice, didn't I? If I can think it, speak it, I could get warm and out dark.

Not far away from her, still not far away at all. She likes me to be like her, she likes that a lot. Grownup land lives in mysister voice with her sensible talk-style.

Maya

Stop jumbling, she said to me, whenever I fearstop. *Stop jumbling and calm down.*

If I can be big now, I'll get mysister talk-style for my mouth.

Can I be big?

I tell myself, *Stop jumbling.*

That's what mysister would say to me now.

Mysister Amber is named for colour.

Ruby, amber, emerald.

On a traffic light she's in the middle.

Don't know what to do without

KIP

She's dead because she's been given the death curse by Old Kelp. If I ever speak about this, I'll end up dead, in here, with her. For what I've done I could be cursed so many times. Old Kelp could kill my eyes for seeing and my nose for smelling. If I speak she'll kill my tongue for talking. She'll kill my hands for touch. Curse my brain for thinking. My heart for feeling. And last is the death curse. The final one that kills the whole body through the veins, turns the blood to clots.

Those must be the colours of the death curse across her face, blotched black, swollen, her purple tongue, the eyes dark and puffed, and this must be the death curse smell.

I get up from the corner of the shed, frozen, shaking. I pull Dagger off her body with my sudden strong arms, and we crawl out of the shed.

Pulling some ivy, I cover the hole in the bottom of the shed door and yank Dagger away. I nearly fall over the rocks along her path and my heart thumps in my neck as the gate creaks shut behind me. I run down the path towards the village. I stop to sick. And again.

I couldn't see her face, for all the swellings and colours of the death curse.

Couldn't see the colour of her hair for the dark, but the light from the matches showed me enough to see her hair wasn't blonde.

So it isn't Lizzie.

But someone else is missing from our village and no one but me has noticed, and I didn't notice hard enough.

I can't stop my feet running towards her home. My feet want to check my eyes didn't get it wrong. Because no one will be in her house and no one will miss her and no one will know.

I'm at her door.

I knock, in case I'm dreaming, in case she's alive, in case she might answer, in case her dead body wasn't real.

She used to leave out sweet-smelling, always-flowering violet flowers.

Her loud face is stuck in my head.

The Quiet Woman, who no one knows at all, is dead.

I turn the handle. It's not locked. Dagger goes inside, slow and quiet. The Quiet Woman never wanted to talk with us, apart from to ask about what she called *local superstitions*. Mam Vann was the one who went round. She told her about the fair, and the Quiet Woman called Old Kelp a crone. She wouldn't give Mam Vann her name, though she was asked for it over and over. Mam Vann talked that all around the village for a long time, her lips tight when saying it.

The Quiet Woman told Mam Vann she didn't want any fuss, didn't want anyone to come round, welcome her, ask her questions. And after that, the Quiet Woman kept herself to herself. She's not even on the list to do the fair, as we don't have her real name.

I switch on the light in her bedroom. There's a grey sheet hanging over something on the wall by the door; I lift it up and there's a mirror hidden under it.

My hands reach out to look through her things because I want to know what she was like before my eyes saw her dead.

The drawers have turquoise underwear, dark blue jumpers, balled-up purple tights and socks. There's a tin can with money notes rolled in it. On her bedside table is a pen with no lid and a brown notebook filled with tiny green handwritten words:

I came here to find myself
I came here to find myself
I came here to find myself

Pages filled with these same words repeated over and over again.

Hanging on the wall above her bed is a glass case with bright butterflies inside it in rows. They've got pins through their bodies. There are handwritten words on tiny pieces of brown paper glued under every butterfly. The words are:

death
dead
deceased
elapsed
expired
finished
late
annihilated
exterminated

Under the Quiet Woman's bed there's a huge empty suitcase and a butterfly net.

Inside her wardrobe, there's a sheet of brown paper pinned with drawing pins over the mirror inside. On the hangers there are purple, turquoise and brown clothes: shirts, skirts, trousers, three dresses, and about five empty hangers. I only ever saw her outside from a distance, wearing a blue frockcoat. It's not in here. On the floor beside her bedroom door are two empty pairs of boots, one pair black, the others bronze. These sad boots will never have her feet in them again. I kick my wellies off and put on the bronze ones, far too big for me. I walk up and down, staring at my feet.

Her dead face flashes in my head. Stepping out of her boots, I cover my mouth and nearly trip over Dagger in the hallway as I push open doors till I find the toilet and sick in it.

In the Quiet Woman's kitchen the kettle's full of water and a green mug has a teabag in it. From the side window, I can see the lights are off in Lizzie's house. Adam must have gone back home. A spoon lies on the counter next to a small metal bowl of white sugar and a half-full jug of curdled milk. A planter tray sits on the front windowsill where she grows violets. The violets are still flowering bright purple. They've got spring in their stems. Their earth is dry. I fill the mug and water them for her. There are lollipop sticks in between the leaves. I pull one out. It's written on, in her tiny writing:

you are wise, so show me who I am

I pull another lollipop stick out, and another. They all say the same thing, like her notebook. There's some kind of blessing or curse in these violets that she put out for her fair and I took to Old Kelp's, these violets that flower and flower and flower.

So the Quiet Woman must have gone to Old Kelp's thinking she'd get some kind of wisdom, and she died there and now she'll never know who she was at all.

Just like we don't know, neither did she.

And I can't find anything in her house to tell me her name.

Dagger is waiting at the front door. He stands up and wags his tail. I cover my nose with my hand. He stinks. I need to get him washed or his smell is going to make me want to sick. I want Mammy's arms and Dad's strong shoulders and to curl up small. But I don't want them to smell this.

I tie a pair of the Quiet Woman's tights over my mouth and nose and that helps with about half of the smell. I run Dagger a bath.

On the edge of the bath, there's a bottle of blue shampoo. I wash Dagger over and over again. It gets the smell off him, and just about does him in.

The bathroom mirror above the sink is covered with a fringed white shawl. The Quiet Woman never wanted to see herself, but she wanted to know who she was. Living here alone with dead butterflies, she must have felt she had a pin right through her body too, and if she looked in a mirror, she'd see it.

Outside our cottage I listen at the front door, and though the lights are on, it's quiet inside. I open the door.

Mammy rushes at me, hugs me and pushes me away. Dad's steaming angry and both their eyes are tired. Wet Dagger tears around rubbing himself on the chairs and rolling on the rug.

They work their voices up and down again. I take my coat off and try not to look at them.

I really want to tell them about the Quiet Woman but, if I do, all the curses will come. They're asking questions and more questions and I don't let myself hear them because I can't speak. Once I do, I'll answer one of their questions by accident. And when they know I can hear, I'll have to go up to Old Kelp's to do the fair and see the shed every single day on my own till it's spring.

I'm shaking. I can smell the death curse on myself.

It's all over my dress.

I tear the dress off and drop it on the floor.

As I cry floods, Mammy rubs my shoulders. She's so close to me, I can't stop myself hearing what she's saying. 'He's freezing cold. And to be this upset . . . Something's happened – do you think he had a fit and he can't tell—'

Dad says, quickly, 'He's not had fits in years.' He picks up my dress and gets a whiff. 'What the flip's this stench off of? Flipsake, that's pure rank.'

He covers his mouth and throws my dress in the fire.

As I watch it burn, my tears blur with smoke.

In bed, I lie stroking Dagger, who's curled next to the sick feeling in my belly. It's too dark so I put the globe lamp on.

There's a bad picture in my head – the face, the tongue, bulging eyes . . . and it shouts in my head like a flash. It makes me want to sick. I keep my eyes open and stroke Dagger behind his ears, and he goes to sleep with his good tooth jutting out.

My eyes droop shut . . .

FACE!

Dagger rolls over. I stroke his soft clean belly and he smells of blue shampoo. I curl around him, and his smell fills my nose with clean. I try to think about bluebells and clean blue sheets and blue fishing nets . . . I close my eyes.

FACE!

I put on the big light and stare at the blue paint on the walls and the blue carpet and the blue blanket and this blue pillowcase.

Biting my lip, I want to cry.

Dad burnt my dress.

I shake Dagger's front leg to wake him up. 'I'd be braver if I was as boyish as Dad wants me to be. Do you remember when Dad made everything blue?'

He blinks at me and tries to settle again, so I fidget with one of his ears. He frowns at me under his ragged fringe.

'Remember. I had a dress-up tea with Maeve – me and you and Mammy. We were sitting her for her mum. Mammy let me dress Maeve up. She was only one, and we were butterflies. She wore a towel and I wore one of Mammy's dresses and you were a fly. When Dad came home and saw me being a butterfly, he hollered and yelled, so you tried to buzz him from being a giant shouter into a little person. But because you can't bark, you also can't buzz, so you couldn't do fly magic right.'

Dagger slumps his chin down and blinks at me three times.

I rub his head to keep him awake. 'And Maeve cried, so Dad went quiet till after her mum took her home. I wouldn't give Mammy's dress back because I wanted to keep being a butterfly and live in a butterfly house. But Mammy and Dad wouldn't stop shouting so I shut you and me in here.'

Dagger sighs and closes his eyes. I let him.

Me and Dagger did noisy games and played chase-fly all over this bed. I tripped and tore Mammy's dress. And I still wouldn't take it off. Two days later, Mammy cut away the rip and made it smaller for me. And a week later, she made me another dress of my own because I needed one to wash and one to wear, but I was only wearing.

When I started wearing dresses, Dad was angry with Mammy for a long time. He made all my things blue because he thinks blue is boyish. But Mammy was glad because I stopped telling lying stories. I stopped because I felt made of truth, like a butterfly is.

But butterflies look so sad when they're pinned through the middle.

MAYA

I learned to be big hearing Amber's voice. Behind her voice, her want for me to be the same as her. Behind her want, her need to not feel alone. Coming here. Changing her mind. Wanting me not to need her. Wanting me to be someone she doesn't need. Can't keep so lost, looking for nothing.

Remember how to think safe in straight lines:

On the edge of this frozen road I'm still in a phone box.

In the dark, it's crimson.

The lines on the edge of the windowpanes smell of rust-metal.

Crimson.

That's the colour for Dead Red.

Dead Red's voice I heard:

Let me see, don't let me see.

Something like that. She said it out loud or in her head, couldn't tell which.

Dead Red's voice was purple.

Forget it.

Forget the dress Dead Red didn't die in.

Forget it's not crimson, not really mine.

Now it's brave grownup talk for my non-mouth.

All learned-up, so remember it properly, sensible now.

The grey moth still skitters around the bare light bulb. It must have hatched somewhere warm, and come to this frost.

I whisper, 'Go to sleep,' to the moth, as if sleep could let death take it gently. It bashes its life against the light-howling bulb.

I whisper, 'Don't look at its wings being singed at the edges, don't care for it, don't hurt for it, don't feel like you *are* the moth.'

Amber would say, *Stop jumbling, it doesn't matter.*

I whisper, 'So make it matter-not.'

Think anything, not Dead Red. Think not crimson dress, think not her purple voice so I . . .

Stop jumbling and

watch the moth bash itself against the light bulb.

Amber taught me how to do sensible thoughts, so I make some up:

It's miraculous how long energy-saving light bulbs last.

Miraculous I've found this small piece of light.

Dust taste isn't a sensible thought.

Banish-it.

But I think Moth *would* taste of dust. I whisper rambles of jumbles at Moth. I talk of cartoons, snowboarding elephants and hanggliding tigers and how even gigantic cartoon animals need to sleep when they're seeing stars and have worn themselves out from so much basharound, so this is even truer for smaller creatures who must get so tired.

This doesn't stop Moth hurting itself on the light bulb.

I uncramp myself and stand up. I reach, make myself taller, try to use my fist to break the light bulb, to save Moth and fill myself with light and electricity and see if the energy from a light bulb would make me hurt-down or glow-light—

Like an unwanted blessing or an expected curse, the telephone rings.

Clangrrrrrrrr! Rrrrrrrrrrrrr!

I say to the loud phone, 'That's not a sensible noise.'

I look at the receiver, resting in the claws of the phone.

Three rings. The receiver is in my hand.

I speak one sensible word into the phone, 'Who?'

Silence.

A woman's voice. The talk-style is the recorded Voice from Paradon.

It speaks: 'Good evening and welcome to my Voice. You have been perceived by the sensor for an unwarranted amount of time. This is not routine. We recognise something is very wrong.'

My small voice says, 'Nothing's not wrong.'

The Voice says, 'Please select carefully from the following options: Press one for the Suicide Squad; two for the Credit Collection Agency; three for Crime Confession, Crime Reporting or anything regarding Criminal Activity; four for Medical Assistance or Psychotherapy; five for Quenchers, Graffiti Removal or Cleaners; six for Global Warming Angst or Sunburn Advice; seven for Intellectual Starvation Intervention; eight for Dissociation Counselling; nine for Afterlife Advice, and zero for Advance Warning.

'Please note that none of these interventions will be available person to person in remote areas; however, you may find our pre-recorded information helpful.

'To hear these options again, please replace the receiver and stay within the sensor range for approximately twenty-four hours, and the telephone will automatically ring.'

'I can't remember all the options; you're being mix-match confusing . . .'

The tone of the Voice doesn't change. It says, 'Please listen carefully and consider taking notes to enable you to make an informed choice when you hear the available options again. If you are confused, insecure, neurotic, unsure, or didn't understand the previous instructions, please replace the receiver. If you are able to be decisive, please press your chosen option now.'

Beep.

I look at the rusted buttons. Close my eyes and press any-which-one.

The Voice says, 'Thank you. You have selected Afterlife Advice.'

'Oh. That's—'

'Please select carefully from the following options: Press one for Nihilism or the Consequences of Suicide according to this theory; two for Consideration of the Benefits of Religious Advice for the Firmly Non-Religious; three if you have already selected a particular Religion, or been assigned one prior to Birth; four for Hopeful Anticipation and how best to support this tendency; five for Comparative Statistics on Afterlife Experiences during Coma; six for the Likelihood of your own personal Afterlife occurring within the next five working days; seven for Parapsychology; eight if you are currently experiencing an Out-of-body Experience; or nine for a Comparison of Heaven, Nirvana, Svarga, Olam Haga, Jannah, Reincarnation, et cetera.'

Beep.

I ask a slow, unjumbled, very sensible question of the Voice. 'What if I'm concerned about the afterlife of someone else?'

The Voice says, 'I'm sorry, I don't understand your selection.'

The line clicks and fuzzes. The phone line sounds like a thousand fracture-voices.

I whisper, 'Hello, hello?'

I think a sensible thought about Dead Red and dial the emergency number printed on the phone.

The Voice speaks at me. 'These services are currently unavailable. Please hold and display patience. Please do not take delays personally. You are calling from an extremely remote area. Please press 888888 if the crisis is now over but you require recorded Praise. If you continue to hold, you may have a delayed response. You are currently number 562 in the queue.'

I say, 'Amber might have wanted me to believe I killed Dead Red because that's what she thought. Then she changed her mind and wanted me to believe I didn't. So I believed her both ways. But want fades. My own thought is that I had opportunity – it was just Dead Red and me. So I might have killed her. I don't remember-big when it's shock or sad or jumble-confusing. My other own thought is that I might not have killed her. So I need the police to help me work out if I had a motive.'

A pause. The Voice says, 'If you check within your locality you may find people nearby who can more rapidly respond. If you have to, please continue to hold.'

I peer through the frosted windows. 'There's no one here but me to rapidly respond and without mysister I don't know what to do.'

After playing high-lifting piano music for a long time, the line clicks and the Voice says, 'In your location there may be some restricted local services, so press one for police, two for fire, three for ambulance, four for coastguard, five for plumbing, six for hazardous waste, seven for postal, highway, electricity and light-bulb maintenance.'

I press one and hold my breath, thinking I don't want to do this, thinking I do want to do this, because I want to know how and why and if. If I find myself out, I need to be punished and not have to think about it afterwards because that's what should happen to murderers. I might even be put safe in a locked room where there's no wind.

I say to the phone, 'If there's no one else, I don't mind being

the jury by myself; I'll be really . . . this is not a jumble word
– impartial . . .'

On the telephone, the piano music changes to a ghostly aria.
Clicks.

The line goes dead.

The phone rings again.

I shout into the receiver, 'Why are you calling so quickly?'

The Voice says, 'Our voice recognition intelligence has not
been able to procure your Identity.'

I laugh and stop. 'What identity?'

The Voice doesn't listen, it talks. 'Unless you have been born
and are thus considered permanently local within a radius of
your current location, you are likely to have left Paradon. If this
was within the last month, please return immediately if you are
registered as Employed and have no Criminal Convictions. After
approval, you should contact your Local Counselling Agency
who may arrange for a Reasonable Adjustment Period. You may
still be entitled to return to your Employment if Counselling is
successful. If you have been away from Paradon for over one
month, we wish you a safe onward life.'

It pauses again, pretend-listening.

The Voice says, 'If you are eligible, we look forward to poten-
tially welcoming you home.'

I whisper, 'I've had more than one month missing Paradon.
So is nowhere my home?'

After another pretend-listen, the Voice says, 'We are aware at
this moment in time, you may be extremely confused. May hope
soon return? Self-determined responsibility is a choice. You may
replace the receiver now.'

The line is full of fracture-noise and the receiver swings.

I have jumbling feelings. I can't understand where the feelings are because they're everywhere, in my bang head the pain is a thudbeat sound, my pinch eyes feel full of paper cuts, my stone shoulders are grit-black, my wave stomach feels like too many jellysweets and my puncture heart feels like a scab.

Now Paradon isn't an eligible home, I want to go back to Amber.

And I think of Dead Red's face, broken and smashed in.

For the first time, perhaps the only time and

I hope the last time,

I cry.

I fill the whole phone box with tears and float to the top, and still can't stop crying, even when my head nudges the miracle energy-saving light bulb. Moth is caught underwater in my swish-hair,

so I cry about drowned Moth.

My tears overflow from a missing pane

I float-drift in tears.

AMBER

He's mine for now, this man who sleeps next to me, his head sharing my pillow and his arm over my thigh. This wavy-haired man, when awake, pants my body into light, this man who had one pair of scuffed trousers: the one pair of trousers I got him out of by putting my hands in the pockets and finding they had holes in the lining.

I've also taken the white shirt from his back, torn it into shreds, tied the rags together, bound him up, and released him from them. We have been, perhaps, too noisy.

His sense of duty to others, of his role as anyone's medic, has abandoned him. I won't let him leave this cottage. He doesn't want to. We're perfectly matched.

I stroke his jaw. I'll keep him naked, because that will mean he never wants to open the curtains. He's disinclined to go outside any more. He doesn't have to return home, whatever home means to him, for anything. I feel for his un-ringed hand, stroke the hairs on the back of his forearm. He doesn't mind at all, being naked. Not when he has my body to put on and wear.

He calls me Gloria because that's the name I've given him. And with the sound of my new name on his tongue, the continuous kneading and caressing of his hands, the curiosity in his face when looking at my naked anatomy, I've become glorious. My body loves my new name. I shine the sun from my eyes and the moon from my smile and he loves the mountains of my belly, my buttocks and breasts. He finds the lightning which flashes through the stars that live in the darkness buried deep between my thighs.

Here in my bed, we storm in shudders.

I don't care what his real name is. I call him Medic because that is what he is and that is how he loves me. He's made of muscle and bone, eyes and tongue, of taut skin, hard and soft, slack and bursting, tufts of hair. He has the cure for any kind of ailment I can feign, and many others he tells me about.

The feelings in my body have become intense. Medic knows how to breathe my gales away, how to kiss me to sunshine and hold me in a pool with rain rippling across the surface. Together in bed, unspeaking, physical, at times almost medical, I feel all kinds of weather over and under and over his hands. No need to go outside with my body soaked, drowned, cloud and storm, a pulse, a hand, his fingers, a fist, a touch that electrifies the air between the whorl of his fingerprints and the flush of my skin.

His eyes flicker behind his eyelids, watching a dream. I touch his lips with my thumb.

He whispers, over and over. Even in his sleep he says it:

'Gloria, love me.' He believes this is love.

'Gloria wants you,' I reply, knowing this is want.

I cook for him. Page after page of recipes. Tonight, as he sleeps, I creep out of bed and select this one:

BOILED FRUIT CAKE

Butter, 4 oz
Brown sugar, 4 oz
Mixed dried fruit, 8 oz

Water, 8 fl oz
Flour, self-raising, 9 oz
Spices
1 egg, beaten
Salt, 1/4 smallest spoon

Grease and caress a round cake tin. Put the butter, sugar, fruit and water into a saucepan, bring it slowly to the boil and simmer for the time it takes for the fruit to moisten and fatten into succulent juicy pieces. Set the pan aside to cool as you consider the process of drying, reversed.*

Think of creases and wrinkles being eradicated by liquid, pulsing fresh, puffing up and out. Consider the notion of steam clustering into drops of water; follow this thought and imagine drips leaping back into a tap, the pipes swallowing the water, and the water from pipes flowing backwards into an eventual reservoir. Imagine, if you need a particularly moist cake, the water in the reservoir raining itself back up into a cloud, swelling it to capacity. And further above, imagine stars and planets floating in oceans.

Setting these thoughts aside, sift the flour and spice into a mixing bowl.

Walk the kitchen in a circle. Repeat as often as is necessary. At the moment you catch the scent of ripe fruit, mix in the fruit mixture, the egg and salt till thick. Put the mixture into the cake tin and bake until a skewer inserted and slowly twisted comes out clean. Turn the cake out in a smooth rolling motion.

* The intention for this cake should involve moistening and softening. The spices used should therefore originate from plants which have once had succulent fruits or berries of their own. If considering any of the nightshades, such as paprika or cayenne, keep the amount used minimal and your thoughts focussed towards the moisture in berries or fruits, unless you wish to involve an additional intention relating to poisoning (though the recipe for Nightshade Pikelets is by far the strongest, in terms of fatal effect).

As I circle the kitchen, the shadow appears again in the cold corner. I ignore it, silence and respect for the recipe contained in my mouth. I'm focussed, awaiting the scent of ripe fruit.

Another circle, and the shadow is more solid. The smell of flowers.

Another circle. Scent of sharp young fruits, unripe, green.

Another circle. I glance at the shadow. It's thickened.

Another circle. The smell of unripe grapes.

Another circle. Green plums. Bitter-sweet.

Another circle, and the shadow walks beside me, a mute companion. I breathe deeply, feeling a sense of continuity with the shadow, with the scents of the fruits which are riper, ripening, and finally . . . the smells of ripe grapes, apricots and plums fill the kitchen with summer.

Gripping the bowl and a bone spoon I can taste the fruits on my lips as I stir in the fruit mixture, egg and salt.

I whisper to the shadow at my side, 'Is it you? Did you write this recipe?'

At the sound of my voice, the shadow thins and disperses to nothing as the mixture thickens.

Medic's cream suitcase contains all kinds of toys to play with. After we've eaten some of the fruit cake, he examines and names all the parts of my body I can't see, using perfectly pronounced medical vocabulary.

He tells me, 'Your clitoris extends deeper into your body than you know.'

I tell him, 'I should know that, not you.'

'Ah,' he strokes my thigh, 'but medical diagrams of the clitoris have been falsified; the bud on the outside is a tiny nub of a much greater, larger organ, in the shape of a curve, which extends deep inside you.'

'So is my organ of pleasure larger than yours?'

He doesn't answer this question.

I don't understand how a man could know this, as I'm sure many women don't. But before I say anything more, he's tipped me onto my back and has his eye to a metal telescope with a bright bulb shining between my legs.

Examining me for a good half-hour or so, he whispers words I can't understand. 'Posterior fornix, anterior and lateral fornices, the columns . . .'

Fondling one of my nipples with his outstretched left forefinger and thumb, he murmurs something about moisture or mucous membranes. I'm beginning to feel boredom and a straining desire for movement.

He says, 'This is something you'll never see. A deep red beauty in the contours inside you.'

I yawn, loudly.

He says, 'Oh. You've spat it out.'

I look down. The telescope has been evicted onto the sheet.

He plugs his stethoscope into his ears, and listens to the pulse of my clitoris whilst moving three fingers in and out of me. I groan and pant with each twist. I shudder from my toenails to hair follicles, as he listens, before, during and after my orgasm.

He reaches a hand to my face. I nibble his finger as he plugs my ears into his stethoscope, and yanks it taut, straining down, pulling. 'You have to hear this particular pulse as well.'

But the stethoscope doesn't reach, as my landscape of breasts and stomach are in the way. He grins at me, his pupils so black they've eaten his irises. He rolls me over and tests the reflexes of my backside with the thud of his hammer and the slap of his palm. Both he and I learn that females can ejaculate.

'I am fascinated by this phenomenon,' he tells me, 'having heard about it, yet never encountered it first . . . hand.' He coughs.

He must have heard about the size of the clitoris, and of female ejaculation while studying at the medical university in Paradon, but I don't ask why he left. I don't want his past, I want him now.

But still, his past steals in while I'm lying in his arms.

He says, 'Once, I dreamed of being a gynaecologist, but men have long been banned from training. I never fitted in Paradon. Seen as a professional rebel though I did little to warrant it. If I hadn't left when I did, they'd have made me want to. I'm not sure I'd have landed if I'd let them push me.'

'Why would a man want to be a gynaecologist?'

'Not necessarily what people think. There are landscapes inside women which look like other planets. It's fascinating.'

I laugh. 'Do you see me as alien?'

'No, I see you as bewitching. The planet Mars is one

comparison, because of the rich colours. But through the reds, the surface of Mars is cold, it barely rises above freezing. On the other hand, the surface of Venus is hot enough to melt lead. But there's also Jupiter – browns, reds, whites . . .'

'What if I was more like Neptune, a cold deep blue . . . would you still—'

'Neptune has methane ice clouds.'

'Do they smell?'

His eyes are far away as he rests his cheek on my stomach. 'You're most like Jupiter inside. I wish I'd known you before, when I was—'

I put my finger over his lips to silence his past. 'Feel my pulse again.'

'You're not like anyone I've ever known. You're so open with your body.'

I smile. 'My legs.'

He frowns. 'Your body. Its moistures are my tutor.'

'Medic?'

'Gloria.'

'What do you see in me?'

'I see your body and –' he runs his thumb over my lower lip '– it is glorious.'

Sometimes, I'm distracted by knowing that he's learning from my body. But my body wants him, so I try to ignore the thought that he's gathering information in order to complete the education he wasn't permitted. And I worry, a little, that he knows it better than I do, for he sees what I can't. But I reconcile myself with the fact that while he may be intimate with my body in an anatomical sense, I'm the one who knows how it feels.

He still keeps to his own expectations of a waking day and sleeping night, even if his waking and sleeping hours both take place in my bed. Tonight he looks slightly worried. He sits up in bed, runs his fingers through his tangled curls. 'What time is it?'

'I don't know.'

'I was trained to know the delicate balance of biorhythms.'

'Well sleep, then,' I say, and he does.

I keep to my own routine. I look over my shoulder at his suitcase full of toys which lies on the floor next to the wardrobe. I'll get out of bed again after one last stroke of his earlobe. I'll release myself and cook enough food to last us through tomorrow. We need to be strong for his experiments and my pleasures, not weak from hunger.

And when I've baked a roast or a meat pie, and made our own puddings, I'll bake the honey cakes for the doorstep.

Medic loves eating puddings and cakes; he says it makes him feel irresponsible. When he finally wakes he will come to me in the kitchen, after the dawn has risen and the morning will be hidden behind the curtains. I'll already have brought in the ingredients, and we'll feast on our own batch of honey cakes; these I'll make with red spice. With the taste of chilli on our lips, we'll go back to bed and I'll knead, fold and beat him as he chants, 'Gloria, my Gloria,' over and over again, singing my new name, the name of my body, into some kind of hymn.

MAYA

Above me the night has shifted into a dark grey sky which hurls sleet at me with sounds of yowling seagulls. Wind-shrieks gust the sleet into rain.

I'm back outside the cottage with Amber inside.

The wind tries to blow me thud-down and swirl-up and it pushes my eyes into blur-blinks till I'm at the front door. I buckle under the wind's meanness. On the doorstep, the honey cakes are covered with weighted plastic to keep them safe.

I knock.

The wind gusts the sound away.

I knock again.

There's no answer.

At the kitchen window, the curtains are closed. The light, off.

The wind blasts me round the side into the garden. I'm blown to the shed.

I lean my head against the wet door. Rain soaks me to it.

I whisper, 'Dead Red, whatever happened when we met, I can't find the lost moment. I'll try to find it. I don't know how. Amber might help me. I'm sorry. It's too late for that to help you.'

There's a tangle of drenched ivy growing up the bottom of

the shed door. I think about Dead Red lying alone and howl along with the wind as tears make my face soaked, or it might be the rain.

The wind has blown itself inside-out and is gone. The rain still cries from the sky. Side door is locked. Bedroom curtain's a crack open. It's caught on a vase that Amber's filled with small kitchen knives.

Kitchen knives like cut flowers in the bedroom. For the first time, I wonder who Amber might be, unjumbled as she is, without me.

Looking through the window, the bedside lamp lights up the bed. I raise my hand to knock on glass. Mysister Amber's in bed, sitting up on cushions, her back to the window. Naked. Rocking. I drop my hand and the rain on the window blurs the cushions she's sitting on. They move. Not cushions: legs.

Rain rolls down glass.

How is mysister sitting up, rocking with her back to me, and her legs stretching behind her?

She bows her head forward and her hands are headboard clasping. She throws her head back, and her dark hair longs itself down her pale broad back.

Another pair of arms
tied at the wrists with torn rags
each headboard end
man muscular arms
mysister Amber's rocking
with rain blurring her
on top of a man in our bed.
I back away from the window
my drench cheeks alight.

I tell myself *no jumbling* and crash around the corner to the front of the cottage and stop.

A boy is crouched outside the gate, looking anxiously at the cottage.

He sees me.

The boy is a ginger-haired, thin, frecklenose. He beckons me follow, follow. He looks me up-down and says in quiet speak, 'Neither of us should be here. No one's seen you?'

My throat is too tight so I shrug-shoulder him.

'You'd know if they had. Come with?' He turns and walks down the hill towards the village. I look back at the cottage with no room for me because mysister is full of man-want.

The scrawny boy waits, taps fingers to lips.

I walk downhill towards him.

His child voice says, 'Can you not howl, or would you bark?'

My throat is dust dry. Don't know if I can speak unjumbled. Don't think I want to.

The boy eyes me again. 'You've not slept well either.'

I shake head and shuffle feet. Try not to eye him back. A child's imaginings could have all kinds of monster wants.

I watch his black shoes.

He holds a foot out. 'You like these, do you? Your paws are too big for them. You've got knackered eyes – want a bed?'

I swallow-words and bitelip myself.

He smiles. 'Right. You can pilfer Lizzie's for me. Not sure I'm up to it after all.'

As I follow him into the village, the rain stops. We move through narrow lanes with houses street-light lit under a dark grey dawn. Waves are roarish as seagulls war-screech above.

On a doorstep are a carton of milk and a bottle of rum. White or brown. I reach for the brown and the street lights go out.

The boy steps in my way. 'Not for you. It's for fair. Mam Vann's round this way soon. Need to get you indoors. Best no one sees me letting you pilfer Lizzie's house. I'd miss my folks if I had to pilfer it by myself all the time. Get scared over all kinds of things I do.' He lowers his voice. 'Need Mum to calm me down. She calmed me good the other night, said my imaginations are too big and wide. Like a great black hat that slips down over my head and makes me hear all kinds of things that aren't really there. That's what Mum said.' He whispers, 'I'd not have been near her cottage that night if it wasn't for Lizzie.'

I try to ask who Lizzie is, but I've got a croak voice.

'Growl something, did you?' As we walk along, he watches my mouth.

I shake my head.

'Good you're not loud. No one else will know you're here. Didn't sleep so well again last night. Kept having bad dreams that there were haunted groans hidden in tree trunks. Mum always says, *After bad dreams everything looks ordinary in the mornings*, so I wanted to check if *sounds* are more ordinary in the morning too. And Mum's right. Didn't hear anything but the wind.' He shivers. 'Listen, though. I'm giving you Lizzie's house. But I'll come round when I want to get out of mine, and I'll see you're not short of food. Deal. All right?'

We walk up a street past doorsteps with jars and bags and bottles. The windows all have closed curtains. The street is so narrow, the houses feel like a crowd.

He says, 'We've pilfered it together. It's ours, only you get to be there for all the time. You've got my best interests. You're my pet grizzly bear. You know, I've always wanted a grizzly. Can you snuffle?'

I sneeze and look at my hands, which have gone brown.

He laughs, looks over his shoulder, says, 'Quick, come with.' He walks faster.

I've got prickle spine: a thin layer of fur rises on my back.

At the end of the street, he hurries me along another row of houses, stops at one, looks both ways, leads me round the back and in through a door. He lock-clicks it shut behind us.

Though I want to drop onto all fours, I don't. Being a bear won't be the worst thing as long as I'm not a bearkind that would ripchild.

He says, 'Bears shouldn't be in cages. But a house might be all right. Bars would make anything fierce. Ever seen a picture of a zoo? There's one in a book at the school. Pictures of grizzlies, all teeth and claws.' He growls, his hands in monster shapes. 'Have you got a whole family of grizzlies where you're from?'

I eye his monster fingers and hope he'll bearwant me without any fierceness.

He says, 'There's water in the taps. I'll run you a sink full.'

I follow him into the kitchen.

'Do grizzlies really drink rum?' He raises his eyebrows.

He looks full of curiosity.

Behind curiosity, he's excited.

Behind excitement, he wants a secret of his own to keep.

A good one, not a bad one; that's very important to him.

Behind a secret of his own, he's worrying about things that feel too big.

Behind his worry, he feels torn.

He feels too small to be torn so he's fighting hard against it.

I have the instinct to hold him, but he doesn't have the want for it yet.

He steps outside. 'If Lizzie comes back, don't let her in, not even if she begs. She's got thick blonde hair and she's really pretty. Don't believe her if she says she's nice. She's bloody not. Growl at her that it's mine now. Ours. The name's Adam.'

Maya

With Adam gone, my limbs lose their fur and strength as I drop on the floor. Slowly, I crawl till I find a room with a bed. One last heave, and I slump onto the mattress.

I dream about being what other people want me to be.

In my dream I'm a bear in a cave. Outside the cave mouth, sunburned leaves fall from trees.

Amber walks in dressed in a party outfit made from flamingo feathers and scratchy silver sequins. She's got a crown made from kitchen knives and there's a black veil trailing down her back.

I charge forward to hug her, growling *mysister*.

My hands have sharp claws.

She backs away, pink cheeks and red lips. She shakes her head with no expression. I growl at her no-move face. She leans backwards and outstretches her arms. She falls off the edge of the cave down a steep drop through falling orange leaves. She shrinks into a flickering pink dot.

I crawl into cave depth and trample-crack a pile of twigs. I settle and the cave is lost to deep black: thick hibernating eyelids of a tired bear.

I wake in this quiet house with thoughts tumbleweeding my head. So I hunt what's real:

toothbrush on a sink

battered sofa

shelf of nature books

coffee table

stained oblong shape on the wall

dented nail

pencil-drawn man and woman swinging a pale pencil-hair girl

dead rose flower.

And the house feelings are wailing:

Someone else lived here and breathed here and she's not here!
The house wailings pull the doorways to narrow, the walls shrink in and in. This house look-hears or feel-smells or touch-tastes me,
and finds: *the wrong person.*
Adam said her name was Lizzie. At this thought, the house air changes, lightens, unthickens. It sighs, *Lizzie, Lizzie, come home.*

With the sounds of upholstery splitting, it creaks architecture and banisters at me. In the kitchen, the light bulb pops.

This house wants her, so my hair is lightening to frizzy blonde and my face tightens and behind this pretty face I think of what Adam told me about Lizzie and feel not-nice all the way through.

Don't like the feeling of not-nice.

So I step outside into an empty street where flakes of snow melt on cobbles.

My hair changes back to deep brown. I look at my hands. I touch my face that's mysister's face.

Outside smells murky. Melted snow tastes of disappointment.
Breathe slower now, *stop jumbling.*

I walk along cobblestones into a narrower lane. Behind the windows are clean rooms with buried doorways.

These empty houses are ghost-homes. The next house I go in could haunt me with a wardrobe-poisoned nightdress, an oven-leak of exorcism, a piano stool that's grown sharp teeth and spike-bummed a child with a wrinkled face. And this bitten grotesque will clink discord tune-style, as he promises alivestars and delivers mildew.

KIP

The Quiet Woman's dead FACE! turns into Mammy's face and I stop screaming but she's next to me on my bed, shaking me, calling, 'Brack, his eyes aren't right – he can't see me!'

She looks more like Mammy and less like the face, though there's still one black blotch under her eye. I want to tell her I can see her but I've got to keep pretending not to hear. The blotch disappears but she looks so worried, I grab her and hang on.

Dad comes in, already dressed, and sits heavy on my bed. 'What's up with him now?'

Mammy leans away and puts her palm on my head. 'He wasn't here. Eyes wide open but he couldn't see – maybe his skull's cracked after all; the doctor could have got it wrong. He said all sorts – blocked ears, inner concussion, cracked skull – I don't think he knew which. Perhaps he's not a very good doctor – look, you feel.'

Dad puts his hand on my head too. 'Not hot. He'll be right.'

'Doctor said to watch for a fever but I don't know – Kip coming back in the middle of the night, crying – and he's not been outside for two days. And now waking up screaming – what if there's something wrong . . .' She turns away from me to face Dad '. . . brain wise.'

'Shouldn't have been out in the cold when he's still sick, is all. Let him sleep. That's his medicine.'

'Call the doctor – his number's by the sink. He said to, if there was any change.'

Dad points at me, says, 'You all right?' and makes an all-right sign at me, pinching his thumb and forefinger together.

I make an all-right sign back at him.

'See.' He says, 'Let him sleep. Why did you let him out that night?'

'I never let him! Sneaked out, didn't he.'

He grins. 'Well, if he's sneaking, he's fine.'

'Oh Brack. I'll get the cakes indoors. You'll not have.'

'I have as well. Why'd you put the cream out for fair? I got that for us.'

'Not while Kip's sick. Nothing too rich.' Mammy strokes my head.

This is a bad lying thing, pretending not to hear when they're so worried about me. It's so bad it makes my belly ache like it's got green pulp in it.

Under the table I hold my honey cake in the palm of my hand. Risen and golden. It smells of honey, ginger, and something sharp. It looks perfect. And it makes me want to sick. I break up the cake, and feed it to Dagger, piece by piece. I point at the crumbs and make sure he licks up every single one.

Mammy's on the floor under the table with me, her eyes angry; she's waving the notepad at me. She's written: *You KNOW that's WRONG!*

I grab the notebook, tear out the page and crumple it. Feeling slumped, I watch Dagger licking his paws.

She says, 'What's got into you?'

Dad says, 'He can't bloody hear you, Dorcas. Let him alone.'

He's sticking up for me and that's usually Mammy's job. He must think sneaking out and not doing what I'm meant to is boyish.

Mammy goes away from under the table. 'What if he's going to have a fit again, and all this is his brain getting clouded and building a storm inside, ready to flip over—'

Dad snaps, 'He just doesn't want to go back to the school, is all!'

'Well, he had the fits when he first started there – didn't cope at all. I don't like him mixing with too many other children; what if they caused it somehow?'

'Kids don't cause fits!'

'Well, I wasn't there, so I've only got things to guess at.'

'Well, stop guessing! He's not had fits for years, Dorcas. Let it drop! Let him mix with the others more, it's good for him. He needs to spend more time with the boys.'

'But he doesn't like the other boys!'

Dad says in his angry-quiet voice, 'Because they bully him for wearing those sodding dresses you make him. It's your fault for wanting a daughter more than a son and that's what he's trying to be.'

She yells, 'I've never wanted Kip to be anything other than who he is!'

I curl up with my arms wrapped around my head.

After Dad's phoned the doctor, he tells Mammy, 'Doctor's wife said he's not there. Not been there for five days. Says he's done this before and come back, but all the same, she was fizzing angry. Gone AWOL, she called it. Took the car, she said. So she's stuck. Not sure he even knows his own phone number, she said.'

'George said something about a grey car, parked up the hill. That's the doctor's, isn't it?'

'What was George off doing?'

'Having a look at one of the cows being down. And I'll bet he never helped it up again.'

Dad says, 'He will have done.'

'So today, we can't agree over anything.'

They both go quiet.

I want to shout and yell and scream because none of the things they're talking about seem important. If the doctor comes, he'll look in my ears and see I can hear. And I'll have to go back to doing my turn at the fair.

Through the window I can see the empty beach. There's a long stretch of wet sand.

Mammy's got her back to me. She's on the phone talking to the doctor's wife about the grey car and she tells her where it is. She says, 'Not seen him of late, but if he does get home soon, get him to drive straight back and check on Kip again. You're a jewel. I'll ask around, and if I hear anything, I'll call you straight off. Thanks, pet, thanks so much. Sorry, but I'm so worried about Kip.'

Feeling jammed full of things I can't say, I slip on my coat and wellies, creep outside and close the door quietly behind me.

It's strange, the way people's faces change when they look at what I've written in huge words across the sand. I'm standing on the best rock, leaning on the driftwood stick I carved the letters with, watching people gathering to stare.

Three of the older boys are up on the concrete ledge. One of them is greasy Pike – last summer he used honey to make a wasp trap in my shoes. I had stings on my big toes. Caddy's there on the ledge too, her mum holding one hand and Maeve holding the other. Jessie comes and joins them. They're all staring at the sand.

Caddy says something to her mum and pulls at her hand like she wants to come down the beach to me, but her mum yanks her back.

Mam Vann comes limping along from the school; she's come out looking for some children to teach at. She sees the group of people, calls something as she goes towards them. None of them look at her. She follows their eyes, reads the words in the sand, and her mouth gets stuck in a straight line.

More and more people join them, not just the ones that are going to the school, but the ones who've seen the beach from their windows.

The wind moans around the rocks.

Mammy and Dad come out of our cottage to see what's happening. Dagger shoots down the beach and runs across the letters but they're so big and clear they don't smudge:

THE QUIET WOMAN IS MISSING TOO

It's dark under the table and I've barricaded myself in with a cardboard box, a stack of bumpy cushions and an old green curtain so I can't see all the people who've come into our cottage. Dagger's out there with the voices because the front door is open and there are rowing grown-ups indoors and outdoors and they're all full of smells to have a go on. To me, they all smell a little bit like chilli and I think that's what was in the honey cakes this morning. They're spiking around the place with angry red voices. I peek out at Dagger, and he's got the spikiness from the cake I fed him as well. He's trying to snap at everyone's legs.

I wish I really couldn't hear.

Everyone's cross with me for telling them loudly without

saying a word. Some of them didn't believe me and called me a wolf crier. Mam Vann went to the Quiet Woman's house. She had a quick look, and came back here fast. Now she's said the Quiet Woman's really gone, they all believe me.

While they're in here talking so loud and thinking I can't hear them, they say some rough stuff.

I hear that:

Mammy thinks I'm very sick and too sensitive to be asked any questions.

Mam Vann thinks I'm full of myself and shouldn't get any attention, even if I tell everyone something they all should have noticed sooner.

Dad thinks I'm rebelling and finally turning normal.

Jessie thinks I'm a little teapot, whatever that means.

And a couple of muttering voices are near where I'm hiding and they're saying Mammy and Dad are wrong for letting me wear dresses. They whisper back and forth that:

'I wouldn't let any child of mine do that.'

'Well, you've got girls and they can wear whatever they want.'

'He'll make the other children turn wrong when he gets hormones.'

'Can we get him kept away from the school when that happens?'

And I want to yell, *I don't know what a hormone is but can I have one now!*

Dad's voice shouts, 'Can everyone stop harping on about Kip, and work out why these two women are missing?'

There's voices coming from everywhere but I can hear Mam Vann best because she's got her teacher voice on. 'If the Quiet Woman asks to have a life all for herself, what does she expect? None of us know where she might have gone—'

Mammy's voice interrupts. 'Is this how you teach them in the school, talking loudly at them?'

I want to tell Mammy yes, that's exactly how she teaches us, by talking at us and reading at us and singing at us and knitting at us and cooking at us and collecting things at us and doing woodwork at us, and ignoring the things that are going on between me and the other boys, but I'm trying really hard to remember I'm not meant to hear.

Mam Vann says, 'We're not responsible if something happens to her. She is.'

A louder voice moves closer – it could be Jessie's but I can't hear clearly above all the others. 'We're responsible for Lizzie, though; now has anyone . . .' The voice moves away.

Mam Vann sounds sure she's meant to be listened to. 'That's right. Now we know there's someone else missing, Lizzie being gone isn't as simple as we thought.'

Another voice says, 'Well, everyone was on about Lizzie having gone to her sister's!'

All the voices mix together and I pick out the nearest ones:

'But does any one person remember her saying that?'

'Did they talk?'

'Did who talk?'

'Lizzie and the Quiet Woman – did they ever talk together? I mean, they live right next door to each other, they could have done, and none of us known . . .'

'But what's to say there's anything to connect the two, other than they're missing?'

'Let's do a thorough search of the Quiet Woman's house – Kip's made a drama of it, but if she's upped and left, we could be fretting over nothing.'

If they read her diary and the lollipop sticks in her violets, they'll know she wanted to go to Old Kelp's.

Dad's voice calls, 'Come out, Kip!'

I don't move.

He pulls a cushion away and drags me out from under the table.

Faces glare at me.

Dad hands me the notepad where he's written in fast jagged writing: *Let's get this straight. Quiet Woman stopped leaving out her fair at exactly the same time as Lizzie, yes?*

He's gripping too hard on my arm. I nod. He lets go of me and goes storming outside and I can hear him shouting to the others, 'Right, we need to get a proper look at her house. And we could do with the Quiet Woman's real name. Anyone got it? We need a name to call!'

Uncle Finn's got his back against a wall and his cheeks are a bit purple. He slips out of the front door after Dad.

As soon as he's gone, the people nearest the door say:

'Now he's got nothing to say for himself. Funny that, don't you reckon?'

'More to the point, why's Pippa not showing her face?'

'What if the Quiet—'

Jessie nudges Mammy, who turns around. Jessie says, 'Maybe the Quiet Woman was sick and needed the doctor? When Pippa set herself to smashing, Lizzie might have run only as far as the Quiet Woman's. And then if Lizzie found the Quiet Woman there, sick, she could have taken her to Fastleigh with her.'

Mammy says, 'Oh!' Her eyes are wide. She looks around the room.

Mam Vann says, 'How would Lizzie get a sick person to Fastleigh without wheels?'

Jessie says, 'Well, if she wasn't too sick, they could have walked it, would have taken them a while, but if she only had a bad elbow or something . . .'

Mammy calls, 'Brack! The doctor's missing too!' She squeezes between people to get to the door, calling for Dad.

Caddy comes in and goes crashing straight into Mam Vann. 'We should phone Lizzie's sister. Maybe they're both there.'

Jessie says, 'Good idea, pet, but no one's got the number.'

Caddy goes over to two boys in the corner who are picking up our telephone and pretending to talk into it. Caddy flicks one of the boy's ears hard with her finger and he grabs her hair and twists. Caddy's eyes water but she's growling, not crying. George pulls them apart and pushes them all outside.

Mammy comes back in and I don't think she's found Dad. She goes to the phone, lifts the receiver and frowns at it, not sure what she's doing. She puts it down again, and looks out of the window.

Next to me, Jessie elbows Mam Vann. 'You've been doing the fair since Kip's been sick, did you not notice the Quiet Woman wasn't leaving out her fair?'

'I never thought anything of it. When it was last my turn, she wasn't living here.'

'Well, you could have asked someone.'

Mam Vann's eyes flick at me, and back to Jessie. With her hands on her hips, she says to her, 'You asking for thunder, are you?'

As they argue about thunder, I swear there's a roll of it outside. I glance at the window.

Mam Vann looks at me again and her eyes narrow.

Quickly, I look away.

Jack wanders in, carrying his fiddle. Mammy's given up on looking for Dad and she's talking to a couple next to the fire-place. Everyone else is still arguing. Jack leans against the table. He plays a quiet tune as he glances around the room, but no one looks at him. The tune Jack's playing is called 'Singing Down the Stars'. Jack's long face is glum, though his fingers flit like they're dancing on the strings.

Nothing feels right; all these people not agreeing about what to do, because not one of them knows that the Quiet Woman, who no one knows, is dead. Her missing name is a hole inside my head.

There's this happy tune and Jack's glum face playing it; the tune should stop because the Quiet Woman has stopped. Happy tune, hole inside my head. People arguing, happy tune, sad face. Mirrors covered. Loud voices. She didn't want to speak. Butterflies pinned in a case. Happy tune. She's dead. I want to tell these loud voices that she's dead . . . They need to know, so all the noise stops. I want to shout it so loud they'll have to believe me—

As I think this, Mam Vann turns to me with glowering eyes, grips my shoulder and pulls me close.

She hisses in my ear, 'You can hear full well. I'll keep doing the fair, for it needs an adult at a time like this. But whatever happens, Kip, you'd best never speak of Old Kelp, never say what's got hold of you, made you go against doing your turn. Now she's taken care of me, kept me safe all these years when there's been no one else to do it.'

Her voice is a harsh whisper. 'Old Kelp's got the gales on her side and a whole lot of rage in her and you'd best believe it'll come storming for you. If she ever has a reason to look at this village hard enough, she'll find whatever she wants to find. Just know whatever you care for now, whatever you love the most, it'll be cursed clean away.'

The room blurs and clears, the tune goes off key and shifts back.

Pushing Mam Vann's hand off my shoulder, I elbow my way to Mammy, grip her hand and pull so she leans down.

My voice shakes as I whisper in her ear, 'What's Jack playing your favourite song for?'

She looks at me like she's eaten salt instead of sugar.

I clap my hand over my mouth.

She grabs my head and hisses in my ear, 'Can you bloody *hear*?'

I shake my head but she pushes me away and sags down on a chair.

Jack's sad face and happy fingers still play out the tune on his fiddle.

The voices talk and bicker and fill our cottage as Mammy stares at her shoes. Her eyes are dark as her lips move, whispering the words to the song:

'We're trying to keep singing
while the clouds are wringing.
Night nudges: tires the day
the sun smudges: drops away.
We all sang,
we sing
and we've sung, till the
stars fall down clattering
and dark clouds come flooding in.
We'll hum awake the moon
for we've sung down the stars.'

I say to Adam, 'Grown-ups should bloody sort themselves out,' and hurl another rock at the sea. The tide's come further in, and all that's left of my carved-in words is: *missing too*.

He follows me along the edge of the waves. 'Well, you've got us out of going to the school today, so we can do what we like. If they have to search for long, they'll use the school to private their meetings in. We might not have to go for a good few—'

'They won't go and look.'

'Look where?'

I glance up the hill towards Old Kelp's cottage. 'Nowhere.' After everyone left our house this morning, they searched the Quiet Woman's house properly first. I asked Dad about what was in her house, and he paled and said, *Nothing that showed anything of her past, or anyone who cares for her.* He wouldn't say anything else, so I think they know she wanted to go to Old Kelp's, but they'll not look for her there. They'll all hope she's somewhere else, but secretly they'll think she's been cursed.

I pick up three stones and hurl them as far out to sea as I can. They splash, not far enough. I pick up some more.

Adam says, 'Where's Dagger?'

'We've fallen out.'

'You've fell out with Dagger?'

I chuck another stone and it lands three waves into the sea. 'Well, everyone's fallen out with me, apart from you. Mammy isn't talking to me at all.'

'She'll talk soon enough.'

'She won't. She says I've gone back to my bad old lying ways and worse than ever. That's what she told Dad, and she knew I was listening. Caddy's fell out with me too, because she likes the school better than me. She said we'd all be there today if I'd told them about the Quiet Woman being missing sooner. Then she put her hands over her ears and sang la la la. Making out she's deaf or something.'

'Why fall out with Dagger?'

'I've got to be not talking to someone too. And Dagger's the one that finds me trouble. Well. His bloody nose does.'

Adam whispers, 'Old Kelp can't have known we were there, else we'd be cursed, but we're not. So there's no need to fall out with Dagger for it. We're all right, eh?'

I look up the hill again, and it feels as if the Old Kelps are watching me from her cottage. My legs want to kick with all the things I need to say, but all I can think of is Mam Vann saying: *Old Kelp's got the gales on her side and a whole lot of rage in her and you'd best believe it'll come storming for you . . .*

Adam walks beside me. 'Make it up with Dagger. You're brilliant for getting us out of going to the school. And it's got Dad out of the house at last. He says everyone's going on about him and Lizzie and Mum again. He thinks it's better if he shows off his innocence and all that. He's searching up the cliffs now, with George and a whole bunch of people. Not just looking for the Quiet Woman, but Lizzie and the doctor as well.' He scratches his nose and frowns. 'Do you think that's another tangle of three? Lizzie's getting busy if it is. Maybe they've all run off together?'

'He'd not leave his car here if he was running.'

'Might do, if he likes running more than driving. Maybe they've all gone to live in a cave together and don't need it. Or they could have stolen a boat.'

'They've already searched the boats.'

Adam says, 'You're as grouchy as Mum. She says she can't hack it. Anyway, cheer up. Part of your job.'

'What job?'

'Being someone's child. We're made to cause trouble. That's why grown-ups have us. We give them a whole bunch of stuff to talk about. Otherwise they'd get bored.'

'Right.' I kick at the sand.

'They'll not admit to it.'

'No.'

'It's the truth, though, eh.' He picks up a small flat stone, runs at the sea, and skims it. It bounces once, twice, three times. He turns to me and says, 'If I tell you a secret, will you plug your mouth?'

'Got to, if you say it's secret, don't I?'

'Look, if you don't want it, I won't give you it. You look bloody miserable. Thought you'd be pleased to have one?'

I kick harder at the sand and make a hole big enough for a rabbit to burrow in. 'You seen what's in George's attic or something?'

'No. Told you, he keeps the curtains shut. What's wrong with you?'

I stamp the sand rabbit burrow in. 'Can't sleep right.'

He hits his forehead with the heel of his hand. 'Ow. That'd do it. Smack yourself on the head. Put some gumption behind it.'

'What's gumption?'

'Initiative. Use a heavy bone.' He smacks his head again and staggers a bit. 'Yup. Do it hard enough, it'll send you stars and you'll sleep.'

I try it as well and stagger. 'Might do it, if I give it a few goes.'

'Let's go and get Caddy to make up with you. She'll want to know my secret, even if you don't.' He turns to walk up the beach.

My feet feel like they're stuck in mud. I say, 'Adam?'

He turns back to face me. 'You do want to know?'

'My brain's ache-full of secrets. I want to tell you something.'

'Go on.'

'Have you ever heard the Quiet Woman's real name?'

'No one knows it.'

'But your dad's much quieter than my dad, and your mum's really shy. I thought maybe they'd have tried to talk to her . . .'

'Quiet people don't have a quiet club where they all get together and don't talk, you know.'

We climb up onto the best rock. Adam sits down, rests his head on his knees and looks up at me, standing in front of him.

I say, 'Don't laugh. I mean it. Or I won't say it.'

He looks at the tears I'm blinking out of my eyes. 'Go on.'

'It's always the quiet ones and that's what everyone says, but I've been thinking about the quiet ones a lot.' I take a deep breath. 'There are all kinds of troubles people who are quiet ones could have going on, and just because they don't talk much, that doesn't mean the trouble's not there.'

He nods. 'That's true enough.'

'Loud people get heard all the time even if they're talking a whole bunch of nonsense. Sometimes they talk so loud because they think no one's listening. After a while they've been too loud, too long, and everyone they wanted to listen has stopped.' I fold my arms and look up at the sky. 'Maybe the quiet ones are quiet because they're waiting for gaps that never come.'

Adam frowns at me. 'Does it matter whose fault it is? Go on . . .'

I take a deep breath. 'What if the Quiet Woman came here and stayed because she'd had such a loud life that she didn't know who she was in all the noise? And she thought this place would be quiet.'

Adam nods. 'That could be right. Keep talking.'

'But what if she couldn't work out anything on her own, or not in the right way? What if she believed someone could help her that wouldn't, and she went somewhere no one will ever search, and died?'

Adam's eyes widen.

I say, 'What if the quiet ones keep having such quiet lives, and the loud ones keep having such loud lives, that no one but me ever works out what's really happened to her?'

He leans back, still gazing at me.

'Last bit. Don't say anything or I'll not get it all out.'

He bites his lip.

'So what if you found out the Quiet Woman was dead? And you've tried bloody hard to forget about it, but it's such a loud thing your head won't let you? And what if you want to tell someone but your Mammy's not talking to you, and your dad has only just started to like you again, and, with him, it's all about how boyish you are or aren't being—'

'Keep *on* it, Kip.'

'If you couldn't forget the horrible dead face you'd seen, what would you do?'

'Wow.' Adam blows out a gulp of air. 'That's a bloody loud kind of secret, Kip. So you've seen the Quiet Woman, and she's dead?'

'Yes.'

'Where?'

'I'll not say.'

There's a low grumble of thunder.

He nods. 'No wonder you can't sleep.'

'Right.'

'So what would I do?'

'That's what I want to know.'

'Kip, pick a grown-up to tell. A quiet one. At least they'll think about it.'

'Who, though?'

'Mum goes on and on about you being her favourite nephew, when you're her only one.'

'She's got enough on her head with your dad and Lizzie and everything that's being said about who's done what to who.'

He looks at me, his head to one side. 'You think like a quiet one, you know that?' He stands up. 'But your brain's booming too loud. Let's see if we can find Mum.'

248

AMBER

My hands are sugar-scrubbed and yeast-scented. I slide an orange and apricot fruit loaf into the oven and close the door with a creak. Outside, there's the sound of distant thunder. Picking up the salt cellar, I lean against the bedroom doorframe. Medic sits on the bed wrapped in black sheets, his wavy hair tangled. His eyes gleam me a smile and I'd like to find this romantic, but I know he's thinking, not feeling. And there is such a difference.

He's grown stubble in the five nights and days he's been here. Our bodies are so different, so of course, our minds must be as well. I know what he's thinking now, though, by looking at his raised eyebrow and the way his eyes are looking at mine. He's considering the diameter of my pupils, so he can estimate how aroused my body is, by doing some calculation according to a concealed formula in his mind.

'Does Gloria love me?' he asks, his voice an ache.

'Gloria wants you,' I say with a smile. 'I've got time and sugar on my hands. Salt in this cellar. Now, why is it called a cellar? It's not deep, underground, dark. More like a tower of some kind.' I run my finger from the salt hole to the base. 'Now, what are you going to do with me for nearly an hour?'

'I could . . .' His eyes take in my full breasts, my hips, my knee slightly bent beneath the black nightdress he tore the bottom half off yesterday so he could watch my legs. 'I could measure you.'

'Measure my what?' I sway against the doorframe.

'Pass me my magnifying glass,' he says. 'You know, I wish I'd always known you. Met you before. If we'd met in Paradon, would we have loved one another?'

'I wouldn't even have looked at you. Nor you at me.'

'I would have—'

'No, you wouldn't. Let me measure that glint in your eye. I'd like to make a comparison of my own. How many grains of sugar does that particular glint compare to? Or perhaps this would be better . . .' I hold up the salt cellar. 'A comparison of glints in eyes, measured not in size, volume or width, but in grains of salt.'

He gazes at my breasts. 'Come here. Who were you, before now . . . Who touched you, before me?'

'Stop it.' I flick my hair off my shoulders.

'How can I deeply love—'

'I don't want deep love.'

He smiles a little sadly and looks back at my eyes. 'What if I love you despite what you want?'

'I could use sugar. So. Sugar or salt? Sweet or . . . stingy?'

He licks his dry lips. 'Stingy, oh Gloria. I really wish . . .'

'That glint of yours has expanded. Salt in your eye.' I walk to the bed and pick up the magnifying glass from the bedside table. 'Let's get a closer look at you.'

I straddle him and measure how the glint in his eye grows to the dimensions of approximately seventeen grains of salt, as he realises I'm not wearing any knickers.

*　　*　　*

When I get the orange and apricot loaf out of the oven, I can still hear the whisper of Medic's voice, that phrase of his: *Gloria, love me.* So repetitive it's sunk itself into my ear canal as a trapped echo.

love me . . .

I stand in the bedroom doorway. Rain taps itself into silence on the window as daylight shines through the dark curtains. Medic sleeps. I've exhausted his body. There's a whisper of words on those lips; some dream dances on that tongue which can make my body sing and shudder.

Crossing the room, I sit on the bed and touch his cheek. He rolls towards me, extends a hand, a whole arm. I stroke the hairs on his forearm and wonder that his skin is so different to mine, the hairs dark and thick: a whole other landscape.

I wonder if I could ever love him. I don't love him now. I've never been in love with anyone.

And that thought is a twist in my stomach. The face of a boy I thought I loved when I lived in Paradon flashes through my mind. And the words he spoke about me when he'd got what he wanted. I throw a black shawl around my body as outside the birds chatter away the rain and cry up the wind.

In thinking I should ever feel love, in thinking I might want to, I could be chasing some ghost.

This thought isn't comfortable. So I go back into the kitchen, which is.

I think about all the recipes I haven't yet tried and the abundance of spices and blends in jars on the shelves.

This is love. A task, a role, a pace.

I stroke the pages of the recipe book and decide that if I find myself wondering a little too often if it's important that I do or don't love Medic, I can easily distract myself.

When I'm baking, I'm in love with the heady scents of allspice, cloves, cinnamon, cardamom and ginger; intoxicated with vanilla, almond, walnut essences; it feels playful, flirting with paprika, cassia, black pepper, cocoa and chilli.

I've got rum and cream: these were new ingredients on the doorstep this morning. So, something rich. The recipe I choose is:

RUM TRUFFLES

Butter, 1 oz
Heavy cream, 6 fl oz
Rum, 2 smallest spoons
Chocolate, 5 oz
Crushed nuts, 1 oz
Sugar, 3 oz

Bring the butter and cream to the boil. Add rum and simmer till the colour of the cream darkens very slightly.

Add the chocolate and nuts, and melt. Watch the colours merging together. Add the sugar. Let the sugar dissolve at the bottom of the pan and just as you smell the tang of burning, plunge in a medium bone spoon and stir furiously. Imagine boats lost at sea in gales and whirlpools, abruptly bring the stirring to a

halt,

and let the mixture become still.

Line a baking sheet with paper and think of the paper as a sail. Spread the mixture flat so the surface resembles a still chocolate sea. As you cover it with tin foil, think of the moon shining across salt water. Leave it in a cold isolated place for a few hours, or overnight.

Cut the truffles into whatever shapes you consider appropriate.* Roll them in icing sugar or cocoa, and keep them inside a tin container until you can hear them either politely chatting to one another or singing sea shanties and siren songs. They are ready to be eaten.

* When considering the shaping of truffles, beware the rum. It is a bawdy beverage which can induce bawdy behaviour. If you wish to overtly encourage this in those who consume the truffles, you may wish to consider making them into the shapes of intimate body parts. If you prefer the bawdiness of the rum to be toned down rather than up, consider more neutral shapes such as squares, triangles or circles.

Medic is still asleep, despite the wind rattling the window. I consider waking him, because he often seems perturbed when he realises he's been asleep for too long in the daytime. My body is wearing his body out with how much it wants him. I wonder if the old woman who once lay in this bed loved her lover, or if it was want.

I think of the bone spoons, and how they make the flavours of anything I stir with them intense and vivid. And even for the sake of some kind of morality, some consideration of the ethics of using spoons made from human bones to cook puddings for myself and my lover to eat, I do think I'd rather not get full of stiff morals or limp ethics in order to sacrifice the flavours.

It could be wrong that this doesn't seem wrong. But cooking is instinctive. And after all, I didn't make the spoons myself. I look at the collection of blades in the cabinet on the wall and imagine actually using the blades on a dead human body in order to extract the bones and make spoons with them. Whichever of the old women it was, the one who called me here or the very first one, she must have truly loved cooking to have done that.

To keep someone's bones when they've died must be love as well. She must have adored her lover to have made the spoons from him. To keep him and cook with him, year after year. Cooking was her obsession. He must have been an obsession as well.

I would have found the internal organs difficult to deal with. She was committed. Too gloopy for me. I've always been slightly squeamish about the idea of the liver, in particular. Such a strange colour. But full of nutrients.

Apparently.

Looking at Medic's arm, it seems thicker, realer, more like a piece of meat than an arm. Fleshy. I take his hand, and explore his fingers with my tongue. He sighs in his sleep but doesn't stir. I suck at a fingertip. Salty.

His skin doesn't smell like cakes or puddings. I sniff my own hand: chocolate and rum. I smell his hand again, and imagine his diet before he met me. Medic has consumed foods which have caused all the cells in his body to react and repair themselves, to split, multiply, regenerate. He will have exercised, toned, flexed and regulated his body to achieve these muscular arms, and he will have consumed the diet he was taught to. He is a medical man, and will have learned from other medics. He will have lived on the perfect balance of vitamins and minerals, carbs and proteins: fish, eggs, white and red meat. And I've been feeding him just a little of those things, a few vegetables, in favour of spoiling him, filling him to bursting with puddings and cakes. All of those years before now, I don't know what he might have eaten, or who might have fed him.

This is why his skin doesn't smell of yeast and butter, flour, sugar or spice. All things nice.

This is not what he's made of.

As hail clatters against the windowpane, I sniff and sniff at his hand, work my way from his fingers into his palm, lick the salt from his wrist, rub my nose on the solid muscle which runs along the back of his arm, kiss it, turn my face, and feel the hairs on his arm rise against my cheek. He smells of fresh meat. Rare steak. I haven't eaten that for ages.

My stomach grumbles, feels hollow, empty. My teeth feel sharp.

So I take a bite, a small chunk of his forearm.

He shouts himself awake, pulls his arm away, and his thick warm blood trickles down my chin.

'Sorry.' I hide my mouth with my hand as I lick his blood from my bottom lip. I suck away the metal taste. 'Accident.'

MAYA

My breathing isn't slow or fast. I'm unjumbled: my eyes and nose and mouth and ears are letting me notice one thing at a time. It's late afternoon, and the sky outside is a gloom place. The sound of hail on these double-glass windowpanes seems blunt. I'm in an empty house and it's used to being neutral, so inside it I feel safe.

It has a sign shaped like a solid flag outside it that says:
Holiday Let

This safe house wants me to let a holiday happen in my head. So I think in straight lines with one-at-a-time thoughts, about what I've learned-up about weather:

Rain wants to be caught in puddles, bowls or lakes, and held. It's desperately lonely.

Snowflakes are made of minuscule teeth which want to eat sound. They can only survive in a crowd with other snowflakes.

Hail is aggressive and wants to slice through whatever it lands on, and feels self-destructive as it melts.

The sun is proud of being reliable and is easily irritated by the blinking of clouds. It also dislikes eyelids.

Fog wants to tumble extremely slowly. It dreams of swamps.

I still can't work out the wind, because it's so full of spite and has no sense of direction. I don't think I'll ever understand what it's for.

When I was alone and outside, the weather seemed impossible and overwhelming and demanding. I wished the sky would iron itself out, and fold up and away, into a sky-sized drawer.

But inside this neutral, unweathered house, the beige carpets are clean and free of fog. The only snowflakes are crushed in the freezer, and the ceilings have no clouds. The rooms smell of electricity, damp air, new carpets and pine air freshener. The surfaces of the empty cupboards, the light wooden sets of drawers, the kitchen counters are all shining. The oven is empty and inside, the shelves gleam silver.

The light bulbs are trapped in round lampshades that look like the sun. In the bathroom, the peach toilet roll is corner-tucked. There's rain in the toilet but only when it flushes. In the kitchen, there's a toaster with a reassuring safety sticker with a picture of a lightning flash that isn't real. The cupboard in the upstairs hall shouts a handwritten sign: CLEAN TOWELS! The white towels are fold-piled like tame clouds next to the water heater that ticks and doesn't work. The brown doormat has green words that sigh: *home sweet home*.

On the kitchen counter there's a roll of bin liners that don't quite fit with neutral because they're sinister-black. There are empty padded clothes hangers polite-bumping in the wardrobes. Inside the hallway cupboards with the doors shut, there are no stars in the dark. The only un-neutral thing is a bible. Its spine is unbroken and it crawls along a bedside shelf.

The small gold-framed prints are of fishing boats, fried-egg breakfasts on blue gingham tablecloths, and there's one of a hot-air balloon in a clear-blue sky.

This empty house isn't looking for someone who should be here. It wants me to slow my thoughts down enough to holiday through them. So because it doesn't want too much, it might try to be a home for me. It's a neutral house with neutral-coloured walls and neutral furniture and neutral carpets and neutral smells and neutral lampshades. This is a perfect, un-haunted, undemanding home.

Now I'm in neutral.

And because there's a *home sweet home* doormat which tells me what to want, I should do things to make this house feel like a sweet home that's mine.

Whatever mine means.

This is not a neutral thought.

But I have to start somewhere. It takes my hands ages to feel un-neutral enough to do what I want them to:

I take all the framed pictures down and stack them in the oven.

Put the bible with the snowflakes in the freezer.

The folded-cloud towels under one of the beds.

The toaster in the sink.

I blow up five bin liners like balloons and put them in the broom cupboard,

and the *home sweet home* mat . . .

I don't know what to do with the *home sweet home* mat. So I sit on the sofa in the living room with the mat and try to feel the bristles with my fingertips. Outside the window, the hail has stopped. The sky has less gloom and the light falls in a wide line across the beige carpet.

There are dust motes in the air. They move too fast to be neutral. They expand to become moths and grow still bigger. They change into silvery drowned maidens the size of my big toes. They swim all round the room, crashbashing into the walls and ceiling, till I whisper, 'Go away, get out of my sweet home,' and I blink the drowned maidens down to moths, and back into dust motes.

My un-neutral smell is creeping through the rooms.

So I find the bathroom again, but it's not where I remember it was. This empty house feels as if there's been no one living here for a long time. No one losing or finding things, no one to think about what belongs where. As I've been moving things around, this house seems to have rearranged its rooms and doors a little. Now I feel as if I'm having a holiday from what I expect to find.

While the bath's running, the water crashes at me that it wants bubbles. Now I'm in a safe house with no people, I'm noticing that everything seems to want something. So I look for something to make bubbles with. I can't find anything apart from a helpful bottle that's fallen out of a cupboard under the kitchen sink. Its label says: *Squeezable Lemon Fairy Liquid*. After seeing what the dust motes turned into, I don't want to imagine what bubbles from squeezable lemon fairies might become.

Back in the bathroom I apologise to the water about no bubbles and it trickles, subdued. The bath wants to be dry afterwards. The plughole's thirst wants to be un-stopped by the plug. I'm getting a bit jumbled, so I go and look for a towel.

I think I put the towels in a bed, and there are three bedrooms. Going in and out of doors that want to open and close, on the first floor I find two identical, twinned rooms, but there are no towels in the beds. Through another door there's a flight of stairs. The banisters smell of fresh varnish, and they lead me up up, and halfway up the stairs, there's a jagged feeling of *leave-me-alone*. I don't know if it's me that wants this, but it's not the banisters or stair-carpet. So I keep going up to the top, and into the third bedroom.

It's the smallest room, with a side table, a children's play-cage, white walls, wooden beams and a small bed. The duvet lies in bumps. I must have laid the towels under the duvet with the lumps and bumps shaped perfectly into the form of a sleeping woman.

I'm about to lift the duvet, and stop.

It *is* a sleeping woman; she's not the towels.

Her light hair is wet, clipped up. Her chest rises and falls.

She wants to stay asleep.

So I leave her alone.

There's a damp towel hanging over the bedpost. The bath wants the towel more than she does while she's asleep, so I take it. I tiptoe out of the bedroom without tripping over her brown shoes.

Downstairs, everything feels as if it wants to be left alone now, because the feelings of the sleeping woman are flooding through the house. I find the other towels under a bed in the room that I thought was the bathroom. I leave them alone. I go back to the ground floor, and think the front door is where the back door was. I leave them alone as well. Feeling a little bit jumbleconfused, I finally find the neutral living room where the un-neutral dust motes live. I lay the damp towel on the carpet where the light from the window has moved to. I sit on the sofa.

I stay still till nothing around me wants to be left alone any more.

I'm made of grey, beige, white, brown and cream.

There's a squeaking metal sound outside, and a call of, 'Binday! Binday!' in a cracked voice. The sky is dimming to evening.

At the window I hide and watch. A man cycles down the lane, a narrow trailer attached to his bike, piled high with sinister bin liners stuffed with rubbish. People have left them next to front doors. The man stops, heaves them onto the trailer, and cycles away. On a rooftop there's a grey and white seagull, pecking at something in the gutter.

I hear the creak of the staircase inside this house.

The sound of the forgotten bath stops.

A plug is pulled. Pipes drain.

Cold drips fall from the ceiling.

Footsteps on stairs.

A woman's voice says, 'Not. Happy.'

A door bumps and clicks.

The woman from the upstairs bedroom passes outside this window. She stops, glances up and down the street, and walks away.

All the reasons she might not be happy crash bam bam in my head.

As I turn away from the window and look at the towel drying on the floor, I don't feel neutral. It doesn't look like a towel any more; it's a white silence screen for projection. It's caught something of mine that isn't neutral.

It's showing me a picture of a piece of soft evidence.

Staring, frozen, I can't screaming-run away.

It's showing me a flickering picture of the crimson dress Dead Red died in.

I've made myself un-think the dress. But now it's here like a burned nightmare. It was my crimson dress and I took it with me when we left Paradon.

The night Dead Red died I must have spoken with her, bond-friended her, given her my dress. And she must have felt safe enough to take off her own clothes, and put it on.

But I can't have been safe.

Dead Red must have been beautiful because she wasn't just killed.

Her face was smashed in.

Was I made of wild-envy?

I snatch the towel back from the floor and it sags white, soft.

KIP

Aunty Pippa's finally come back home. She's taken her damp hair down from a clip, brushed it, and now she's plaiting it. Her perfume smells of oranges.

I look around the room. There's a typewriter and a rolled-up bathmat among the books on the shelves, and watercolour paintings of toadstools on the walls. There's a shelf full of bottles of her perfumes and jars with crushed leaves and petals in oil. I stroke the prickly fabric on the red chair I'm sitting on.

Aunty Pippa hasn't said anything since I told her I saw the Quiet Woman, dead.

I say to her, 'Are you all right?'

She nods. 'I just need to think about what you've said . . .'

Adam comes in from the kitchen with three glasses of milk on a small tray. He switches the light on with his elbow and squeezes between the oval coffee table and the sofa. He puts the tray down, sucks spilled milk from his thumb and says to his mum, 'It takes you a while to remember all that psychology stuff, doesn't it?'

She nods. 'It was a long time ago.'

Adam hands me a glass of milk, puts one on a coaster in front of his mum, sits down and drinks his.

Aunty Pippa says, 'Kip, are you hungry? It's nearly teatime.'

'No thanks.'

She reaches into her pocket and passes me a tissue.

I say, 'I'm not crying.'

Aunty Pippa waves a finger. 'No. I've got it. How you're thinking about death is what's hurting you.'

'It's not hurting me—'

'If she's really dead, it won't be hurting the Quiet Woman.' She leans back against the brown velvet sofa.

'But isn't being dead the worst kind of hurt there is?'

She sighs. 'Sorry, my techniques weren't ever properly tested. I've got an old textbook somewhere, but I'm not so great at finding things . . .' She glances around the room. 'I'm going to help you. But,' she leans forward, 'no taking your cousin anywhere you shouldn't, especially not at night. Never again?'

Adam's got up and he's rummaging in a bookcase with his back to me. I can see from his ears he's gone pink.

I say, 'I keep seeing her dead face over and over – it was all these horrible colours, like it had been hit or bashed or run over or—'

Aunty Pippa says, 'So you couldn't even see her face clearly?'

I shake my head.

'As if she was an inkblot. And you projected your own fears. I can tell you believe you've seen her, but we all think about things we're frightened of. It's how quickly we can put them out of our heads that matters. Resilience. Now, think about who she was.'

'I don't know who she was.'

'So you feel . . .' She raises her hands, palms up, and waits.

Adam leaves the room, closing the kitchen door behind him. I hear running taps, then silence. His shape behind the glass of the door disappears, and there's the sound of another door closing.

Aunty Pippa says again, 'So you feel . . .'

'Bad . . . I mean, guilty.'

She puts her hands on her knees, leans forward, and frowns at me. 'For not knowing her?'

'For not noticing she wasn't alive when I was doing the fair.'

'Did you notice her when she was alive?'

'Not really.'

'So why notice her now she's dead?'

'She isn't meant to be dead. She's not old. And she's not buried.'

'Was she old or buried when she was alive?'

'Of course not.'

'And she still isn't old or buried now.'

'But she's hidden—' I bite my lip so I don't say where I saw her.

'Was she hidden away when she was alive?'

'Yes. She hid herself in her home. From all of us.'

She clasps her hands together. 'So nothing's changed for her then, has it?'

'But she's dead!'

'Some people want to be dead. She might well have done. Melancholic, running away, holing herself up in a village where she knows no one, hiding . . .'

She reaches over the coffee table and puts her hand on my knee. 'What do we know about the Quiet Woman? Nothing really. And that was her choice. I asked her what her name was, your mum did as well, but she wouldn't speak. I'd really wanted to talk to her, because I thought she'd come here from Paradon, where I grew up. But she skulked her eyes to the floor, before slipping back to her solitude. I'd say she was pretty miserable alive.'

I drink the milk and curl up in the chair. 'I'm hungry.'

Aunty Pippa stands up. 'Ah, good! You're tired and have your appetite back. Close your eyes. How's it feeling now – that head of yours?'

As I close my eyes, Aunty Pippa puts her hands on my shoulders. They're warm and solid.

She asks, 'Can you see her?'

'I can't see her dead face, but . . .'

'She looks the same as when she was alive, doesn't she? Not old, not buried, and hidden. Just what you said.'

I open my eyes. 'She does look the same. How did you do that?'

She squeezes my shoulders. 'Verbal inkblots. Daubing the real over the imagined. It's a theory I tried to adapt for a particularly important essay but it didn't go down well at all. But anyway, Kip – *you* need to think of these words: *Not old, not buried, and hidden.* Try that every time you think of the Quiet Woman, for now, and you'll sleep better soon. It's quite usual for imaginative children to have nightmares when people who live near them go missing. Realities do merge sometimes. Mine are, all the time at the moment. Suspicion is like glitter: impossible to wash off, and glued on with a type of false guilt.' She stares at the floor.

'Why aren't you off searching with all the other grown-ups?'

'I'm not keen on herds. You know, the Quiet Woman may well turn up dead sooner or later. Possibly cliff-topped herself and she'll be washed up on the shore. Best to keep off the beach, Kip. I expect they'll check it at low tide.' She glances at the window. 'The light's gone, so they'll have to call off the search till tomorrow.' She pats my arm. 'Get yourself home, so you're back before your mum. She worries about you.'

'She's not talking to me.'

'She will, when she's ready.' As she sees me to the front door, on a small crowded table, between a tangle of wool and a folded umbrella, is a black glove that matches the one from Lizzie's doorstep. I pick it up.

She says sadly, 'Finn's stray glove. I can't find the other one. It's a bit lost on its own.'

MAYA

Neutral wants to be calm and make space for thoughts to spread out in colour. It doesn't know I don't want them. It's night outside and the twin mattresses in this room are covered in crackling plastic that won't sleep-sink me. I try another bedroom, where the mattresses have foam covering. Each time I shift there are lumps in the foam.

So I creep up the wooden stairs to the bedroom on the top floor with the smallest bed and lie where the sleeping woman lay. The smells on the pillow are oranges and shampoo hairsmells. If she was here too, I'd forget anything that's not about her. I'd even un-learn neutral.

Especially if she's still not happy. The pillow doesn't smell of happy.

Across from the bed, there's a blurred picture flickering on the blank white wall. So this is what happens when I'm on my own and neutral. My brain sends pictures out, not always what I want to see. They're just whatever's there. Projected onto blank screens like flat white towels or light walls.

The bright colours of the picture tighten and hum. My sister is in a twin bed across the room from me. Yellow bedspread. Gold lampshade. There's a curled tangerine peel on a plate by my bed. Our mother sits in a chair between us. She's wearing

267

yellow-red striped pyjamas and a pink dressing gown. I can't hear it, but I know her voice is a night bird. She's telling us a bedtime story of bears. I know I'm her good child and she wants all good children to go to sleep.

Now, this mattress feels not too crackle-loud or lump-quiet, but just right.

With a sharp talk-style, a female voice says, 'I'm getting my own back.' The neat-haired woman who was asleep in this bed is here looking down at me.

I sit up, blinking, from a crimson dream. She's switched on the bedroom light and I can tell from the window that it's still night outside.

She says, 'It's been niggling at me, are you staying here long?'

Still half in sleep, I ask, 'Is it your house?'

She looks at the door. 'It's owned by someone who's only ever seen an enhanced photograph, hired out by a Lets Agency. Paradon way. From there, aren't you?'

We scowl at each other.

She unscowls her face first. 'Ah. You're from Paradon, but *not* from the Lets Agency. You're not meant to be here either.' She sits on the bed.

I sniff her pale jumper for orange smell but it's been covered in lemon.

She wraps her arms tightly around her smells. 'You smell quite odd yourself, you know. Have you gone feral?' She shakes her head. 'This house is mine, as in borrowed in autumn and winter. It's not strictly allowed, but no one knows I come here.'

She wants me to go. She wants me to stay. I don't know which to do, so I claw at the duvet and say, 'Are you all right?'

'Not really, and neither are you; it's all in the eyes. You even look a little like me.' She looks at me closely. 'Actually, a lot.

268

But the thing is . . . the thing is . . . The get-out-of-this-house thing. Right now I really need privacy.' Her eyes anger-flash. 'Oh, maybe that's not what I need. I could really do with a chat, could you listen?'

My eyes give her anger-flash back to her. 'I can do anything you want.'

She leans away from me. 'Are you angry? You sound—'

'I'm not angry with you.'

She beams. 'Ooh. I'm not angry with you either!'

We smile light at each other.

She relaxes. 'So good to talk. Someone else who knows Paradon. Thing is, once here, I adapted to fit in, and married Finn – who'd always lived here. It was easier when attached. I was toned down and pleasant. But he'd liked my differences. Back then, he thought me exotic. I do have a frog tattoo on my bum, and tattoos are rare here. It's widened over the years and now it's more like a toad.' She laughs. 'Exotic fades. All these years, he must have seen me as a shrivelly quiet wife. That wasn't how I felt, but it must have been what he saw . . .'

I look at her closely to check if there's anything wrinkled or dusty or rotten about her, but there isn't. She's clear blue and jagged. Her sharpness is protecting her softness because it's bruised. So I tell her, 'You don't seem shrivelly at all.'

She smiles. 'That's so kind of you to say, thank you. Anyway. Him and another woman. Lovelier, fiery, lived here all her life, independent frizzy-haired Lizzie. With her lovely name that sounds like a swarm of lovely bees.'

'It does when you say it like that.'

'He's hankering for her. It's almost unbearable.' She looks at me closely. 'Now, how did *you* end up here?'

My bam crash thoughts about what to say don't let me say anything.

She says, 'All clammed up. I was like that as a teenager too. But I wanted someone to break in. The reason you're here in a completely empty house. Ah, got it. A presence that's upset you. You're seeking absence.'

Downstairs in the kitchen, she makes tea in a grey teapot. She talks about popping home for some milk, but doesn't. She puts three cubes of sugar in her mug and stirs.

I watch her and can see: she wants to talk more.

And behind that, she wants to be heard.

And behind that, she wants to remember who she used to be.

And behind that, she wants to belong.

And behind that, she wants someone vulnerable to care for.

And behind that, she wants someone to care.

She says, 'I'm starving,' as she rummages in the cupboards and finds a tin behind some mugs. She says, 'Digestion,' as she puts neutral biscuits on a plate. She puts a mug of tea on the table in front of me and sits down clutching hers.

I watch her break a biscuit in half and she says, 'My name's Pippa.'

'Maya. Why did you leave Paradon?'

'It was university that finished me off. Religion and Psychology. Mainly Psychology. I failed. With enormous debt, I felt endangered and unemployable. Paradon is still . . . functioning *well*, is it?' Her eyes widen.

'It's beautiful.'

'Oh dear. Over-empowered and still erupting. It'll melt down one day. And yes. It's always extremely beautiful.'

I look down at my body. She's seeing me as wearing a crochet jumper and skirt, made from grannysquares and motherlove. The colours clash.

Pippa looks out of the window where the sky is still thick

with night. She stares for a while, and says, quietly, 'Tomorrow will be the second day. Everyone apart from me will be searching for people who've gone missing. And I'm not searching for anyone at all, and I've found you. Sometimes life takes such turns.'

I nod without wisdom.

She says, 'You know life – when these turns twist into dark corners, there must be light somewhere.'

My heart floats. 'The neon lights of Paradon. The reflected sun and moon. This village feels so dark.'

'No.' She shakes her head. 'No, I thought that too, at first. But this village isn't dark; it's just not lit up. I'm holding out for a torch. And a torch isn't ever sunshine or moonlight, it isn't even neon. It's something much more . . .'

'Yes?' I wide-up my eyes to drink her torch-thoughts in.

She smiles at me. 'We all need to wake up. All of us, wherever we are, in rich bright cities or eroded villages – everyone who's ever truly alive is only looking for hope.'

There's a punch-ache in my gut and I don't know if it's mine or hers. I whisper, 'Sometimes what everyone's looking for makes the world feel impossible. I don't know anything about hope.'

Pippa says, slowly, 'That's really sad. There was this box in an ancient story, full of everything that could possibly go wrong. The box was emptied and everything did go wrong. The last thing left inside it was hope. And the hope didn't get emptied out. Didn't jump up or make itself known. Because hope needs to be kept inside something. It's quiet, some might say, shy.'

She pats her chest and looks at me. 'Oh, you look upset.'

I feel like something I should want for myself is cracking open. Breaking, not hatching. She wants me to speak, and I choke, 'Trying to want but I don't. Learning myself is breaking myself. You're easier than crimson thoughts. Your wanting is safer, bigger . . .' My eyes fill with tears. I look up at the ceiling and they disappear.

She laughs and her face fills with light. 'You're adorable. I might have to take you home with me.' Her smile dances warm colours through her voice. 'You're so like I was. I've always wanted a daughter.'

AMBER

The kitchen cupboards contain heaving supplies of jams, dried fruits, sugars, several varieties of flour. Looking through the recipe book with the shadow standing beside me, I try to decide what to make next. The shadow of a hand falls across a recipe as I turn the page. It's a recipe for Mincemeat Cake. Perhaps the simplest recipe in the whole book. The shadow hand points to the top of the page.

I reread the title:

MINCEMAN CAKE

Butter, 4 oz
Soft brown sugar, 4 oz
3 large eggs, beaten
Minceman, 12 oz
Flour, self-raising, 7 oz
Milk to mix

Cream together the butter and sugar till light and fluffy. Beat in the eggs little by little and add the minceman.

Fold in the flour, mix well, adding sufficient milk for a dropping consistency.

Put the mixture in a greased and lined cake tin and bake for a short time, lower the temperature of the oven and continue baking till the cake is firm and shrinking slightly.

When a skewer comes out clean, cool the cake, and turn it out onto a wire rack. Feed to the birds.

The hand fades away.

The shadow is a thickened dark figure in the cold corner, pacing up and down. In the six nights Medic's been here, it's become more and more solid. I've learned not to speak to it, as it often fades away when I do. It never leaves the kitchen. It appears when we're here together in silence.

I reread the recipe. This must be how the old woman disposed of her lover's body. The lover whose bones I'm now cooking with.

At the open bedroom door, the shadow and I stand side by side, watching Medic sleeping. As I glance at the shadow, the morning light filters through the kitchen curtain and it disappears.

Looking at Medic, I wonder which part of him would weigh twelve ounces. I get a chopping board and sneak round to his side of the bed. Gently, carefully, I move his left arm so it lies flat on the mattress. I place the chopping board under his limp, outstretched hand. I think of all the bones in the hand and realise that to get twelve ounces of actual meat, I might need a bit of his arm as well. I move the chopping board up, so the white flesh of his forearm lies exposed. I go to the cabinet, take out the meat cleaver, and creep back to the side of the bed.

As I raise the blade, he sits up quick as a whip and grips my wrist, his eyes cutting into mine.

I drop the cleaver, bang on the floor.

'Sorry.' I blush under the spark in his unblinking eyes.

I say sweetly, 'It's just you're so . . . delicious, I could eat you. I only wanted a little bit, not every bit. And you don't use your left hand much.'

I don't feel glorious because in the living room there are cracks in the walls and I've walked into the sewing box and now there are pins in the carpet. It smells damp, the fire isn't lit, and the light bulb is flickering. The thing which is making me feel the most inglorious of all is that Medic is standing naked next to the draughty window and he has goosebumps. His pasty skin looks like raw chicken.

I'm annoyed with myself that I can't stop staring at the criss-cross of sticking plaster he's put over my bite, but I'm much more annoyed with him, because he's attempting to lecture me.

'Couldn't you leave more of the puddings you bake outside, instead of eating so much—'

'You've been spying on me.'

'It's concern. You're obsessed with cooking and rarely sleep. It's unhealthy.'

'You know nothing about my health.'

He frowns. 'Oh, believe me, I do. If you insist on baking so many cakes and puddings, use more of the margarine instead of so much butter, so at least you'll get some vitamin D. Can we both have a complete break from sugar for a while?'

'Don't tell me what to cook.'

'We shouldn't row.'

I gasp. 'This can't be rowing. This is dull. Is this rowing?'

'Isn't it?'

I glare at him. 'This isn't what I wanted you for. I feel . . . examined.'

He steps around the pins on the carpet, stands behind me, puts his hands on my shoulders and breathes into my hair. 'But I care. If you're craving blood enough to actually bite me . . .'

'Care is so domestic.' I elbow him in the rib, break away from him and lean my arm on the mantelpiece. 'Go and find someone else to lay on your slab.'

He folds his arms. 'My slab?'

'You only see my body. And don't medics dissect bodies, examine them, aren't there body farms and labs where you lay corpses out in lines? Is that how you got such an intimate knowledge of female anatomy, dissection?'

He shakes his head. 'Love, I learned from books. Online journals. Case studies. Body farms are for forensics, not medics – and it's not like that. Not with us. This is—'

'What? This is what, exactly, precisely, medically? A temporary tremor of some lobe or another? A heart flutter requiring investigation? An overexcited gland, an agitated nerve? Don't call me, or this, love.'

'I could give you some tips about willpower?'

'My willpower is extremely powerful. It wills me not to change anything about it. Paranoia about weight is much more unhealthy than weight itself. And I thought you liked grabbing handfuls of me.'

'I do. But I've heard of people on restricted diets craving iron, and it stands to reason that if you're craving blood, or . . .' he swallows, '. . . flesh, something's seriously lacking. You shouldn't risk—'

'How dull.'

'Don't you worry? We've always been careful.'

'We?'

'What?'

'Who is this careful pair that isn't you and me?'

'Gloria, love me.' He opens his arms.

'Not playing.'

He looks at the floor. 'Slip of the tongue. I meant, we, as in . . . my craving for sweetness, and what my willpower allows my body to consume.'

'Liar. Don't split yourself into pieces to disguise your . . . wife? Or is it a man you live with?'

He picks at the sticking plaster on his arm. 'Wife. Are you jealous?'

'If I was, you wouldn't still be standing. Has she never bitten you?'

'Not to the point of drawing blood. Now, how would you want me,' he steps towards me, looking out from under lowered eyelids, his eyes glinting, 'if you happened to be jealous . . .'

I step towards him. 'I might want you laid out on a gurney, anaesthetised, your legs in stirrups. I'd be there, white-masked, a scalpel in my hand.'

'Would I lash out?'

'You might try. But you wouldn't be able to defend yourself.'

'Oh Gloria, love me. Ouch.' He's stepped on a pin.

He extracts the pin, puts his hand on my waist and pulls me towards him.

I say, 'Gloria wants you. And after I've had you, I might want your wife as well.'

'You wouldn't like her,' he murmurs, licking my neck.

'I might.' I let him lick. 'But I'd doubt she'd like me. Tell me the most exciting thing there is to know about her.'

'In Paradon, she collected cans of paraffin and wouldn't tell

me why. She insisted we brought them with us when we left.'
His eyes seem far away.

I ask, 'Paraffin's *very* illegal, isn't it?'

'Black market of course. But she always says, *Out here, no one is looking.*'

'Then you should thank her.'

'What for?' He nips my earlobe with his teeth.

'She's just made you much more interesting.'

Two hours later, Medic rushes naked into the bedroom as I'm brushing my hair. He grabs clothing from the floor, covers his pasty skin and rushes back out.

I follow him through to the kitchen to be met with the front door slamming.

Raising the curtain a little, I can see Medic outside on the path next to the wall, fighting with a woman. Well, she is fighting. He is being fought with.

She's dressed in grey and blue woollens. Her skin is dark, her eyes gleam brown, and her chestnut hair is a tumble of shining curls. And the way she looks at him, I can tell she believes he belongs to her. This is his wife.

He's squinting; his eyes are unused to daylight. The sky is white, and he's wearing one of my black nightdresses. The arms are too short and the skirt hem stops just below his knees.

She grabs it; she will tear it from him; she doesn't understand. He won't explain.

And watching them, I see past the ridiculous. This isn't want, this isn't two bodies, this is love.

She's a flame. She rushes at him, she retreats and then flares, he rushes at her and she burns. She grips his forearms and pushes him away, she clenches and unclenches herself, she tries to release him, she hates him, she loves him, I can see she is frightened, she needs him, she doesn't need him: this is what she must be saying. She wants him to tell her where he's been and who with and why for this long, but she doesn't want to hear the answers.

It's her face, not his, which shows the most expression. She uses her eyes. She opens them wide, cries from them, pleads with them, shouts through them. She uses her eyes in ways that crumple him, she knows how to do this; she knows him.

He glances at the cottage, he knows I'm watching.

She questions him with her lips and her hands, and he tells her answers she doesn't hear or believe. He touches her hair. Once, she lets him and again, she pushes him away, puts her hands to her mouth; he puts his hands on her shoulders, she lets him. She cries onto his chest. He pulls her close and kisses her head.

He looks over her head at this window, at me.

That is a look that says goodbye. That is a look that tells me this was inevitable. That is a look that says, 'I belong with this woman, crying into my chest. And you have to be sliced away. Dissection.'

I drop the curtain, find his car keys, the remnants of his clothes, his stethoscope and other medical implements and hurl them inside his cream suitcase. I throw it out of the front door into the grass.

I shout, 'Spineless!' as I slam the door and lock them away in this world which exists for him with her without me.

Taking my clothes off, I get into the empty bathtub. I put in the plug, turn on the spitting hot tap and lie back. A burning redness spreads up my body to each hair on my head and the tips of my fingers and I can hear one or other of them banging on the front door.

Scalding, sinking, I say, 'Go. Away. I don't care. Gloria wanted him. He wanted Gloria. Amber. My name is Amber, my name is Amber.'

As I towel myself dry, I can feel they've gone. He's gone. He's gone home; he's gone home with her. They will talk about *us* and *ours* and *we* and these are words I didn't want from him.

He doesn't even know my real name. So there will be nothing he can say about me, Amber. He can speak of Gloria as a body; how the body felt, what he discovered, uncovered, why he experimented, what the results of his experiments were, all the things which interested him. But Gloria's body is still my own body, whatever name I give it. Will he talk of my body with his wife, will she ask? I lean my head into my towelled hands and groan.

I whisper, 'Medic, say nothing, this body was never yours.'

Looking in the bathroom mirror I tell my body, 'Stop this ache; you need the rest of me, my brain to think, my mind to know, my heart to beat and beat and beat.'

Yet my body grieves the loss of touch. Nothing more. It's just a body. Not the part of me which could ever know love as well as want. That part is hidden away somewhere, buried so deeply I've forgotten where I put it. It doesn't want to be found. There were only boys, before him. Boys who spoke to others about what they'd done to my body, and if they were too drunk or high to remember, or I hadn't wanted them and shoved them away, they made up unpretty lies.

Whenever a spark of love crackled in me, I buried it somewhere in one of the veins near the back of my lungs. It may have stirred a little, moved along, got caught flickering in some artery. But wherever the spark lodged itself, I know the human body is a damp place, and its bloods are the dampest. They can easily extinguish unwanted flames.

When night comes, I bake a batch of honey cakes and use a jar labelled All or Nothing Spice. My intentions are confused; the air fills with scents of a whole variety of mismatched herbs. It's baking hot – the whole kitchen has become an oven and is baking me inside it. Even the cold corner is warm. Empty.

I say, 'So now you've finally got me alone again, you've gone.' Nothing flickers.

Feeling deserted, I look at the table of spices in the recipe book:

All or Nothing Spice: Shuffles thoughts to opposites: wrong/right, interested/asleep, soft/stabbed, low/soaring, flight/burial, etc.

I pick up the jar again. It's a speckled black and white mix. It smells of a whole array of combinations – ginger, curry, aniseed, mint, sage, camomile, clove and bergamot. I close one nostril and then the other with my thumb. My left nostril can smell it and my right nostril can't.

As soon as the cakes are ready I feel dislocated. My thoughts are of Medic. He didn't come near the cooker. Didn't look at the recipe book.

My hands pick up the bone spoons one by one. I stroke them and think about how these bones have never felt cold in my hands; there's always been a flicker of energy around them. My hands were made to touch them. These are the bones that I love. Not any living person's bones locked away inside the damps of a human body, buried too deep to touch.

Medic didn't even notice these spoons. He should have done, because he's a medic and because these bones demand me to touch them, cook with them, stroke them and clean them and love them and wonder at the flavours they bring out. Medic could have recognised them for what they are, if he'd just looked beyond what caught his interest. If he'd allowed himself to really see what drew me away from the bed each night.

Inside my veins, my blood feels too hot. So I open the front door and the heat from the kitchen blusters out into the freezing night like warm fog. The night sky changes from black to charcoal. The sun's drowned under the sea. The tightened clouds make the air tense. In the distance, seagulls scream.

We were bodies. Skin and flesh but nothing deeper.

We didn't love the bones of each other.

Neither of us could say that.

KIP

Mammy and Dad are still in bed as I get dressed and take Dagger outside, stepping over the packs of caster sugar and dried fruits left out for our fair. Dagger looks confused; he's got used to me sleeping in. The clouds are so thick it's more like night than nearly dawn.

As I do up my coat, Dagger looks at me with his head to one side. I say, 'Glad we've made up. Missed you. If you could lean on Mammy and make her talk to me again, that'd be a good thing.'

He jerks a silent bark at me and I rub the top of his head.

'Come on. Let's see if we can wake Adam.'

The downstairs curtains at Adam's house are closed. His bedroom window on the first floor has a mobile with planets and explosions hanging from the grey ceiling. I pick up some gravel from outside someone's house and throw a small stone at his window. And another, a fistful. They clatter on his window but no face appears.

Uncle Finn opens the door. He looks tired, and is wearing his old red dressing gown, not the multi-colour one Aunty Pippa knitted him last year. 'What is it?' He looks up and down the street.

'Is Adam in?'

'He'll be still asleep. Early, isn't it?'

'Sorry.'

'It's all right. You feeling better than you have been? Must do strange things to your head, not being able to hear so long.'

'I'm fine.'

'Good, good.' He steps away from the door. 'You wanting an early breakfast?' He looks down at the three jars of honey on the doorstep. 'I could do us some eggs before I have to get on?'

'It's all right. Just wanted to talk to Adam.'

'You get him out and about later. He could do with seeing things wider than these four.' He knocks on the wall beside the door.

'Sorry I woke you.'

'You didn't. Is Pippa round at your place?'

'No – she's not here?'

He sighs and says, 'She took off really early this morning. Said she'd be somewhere I'd not think to look for her . . .' He shakes his head. 'Coming in, then?'

'No. See you later.'

'If you see her on your travels, tell her I'm missing her. Tell her I said to come home.' He closes the door.

I look up at Adam's window, and don't really believe he'll have slept through a rattle of stones.

At Lizzie's house, there's a light on in the hallway but the door's locked. After about thirty knocks, Adam opens the door.

I follow Dagger as he shoots in, trailing his lead along the hallway. He disappears into one of the rooms. Adam closes the door and sits on the floor in the hallway.

I sit opposite him. We look at each other, neither one of us smiling.

I say, 'Well, we're both glum.'

He nods and ties and unties one of his shoelaces. 'I had a brilliant secret. But it's gone.'

'Thought you might be—'

'And Mum's gone strange. She went out late last night, and when she came back home in the middle of the night, she sat on my bed. Talked for ages, but I fell back to sleep. Kept waking up and there she was, talking quietly.'

'About the Quiet Woman, or Lizzie and your dad?'

'No. Mainly boxes. Torches. Boxes again.'

'Boxes?'

'I had cardboard dreams.'

We look at each other for a while and neither of us smiles.

Adam says, 'Kip, I don't think they're going to be all right. When they're both home at the same time, they're paying me far too much attention. If I'm nice to Mum, Dad frowns at me, and if I give Dad a hug, Mum folds her arms. We're all bloody miserable.'

I say, 'Can't understand grown-up heads. Mammy keeps talking loudly about disappointment. She's disappointed Dad took the teabag out of her mug too quick, and he doesn't know after all these years she likes it strong. She's disappointed that the searching has gone on for two whole days and today's going to be the third. She's disappointed that the only thing that's happened about the three missing people is that we've found out that the doctor's not really missing.'

'Where is he?'

'His car's gone now, so Mammy called his wife again. She said he was back home but wouldn't say where he'd been. And Mammy's disappointed she hasn't had any time to herself, that she's not had the time to see your mum, that Dad hasn't been able to go up to Jock's for more coal, that she's not had time to fix all the things that are broken . . . She's disappointed that some people lie to her . . . and that's the worst one because she means me.'

'What's broken?'

'Don't even know. Mam Vann's angry with me. Every time I see her she glares at me like her eyes are blazing holes.'

Adam says, 'She's just mad with you for not finishing your turn on the fair properly. We could make her eyes into blazing holes easily enough. Hard to know if someone's setting fire to your eyelashes if you're asleep when they do it.'

Dagger comes tearing into the hallway, jumps over my legs and leaps up at the back door, jerking and jerking. Someone's coming. We scramble up, I grab his lead, and all three of us shoot into Lizzie's bedroom. We crouch on the floor behind the bed. I hang onto Dagger though he strains to get away.

The door bangs. There are footsteps in the hall.

Two voices come into Lizzie's bedroom.

One voice says, ' . . . don't want to live here. Prefer sweet home.'

Aunty Pippa's voice says, 'They'll be searching the Lets soon. Anyway, this one's more . . . vacant, now they've searched it for a second time and found nothing. I'm hoping permanently. We won't be disturbed here, come spring or summer. It'll need a good clear-out over time. We'll get rid of all her things, but—'

Adam stands up. 'Mum, what are you doing with Grizzly?'

I stand up too. There's one of the Old Kelps. Her wrinkled mouth opens at the sight of me. I push past Adam to the bedroom door.

Aunty Pippa drops two suitcases; they thud on the floor as she grabs my arm. She says to me, 'Now stop. What?'

I pull away but she grips on too hard.

'She's . . . she's . . . a double of . . .' I stare at the Old Kelp, who's looking back at me with trouble storming in her eyes. I can't speak her name for fear of her.

Aunty Pippa says, 'Oh. Not sure if I . . .'

The Old Kelp says, 'Not a double.' Her voice is low and eerie.

Adam says to the Old Kelp, 'Don't growl at him.'

The Old Kelp speaks with three voices in one word: '*Him?*'

Aunty Pippa says to the Old Kelp, 'Ah, the dress. This is my nephew.'

The Old Kelp's voice sounds like curses, like the shrieks of wind. 'Seen her. Takes cakes. I'm not never a double. Double would never flicker deadness. Ghosting. Double would be one of us not dropping dead. No doubles. Not a doppelganger . . . too many things to be, not at the same time . . . daughter, double, bear . . . can't be here, not with all of you!'

Adam says to her, 'Stop *growling* at Kip!'

Aunty Pippa ignores him and turns to the Old Kelp. 'It's all right, you just need to . . .' Her voice trails away as the Old Kelp looks up at the yellow ruffled lampshade, her face warped, twisted. She's swaying like she's set to stamp down mad thunder.

The Old Kelp's head twists down to look at Adam.

He says, 'Grizzly, where did you go?'

I say to Adam, 'You're calling her—'

Aunty Pippa looks at me as she says, 'She'll be all right over time. She needs a proper home, proper parenting . . .' She frowns and asks Adam, 'Why are you calling her Grizzly?'

Adam says, 'She is one. Escaped from a zoo and came here. Got to keep an eye – make sure George doesn't go after her for a taxidermy hybrid.' He reaches for the Old Kelp's arm.

I back away from them all and yell, 'Don't touch her!'

The Old Kelp groans like her many voices are building a gale inside her.

Aunty Pippa looks at her, still concerned. She says, 'Oh, come on, Kip. She's a lost girl who's desperately shy and needs somewhere to live. Needs to find hope, somehow.'

'Grizzly could stay with us?'

I shout, 'No!'

'If your father left,' Aunty Pippa says to Adam. 'I'm working on it. But we'll stay here for a while. I've got our things. Most of your clothes, some of your toys and books . . . well, we'll need to go back. I forgot our toothbrushes. And . . . socks. Damn.'

'We're leaving Dad?'

She sighs, 'Sorry, Adam. With him bloody helping them search for Lizzie, I can't stand it. So we'll have her home – she should do something for us, even in absence. And you shouldn't have to cope with atmosphere. It's best. For now. I'm sorry, really.'

Adam covers his face and sits on Lizzie's bed, his shoulders jerking with sobs. Aunty Pippa sits next to him and leans his head against her chest.

The Old Kelp slides down next to them, tries to make herself seem smaller. Her face is like a skeleton and she closes her sunken dark eyes. Adam's crying all over his freckles, and Aunty Pippa's dressed neat and tidy in her woollen skirt and jacket and pearls. They look like a group of people playing a deadly game called 'unhappy families' where someone has to die.

The Old Kelp's eyes are only half closed. There's a creepy sneer on her face.

I grab Dagger, and run.

As I rush into our home with Dagger, Mammy's standing in front of the fire staring into the flames. I go running right into her, and she starts, puts her hand on my head, remembers she's still angry with me and pushes me away. 'Finally, you're back. What now?'

'There's an O . . . O . . .' I pant. 'I can't speak her name, but she's with Aunty Pippa and Adam – she's cursed their eyes to see her as . . . a grizzly bear and a girl . . .'

'When will you stop?' Her voice is stone calm.

'Stop what?'

'Lying to me.'

I gasp, 'I'm not – not about this—'

'I've had enough.' She pushes past me, goes to the front door and puts her coat on. 'Enough of you acting sick when you're well, and enough of you lying when I've brought you up to be truthful. I'm doing my best.' Her lips are a straight line but her eyes are shining like she's about to cry. She gets the box of keys for the Lets out of a drawer, puts it in her canvas bag and slings it over her shoulder. 'I've got to go and catch up with the others. We're searching the rocky side of the coast and the Holiday Lets. There's another group searching the tunnels now the tide's out. Then that's it. We'll have looked everywhere there is to look by midday. Don't lie to me, Kip, I can't take it. I'm so tired my eyes are seeing everything in black and white.'

I try to slow down my breathing. 'I'm not lying . . . don't want you to go there in case she curses you, but I—'

She shakes her head, her eyes full of tears. 'Stop it. Now.'

'It's not a—'

'Not one more word. You're either truthful, or you're a liar. What do you want to be, Kip? Clearly you're old enough to decide for yourself.'

I reach for her hand but she goes outside and slams the door.

On the table, there are two empty plates and on my plate a honey cake is looking up at me, waiting for me to eat it. I pick it up and sniff. It fills one of my nostrils with a whizz of smells. I throw it in the fire and watch it melt in the flames.

AMBER

I hold out two fingers: a gun. I say, 'Bang bang,' and fire, twice. My reflection doesn't flinch.

I tell it, 'Not dead, then. That game doesn't work.'

I look over my shoulder at the bed: the wrinkled sheets, the lamp I've knocked over in my sleep, the crumpled clothes I haven't bothered washing. Looking back at my reflection, I say, 'Alone is nothing that will kill you. No one to answer to and no one to ask. No one to say anything at all.'

I'd like to pretend to myself that I've never cared what anyone's said about me. Boys have sly tongues. Bitch. Slut. Whore.

But. I turn my face to the side and watch my reflection in the mirror. The eyes. Unflinching. 'Well. Not caring. Let's pretend. Or let's tell the truth. I. Don't. Care. Which would be a lie now, wouldn't it? Isn't honesty gorgeous.'

I wonder what it would be like to have a metallic self-destruct button on my bottom lip. I could explode myself and all the words that shouldn't ever have been spoken. The names I've dragged all the way here with me. They pop and fizzle in my head like dented fireworks.

Boom. Fttt.

Just . . . blow them away. I shoot myself again. Bang bang. No one speaks ill of the dead. It's somebody's rule. Not mine.

Mine would be not to speak ill of the living, and certainly not the most living people of all: the ones who've been most alive.

I decide not to self-destruct yet, and blow my reflection a kiss.

The shadow has never appeared in the daytimes. While Medic was here, it seemed more and more human each night, though the face still had no features and the edges of the body blurred.

Tonight it's back.

I tell it with certainty, 'I'm not afraid.'

I hear the sound of a laugh.

One crack, *Ha.*

I spend an hour sitting on the kitchen floor by the oven, watching the shadow thicken. I try to remember the build and height of the shed woman, but I only ever saw her lying down. I'm thinking the shadow might be her ghost. I could go out into the shed and look. Measure her with my hands or a tape measure or a sheet. Draw a line on the wall in the cold corner to compare the heights. But I'd need to be able to stomach human decay. My eyes don't want to see, my hands don't want to touch, and my nose doesn't want to smell.

I feel certain that the shadow is her ghost and she's condensing herself, building and thickening so she's capable of speech.

And what would she say?

I ask aloud: 'Bury me?'

The shadow seems a little taller.

'Lock me away in roots under the soil? Banish me? Exorcise me?' It edges towards me.

I say, 'You need somewhere no one would ever find you, even if this whole place is burned to ash. I've been thinking about Medic's wife collecting paraffin. All she'd need is a match. Boom bang fttt. Then, there would be more bones. Yours. And probably mine.'

The shadow is silent and its edges curl like smoke.

In the garden the torch shines a line along the soil where a few tiny shoots are pushing out of the earth between broken dry stems. I hack and thud and bang the rusted spade on the earth, but still can't get through the unyielding soil.

Giving up, I come back indoors and say to the shadow, 'I'm trying to do what you want. So you can go to sleep in warm flames, or shoot off to some foggy heaven and follow whatever afterlife rules you're inclined towards. I don't want to call you a ghost because that word's used to scare children and I'm no child. Anyway, you look more like a shadow than anything ghoulish to me.'

Again, the laugh cracks, *Ha.*

Alone, I'm talking to shadows and reflections.

Other people's thoughts, bodies, voices, make a house full. All of the dishes, pans, the oven trays, the cake tins are made in sizes meant for more than one. I didn't realise that sharing food adds to the texture and flavour. I can't eat tonight. Meringues are powder, jam is glue and cocoa tastes like mud.

I am full of dread: an outside-is-too-cold, inside-is-warm-and-safe feeling. The fir trees up the hill stand too close together, like an army of spikes. As I look out of the bedroom window, even in the dark, they seem to move a little closer to this cottage.

I'm overwhelmed by thoughts of the dead woman, the shadow in the corner and the threat of an angry wife.

But I tell myself, 'I'm the sister who was never afraid.' I try to avoid my emotions, but thoughts of Maya creep in and sting my chest:

Where is she? Ouch. Is she safe? Ow. Is she still alive? Aaaaah. Who is she?

I have to bury these thoughts.

It's still a couple of hours till dawn and the shadow moves closer to me as I slide the honey cakes into the oven. My heart booms but I won't let fear show. I think it's the old woman's ghost. No, now I think it's the ghost of the dead woman in the shed.

I hear the laugh, *Ha.*

My heart misses beats.

I ask, 'What do you eat?' The sound of my voice calms me down. So I say, 'You've probably eaten my hunger and that's why I'm not hungry.'

I say, 'The soil's thawing but still solid. Burying isn't easy; it's not like baking plums under a piecrust.'

After silence, 'Well, now we'll both be silent. So we'll have the same kind of hunger, won't we?'

I'm glad there's no answer.

A feeling of anger crackles as I'm drawing the honey cakes from the oven. Coldness spreads across my neck. I put the wire racks on the table, tilt the trays of warm honey cakes onto them.

The shadow's hand hovers next to my cheek.

I say, 'So you're still here. Touch me. Slap me. Stroke me. What do you want?'

It doesn't do anything.

I sit at the table. 'I could make choices. Leave here or stay. If I leave, you'll be completely alone.' I put my hands on the mortar. 'I could smash this up. I could break the bone spoons. Every one of them. Would you let me, or stop me? Snap. Crack crack.'

Glancing at the corner, the shadow has crowded itself back there. It seems yet more visible. A human shape, made of thickened smoke.

I ask, 'Which dead woman are you?' and wait.

Nothing.

'I didn't realise you mattered so much, till now. Which? Is this your recipe book, are these your spoons? Or if I said I might tear up your crimson dress, would you care more about that?'

No reply.

And it strikes me like a slap, that for a long time, there have been these two dead women in my life, and now they feel far more constant than either of the live people who've lived with me here.

And I also know that this fear might be a symptom of hunger.

So I eat half of a steaming honey cake and have to lean over the sink because my body is too quickly warm. Turning around, I look at the mortar and pestle, and the orange ceramic jar that houses the bone spoons, the two biggest shaped like femurs, thin bones, long bones, small ones, and a fistful which must once have been ribs.

I pick up a rib spoon and cross the kitchen to the thickening shadow. My voice shakes a little. 'You might not be the ghost of either of the dead women. You could be the ghost of these bones.'

KIP

Mammy wakes me. 'Kip, take Dagger out. He's been scratching your door. He needs to piss.' She goes out of my room.

'It might be all right if it's this early,' I whisper into Dagger's ear as I put on his lead. 'The Old Kelp with Adam might still be asleep.'

Dad told me that yesterday morning when the Holiday Lets were searched, they thought someone had been in one of them. The key was in the front door, and Dad swore Mammy would never have left it there, so someone must have pinched it from her. Inside, there were blown-up bin liners in a cupboard and when they popped them, they smelled of bad breath. No one thinks Uncle Finn has done anything wrong any more, as he joined in with the searching. He was there first at the school to meet everyone who was searching, each morning for three days. I heard Mammy say he's looking sicker than ever.

Dad said last night, *I know him the best and if he'd got something to hide, he'd have steered well clear and hid it.* Jessie's been saying to anyone who'll listen that Aunty Pippa didn't help because she can't bear to be near Uncle Finn.

So they've searched the woods and the ditches, the roads, the coast both ways, the cliffs, the fields and farms, the tunnels, the Lets and all the woods around here. At low tide, two of the grown-ups were on the beach walking along the tidemarks. There was just seaweed, driftwood, jellyfish and seabirds that were so dead even George wasn't interested. They've called off the search in our village, and sent a couple of people off to look further away. Everyone must be thinking it, but no one will speak it for fear of being cursed. No one will ever look at Old Kelp's cottage.

I get dressed and go outside. Mam Vann is coming down the hill wheeling the basket, getting the fair. She hasn't seen me, so I duck through an alleyway with Dagger. He pulls me the ways he wants to walk, so I follow him.

Something's moving. It's Uncle Finn. He creeps up a lane like an old stray cat. I follow him, to see where he's going.

He's wearing a rumpled brown coat over his grey pyjamas and black wellies. In the morning half-dark, under the dim street lights, he looks like a man made of dust. He reaches the end of the lane and turns into the next row of houses. Me and Dagger watch him from the corner. He steps quietly and ducks under windows.

I think he's going round to Lizzie's house to see Aunty Pippa and Adam, and I hold my breath, because the Old Kelp might still be in there. I think she'll curse Uncle Finn for the tangle of three, and I should stop him going in . . .

But he doesn't go in. He creeps past Lizzie's.

He goes inside the Quiet Woman's home. We wait at the corner for a while. When I hear the door click, I look round the corner and see him come out again. Dagger jerks a silent bark.

I step towards him and say, 'Why are you going in her house?'

Uncle Finn looks over his shoulder at me and his neck is blotchy red. He leans on her door, breathing hard. He speaks between breaths. 'Not now . . . not with Kip. Slow, slow.'

I grip Dagger's lead. 'Did you kill her and hide her body?'

'Kip, ask your dad. He'll tell you, I'd never kill . . . anyone.' He looks confused. 'And why are you saying kill?' His face is purple as he looks at me.

My voice shakes. 'The Quiet Woman's dead.'

He looks at me as if he can't see me proper. He glances at Lizzie's house and takes a deep heave of breath. Coming towards me, he grabs hold of my arm, and walks me halfway down the lane.

He turns me to face him. 'Only Lizzie knew the Quiet Woman, said she'd had a lot of pain, left it behind her. They used to sit up through the night in that house. *Talking deep talk*, Lizzie said. I just went in, to think of Lizzie.' He wheezes a little, shakes his head, confused.

Too fast, he grips my arms so hard I can't move. 'Dead. You're sure?'

I nod.

His voice slurs, 'Just her that's dead, not Lizzie?'

'Her hair wasn't blonde.'

He's shaking his head, breathing hard. 'If it's now, Kip, remember . . . will you?'

'What?'

'That . . . it's not your fault . . .'

'You're squeezing me too tight!'

He lets go of one of my arms and I drop Dagger's lead.

Uncle Finn staggers, grips his own arm and crashes down on top of Dagger. He stumbles up again, but Dagger lies rock still on the cobbles. I rush down to him and lift his head. He won't open his eyes.

Uncle Finn limps away down the alleyway, stops and leans on the wall of one of the houses. I feel Dagger's neck for his pulse, but can only feel the heartbeat in my own throat, as Uncle Finn falls.

I shake Dagger but he doesn't wake and at the same time I shout and yell for help for Uncle Finn. Three front doors open and people rush outside and cluster around crumpled Uncle Finn.

I press on Dagger's chest pretending my fingers are his heartbeats, but I need someone to help me. Mammy always says people are more important than animals. But I don't believe her because if Dagger dies I won't want anything to do with anyone, not ever again.

I bang on George's door till he opens it, pulling on his velvet dressing gown and looking angry enough to stuff me.

Carrying Dagger, I push past George into his chemical-smelling front room. I gasp, 'You've got to make him better!'

'What's happened?'

'Got fell on by my uncle and he won't wake up.'

'I'm not a veterinary—'

'Neither's anyone else. But you know how animals work, all about their insides. You can find the broken bit – might just be a bone. Can you fix it and stitch him up quick? I'll stroke him so if he wakes he won't bite you, and he's just got one tooth so it won't hurt too much—' With my elbow I nudge a box of gloves and his skinning knives along his table and yell, 'Mend him!'

George leans his hands on the table. 'Kip, I only make dead ones look good. Can't make them live again. Look – I don't even use the bones apart from the skull. I've got to make them all over again.' He waves at a shelf where there are small animal shapes made from plaster and wood wool.

I lay Dagger on the sofa. I sweep all the wire, bottles of glue, wax and a bag of clay to the edge of the table. I move George's bodhran.

He grabs it off me. 'What're you doing? You don't go touching other folks' music!'

I'm crying. 'Get Dagger on the table. Mend him.'

'Heck's sake.' He crouches down and looks at Dagger. 'I'm a bloody taxidermist; I can't mend him till he's dead! Look at him, he's still breathing!'

'He's breathing? Check he's mended himself!'

On the sofa Dagger staggers to his feet, blinking, and drops down again.

George scratches his beard. Flexes his fingers. 'He'll yelp if there's a bone broke.'

He lifts Dagger off the sofa and lays him on the table. He kneads up all four legs and along Dagger's spine with his fingertips, his eyes closed, nodding. He goes over his ribs as well. 'Nothing. Just winded and winded bad. He'll be right after you give him some quiet petting and a hot-water bottle. Stronger than you think, dogs are.'

I wipe the tears off my face. 'See, you do know what to do.'

'Oh, I know how bones feel when they're broke, but that's about as far as I get. When they're dead, it's their true character you want to bring alive. Now when the time does come for him . . .' He smiles at me with the corners of his mouth.

'Stop it.'

'Well, he'd be right fearful in a pose where he's fighting off a bat or some kind of nocturnal. He'd look good with his dark scrappy fur and long claws. Bats' wings are a good texture. Have him fighting them off brave. Or I could try a rat. Look at them.' He points at a high shelf where there's a taxidermy of three rats climbing a branch. 'Nice strong fighting pose for Dagger, and a rat quaking at his feet . . . Now would I give him a full set of teeth, or shine up the one he's got . . .' He rubs Dagger's head. 'That's what this one'd want, isn't it, chum? For he's a fighter.'

I pick Dagger up from the table. 'You're not having him.'

'No use to me alive, Kip. Though I daresay that's the way you like him best. But when the time does come . . .' His eyes glint as he grips one of Dagger's front paws. With his other hand, he reaches out and grabs a piece of wire from the table.

I remember what Jessie said about George having something in his attic, and him not letting anyone go upstairs. There's a green door with a key in the lock.

He's seen me looking. He goes to the door, clicks it locked and puts the key in his dressing-gown pocket. He turns to face me and folds his arms. He says, 'Keep brushing his fur, Kip. Keep it nice for me.'

I hold Dagger tight and say, 'Go and stuff something wriggly.'

Dagger's on my bed with a hot-water bottle, wrapped in a towel. My eyes are puffed up and my throat's sore from crying.

Mammy sits on the bed next to me, stroking Dagger's head. 'Just spoke with your dad on the phone. He's going to sit with Finn. I called the doctor but his wife says he can't come. Pippa's there now, Adam as well. But it'll be strained.'

I stroke Dagger's rough fur on his neck. 'Will Uncle Finn be all right?'

'I don't know.' She swallows.

'Is anyone else there too?'

'Not as far as I know. Look, I've been angry, but you'd never lied to me that convincingly, not even when you told stories all the time. They were always about other people, other things. But this time I thought you were so ill—'

'I'm sorry.'

'What for?'

'For pretending I couldn't hear.'

She kisses my forehead. 'Forgiven, forgot. Listen, I've made up a song to make Dagger feel better.' She leans down and sings into his ear:

'When Kip's grown taller,
he'll wear a swishy fishscale dress,
Dagger will spin around;
he'll make blobs of doggish mess—'

I interrupt her. 'Why does Dad mind me wearing dresses but you don't?'

She stops singing. 'I spent a whole chunk of my own life trying to be what someone else wanted me to be. I don't want you doing the same.'

'What did you try to be?'

She takes my hand. 'After Mum died, Dad got me looking after him when I was so small I believed that was my job forever. If I left him alone for a moment when he didn't want to be, he'd cry or wail, or fall and hurt himself, and I'd feel so bad. If he'd not died so young . . . Well, all of me would be for him, and I'd never have had anything my own. But sometimes even now, I feel awful for not looking after him well enough. But if he'd lived, terrible as it is to say it, I wouldn't have been able to marry your dad. Or to have you.'

'I'm glad you had me.'

'Wouldn't part with you.' She kisses my head. 'Not till the day you're ready to go. And even then, I hope you'll come home often. Not like Morag.'

'Your sister?'

'Your other aunty. I'm sad you've never got to meet her. At first everyone thought she'd run off with one of the summer people – some man or another she'd liked the look of. But it was a spring woman Morag had met, that she loved the heart of. Wasn't long after Morag left the ugly talk got round. There was nothing of love spoken, though love was what it was. She'd promised herself to a farmer's son, just months before she ran off. No one likes it when someone switches like that; we think they're one thing, they turn out another. It unsettles people.'

Her eyes are far away. 'Sometimes I wonder if everyone thinks change is dangerous. We're all so afraid of it, because it's fear that makes talk turn ugly. We're even afraid when people do so little as to change their minds. I'm ashamed to say it, but I joined in with that ugly talk about Morag. I was angry she'd left me behind. Wanted to follow her, and she wrote me to, but I couldn't.'

'Why not?'

'Someone had to look after Dad.'

Dagger lets me rub his belly.

Mammy says, 'That's a good sign, him rolling over like that. Wouldn't do that if it hurt him to.' She strokes my hair. 'Kip, what I'm saying to you is: you can only ever be yourself.'

Dad comes back in the middle of the day and clatters around the kitchen. He comes into my room with egg sandwiches on a plate and puts them on my bedside table.

I ask, 'How's Uncle Finn?'

'He pushed himself too hard. He's not good. I'm leaving them to it. Pippa says she wants time with him, and he wants her to have it. Just shows it's never too late to patch what might look broken to others.'

I stroke Dagger's ears and look at the shell shapes inside them. He shakes his head like he felt my eyes burrowing in there.

I can hear Mammy and Jessie's voices talking in the living room. Dad looks sad about Uncle Finn. I don't know what to say, so I get in the tunnel I've made with my duvet.

Dad sits on the bed and rocks it. I'm tunnelling in outerspace but he's found my head in the tunnel with his hand. There's not meant to be touching in this tunnel because of zero gravity and zeroed hands in puffed-up gloves. There's meant to be milkshakes and exploding planets and atoms and fizzing sweets and I should be wearing a tin-foil dress and lead shoes and my head should be in a glass bubble with three tiny silverfish that clean my teeth.

But it's not working proper because Dad's hand is on my head.

He says, 'Listen up, Kip. A couple of the lads set off to Fastleigh yesterday, to see if they can find Lizzie or the Quiet Woman there. It'll take time for them to search and come back. But if they can't find the two women, they're to get the police to come back with them. Your mammy and Jessie reckon it's pointless, but everyone else knows it's the one thing left to do. If the police does come here, don't say a word to him about Old Kelp. She's not to be talked about, and he's to be kept away from her cottage.' He whispers, 'Some say she's getting stronger, and great cruelty can come with great strength.'

MAYA

I dream that ghost stories are coming for me.

Bed. Bed. Bed. Can't stop my heart beating pale. I can smell the sound of a tambourine, hear the sight of a double bass, smooth, fat, plucked, thuck thack thrum. The duvet is heavy and made of air, it floods cold smoke over my body as I roll over and when I'm still, it clamps me like thick rusted steel. Bolted to bed.

I'm dancing on pointe, spinning, twirling, spiralling myself in an attic room filled with the sun. At the same time, I'm a clothes moth, grey, shut in a wardrobe, crawling through holes in black clothes, dust clumps in my wings and my heart.

Pickled eye whites in a jam jar. Marionettes with string ballerina dreams eating fingernails roasted on top of a marzipan pie.

The sound of a child's voice, singing:

'Grilled limping soldiers with crusted moustaches.

Snot white and rose dead and criss-crossed eyelashes.

Needles are pinning your hair to the floor . . .'

I shout, 'NOT the floor – it's a pillow!' And I tell myself, oh quiet, now I'm a soak wet head . . .

Still the child's voice:

'Triplets of corpses with eyes blind and white,

Mouths stapled shut with ears plugged by the night.'

I say, 'Stop it singing,' and the voice is gone.
It stops so suddenly it might have been my voice.

In a small bed. A tiny spare room full of spare things. A dented wardrobe filled with deflated blue beach balls, curtains closed make everything grey, dust smell, lavender smell, broken lamp, grey-lilac tablecloth with greying daisy chains, grey-white walls, crack glass picture of gulls, spare clothes folded: pyjamas cardigans jumper grey skirt, socks, five broken chair legs tied up with string.

Try to see all of it, fill my eyes and learn it up. Being alone and spare makes my head shriek thought-gales and there's the picture blown in of Dead Red, lying on the floor.

Stop it jumbles. Stop it thinking about Dead Red.

The dress leaks red in my head.

When we left Paradon, I packed the crimson dress in my bag, rolled small as a secret.

The colour was so singing I couldn't leave it behind.

I was meant to have worn that dress the night of Amber's last birthday party. She was wearing: silver-sequin shift-dress, pink-heeled shoes, faux-flamingo jacket.

Our parents never thought Amber was beautiful. She wanted to be.

As I helped her get ready, I stood behind her at the dressing table, up-doing her hair and crystalling raindrops through hand-made curls. She was eyeing herself in the mirror. She sank down glasses of fizz bubbles and toasted her reflection. She shone.

I said to her with a smile crowding my voice, *You look pretty, gorgeous, dazzling.*

She waited for me at the front door, and she was calling and shouting up the stairs, *We have to go now!* I was in the bathroom. I flushed the toilet. I was confused because Amber wanted me to go now, but I should quick-change into the crimson dress. I pulled it out of the wardrobe. The colour was singing like opera, like red angels, like bright dance.

Our mother had bought it for me and wanted me to wear it at Amber's party. She always bought me and Amber lovely clothes, filled our wardrobes with colours and textures. She wanted daughters who dressed up nice, made her proud. But that night, our mother was working late; she wasn't going to be at the party.

Her want shrank.

Amber would see me as being dressed just like her. Twin and identical. She always did. Everyone else would see whatever they wanted to see.

Amber was glowing so bright I could feel her glow all the way from downstairs by the front door. So when she shouted again, *Come ON, Maya!* I shoved the dress and our mother's want back in the wardrobe, ran down the stairs and we left to go to the party.

Parties: too many people and jumbles: noise chaos, blur-colours, want. Fear flooded and sound from speakers head-churned me. People want too much, too hard, my breathing was high-throated.

Amber spun under chandeliers. She was made of sparks, hot dancing. She came over to me, hiding behind a fern. She whispered in my ear, *I don't mind if you slip away. Can't keep an eye on you when the focus is on me.* She blew my nose with the smell of fizz grapes.

So I cornered myself in the cloakroom till time struck to go home. I hid inside other people's coats; they were a soft wrap around me.

In this sad house my alone is the weight of heavy grey. Going down the steep staircases, I pass narrow shelves, dusty books, pompom chicks, elastic bands in a plastic tub, antique clarinet, stuffed toy carrot, picture of planet explosions and bongo drums.

In the kitchen, as soon as Pippa looks at me, my own thoughts jump into the sink with her hands and froth and pan handles.

I'm her good good daughter. I've learned it all up.

She's wearing a green and purple crochet skirt and matching cardigan with a pale pink blouse tied with a pussy bow. She's got pearl earrings and stockinged feet. She wipes her hands on a plaid tea towel and stirs a pot of glubbing porridge.

I look down and I'm wearing a patchwork dressing gown.

The front door bangs, footsteps crash.

Adam springs into the kitchen, yells, 'Morning, Grizzly!' and dashes out through the other door that leads to the hallway and up the stairs.

Fur grows under the dressing gown.

Pippa says to me in a mother talk-style, 'Stir that.' She nods at the pot on the stove, follows him and looks upstairs through the banisters. She calls, 'Where have you been?'

Adam's voice shouts, 'Nowhere!'

'Be quiet! You'll wake your dad!' She comes back in.

I shake growls away, smile at Pippa and ask, 'How is he?'

She grips the spoon, gives the porridge a stir and reaches up to a shelf piled high with mismatched bowls. I sit at the table next to a basket filled with fabric scraps and a half-finished patchwork frog.

Pippa clinks a pile of bowls on the worktop beside the cooker. 'The doctor phoned. Really early. Said he still wouldn't be able to come over this way today. Perhaps tomorrow, he said, but, oh Maya, he didn't sound sure. I've got this horrible feeling he's not coming at all. Something in his voice . . .'

I ask again, 'How is he?'

'I'm over-tired. Finn—'

'I meant Adam.'

'Well, he doesn't like all the chopping and changing, move out, move back. But I do have a sense of responsibility. I'm so glad you're thinking of Adam too.'

'Why does he want a bear – does he need affection, or courage?'

She fills two bowls with porridge and takes them upstairs. I keep thinking of Adam. He's filled with emotions he doesn't know the names for. I look at a picture that's pinned to the wall. He's drawn two explosions with oranges and yellows. Between the flames are dotted black lines that look like stitches, sewing all the sparks together.

Pippa comes back into the kitchen again with one bowl. 'I'll have Finn's, then. Ooh, sorry, are you hungry too? I haven't made enough—'

'Not yet.'

She nudges a teddy bear off the chair next to me and sits down. After three mouthfuls of porridge, she says, 'No one's overhearing?' She glances at the door to the stairs.

I go and check. The stairway is empty. The silence seems thick. 'Only me.'

As I sit down next to her again, she says, 'If Finn dies, you'll help with Adam? He's already so attached to you. This timing is terrible, but Maya, sweetheart, you're what I've always dreamed of, so helpful.'

I hear my voice say, 'I'll always be here for you.' This feels wrong, because unless I stay with just one person, my promises don't last. I've avoided going into Finn's room so far. Soon I won't be able to stop myself. He wants something he isn't ready for yet. On the stairs just outside his room, there's a feeling of something straining and inevitable. A gap in the air that's waiting.

There's a sound from outside, and Pippa grabs a plate and

goes to the front door. She comes back in with three of Amber's honey cakes. 'Don't think Finn will eat his,' she says, sadly. Her face clears. 'Ah. You will, though.' She puts a cake on a small plate in front of me. She takes a bite from hers and chews.

I eye the cake.

Pippa glances at me.

Adam comes into the kitchen. 'Dad's awake. He's thirsty.'

Pippa says, 'Does he want tea?'

'Just water.'

'I'll take it. Have your cake.' She strokes Adam's shoulder, and kisses the top of his head. The pipes rattle as she runs a glass of water and goes upstairs.

On his last mouthful, Adam looks at my cake and says in a muffled voice, 'Is Mum making you eat Dad's?'

'She tried to.'

He smiles. 'That sound, that one's my new favourite. You're the best growler ever.'

He picks up my plate. 'I'm full with two breakfasts. Do bears eat cakes?'

'Not if they're suspicious of their sister's cooking because of a foggy steamed pudding.'

'Wow, you're getting louder all the time. That was a good one. A roar. Come with.'

In the downstairs loo I'm on all fours watching as Adam crumbles the honey cake into the toilet bowl. He looks up at a dusty taxidermy duck with a light bulb in its bill and whispers, 'Not a quack,' as he tries again and again to flush-handle.

As I shuffle around, Pippa's standing in front of us in an arm-fold. The empty plate falls from Adam's hands and clang-floors itself without a smash.

He dodges past her and goes upstairs.

I swallow a growl she won't want.

She says in a gentle talk-style, 'Oh my love, you've got a food thing. Don't make Adam your co-conspirator. I need to really look after you, don't I?'

KIP

My bedroom door closes and wakes me.

Mammy's left a new purple dress hanging over the end of my bed. It's gathered at the waist and the skirt is long and wide, with white kisses stitched criss-cross along the hem.

Mammy's sewing machine was clattering late last night, and she'd said if I promised I'd go back to the school today, there would be a surprise this morning on the end of my bed. Saying I'd go back made her smile.

The school is open again because everyone's back to normal, not searching or hunting or talking too much. They're all just waiting for news from the lads who went to Fastleigh.

Adam was round again yesterday. When he said, *Grizzly's living with us now*, I was too scared to go to his house. So after tea we went down the beach instead. I'm too frightened to even tell him it's really the Old Kelp. If I make him see her as she really is, she'll curse away his eyes.

Last night I stayed awake, waiting for Mammy's machine clatters to stop and for her to go to bed. I found Dagger's hidden weaponry in the fur of his paws: his claws are like little knives, so each time I thought of the Old Kelp, I imagined Dagger's claws tearing through my thinking-pictures. Now Dagger's my secret weapon, I feel a bit better protected.

Mammy and Dad are talking in their room as I get out of bed and take off my nightie. It's too grimy to wear any more. I put on the new purple dress and do giant steps around my bed.

Dagger watches me, his eyes gleaming under his shaggy fringe.

I hold the skirt of the dress wide and swish around the room. I twirl and spin and stop, stand up tall to look in the mirror on the dresser, turn around and curtsey and bow to Dagger.

I rub his head and touch his nose. 'Cold and wet. That means you're much betterer. So. New dress, like it?' I sit on the bed next to him, and he paws at my leg. 'I do too. But no slashing it up. This one's my new favourite. I'm going to call it . . . my best-till-last dress.'

Dad comes in and doesn't look at my dress. He sits on my bed. 'Letter for you.' He hands me a sealed brown envelope with my name printed on the front in neat capital letters. I tear it open. It says:

Dear Kip.

Good for you, you're always the best there is at getting us out of it.
Hope you didn't get too dirty. Bet you did.
Have you heard the news about the police?
I'll come outside if you come round mine later, so you don't have to see Grizzly. Don't tell anyone about her, I promise she's good and won't hurt a flea on you or Dagger.
Kidding. I know Dagger doesn't have fleas.
Dad is worse than ever sick.
See you later

Adam

Dad's saying, 'I'm off to Jock's farm.'

'What about Uncle Finn?'

'He's bad. But he says, *Life has to go tramping on.* If there's another turn for the worse, I'll get Jock to drop me straight back. If Finn stays level enough, I'll be back in just a few days. I want you to look after your mammy for me.'

'What's happened about the police?'

'News travels fast when you're sleeping, does it?' He nods at the letter in my hand. 'The lads we sent to Fastleigh got back here late last night.'

'Did they bring the police with them?'

'No, but they've brought news. He's long gone. There's not been a policeman there for years. They thought he'd moved over here, and we thought he lived over there, and there's not a police in the whole area they know of.'

'So what's going to happen about the Quiet Woman and Lizzie?'

'Well, that's the other thing.'

'What?'

He stares at the floor. 'While they were there, they saw Lizzie. She's right as rain. Living there now, she says. Not wanting to come back. She asked them to pack up her house and get her things sent over. Didn't offer them anything for their trouble though, so I'd not think they'll bother—' He glances at my dress and looks away again, quickly.

'What about the Quiet Woman?'

'They asked Lizzie about her, and she wouldn't say much, but she did say, *She won't be back either, and there's nothing to worry about.* So that's all right. Lizzie and the Quiet Woman are accounted for.'

I whisper, 'But . . . she can't be fine. Maybe Lizzie's just saying that, because it was her who—'

Dad's voice is sharp. 'Kip, it's all settled. Lizzie's fine, the Quiet Woman's fine, and you're well again. Your mammy's feeling proper blessed.'

'But the Quiet—'

He shakes his head. 'Mammy's been so worried about you, so let her have that. We've much to be grateful for.' He nods at my letter. 'Who's writing to you?'

'Adam. He's worried about Uncle Finn.' I fold up the letter and put it under my pillow.

'I am as well. Poor kid.' He finally looks at my new dress properly.

I bite my lip. 'Don't say anything.'

'But—'

I fold my arms. 'Up to me, isn't it?'

He frowns. 'Just let me talk. If you're a, you know, a . . .'

'A what?'

'A travesty or some such.'

'What's a travesty?'

He looks at my dirty nightie on a pile of dirty clothes. 'Look Kip, if you'd bloody tell me when things get rough for you at the school, I'd come in and give the lot of them what for. I've heard the way some of the kids talk about you. That Pike lad is a little sod – I'll clobber him—'

'I'm the best there is at hiding.'

'Well, you shouldn't have to.'

'Well, I do have to.' I crouch and look under my bed. 'Where's my pencil case?'

'Wait up, Kip, not today.' Dad stands up.

'But I promised Mammy I'd go back.'

'It's not open. Jessie knocked us up over a half-hour ago, said she'd been to the school to light the fire for Mam Vann. She's saying someone's made off with the school's coal. There was a couple of sacks or so left. But now there's none at all. So it's closed again till they've got more in.'

I open my eyes, wide as I can. 'Who'd nick coal?'

Dad has a spark in his eye. 'Can't imagine.' He picks up my nightie, shakes it and holds it out. 'My, but this is filthy. All these black smears. Looks like you've been cleaning my trailer with it, in time for me to dirty it up with a load more coal. I'll sneak it into the wash.'

'Thanks.'

'You know, I could've sworn I heard this strange squeaking sound really early this morning. And not that long after, I heard the front door.'

'Funny, that.'

'That's what I'm thinking, Kip. You know, we've more coal left than I thought. You and Mammy had best keep the fire burning all day and nights as well while I'm away, so there's room for the coal I bring back.' He pats my shoulder and his hand feels strong. 'You'll keep warm. See you in a few days. Look after your mammy for me. And I mean that.' He gives me a look that says, *Don't fret her.*

I follow him out of my bedroom and watch him put on his red wool hat, warm coat and gloves. He slings his bag over his shoulder.

On the doorstep are our honey cakes. I bring them in and put them on the table. Mammy comes out of the bathroom, still in her dressing gown. She hugs her goodbye around Dad.

Dad grabs his honey cake to take with him. 'You pair take care of each other. I'm gone.' He winks at me.

As he kisses Mammy, she touches his cheek.

At the front door, me and Mammy hold hands as we watch Dad pull his empty trailer away. Even when he's out of sight, we squeeze each other's hand. We're making a beating heart with our fingers as we listen to the squeak of the wheels.

MAYA

Stepping up the stairs my feet make no sound. There's a small framed mirror that hangs on the wall outside Adam's bedroom. I wonder if, as much as we eye them, mirrors look back. If they want to steal something from us for themselves. I look in the mirror and my face is still Amber's. And here again is the red flash. A swirl of ghost faces. They shift, change drift. Mouthing two words I can't lip-read.

These ghosts aren't just in the cottage with Amber.

They're wherever I am.

I look away.

So I still see myself as Amber. My glass-mirror-face is her face. Even without her in this house, even not living with her, talking to her, she still wants more from me than anyone else. I'm still hers.

And here's something Amber would be happy about – this want I have of my own: to know what I really look like. I want to see my true face archaeology: high-low brow, wide-narrow lips, plump-hollow cheeks, broad-narrow nose, dark-light eyes, thick-fine eyebrows. A wish to see something I've never seen, beauty or ugliness, emotion-jump or neutral-still, anything. If I could want to see myself for long enough could I make my eyes into spades; can eyes dig?

A wish and I don't know if it's mine or borrowed:
that mirrors could dig deeper than reflections.

I don't breathe in the hallway as I try to pass Finn's bedroom on my way up to the spare room. The air in the hall is moving, and the door's open. His voice calls in a weak talk-style, 'It's you. Still here, then. Best cuppa I've ever had, the one you made me yesterday. At least, I think it was you. I was barely wakeful.'

He wants me to go in. So I do.

Inside the white bedroom he lies in the middle of a double bed. Pale crumpled sheets cover his body. The light grey curtains are closed and the window behind them is wide open. Cold blows into the room.

I stand in the doorway. 'Pippa's been making your tea, not me. She's feeling helpless. Where's Adam?'

'Shut himself in his room. He's upset again, poor sod.' Finn places a hand on the mattress, pushes and falls back on his pillows. Beads of sweat cover his forehead and upper lip. 'You'll need to be calm if you come in here now. Can you be calm?'

'I can be calm for you.'

'So set yourself down.' He weakly pats the edge of his bed.

I go into the room. 'I'm sorry you're so ill.'

'I'm dying. You're a strange presence in this house.'

'Am I?'

'You are.' He tries to sit up. 'It's good. That you're here, I mean. They're going to need you. And maybe now, with you finally coming into this room, this is the moment I need you as well.' He struggles to move back against the pillows.

'Let me help.' I reach to rearrange his pillows but before I can grasp them he pushes himself and leans back, heavily.

He says, 'Now I can see you as much as you can see me. And you can see more than you're saying. So tell me.'

'Your body's exhausted.' I sit on the edge of his bed. 'And behind that, you're desperately frightened.'

'You're too sensitive.' He frowns, and I can tell he's changed his mind because he doesn't really want to know all the things I can see.

'Am I?' I say, again.

He swallows, hard. 'Like I said, you can see more than you're saying. So, do you think I've got more to fear than you right now?'

'Is this a game?'

His eyes, though deeply tired, have a smile crouching in them. 'Perhaps I need one. You're sleeping in the room above me, yes?'

I nod.

'You shout in your sleep. Look up.' He raises and drops his hand.

There's a hole in the plaster ceiling, and I can see the floorboards above us. His fingers stroke and pinch at the sheet.

'Sorry I disturbed you.'

He smiles. 'Awake, you're nowhere near as frightened as you are asleep.'

Now I feel helpless as his eyes thin me and widen me as they try to focus. I glance down at myself and I'm wearing white drapes.

He moves his head and his eyes clear. 'You look fresh. Like you're beginning. Young. There's light all around you. A glow in your eyes. I must look terrible to you?' He puts his hand over his chest and rubs.

'Not terrible. You look like you're ending and you're afraid. I'm afraid of never being able to begin. Never knowing what hope feels like, or finding anything to hope for.'

He smiles, and his eyes shine. 'Well.' He sighs. 'You will. You're still young. Now, sensitivity. Kind of makes you more-than-alive. Over-alive . . . And what's the alternative?' He blinks at me. His eyes mist and blur me, and I feel more solid as they focus again. 'Yes. You're damn right I'm scared. Do I win a prize?' His laugh turns into a wheeze.

I reach to touch his hand, and his eyes blink away tears.

Breath heaves in his chest. 'There's something about you. It's comfort you're giving me. And that's what I've been wanting since being stuck here in this bed, a comfort that's not a one-way flow like sympathy. Your troubles meet mine. I've heard you shout out "murderer", "blood", "crimson", "burial", all kinds of brawling going on in your head when you sleep. But listen here. Others see what they want in you, and you can tell what it is they need. That's some gift.'

'It feels like a curse.'

Sweat shines on his forehead. 'If nothing else, I've learned that what happens to you, it all depends how you think about things. Like falling in love. You can love, but falling isn't the best way to go about it. Better go into it with your feet stepping sure, and your head high, but not up there in clouds or the like. Watch out for the things you might trip over. It's not about who you are or aren't . . . Try thinking the opposite . . . to what you're thinking.'

'So the opposite would be that I already know who I am. That I will find some kind of hope. That I'm . . .' my voice cracks, 'safe, to other people, even when what they want from me isn't always safe?'

His breathing fights with his words. 'That's the way . . . Everyone chooses what to want, not a single other bugger chooses that for them. So all you can do, missy, is to get in control of yourself more. Same as what I need to think . . . to get away from this god-awful fear. Death as an end. An anti-life. An opposite. Death being so close . . . while I'm dying . . .'

I hear myself say, 'You're more alive now than you've ever been.'

His eyes close as I stroke his fingers. His skin feels transparent. He says quietly, 'More alive than ever . . . Like being touched by life, the feeling of your hand. Touched by a guardian I've never known . . . never needed . . .' His breathing slows.

Slows more.

And is gone.

There's no smell, no colour, no taste, no sound.

With numbness, I cover his face with the crumpled white sheet.

White sky glows into the room between the curtains as a sharp wind blows in. I look at Finn's body. He seems like a statue; beneath the sheet I can see the veins and muscles in his legs. The room is filled with moving air and white light. Tears come to my eyes.

I place my numb hand over his forehead till I can feel the still air between the sheet and my palm. My voice says, 'Rest. Silence . . .'

The pale grey curtains billow like sails.

'. . . a journey.'

My legs ache, as if they've walked a lifetime that isn't mine.

There's nothing right about death. It shouldn't be allowed. And it's allowed, but it's not right. Nothing's solid; death wrenches the air in half, a lightning jolt, sent and returned, straight down the middle. There's charred absence: the black hole of a heartbeat, stopped.

Time has clawed itself backwards.

As if this is the first death I've seen, the world has shapeshifted around me.

There's more he must have wanted.

There's more he could have been given.

There's a bruise spreading in whatever rock this home is built on. There are no stable enough foundations to raise anyone from death, walls aren't bricked strong enough to keep out illness, and somewhere high above the roof is the sound of an icicle wind.

My eyes see too bright and too dark.

There must be a rip in the sky.

Bang, bang, bang. Adam wakes me, knocking on the doorframe to this spare room.

He looks small, thin. 'Grizzly, I want a proper cuddle.' He's crying as he plods over to the bed, gets in and curls up next to me. I put my hand over him. It feels like a clumsy paw.

His talk-style is choked. 'Dad's dead,' he sobs and sobs, his tiny frame jerking with loss. I pat him for a long time, till he quiets into sleep.

Faint-hearted without light, I promise in a whisper, 'I'll carry his death with you, because I can feel how heavy it is.'

He's curled, locked in sleep.

I forget all my promises.

The memory of the other death drags at me like an anchor: Dead Red. It's sunk in a hidden place. I sink myself to find it.

I'm back in the cottage, in the living room beside the fire.

Sewing up a hem with the smells of ashes and honey.

My dream is in black, grey, white.

The sound of the front door opening. The smell of nightfrost.

I think it's Amber, come back from her walk.

In the kitchen the light's off.

In the shadows a woman with dark hair stands on the door-step.

The sky is filled with deadstars behind her and a chill wind blows in.

She steps into the kitchen, sees me, covers her mouth.

Behind her, a light-haired woman runs up the path.

She bends down and picks up a grey rock.

She comes in and grabs the woman's arm, tries to pull her back towards the front door, says, 'No, no, you can't go in here. Come away. Now.' Her voice tastes of charcoal.

I don't move. I'm shifting inside, can't speak feelings from both of them.

The woman with light frizzy hair watches me.

For her, I'm stretched old, angry, my heart aflame.

But the woman with dark hair is stone-frozen.

For her, I'm curving, made of glass and infinity.

The fair-haired woman presses the rock into the dark-haired woman's hand, and backs towards the door.

The woman grips the rock but doesn't take her stricken eyes from mine. 'Go away, Lizzie. I have to see.'

As I take a step towards them, Lizzie gasps and runs away, leaving us alone.

The woman stands half in shadow. Her chest rises and falls like that of an animal, trapped. She glances at my hand, and back at my face.

My own hand is clenching a rock, the same rock she clenches in hers. I can feel her heart, not mine, wavering in my chest. My face feels made of glass. I've changed into a mirror image of her. I can feel what it is that she wants, and fears.

She wants to see herself.

Not as layers of behind and behind and behind.

Not as a flat mirrored reflection.

She wants to see everything.

Her despairing voice says, 'Finally, I'm faced with myself. So turn on the light.'

Bang bang.

Maya

The night I killed Dead Red in black, grey, white.
Bang bang.
My left hand reaches and switches the kitchen to light.
Colour.

I'm pulled into Adam's dream. I'm a bear cradle-nursing a newborn cub. I'm in Finn's dream, calm. My grey curtain wings flap as I sing him into a coffin that turns into a small empty rowing boat, and slides away on a sea made of grains of salt. I'm in a daughter dream with Pippa, looking at an ancient album. In a creased photograph, I'm in sepia at her side and my face is blank. There are strings of enormous pearls around our throats, and the taste of strong tea.

Turning around, I'm a twin sister, holding hands with Amber, gazing into a mirror where we turn into joined shadows made from blackened ash from the sun that's blazing, a white river flowing through flames. I want to dive into the river, but Amber pulls me away and we're running through nights and days, into wilder landscapes, the rain beating us. My teeth feel an ice-cream sting. I'm scared of the wind till we stop and take shelter next to a wall of weatherworn stones, mountain high. The sky rumbles through thick grey clouds but we're together.

The same and together and everything is safe.

Now I'm alone. In the grass is a dented telescope. I hold it to my eye. In the distance, there's a horizon made from a sea which sounds like a surging orchestra. There's a thick-weave forest on a hill. A crimson flash between trunks of trees. The raindrops on the telescope lens burst the crimson. Earth browns and sharp greens flood, and the colour I want to magnify is gone.

AMBER

In the middle of the night, the honey cakes are on wire racks, cooling. I sit at the kitchen table grinding the pestle in the mortar, crushing peppercorns on the inside of someone's head. I'm thinking of Medic and his wife. Two of them. Three of us. One of me. I crush and pound and beat the peppercorns. Two of them. Three of us. One of me. Two of me and Maya.

One of me and Maya.

One of me.

Me and a shadow who doesn't speak.

No one to say my name.

I feel nameless. Spare. The pastry edges that are cut off and put in the bin.

A draught crawls through the cottage and everything creaks. My hands have run out of peppercorns. I want to move. Bring warmth through me; remember this is my home. Remember I couldn't love Medic. I won't let myself care enough. So I'll never feel love. Never give anyone anything they can hurt me with.

Because I know what it feels like.

At school when everyone else was in class, in a corridor kissing a boy. A door opening, footsteps. The boy pushing me into an empty classroom, my first boy. His hand up my skirt. Sharp pain. Kissing, still kissing. When he took his hand away. His scream.

My blood on his hand. Him, gone. Seeing him outside later in a circle of boys. Hearing him laughing his scream away. My nickname for years was *bloodhand*. So many boys whispered it, sniggered it as I passed, shouted it whenever I was on the school stage, in a group of singers, dancers, any assembled horde of girls who smiled and were photographed, and I was there. Making myself untouchable.

And things that hurt will keep happening over and over again until everything goes numb and nothing hurts or something changes. Bloodhand. Bloodhand. Bloodhand.

The kitchen light bulb blinks dark and light again.

I whisper, 'Come on, Amber. Don't let yourself get eaten up.'

Soaking up the scents of the spices, I stroke the recipe book, clean the bone spoons, polish them, put them back in the jar and rest my head against the cool stone wall.

The shadow in the corner stands still and quiet. I tell it, 'If you can hear my thoughts, don't you dare laugh at me or feel sorry for me.'

The shadow is without eyes, without face, without name.

I get out a pie dish, and find the recipe I want to try next:

NAMELESS PIE

Pastry:
Flour, self-raising, 12 oz
Salt, 2 pinches
Caster sugar, 1½ oz
Butter, 6 oz
Water, 3 fl oz

See instructions below regarding ingredients for Filling

Prepare the pastry to become a container; its job is to provide a receptacle and to keep the filling hidden and quiet.

Sift the flour and stir in the salt and sugar. Break the butter into pieces with your fingertips and as you rub it into the flour, think of bindings, of eggshells, membranes, glues. Once the binding thoughts seem irrelevant because the mixture resembles crumbs, stir once or twice more, as you imagine birds in flight have resentfully dropped the crumbs into your bowl. Stir in enough water to enforce the holding intention that is to be contained in the pastry. Divide the dough into two, and roll out circles.

When you are at an emotional impasse, allow all of your confusions and misunderstandings to flow into your fingertips. Allow your instincts to be your guide, but remember that the cooking of a Nameless Pie may result in something or someone being named, and their identity brought to the fore. Allow your fingers to select only the ingredients for the filling* that your hands reach for. Be unstinting regarding quantities.

Press one pastry circle into a pie dish. Spoon in the filling, and think of two opposing weights, one above, and one below, as you lay the circle, pressing and sealing the edges. Think of eggs being warmed by feathers, a period of incubation, a violent hatching, and the naming of newborns. Cramp the edges with the prongs of a fork, constrict the surface *with milk and restrict with caster sugar. Make a small slit in the centre of the pie, to avoid premature explosions.*

* *The effect of consumption is unpredictable. It is dependent on how generous you are able to be when allowing your hands, and not your mind, to make choices.*

For the filling, I steam apples, dried apricots and prunes, segments of oranges and grate in a shrivelled lemon. With a bone spoon I stir in cocoa, icing sugar and some of the crushed peppercorns. I mix it together, spoon it into the pie and hide the sticky filling under the thick piecrust.

As it bakes, the shrieks and wails of the birds outside call me. Dawn has come too fast. I haven't yet put out the honey cakes.

Wrenching open the front door, I put them on the doorstep.

I hear the gate creak and look up. A small elderly woman wheels through a large wicker basket, filled with ingredients. She closes the gate behind her, and grips onto the basket again.

Slamming the door, my palms soaked in sweat, I lock myself in. I don't know if she's seen me.

Eventually, she speaks from the other side of the door. Her voice sounds awestruck. 'Such the smallest thing, seeing a door closing.'

I exhale, and rub the sweat from my palms onto my threadbare jumper.

Still she speaks, 'Showing me you're still here, watching over us all. Makes me feel not so alone. You've always been here. Longer than time. Older than age.'

The next night thickens outside and I imagine my thoughts buzzing in the powders as I sift flour, bicarb, baking powder and salt for the honey cakes into a bowl. I sprinkle in finely chopped dried mint as it matches my intention – come clean, come clear, get it off the chest. Let the cake-eaters have the need to confess whatever damp guilts they have, let guilt sludge up in their digestive tracts and be crapped out, because that's what's best to do with guilt. I'm sure guilt must cause constipation.

I grease the cake trays and turn around.

I look at the flickering shadow in the corner. 'If you're listening, I'm going to confess to you. I'm feeling guilt because I'm desperately missing Maya. I know how she felt now, living here. Because I've felt the same.'

The shadow is thicker than ever, yet more human. It thickens . . . I can see hair. Features. It's a man in breeches and a waistcoat. A wide-necked pale shirt. Worn lace-up boots. His dark eyes glint. I grab one of the rib spoons and he rubs his chest.

'You were the old woman's lover, weren't you?' I say.

He looks at me, and is closer.

I step back.

He's still closer.

His face is about ten inches from mine. His eyes are intense, unsettlingly deep. Unbelievably beautiful.

'Which old woman's lover were you? The one before me, or one of the others long before her?'

He doesn't answer.

'What do you want from me?'

His voice is deep, echoing. 'You have to bury her. Not just forget.'

I shake myself.

He's still here.

I say, 'The woman in the shed?'

'Properly. Don't ignore what you can't see. There's reasons bodies should be under the earth. It's undignified, aside from anything else.' He frowns and says in a harsh voice, 'She's needing burying.' He watches me, and I can see how big his lips are, and I imagine what it must have been like, when they were alive, moist, warm, to kiss them.

I say, 'How did you die?'

He looks at the bone spoon in my hand. 'You know I'm not really dead.'

I hold out the spoon. 'Not so long as these are being used?'

He smiles with half of his mouth. 'Love the way you touch them. Almost a caress at times . . .'

'You can feel it?'

He looks down at the floor and back at me again, with aching eyes. 'All the way through.'

I flush all over. I never realised a ghost could be so charismatic.

He interrupts my rapid heartbeat. 'Now that poor lass out in the shed . . .' He glowers at me intently, into me . . . with eyes that seem at the other end of a long corridor, but are somehow so close to my own that I'm falling out of myself and into them. The kitchen shifts, swirls around those eyes . . .

I look away. 'Did you kill her?'

He doesn't answer.

So I say, 'You know most people think silence means yes. Is there a justice system in the afterlife, or can you do what you like, as long as you only harm the living?'

Still, no answer. Just those eyes . . .

'Did she want to die?'

He says nothing.

'Well, if you're a murderer, a suicide assistant or a euthanasiastical type, I'd better be careful what I wish for with you around. What's your name?'

He finally speaks. 'Gilliam. And you're not Gloria, you're Amber, who is glorious.'

'You've been paying attention.' I put the bone spoon down on the table.

He's beside me. I can feel his breath on my neck like a sigh. My pulse thuds as he whispers, 'I've been lover to all of the women who've baked in this kitchen before you. And you'll not be the last. That you'll not mind, when the time comes.'

I close my eyes and match my breathing to his.

His lips speak into my ear, 'Last night you wondered aloud if I could hear your thoughts. The answer is, no. I can't. I can only hear what you say.'

As I open my eyes, he's a faint shadow flickering in the corner. A feeling in the air of a purpose, fulfilled.

And I am left, wanting.

I go into the bedroom, throw myself on the bed and hug the duvet with my legs. Grabbing the pillow in my arms, I whisper, 'Oh Maya, please come back. I'm going to be in love and it's bound to be terrible.'

I take the honey cakes out of the oven and think about the Nameless Pie and how it was meant to result in something or someone being named. And now I know the name of the ghost who's been living here with me all this time.

I whisper into the steam that comes from the cakes, 'Honey scent, remember bees, buzz away to find my sister, make her safe, and bring her back. Find her, and bring her safe, back to me.' Over and over again I whisper it into the breath of the cakes as it rises like a mist.

Once the cakes are outside, the dawn creeps through the curtains and across the kitchen, changing shadows from dark to pale grey. I eat scrambled eggs and cheese from a pan as I sit on the floor and lean my head back against the front door. I think about what to do about burying the dead woman.

There's the sound of a walking stick and heavy footfall on the path, as the woman comes to get the honey cakes.

Her cracked voice speaks on the other side of the closed front door. 'Old Kelp, I don't know if you can somehow see me or the like.'

She waits, and speaks again.

'Know you won't answer me. But I'm feeling so blessed to have seen a sign of you. I've always felt we've got this link.'

She pauses again, and I can hear her sniffing. 'Mmm. Mint. Well, that's a good clean herb. See, you do no bad. Got no trouble from you myself in all these years. Feel it's a kind of sisterly bond it is we've got. Till tomorrow, then.'

'Wait,' I say, in my most dramatic voice.

Her voice is full of reverence. 'Old Kelp . . .'

This is going well.

I announce in my deepest, most powerful voice, 'There is a body.'

'A bod—'

'You heard.'

'A body of water – are you set on sending us another flood?'

'You promise to listen but never to speak?'

'I'll swear it to you, over and over if you want me to.'

'A body in my shed.'

'Oh. I might need to mention it to just one other person if you're wanting me to help with that, my arms aren't quite as strong as—'

'Hold steadfast and faithful and I will smile all over you.' I wince. That didn't sound quite right. I leave a dramatic pause and make my voice stern and low. 'You must bury that body. It will . . . be unpleasant. Unpleasant as . . .'

I don't know what religion she might be. So remembering what I learned about hell at school, I try to cover various possibilities quickly, in the hope they'll blur together and she'll grab onto one which means something to her. I take a deep breath.

'. . . an inferno next to a lake of blood and guilt, filled by twin rivers – one of fire and one of ice, as roasting as hellfire fuelled by rocks and stones, as destructive as a devourer's teeth, your soul, breaking like a firelighter in order to light a candle which will never extinguish . . .'

I'd no idea I'd taken in so much hell at school.

She's silent. I might have scared her too much.

So I say, 'Repeat this: The lives of the faithful are filled with inexplicable trials.'

She sounds worryingly repentant as she repeats it over and over again.

Taking a deep breath, I announce, 'The body met death, because she crossed my threshold. Stoned, with a rock. Death by way of rock and a crashing floor is brief, but others will suffer far worse by my hand, if they so much as touch the handles of my doors. Say it. Again!' My voice booms.

She murmurs, 'The lives of the faithful . . .'

In my most punitive voice I say, 'Bury her, and remember that faith is at its most powerful when it is unspoken.' I slide the key for the padlock on the shed through the gap under the door.

She's quiet for a while.

She finally speaks. 'I know the right thing to do. It'll be done within two days, if I'm not mistook. Leave it with me.'

I decide to sweeten the air in the kitchen all day with the flavours and scents of the richest puddings. Hunting through all the cupboards, I find an ingredient I've never tried before. Black sugar.

I read the recipe that wants it:

DARK CUSTARDS

Double cream, 10½ fl oz
Vanilla essence, ½ smallest spoon
Brown sugar, 2 oz
Black sugar, 1½ oz
Salt, pinch
Egg yolks, 4

Warm the double cream, vanilla essence, brown and black sugars and the pinch of salt in a saucepan. Consider the texture of the cream mixture, as you imagine the sugars and creams combining in a rolling boil, but do not reach boiling point. Instead, allow your mind to gain a sense of the movement within the pan, and any situations it may call to mind. Allow yourself to feel tantalised by the effort of almost reaching a rolling boil, but not quite. Stir, until the sugar has been absorbed into the cream, and allow your mouth to salivate as you lick your lips. Do not dribble.

Take the saucepan off the heat, and let the warmth in your face and hands spread throughout your body. Allow sensual memories to surface as you beat the egg yolks, and keep these memories at the front of your mind as you whisk in the hot cream mixture.

Strain into a jug and pour into two medium-sized dishes. (Or more than two smaller ones if there

are to be more people present – but please note:
unless you have boundless energy, and aren't prone
to embarrassment, it is advised to stick with two.)

Put these dishes in a deep roasting tin and pour
in enough boiling water to come halfway up the
dishes. Bake in the oven until the custards have
just set. Remove from the oven and wobble them
gently. Consider the texture of human skin and the
taste of caramel. Inhale the aromas.

Put the dishes in the fridge and cool them for a
good few hours, while you and your eating companion
entertain yourselves wherever your inclinations lead
you.*

Consume from your companion's surface.

* The combination of brown and black sugars with
cream are a purely skin-deep aphrodisiac, which
may wear off rapidly if there is no sense of
connection beyond the physical.

I wait for the night, for Gilliam to become visible. It will be
gradual, slow, delicious. I imagine kissing his smoky lips to
warmth and my body flushes, heats, moistens. And I smile to
myself at the thought of having a lover who comes to me at
nights, and leaves me the days for myself.

Even if he killed the woman in the shed, I'm not worried
about him ever harming me. Because I know what to do if he
frightens me. He feels me touching the bone spoons, so I'll pick

one I don't use too often for cooking, and break it. He'll feel it, as he said, all the way through. Gilliam will be a lover who won't ever talk about me to anyone else.

Because my hands could break his bones, his words will never hurt me.

MAYA

Pippa switches on the hallway lights as she comes downstairs in her dressing gown. She says, 'I thought I heard you. If you're not able to sleep either, next time, come and get me.'

I'm sitting on the floor, staring at the telephone.

She looks down at her hands and says, 'Sometimes, I wish I had a religion. To be able to believe there's an afterlife would be such a comfort. Will you follow me?'

I follow her as far as the kitchen.

We sit at the table together as she unravels and re-ravels balls of wool with fidgety hands. She finishes rolling a green ball and puts it next to an orange one.

She speaks in a rushing talk-style, 'I'll forget if I don't speak tonight, while all these memories are visiting. Remember them for me?'

I prepare a wall of shelves in my head.

Her eyes are bright but her face is full of clouds. She tells me about her wedding day. They married, barefoot at her request, on cold flagstones. She calls the place they were married: 'the nearest village that's still churched'. She says, 'We danced all the way there, and limped all the way back, and though neither of us held firm to any particular religion, I don't think any deity objected. Apart from the thunderstorm, the burning barn we passed, and then later, our entire wedding party being almost drowned by torrential rain on the way home, it was the best day I've ever known.'

I add filing trays to the shelves in my head and begin to fill them.

'But,' she says, 'after the ceremony, Finn was always like an eel; he seemed comfortable and quiet in the darkest corner of any room, though he smiled whenever he heard me laugh. But,' she sighs, 'and this is the thing, he was always an eel. And after a fair few years, he seemed to *lurk*.' She tells me he'd kept looking at Lizzie. 'And when Lizzie finally looked back at him . . . Well,' she says, 'well. He slipped through my hands and slithered away and back, away and back, like I'd always hoped he wouldn't.'

I turn around in my head, put up more shelves, and add archive filing boxes.

Pippa speaks of walks she went on with Finn. Of climbing steep hills, and the colours of the fish he caught and the stink he brought home on the jumpers she'd knitted for him. She tells me about the smells of their home in the spring: of paint and cut grass and salt and varnish. She talks about the shapes of clouds in a mackerel sky, of icicles and frozen pipes.

She tells me about annoyed words and avoided conversations and the lies Finn told her that she'd rather forget.

So in the small room in my head, I add a shredder that grinds up annoyances, avoidances and lies. This lightens her.

She describes Finn's kisses when he loved her most, and how he once tried and messily failed to make a meringue. She tells me she never forgot the pain of childbirth, though Finn always told her she would.

Her memories creak and strain and cramp as I shut them safely away.

Pippa's face clears.

A feeling through the kitchen of high-lifting thin air.

She says with a smile, 'Whoosh. Now it's your turn to talk.'

My hand is clutching something heavy, but I look at my palm and it's empty. 'I've got this invisible rock in my hand.'

She nods me encouragement.

I say, 'Maybe it's guilt. If I need to confess, to talk to the police, what will I have to do?'

'Oh darling. You're still so unsettled. Police can't help you with that.'

Ignoring the weight of the rock, I lean my head on my hands. 'Does punishment feel like relief?'

'Law isn't like maths. There's no definitively right answer to much in life. Not when you consider all the points of view that could possibly be involved.'

I put my right hand on the table, palm up, and stare at it. 'The weight of a guilt rock feels mine and not-mine. I didn't get the right answers in maths anyway.'

She laughs. 'Neither did I.' She scoops a ball of white and black flecked yarn up off the floor and drops it on the table. 'There was only the one policeman, but he's long gone.'

'One?'

'There's nothing he was ever really needed for. We've both come from somewhere that seemed to need hundreds of police all the time.'

I clench, unclench my right hand. 'But where is law?'

Pippa says, 'Where there's crime.'

'There must be crime wherever there are people.'

'Ah, but there you have it. There's the hope.'

I say again, 'But where is law?'

She says again, 'Where there's crime. Meaningful crime.'

'Not here?'

'I've been here long enough to notice that punishment's not necessarily the best response. See, hope.'

'Hope?'

Her face brightens into a smile. 'It never was going to be in somewhere designed to be as exceptional as Paradon. Hope's too quiet a thing. It would never have hidden itself there. It's here, in places like this.'

It's dawn and I still haven't slept. I'm lying on the spare-room bed. If I stare at this blank ceiling for long enough, thinking about hope, perhaps I can make it appear. It would be a quiet, salty thing. It would small-big itself fast. It would be a white lump of hope I could hold in my hand. I'd hide it under the bed because it would be shy. I've been lying here for ages but I don't think I can do this, not in a house with other people and mix-match feelings.

The sound of the telephone sharp-ringing cuts the air all the way through the house.

I run downstairs with small hope grains clumping:

the phone's ringing for me,

somewhere else, somehow else,

the guilt rock I'm dragging has been sensed,

and there really still is one policeman,

calling this phone, trying to find me.

As I get to the last flight of stairs I hear Pippa answer the phone.

I go halfway down the stairs.

She says, 'That's so kind of you. I'll send him round after lunch, so you can fit it there, if that's all right. I'd like him out of the house. They're coming with the coffin this afternoon.'

It's not the one policeman.

My feelings jump to somewhere else, I don't know where. Hope dissolves.

I sit on a stair and watch her through the banisters.

Pippa listens again, says, 'Thank you. I'd like that.'

After another pause she says, 'Yes. Adam wants to see him too. Thanks. Really, thanks.'

She hangs up the phone and looks up at me between the banisters. 'You know I've never known people to be so kind. Especially when they've not been asked. And because you're here, being so kind to me, I'm seeing kindness everywhere. Dorcas has made Adam's suit jacket for the funeral, so now I've only got my skirt to finish. A couple of the others are coming to do a blessing for Finn after dusk.'

'Is everyone here kind?'

'Not all. But they're familiar. Adam's back in bed again.' She sighs. 'I'd only slept for a couple of hours when he woke me. He was crying his eyes out, in case you ever went away.' She looks up at me. 'You didn't sleep at all, did you?'

'No. I keep trying. There's something I need to dream.'

Her talk-style is gentle. 'What is it?'

She comes away from the phone and sits sideways on the bottom stairs. She waits for me to speak. Her silence stretches like a stroke. She wants me to talk, wants to know, wants to look after me and so the words come. 'Pippa, I killed someone.'

Her eyes widen.

'I can't remember exactly what happened.'

She says, softly, 'Then how can you be so certain?'

'No one else was there.'

'Where was there?'

I look down at the fluff on the stair carpet between us.

She leans to catch my gaze. 'What can you remember?'

I take a deep breath. 'Me and her, face to face in the dark.

Both of us had a rock in our hands. And the next thing I remember is that the light was on, she was dead on the floor in front of me, wearing a dress that was mine, the rock stained with blood lying next to her head.'

Pippa says, 'It could have been self-defence. Or do you remember wanting to kill her?'

'I don't remember ever wanting anything. Apart from now, wanting the guilt to go away. It's a rock in my hand, stones in my stomach, gravel in my throat – and I want it to be sand.'

'Because sand blows away.' She nods, slowly. 'I would argue diminished responsibility. Definitely, if you're suffering amnesia. I want to help you.'

'How I can find out what happened?'

She leans back against the wall, still looking up at me. She speaks in a calm talk-style. 'You've got the right idea about dreaming. The memory will be there somewhere but your unconscious is protecting you. We could try hypnosis.' She rubs her neck. 'Sweetie, don't look so scared, I can't make you do anything you don't want to.'

'I'm not so sure about that.'

She smiles. 'I don't believe for a moment we'll find anything that proves you're a murderess. Quite the opposite. You're far too gentle by nature.'

'What if my nature's changeable?'

She stands up and leans on the banister. 'I'll help you after tomorrow. When the funeral's over. Just for now, we both have to keep ourselves ticking over. So, precious. Practicalities. You'll have to stay upstairs again this afternoon. Try to sleep a little then, if you can, but no foraging for now. They're coming from Fastleigh, laying Finn in his coffin. He arranged it all, long before he died. Never told me. My poor boy.' She shakes her head, and

341

I don't know if she means Adam or Finn as she wanders unsteadily into the kitchen.

I can hear muffle-voices in Finn's room below me. The sound of hammering. Silence. More quiet talking. At the spare-room window I look out over mossy rooftops and smoking chimneys. My stomach is hoarding stones.

The sky is white-clear and clean. I whisper to it, 'Don't believe Pippa can help. She wants me to be innocent.' My eyes salt-sting me. I know it would only last while I'm with Pippa, wanting me to believe in my own innocence.

A gull flies pale across the tiled rooftops. I whisper again, 'What happens here, to people who've done something terrible? Could long silence grind guilt to sand?'

Across the narrow street in the window opposite this one, the attic curtain that's always closed is open. There's a middle-aged man washing the window with a cloth. I move closer to the curtain so he can't see me. He leaves faint smears on one of the windowpanes and turns the dirty cloth over and over in his hands. He disappears from the room. But there's another man there. He's standing completely still, looking out at me. Hanging from the ceiling all around him are unflying doves.

The man's frozen. Even his face doesn't move.

I wave-hand him.

He doesn't wave-hand me back.

He's wearing a uniform with arrows on the shoulders that point to his arms. Under a peaked cap, his eyes look like smoky marbles. They . . . are smoky marbles. His skin shines with a pale blue under-tinge.

The middle-aged man comes back into the room and polishes the dull silver buttons on the man's uniform. He dusts the peaked cap with his mouth moving slowly as if he's utter-speaking penance. He picks up a small paintbrush and dab-paints the edges of the man's eyes. He comes to the window, wipes each of the panes clean, closes the curtains again and pegs them shut.

The only policeman there was stands in that attic room, stuffed like the doves.

A taxidermied policeman.

KIP

George and three men in black glasses and brown suits carry Uncle Finn's coffin through the village on their shoulders. There are bunches of herbs and trails of ivy on the coffin. On top of a wreath of holly is Uncle Finn's cloth cap with his fishing flies still stuck in.

People join us behind the coffin, talking quietly, or walking in silence. I look at the coffin with Uncle Finn's body lying closed away inside it. The last time I saw his body, he was alive and living in it. I pull Mammy's arm and whisper in her ear, 'He said it wasn't, but is it my fault?'

'Is what your fault?'

'That he died.'

'Oh Kip, no. You called for help and people came. Everyone knows that. You might even have given his heart more beats before it stopped, getting help to him so quick.'

'But I might have upset him.'

'People upset each other all the time. He was killed by his heart, not by you.' Mammy squeezes my hand.

Adam and Aunty Pippa walk behind the coffin, both dressed in white outfits.

I ask Mammy, 'Why do the most important mourners wear white?'

She says, quietly, 'When someone dies, those closest to them have to learn how to live. Sometimes when someone you love dies, it's like the sun blinks itself shut. White's a blank picture. White's so mourners can see colours as soon as the sun opens for them again.'

Aunty Pippa's left some threads coming out of the seam down the back of her jacket. Mammy won't let me go and pull them out for her because, she says, 'it'll give her something to fidget at later'.

We're passing Old Kelp's cottage so I'm hiding beside Mammy. Mam Vann's a bit late as she catches us up, breathless. We all walk behind the coffin. My hand's holding tight to Mammy's.

She grips my hand back and says, 'Kip, you're really shaking!'

I whisper, 'I'm scared to go past here.'

She puts her arm around me and says, 'I'll take care of you.' She doesn't look at Old Kelp's cottage as we go up the path to where the hearse is parked.

Uncle Finn's to be buried at Fastleigh in the yard with a church where he and Aunty Pippa got married. Dad's been allowed to drive Jock's tractor and his biggest trailer, so a fair few of us can go.

Mammy stands on her tiptoes and looks up at the lay-by, squeezes my hand and whispers, 'Your dad's not made it back yet. He'll turn up soon. He'll not cry for his brother, though he'll be sad on the inside.'

'Is not crying brave?'

She sighs. 'No Kip, he's just private, that's all. He'll cry with me, when there's no one else to see it.'

The hearse looks a bit dented but the metal fittings are shining so they look brand new. We gather on one side and no one speaks as one of the men in brown suits opens the back doors.

We watch them slide in Uncle Finn's coffin.

One of the men gets in the driver's seat as the other two close the back doors and stand with their heads bowed and their dark glasses looking down at their brown suit buttons. Their hands are clenched together over the fronts of their trousers.

George goes around to the driver's side of the hearse, ducks down, and stands up straight again. He raps on the driver's window. The driver winds the window down and George leans in and says something. The driver takes his dark glasses off, looks in the mirror, smoothes his bald patch, opens the door and steps out. He kicks at the back tyre, walks to the front, and kicks that one too.

I tug at Mammy because I want to go and look at the wheels.

She whispers in my ear, 'No, stay put. It's a solemn moment.'

Adam isn't having a solemn moment. He goes round the other side of the hearse as well, looks at me and says loudly, 'They're flat.'

George turns to the men in brown. 'So you've got Finn all the way up from our village in a different box to the one he asked for because you've run out of the right wood, one of your men's off sick today, and now your wheels are done in. What do you do next? Phone the doctor to see if he'll bother coming over to stop him dying?'

Adam climbs on the bonnet and lies back against the window.

Jessie has a look at the wheels. 'You can't short-change Finn because he's not here to quibble you for what he paid for. Well, this puts me off from setting up a funeral while I'm alive, if this is the kind of shite I'll get when I've kicked my own bucket over!' She ducks down and looks more closely at the wheels. 'They've only been slashed!'

A whole bunch of people flurry to look at the wheels.

One of the men in brown asks the others about a spare, and they shrug and say something about even if there was one, they'd need two. One of them says loudly, 'The wheels were fine when we parked it here.'

Aunty Pippa puts the palms of her hands on the long hearse window and leans her forehead against the silver line that runs along the hearse roof.

Mammy puts her arm around her shoulders.

I climb on the bonnet and sit with Adam. I lean back against the windscreen too. He nudges me gently and I nudge him back. We lie looking up at the thick grey clouds and listen to everyone talking loudly at the same time as each other and finding no sense about what's to be done.

I say to Adam, 'We could take him up to our own graveyard by the fir trees.'

'He didn't want to be buried here.'

I swallow. 'No one else who's in your house coming with us then?'

'Grizzly?' He glances around and whispers, 'No. Mum says she's best kept hid till she's more settled. Everyone talks, and she's so amazing, they'd all want to see her.' He says louder, 'If we go to our own graveyard they'll have to carry Dad all the way round the wood, all uphill, it's a fair walk.'

'We can't leave him here in a broken hearse.'

Mam Vann's listening. She says, 'From the mouths of boys!'

Everyone goes quiet and one or two of them frown at my best-till-last dress.

Mam Vann says, 'If some of us run back down the village for spades and wood for burning, we'll be able to get a grave dug in our own graveyard, and Finn in the ground before the light's gone from the sky.'

George nods. 'We could get that done. What do you think, Pippa?'

Aunty Pippa says to them, 'You two coming round last night with that great barrowful of herbs for last rites, well yes. That was kind. But just because I don't know how to bless him myself . . .' She sobs and can't speak.

Mammy pats Aunty Pippa's shoulder. She says to Mam Vann, 'What she's saying is that you're not in charge of his burial.'

Mam Vann hurries away to have another look at the tyres.

Aunty Pippa says to Mammy, 'Well, that was above and beyond any kind of last rites I've ever heard of. I mean, they said the herbs were to go inside the coffin as well – I couldn't watch them open it, I'd already said goodbye. Is that terrible?'

'Well, so he's been blessed. That's only a good thing. It doesn't matter that you didn't know how. I wouldn't either. We'll get him buried somehow. Today.'

I hear the sound of a tractor and look up the hill. It's Dad at the wheel, and the tractor's pulling a huge trailer. I say to Adam, 'If we put your dad in the trailer and all get in and huddle his coffin steady so he doesn't fall out – we can take him to Fastleigh.'

Mam Vann's heard me. She shouts, 'A trailer for a dead man, that's no dignity. You'd be better off putting his coffin in a fishing boat, sending him off out to sea and asking him to fish out a working pair of wheels! If we all do it, we can get a grave dug. Adam –' she leans on the bonnet '– you'd like him buried nearer home, wouldn't you?'

'Mum says we'll get to Fastleigh sometimes . . .'

'You'll not get there often.'

Adam puts his arms over his eyes.

Mammy says, 'Let him alone. We'll get him there when he wants to go.'

Mam Vann says to Aunty Pippa, 'If he's buried nearer, you can visit him, you know. We can all keep an eye . . .'

Aunty Pippa comes to the front of the hearse and rubs Adam's shin. 'Dignity. Perhaps later on it might nag at me . . .' Mammy gives her a hankie and she wipes her eyes. 'But Finn wanted to be buried where we married. Well. He did when he wrote it all down.'

As Dad slows up in the tractor next to us, Mammy shouts over the engine rattles, 'Brack, the hearse is done in! We'll have to get Finn up in the trailer. Take as many of us as you can fit, to hold him in place.'

Dad watches the three men shuffling around by the back of the hearse. He calls loudly back to Mammy, 'We'd best take the three blind mice along, so my brother can at least be carried to his grave proper.'

MAYA

This sad house is finally empty of other people. In a sleepless curl under spare blankets, I feel big-small. My insidehalf is walking a tightrope wire with a clock ticking at one end, and my outsidehalf is bed-huddled at the other.

Along the tightrope wire are air-hanging moving pictures. There's Amber and me in our lilac flowery dresses. Amber's holding my hand as we attic-window-sing at pale clouds. We're sure with light-breathing we can fly.

Further along the wire, we build chair and table empires. Amber's the ruler because she's cleverest. She pirate-swashes our bathwaters into oceans, climbs our stairs into ladders, smears redyellowblue paints into greenpurpleorange pictures, and sings us into queens. Our toys are removed and replaced as we grow. Our rattles and blankets, stuffed toys and mobiles are pine-disinfected and sent to a nursery.

Further still along the wire, there's a louder ticking sound as our parents fill the playroom with alphabet and number bricks. There's sinister nursery-rhyming music.

Next there are picture books, bubble blowers, green calcula-tors, neon crayons, and a tower-stack of sugar paper. We draw our own seasons, over and over again, and wave torn raindrops at the sunshine.

Balance balance. I try not to fall as I watch me and Amber hand in hand by a gleaming blue river. Our parents take stop-photos as we walk, balance, listen for ticks and clicks. Their once-a-year photographs are pegged along the tightrope wire. They're all of our silhouettes.

This is real innocence: memories with no meanings pegged to them.

My insidehalf sways alone on this high wire, trying to breathe myself weightless. My outsidehalf is stone-heavy, a rock in this bed. I'm pulled up and falling between sky-height and bed-depth.

It's not our parents, or Paradon, but Amber I'm missing now.

The village is an empty echo. I walk narrow streets, trying to remember the way outoutout to Amber.

This alleyway smells of clean laundry. As I tread silent cobble-stones, daylight makes me a float-head. I turn a corner and the next lane looks the same as the one I've just walked up. Turning back, the street I've walked along is one I've never seen before. The houses lean forward so I'm in a tunnel of buildings, the rooftops leaning closer together. The houses eye me with windows; they don't want a flood and my hands feel like rain.

I breathe in jumble colours and flavours. Bricks taste of paprika and mustard. Pastel-painted walls and windowsills are ice cream vanilla, strawberry, and grey tastes of liquorice.

Remembering when I left mysister, her shout-smash: *What are you? Who are you, without what other people want?*

She didn't know my new feelings that jump don't have guard-walls, they've only got eggshell around them. I didn't tell her. She didn't want to know.

I stop, and cover my eyes black to think. Need to find some-thing to tell her, because mysister wants. Think with no jumbles.

I've learned-up some sensible things of want to say:

I want there to be a home for me, somewhere

and behind that I want to know what I really look like.

I want to find out for certain if stars are dead or alive

and behind that I still want to be able to give others what they want.

I want to bury rock-heavy feelings in dug-out earth holes.

And the biggest one I can think of is that:

I want something to hope for.

That's a lot. I should draw pictures of all these things and peg them to myself, so I don't forget them as soon as I'm with Amber. Make them all into little bright-coloured want flags.

I open my eyes and there's nothing in my hands to draw with. So I keep walking through this wind full of spite. A rusted bike leans against a wall. The thickness of clouds is the swarm-sound of bees. A line of damp pillowcases tastes the flavour of teabags. I turn into another alleyway, where a seagull-wail smells of yeast.

I don't even know if Amber will want to see me.

And that could easily mean that she won't.

I walk towards the cottage.

Dead Red drones in my eyes, not my ears.

A crow croaks as it flies out of the garden. The kitchen curtain moves.

At the front door, I reach for the door handle.

Amber wrenches the door open, shrieks my name, and I'm inside the kitchen.

I splutter, 'It mustn't have been me. Motive undoubt,' I gasp, though Amber's happiness crashes into me so hard, I almost stagger. I try again. 'It wasn't me . . .' My jumble words are squeezed fat to thin as they crumble in my throat. So I change what I'm trying to say. 'Are you alone?'

She nods, beaming. 'For now.'

I try to get the right words to be the right width in my mouth. I bundle them up and spit them out, 'Amber, I must have killed Dead Red.'

Amber's voice sounds golden. 'No, Maya, it doesn't matter now, her body's gone. You seem so strange . . . and thinner.' She touches my cheek. 'You're freezing. Where have you, who have you been?' She frowns at her hand. The colours blue and purple flash in my eyes.

All my want flags have gone; I've forgotten what they are.

I steady myself and know that my eyes are seeing as Amber's eyes, because all the things that are important to her, glow. I look around the kitchen at the shimmering recipe book, the luminous bone spoons in the orange jar, the pestle and mortar drying in a gleam on the draining board, and there's a shine in the air over the unmade bed she's moved out of the bedroom and into the kitchen corner.

KIP

As we bump and rattle along in the trailer, the herbs keep coming off the coffin lid. Mam Vann doesn't care about putting her hands into whoever's lap the herbs have landed in, as long as she can put them back on.

George keeps letting go of the coffin to grab Mam Vann so she doesn't get shaken off the trailer into some passing field.

She's saying, 'The herbs have to stay put; they're his blessing and doesn't he need one?'

George mutters, 'But the stink of them is more like a curse.'

Mam Vann hisses back at him, 'You're one to talk about stinks, George. Been handling something gnarly, have you? You could have at least washed your hands.'

Aunty Pippa's sat up the back of the trailer. Mammy's on one side of her, holding her tightly, Adam's on the other, gripping her hand.

The three men in brown suits keep Uncle Finn's coffin steady. They're concentrating hard and won't talk to us when we ask them anything. When they'd heaved the coffin up onto the trailer, Jessie asked them, *Are coffins always that heavy?* Two of them shook their heads and the other one nodded, which means they don't know.

We're coming into Fastleigh, and can see the church spire not

354

far up the hill. As we pass a row of shops, the people out in the street lower their heads, though their eyes are still having a good stare.

One of them is the Quiet Woman.

Alive.

She comes out of a shop, arm in arm with Lizzie. I take my hands off the coffin and spin around, staring at her.

She looks back at me and nods. She's real, not a ghost of herself, not a dead body in Old Kelp's shed.

Lizzie rushes her hands to her mouth as she looks at the coffin. She sees Adam and Aunty Pippa dressed in white, juddering along. Her face breaks into tears and the Quiet Woman puts her arms around her.

As we drive on, I watch the very alive Quiet Woman sit Lizzie down on a bench. A whispering between Jessie and Mam Vann tells me they've seen Lizzie as well. Mammy's showing Aunty Pippa and Adam two black swans in a pond on the other side of the road.

As soon as we're at the yard next to the ancient stone church, Dad stops the tractor and kills the engine. I can hear crows in the high trees and my ears are ringing as Dad lets down the back of the trailer. He gives Aunty Pippa and Adam a hand down, gets Mammy down next and lets the others scrabble off the trailer themselves. Mam Vann waits to be helped.

The three brown-suited men and George get Uncle Finn's coffin off. They carry it steady on their shoulders through the rusted iron gate. Adam, Aunty Pippa and Mammy follow the coffin in.

As the others go in after them, Dad helps Mam Vann down. I say to him, 'I've got to go. Be right back.'

He nods towards the edge of the yard. 'There's bushes over there, be quick about it.'

Mam Vann says, 'Can't you tie a knot in it? All of us need

to go, but we're late e-bloody-nough . . . got to get Finn six foot under, and covered . . . Brack – he's off the wrong way – where's he going?'

I run back down the street, towards the row of shops.

Lizzie and the Quiet Woman are still sitting on the bench. Lizzie's sobbing, and a couple of men have stopped next to them.

The Quiet Woman has her arm around Lizzie and she's shaking her head at them, saying 'She's had a shock. I'll take care of her.'

'You're alive,' I say to her as the men walk away.

She has a strange voice, as if she's only just learned how to talk. 'You're . . . you're the girl who was taking my violets?' She pats Lizzie's shoulder.

'I'm . . . I'm a . . . Kip. I saw . . .'

Lizzie sits up, her cheeks flushed. 'Kip, what happened to Finn?'

'He had a heart attack.'

'Oh Finn. Your heart . . .' She sobs against the Quiet Woman's neck.

The Quiet Woman says to her, 'If they're for burying him here, you'll get to say your goodbyes at his grave. Every day if you're wanting.'

Lizzie nods, still crying.

I say, 'I saw you dead.'

The Quiet Woman looks at me, sharply. 'No you didn't.'

'I did. Your . . . face, it was . . .' I cover my mouth.

'I'm not dead.' Her voice is angry. It softens as she looks me up and down. 'You must have seen me in some nightmare.'

I say quietly, 'You were dead. I thought it could only be you. So it's someone else who's lying there in Old Kelp's . . .' I bite my lip so I don't say any more.

She's paler. 'That cottage. See all things in there, that's how I'm remembering—'

My heart thumps as I whisper, 'You went inside?'

Her eyes look up into the sky. 'You saw me, dead. So I'll tell you. Pain shouldn't be carried like bad luggage. It was for me, like that.'

She strokes Lizzie's shoulder, who grips onto her tightly. 'Different for Lizzie. She saw a crone, her claws hot pokers, fit for killing her. She showed Lizzie that loving someone she couldn't have was burning her up. She'd wanted to leave, but felt she couldn't. When Lizzie saw that crone's fire, she knew she had to. Is that right, Liz?' She shakes her a little but Lizzie's still crying too much to speak.

I say, 'But I saw you.'

Lizzie wrenches herself up, pushes away the Quiet Woman's outstretched hand and goes into one of the shops.

The Quiet Woman looks closely at me. 'Perhaps for you it's a meaning – all I know is in that cursed place, I saw myself. What I saw was like a mirror, but wasn't one. It was another person standing in front of me. Imagine you met yourself, and saw all the things a mirror can never show. I saw all of those things and more, in a woman who looked exactly like me, who came towards me and stood in front of me. Myself, un-reflected. A mirror that shows too much would need to be smashed. So I smashed her. Broke the face that was my face and ran without looking back. As you see, I'm not dead. But I saw, in that face . . .' her voice cracks, 'I wanted to be.'

'You don't still want to be dead now?'

She frowns at the grass growing between cracked paving stones. 'I can only believe you caught something left there, of what I saw. A jagged piece, fallen away. Because as you see, here

I am. You can pinch me.' She smiles a little as she holds out her hand.

I touch her blue frockcoat sleeve; press hard with my fingers and feel her solid arm. 'None of us know your real name.'

The Quiet Woman lowers her voice. 'Only because you believe you saw me dead. You'll know I'm alive true, if I give my name. It's Decesso.'

'You never told it to any of us.'

White sky reflects in her eyes. 'Why would I tell it? Decesso means death. Someone was having a joke for my life, when I was born. Threw me and my name away. Some parents give life without wanting it. Accident of a life, that's what I was.'

Lizzie comes back from the shop and thrusts a bunch of white lilies into my hands. 'I can't go. Not with Pippa there, Kip. Take these.' She crouches down and puts her hands on my shoulders. Her eyes shine. 'Put them on your uncle's coffin, for me. Now. Before they've covered him with soil.'

Decesso looks at the lilies and says to me, 'The person who's really dead must be stilled. And I'm learning to still myself here, alive.'

All the way home in the trailer, Adam's head rests against my shoulder and he doesn't speak. We get back to the lay-by at dusk.

As Aunty Pippa takes Adam's hand, he turns to me and says in a choked voice, 'You'll come round tomorrow?'

'I will, but can you come outside?'

He nods. 'See you tomorrow, then.'

Most of the other grown-ups follow Aunty Pippa and Adam back down to the village.

I'm crouched down next to Mammy. We're watching Dad try to patch up the wheels on the hearse before he takes the tractor back.

I hear George's voice say quietly, 'Not a hitch.'

Mam Vann's voice replies, 'Shush it. All's well and quiet when it's good and buried.'

They follow the others down the path.

When Dad's gone with the tractor, me and Mammy walk down the path towards Old Kelp's cottage.

Mammy says, 'You were good today, Kip. Lovely you got those lilies for Finn. Touched, Pippa and Adam were, and your dad was as well. I could tell.' She nudges me. 'You made me mist up.' She fans her eyes.

'Mammy?'

She stops walking. 'You're shaking again. What is it?'

'Can I . . . look in Old Kelp's shed?'

'No, Kip.'

'Just quickly, while you're here too?'

She holds both of my hands which tremble in hers. 'If we do, will it make you stop being this terrified of going past her cottage?'

'Depends.'

'We'll have to be so quiet.'

At the shed door, the padlock's got the key in it. Mammy nods, and whispers, 'Quick!' as we open the door. Her eyes are wide as she looks over her shoulder at Old Kelp's windows.

She steps inside, with me close behind her, covering my nose. On the floor is a pile of crumpled dustsheets on a mattress. I whisper to Mammy, 'There's nothing but a smell.'

She's shaking too. She whispers, 'See, there's nothing here at all.'

We don't speak till we're out of Old Kelp's gate.

Mammy glances over her shoulder at the cottage, and back

at me. She's still pale as she says, 'So. Are you all right now?'

'There was someone in there, before.'

'You've not been—'

'I thought it was the Quiet Woman. She was dead, her face blackened. How can she still be alive? Did you see—'

'I saw Lizzie with her, yes. And that's proof she's alive. Can't be in two places at the same time. You're never to go there again, Kip. No matter what happens. You know about all the curses.' As she looks at me, her face softens. 'If you thought the Quiet Woman was dead, and you've found out she's alive, that's only a good thing.'

'It won't be this way for Uncle Finn, will it?'

She sighs and says quietly, 'No, no it won't.'

As we keep walking, both silent, I think about Uncle Finn not being here any more, and not being here ever again. My eyes spill a little.

A seagull cries.

Mammy breathes in hard, like she's just woken up. She squeezes my hand. 'So. We need to think of something really nice to do for Adam. Got any thoughts about that?'

She swings my hand as we walk down the lane.

I tell her, 'He likes anything that could explode all over outer-space. He likes cracked atoms the very best.'

'I don't know where we can get him one of them.'

My mouth's jabbering about all the things Adam might like. It won't stop talking now the Quiet Woman's alive again, and my mouth jabbers so much it even tells Mammy, 'Me and Adam got high.'

She stops walking. 'I'd have never thought you two were on drugs.' She lets go of my hand. 'Where did you get—'

'It was—'

She leans down to me and grips my arms tight. 'Well, no

wonder your imagination flew so high. Thinking you've seen a dead body in a cursed place. You're far too young to be messing with your head. Was it hallucinogens, natural ones, like mushrooms?'

'I didn't smoke a mushroom, it was—'

She squeezes my arms hard. 'Not anything that's going to twist up your still-growing brain?'

'My brain isn't twisted.'

She lets my arms go. 'Good. I don't want you going simple on me. I'll be wanting promises out of you for this.' She straightens up and looks into the sky where the clouds are chasing each other along. Her curly hair blows across her face and I reach up and pull it away from her mouth.

She looks down at me. 'So, what will you promise?' She doesn't speak for a while, but keeps looking at me for an answer.

So I promise her, 'I won't ever smoke cinnamon sticks again, and I promise not to mind going past Old Kelp's any more and I won't go through her gate till it's my turn on the fair again. If you want me to help Dad at Jock's farm when I'm bigger, I'll do it, but only as long as I can still wear a dress.'

When I look up again at her, she's smiling to herself as she takes my hand. The rest of the way home, I swish and swish in my best-till-last dress, looking down at the kisses she's sewn on the hem.

MAYA

In the bedroom with Amber only a door-width away, I can sleep.

A dream of a small place, underground.

I'm inside a satin-lined wooden box. Rolling over in a flickering half-light, Finn's face is opposite mine, his eyes closed. He's humming a slow song.

I lay my cold cheek against his. As he hums, I'm in his dream. We're lying in a rowing boat, leaving people we've loved behind us on some shore. Pieces of our hearts are tied with bright strands of wool to the necks of seagulls. They're pulling us away.

I'm myself and Finn, neither and both. Our bodies rock, we're tipped out of the boat and we fall through salt water, our hands cling to each other as we slide through sand, and we land

grey shroud swaddled,

inside a satin-lined wooden box.

Under the soil is the quietest place in this whole world.

We're darkness.

Something inside me stretches, lengthen-narrows, wide-tightens, restless. Rolling out and away, I'm not underground any more. I run, flags waving from my fingertips.

The next dream lives behind an ice door.

Opening the door, I'm in the living room in the cottage. I'm sewing up the hems of the old woman's clothes. The needle spikes my thumb. I drop the black cloth and look at my hands, full of pinpricks.

I don't want, too much. Don't want Amber to be outside. Don't want to be here alone. Don't want this scared fast-breathing. I'm missing Paradon.

I go and find my crimson dress. It's a colour that sings.

It's dark in a drawer, rolled up, almost forgotten.

And beside the fire in the living room, I shake the dress out of its curl. The stretchy fabric isn't even creased. The colour sings brightness and shouts red as it explodes the smell of roses.

Holding the dress up, I think that wearing a song in this colour, I might be beautiful. That with the shout of red I could be magnificent. And with this perfect scent of roses it would make me laugh for the longest time, to find out I'm ugly.

I'm here alone, with no one to change me.

No one to look at me and see what their own eyes can imagine or design.

I put on the crimson dress.

The ice door closes this dream away, and there's another one.

The sunken picture I've been looking for:

Two blurred shapes.

It's the kitchen of the cottage in black, grey, white. Two young women stand opposite one another in shadows, each with a rock clenched in her hand. The one with her back to the front door is Dead Red. The one with her back to the living-room door is me.

I walk slowly around them.

Dead Red speaks: 'Finally, I'm faced with myself. So turn on the light.'

My left hand flicks a switch.

Colour.

Dead Red is staring into my face which has changed into hers:

Unscreamed screams, uncried tears, unspoken words, damaged hopes and unanswered questions –

despair.

Something's wrong.

I'm still wearing the crimson dress.

Not her: she's only seeing our faces.

We step towards one another.

We take another step as we both raise the rocks in our hands.

I watch as one of us kills the other.

But it's the wrong way around.

I wake on the bedroom floor next to the old woman's wardrobe, lying where Amber folded me in blankets. I stare at the cabinet on the wall for a long time, looking at the surface of salt that coats a rock which is a disguised murder weapon.

A white, salty thing.

I want to cry. So I let myself cry till I stop.

Getting up, I look in the mirror at my face that's Amber's face. There's the flash of red and ghost faces swirl up in a mist. Their mouths move as they urgent-speak two words.

Now, I recognise the words. I tell the ghosts, 'I know,' and their mouths stop moving. The ghosts shift, fade, and are gone.

The smell of honey fills the kitchen with bright-smell. The light's dawn-stained through closed curtains.

Amber's duvet-buried on the bed in the corner. She's saying, ' . . . but I wish I could. There was something there . . . almost a whisper of your hand.'

She upright jerks and stares at me through shadows. 'Maya.'

'Who are you talking to?'

She looks at her pillow, and whispers, 'No one.'

'When you came back from your walk . . .'

She blinks at me and rubs her eyes. 'Which walk?'

'On the night of Dead Red. You said you felt her fall through your arms.'

She puts her hand on her chest. 'I was so relieved when I saw you.'

'Why?'

'I thought you'd been hurt, even killed. I ran all the way back. But there you were, alive. And there she was, dead.' She looks at the kitchen floor.

'When you came back in, I was still wearing black, wasn't I?'

'Of course. That's what we wear here.'

'So you came in, expecting to see me hurt or dead, but you wanted to see me looking exactly as I did when you left me.'

She outreaches her hand.

I sidestep away. 'Tell me! You wanted to see me alive?'

She eyes me with an intense-stare. 'Of course I want you to be alive. I always will. You're my sister.'

I bury my face in my hands.

Amber says in gentle-speak, 'Dead Red's gone.'

My voice is sob-thick. 'Face gone. Broken, smashed.'

Amber frowns at me. 'What is this, Maya?'

Pacing the kitchen, I circle-turn in the corners, whispering, 'I'll never know what I really look like.' I say it again, again.

'What's wrong with you?' Amber gathers the black duvet around her and shuffles forward. She sits, bed-edging.

I stop breathing.

'Maya, you're ashen. Please. Come here.' She beckons me.

My heart-bangs stop as I cross the kitchen and sit next to her. Her cheeks are flushed, her shoulders are sleep-warm, the rest of her body is bundled in the black duvet.

She breathes.

I'm just pretending to.

We're holding hands to make a bridge between separate places.

Amber says, 'Maya, I need to tell you. I'm in love – I feel so alive.'

And because she has to want me to be alive for the rest of her life, I swallow the ghost words: I'm dead.

EPILOGUE

That's how I came to find out it was me who'd died, wearing crimson, that night on the kitchen floor.

I spent up a life without being seen as myself. I don't think it was ever meant to be a life that was mine; it was designed for other people. If I ever made them truly happy, I'm not sure I noticed. The people who can see me now are those who deeply want to believe in an afterlife. They don't realise I'm dead, and still see whatever they want. That's the thing about the enhancement of any kind of mirror – polished glass or pathways. They're designed to keep reflecting.

My thoughts became clearer, after the shiver-like shock of realising I'd died. Now, I'm much less frightened.

I've found the wind is often spiteful, and only goes where it wants to, but it exists to carry travellers.

Eyeing its direction, I managed to visit our parents, just once. They couldn't see me. They've decided how they want to remember us, and we're frozen in time. They've decorated our bedroom with a mural, copied from a photograph. We're holding hands with sunshine behind us. I'm painted silver-light, Amber's rust-red. We're twinned silhouettes with no faces.

Adam has now perfected his own bearish roar, and though it baffles Pippa, he still swears to her I'm a bear. Pippa and I often go to Lizzie's abandoned house to talk and rage in private.

Whenever I'm fading, I go to Amber, who always wants me to be alive. I get out of her way when she's finished cooking, as she often takes a bone spoon with her to bed. She tells me she's in love with a ghost who can't physically touch her, because he used his hands to bully when he was alive. She tells me, in the talk-style of a ghost expert, that sometimes one or other or even all of the senses are removed by death. My own senses still jumble more than ever. I've never seen Gilliam myself, but since living without me, Amber's developed a vivid imagination.

People often see what they want in others, and not always the person who's in front of them. No one can ever be everything someone needs, so people find what they can in fragments to avoid despair. Someone whose insidehalf wants to be cared for will seek out caring people. Someone who's never been given enough love will send their outsidehalf crashing across landscapes, chasing someone they believe will make them feel it. Someone who wants to die will see death all around them, till they meet their own.

I've no face that's my own; no one sees me as I am.

So, I have to see everything.

My eyes are over-alive. With them I inhale rain and gales, sunshine and crackle-leaves, flavours and smells, emotions and sounds. I collect and store and lose and hoard and drop and find everything there is to see.

I've been searching wide-high, and have found something that's really my own. Out in the stars, I'm weightless, dancing. All of the stars are alive. There are smells that are the clang of great bells, and music made from dark blue. There are clouds of echo-pulses and the tastes of winter frost. With my eyes closed or wide open, I can let myself be blown by the wind, all the way there.

And hope. It's not found in a place, or in anyone else. It isn't anything we can imagine or design. It's found when there are no mirrors reflecting what we believe we want to see.

ACKNOWLEDGEMENTS

Lucy Luck for her uncanny ability to see the bigger picture, and her continued support and wisdom.

Suzie Dooré for having such a fine eye for detail and dry sense of humour. Francine Toon for her intelligent thoughts. Carole Welch, Rosie Gailer and all the brilliant and lively staff at Sceptre.

Anne and Alan for travelling to join me, even when the journeys were hard. Caspian, Ben, Orlando, the two Fionas and Kirsty for their many kindnesses. Willow, for already writing her own books at the age of four.

Tom for his critical eye, writing nest, and research suggestions, Kate A. for her gentle support. Paul for his sympathetic ear, Sarah for her quirkiness and knits, Andy, Steve and Sophie for their many enthusiasms. Mike, Charlotte, Will, Peta, Nicky and all the staff and students at Barts.

Anna McGrail for reading something that wasn't ready to be read, and still having such clear questions.

Mark Slater and Catherine Smith for their continued support of my endeavours. Woody, Lucy, Noel and David for their late-night feedback, loan of books and *New Scientists*. Rosie and Sue for their constant friendship and humour. Jac, for having dreams of red feathers.

Jess Eaton, of Roadkill Couture at Eaton Nott for advice about taxidermy. www.eatonnott.co.uk. Dr R. Jarvis for medical information.

The recipes were adapted and rewritten based on a variety of sources, including online magazines, the *Woman's Weekly* and a booklet containing cake and pudding recipes that I bought in a shop in Cornwall.

Huge appreciation and much love again to Kakey, for putting up with my long mental absences while writing this book.